"YOU'RE SO LOVELY,"
HE WHISPERED.

He nibbled her bottom lip. Sensations began to rise, as faint as the light from a distant star at first, but with each passionate draw upon her lips they grew stronger. He slid a hand to the nape of her neck and deepened both the kiss and their embrace—inviting her, bewitching her with his lulling power.

When his hands began to roam ever so gently over the back of her dress, the heat in his palms seeped through to her skin, warming the new woman blossoming within. He lowered his kisses to her jaw and throat, and her soft gasp of pleasure mingled with the whispers of the trees. Hands as gentle as the night mapped her waist and shoulders.

"Yes," she whispered. "Yes." His heated kisses were making her lose sight of who and where she was.

But she didn't care.

THROUGH THE STORM

BEVERLY JENKINS

AVON BOOKS
An Imprint of HarperCollinsPublishers

This is a work of fiction. Names, characters, places, and incidents are products of the author's imagination or are used fictitiously and are not to be construed as real. Any resemblance to actual events, locales, organizations, or persons, living or dead, is entirely coincidental.

AVON BOOKS
An Imprint of HarperCollins*Publishers*
195 Broadway
New York, New York 10007

Copyright © 1998 By Beverly Jenkins
Inside back cover author photo by Glamour Shots
Library of Congress Catalog Card Number: 97-94938
ISBN: 0-380-79864-6
www.avonromance.com

First Avon Books paperback printing: August 1998

Avon Trademark Reg. U.S. Pat. Off. and in Other Countries, Marca Registrada, Hecho en U.S.A.
HarperCollins® is a trademark of HarperCollins Publishers Inc.

Printed in the U.S.A.

HB 05.14.2023

This book is dedicated to Christine Zika—
remember to allow yourself joy.
And to Alex—because he is always there.

Now rally, Black Republicans
Wherever you may be
Brave soldiers on the battle-field
And sailors on the sea.
Now rally, Black Republicans—
Aye rally! We are free!
We've waited long long
To sing the song—
The song of liberty.

"The Song of the Black Republicans"
The Black Republican, *New Orleans*
April 29, 1865

Chapter 1

Georgia, 1864

When house slave Sable Fontaine was growing up in the mansion that was her home, it had taken fifteen male slaves to care for the rolling green lawns surrounding the estate. Under the watchful eye of the head gardener, an equal number of young slaves had trimmed the trees and sculpted the shrubs. They'd planted lush, fragrant flowers every spring, adding color and beauty to the genteel, pastoral surroundings, and every year the sprawling white house had been freshly painted so that its stately columns anchoring the wide front porch stood like monuments gleaming in the Georgia sun.

Now the Fontaine lawns and gardens were overgrown with weeds. No one had trimmed the shrubs or trees in three seasons, and the lush flowers hadn't been planted for years. The house hadn't been painted either, and it gleamed no more. Because of Mr. Lincoln's war, no slaves could be spared to perform such inconsequential tasks. Everyone was too bent upon survival.

When the conflict began, no one imagined the war would drag on for years or that families in the South would be reduced to living no better than their slaves. The thought that there would be food riots in Charleston

1

and Mobile, or that the Southern way of life would be destroyed, had been unthinkable. The South's sons and fathers rode off to war in 1861 filled with the pride and arrogance of their class. It was now 1864, and the prideful and the arrogant were deserting in staggering numbers, weary of fighting, starving, and dying. Adding to the turmoil were huge numbers of escaping slaves—men, women, and children who weren't waiting for the yoke of enslavement to be officially lifted. They were slipping away all over the south, many attaching themselves to the advancing Union troops. Sable's great-aunt Mahti said you could smell freedom in the air.

For Sable, though, the long anticipated, sweet scent of freedom had become fouled. Even as the marauding Yankees marched deeper and deeper into the heartland, tearing up the railroads and forcing families to flee, the buying and selling of slaves continued. Yesterday, she'd been sold too.

Some would say a twenty-nine year old female slave should be flattered to fetch the comely sum of eight hundred dollars, especially with war on, but Sable felt no such pride. The buyer, a man named Henry Morse, would not treat her well.

Sable's mistress, Sally Ann Fontaine, had announced the sale at supper last evening. Sable had stared at her in disbelief. Her anger flared as she held Sally's triumphant eyes, but Sable knew her feelings would make no difference. In the end only numbness remained, a numbness that gripped her still.

Now, watching the sun set, Sable stood on the wide front porch contemplating her future. She felt someone step out onto the porch behind her and knew without turning that it was Mavis.

"How are you, little sister?" Mavis asked softly.

In spite of Sable's mood, the salutation made her smile. The half-sisters had been born less than six minutes apart and Mavis never let Sable forget who'd drawn breath first. Sable's love for her knew no bounds, but contemplating Mavis's query made the numbness return. "As well as can be expected, I suppose. How about you?"

Sable turned and peered into the face that in many ways mirrored her own. Mavis's brown eyes were red-rimmed and swollen as she confessed, "I can't stop crying."

Sable turned away. She ached too but knew tears were a waste of time; they would not alter her fate.

Mavis announced bitterly, "I told Mama I'll never speak to her again if she goes through with the sale, but she won't change her mind."

Sable didn't expect Sally Ann to relent. The mistress of the household had never hidden her dislike for Sable, mostly because of what the bronze-skinned, green-eyed Sable represented. Sable's mother, a slave woman named Azelia, had given birth to Sable six minutes after Sally Ann gave birth to Mavis. Both baby girls had been fathered by Sally Ann's husband, Carson Fontaine, just as he'd fathered Sable's older brother Rhine and Mavis's brother Andrew, two years earlier.

Mavis interrupted Sable's thoughts. "I'll help however I can."

Sable knew she would. Though society forced the two women to walk in different worlds—making one mistress and the other slave—they'd shared everything all their lives. When Mavis had lost her beloved husband, Sanford, six months into the war, Sable had held her while she cried.

Mavis stepped around to look into Sable's eyes, "I know you're thinking of running, but there must be another way. The roads aren't safe."

"Safer than having Henry Morse as a master?" Sable retorted.

Rumors surrounding Morse's treatment of his female slaves linked him to at least two mysterious deaths that had taken place last year. The local constabulary had eventually charged a young male slave on a neighboring plantation with the killings, but most people, Black and White, questioned the validity of the official findings. The slave had been hanged as punishment, in spite of protestations from his owner, who'd loudly proclaimed his man's innocence.

Mavis spoke again. "Well, if you do decide to run, don't worry. I'll make certain Mahti's cared for."

In spite of Mavis's assurances Sable did worry. Since receiving Sally Ann's news, the fate of Sable's great-aunt had been weighing heavily on Sable's already over-burdened shoulders.

Mahti had been captured by European slavers and brought to America at the tender age of eight. Now, over sixty years later, she appeared destined to die without ever seeing her homeland again. She'd been ill for some time and although Sable knew Mavis would do every-thing in her power to make Mahti comfortable until the end, Sable could not leave her; it would break her heart. Were Sable's brother Rhine there, maybe the two of them could concoct a plan to secure Mahti's safety, but two years ago Rhine had gone to war to serve as per-sonal valet to Andrew, Mavis's older brother. No one had heard a word from either man since then.

So Mahti's future remained unsettled. Sable didn't want her aunt to die without a final farewell caress from Sable's hand to ease the passage home. Six weeks ago, she'd been given a chance to escape with the Fontaine's head butler and driver, Otis, but she'd declined because of Mahti's health. Otis had forged himself a pass, "bor-rowed" the last working carriage the Fontaines owned, and driven himself to freedom. With him he'd taken his wife Opal, who'd been the Fontaines' cook and head housekeeper for over thirty years, and their fifteen-year-old daughter Ophelia, the kitchen maid. Sally Ann had thrown a fit upon finding them gone, but Sable had smiled inwardly, hoping they'd reached freedom safely.

Sable had been a slave all her life and dearly wanted

to be free, but she wouldn't leave unless she could take her aunt too.

Sable's face took on a distinct show of dislike as Henry Morse's fancy black carriage drew up in front of the house. As he got out and headed up the long winding walk toward the porch, Mavis drawled brittlely, "Two years ago, trash like him wouldn't've had the gall to call at the front door."

Sable agreed. Like Black women all over the South, the Fontaines' housekeeper Opal had set very high standards of etiquette for family and visitors alike. A man of Morse's pedigree and reputation would never have set foot in her parlor. He'd have been received at the back door or not at all. Times were different now. With everyone in the South, Black and White, starving and clad in rags, the prewar caste system had been turned upside down. While the scions of the first families were on the front lines fighting and dying to preserve their way of life, back home men of questionable motives and character were forming a new class of Southern aristocracy. If the rumors were true, Morse had made a fortune over the past few years by buying up the property and slaves of planters who chose to flee the South in advance of the Yankees. Families who'd once shunned him because of his dirt-poor beginnings were now inviting him into their homes, in case they needed to make similar deals.

By the time Morse reached the porch, Sable had schooled her features into the blank mask behind which she'd been hiding her emotions since she'd become aware of her true station in life at the age of twelve.

He tipped his expensive hat politely as he stepped onto the porch. "Evenin', Miss Mavis. Sable."

Mavis nodded curtly and went back inside.

In spite of Henry Morse's evil nature, he was a handsome, middle-aged man. Tall, with jet-black hair and matching black eyes, he had a charm that could melt even the iciest belle. For the past few years, desperate war widows had been tossing themselves at him like corn to a rooster.

When Sable didn't acknowledge his greeting, he asked her with a grin, "Cat got your tongue, green eyes?"

She hated his pet name for her. Coolly, she asked, "Is Mrs. Fontaine expecting you?"

He ignored her question and reached out to stroke her cheek. She stepped away. She hated his touch.

He drawled, "You'd think you were a queen the way you act toward me, Sable. Even with all that education, you're still a slave, you know."

"And with all your money, you are still trash, Mr. Morse." She swept past him. "I will tell Mrs. Fontaine you are here."

"Hold on a minute, gal."

She stopped and turned slowly back.

A low rumble of malevolence entered his voice as he warned her softly, "You're going to be mine real soon, you royal bitch. We'll see how uppity you are then."

She held his cold eyes with her equally frosty green ones before continuing into the house.

After Otis and Opal's escape, the role of butler had fallen upon Sable's shoulders. Because she also did the bulk of the washing, cleaning, cooking, and whatever else Sally Ann needed, the days seemed endless. Otis and Opal weren't the only ones who'd gone. Of the three hundred slaves Carson Fontaine had owned prior to the war, fewer than fifty remained. All but a handful were children and oldsters. According to the whispers in the quarters, most of the runaways were attaching themselves to the advancing Yankee army. There were said to be thousands of Blacks seeking freedom and safety with Lincoln's troops.

As Sable wound her way through the big house to find Sally Ann and announce Morse's arrival, her footsteps echoed eerily. In the old days, the place had bustled with life, but now the silence was ever present.

Sable found her mistress in the kitchen yelling at the poor young girl, Cindi, who'd taken over Ophelia's duties. At Cindi's feet lay the shattered remains of one of Sally Ann's wedding plates. In her eyes were tears.

Sable interrupted the tirade. "Mrs. Fontaine."

The furious mistress whirled on Sable. "What?!"

Sable's face remained impassive. "Henry Morse is here to see you."

The lady of the house turned her angry brown eyes on the girl once more and threatened, "I'll deal with you later," then ordered, "Sable, get this mess cleaned up."

She sailed out.

As soon as they were alone, Sable looked across the kitchen at the distraught child and held out her arms. Cindi ran to Sable and burrowed into her arms. "I didn't mean to break it, Sable," she sobbed.

"I know, I know. She's a mean old bat, isn't she?"

Cindi nodded vigorously against Sable's waist.

Sable spent a few moments stroking her small head, then said, "Maybe when the Yankees come, they'll eat her."

Cindi looked up, smiling.

Sable smiled down in reply before adding, "You go on back to your nana. I'll clean up here."

After the youngster's exit, Sable swept up the shards and deposited them in the waste bin out back. When she came back inside, Mavis was finishing up the dishes. As had befitted the women of her class, Mavis had never been allowed in the kitchen during the years before the war, but times had changed. Now Mavis helped with many of the chores and housework, while Sally Ann—or Silly Ann as she'd been dubbed by the old slaves—spent her time bemoaning the lack of a qualified dressmaker and anything to eat except collards and yams.

When Sable picked up a towel to help Mavis, her sister said in a conspiratorial whisper, "No, I'll do this. Mama and Morse are out on the porch. Go."

Sable tossed the towel aside and slipped back outside. She had to hear what they were saying. Moving carefully and quietly so she wouldn't be detected over the sounds of early evening, she skirted the side of the house until she reached the porch.

When the Fontaine mansion had been expanded fifteen years ago, the slaves who had done the work had purposefully left enough crawlspace beneath the porch to allow a person to hide there and listen to what was being said above. Since masters rarely informed their slaves as to the daily goings-on in the world, the enslaved populations were forced to glean information in any way they could. Since slavery's inception, spying had been a tried and true method.

Sable hiked up her ragged dress and scooted on all fours under the porch. Plant debris and damp earth covered her palms and knees but she paid them scant attention. Sally Ann escorted her guests out on the porch with such regularity that in the old days, the house slaves had ensured someone would be stationed at this listening post every evening.

Sable settled into position. She forced herself not to speculate on the snakes and other vermin that might be living nearby in the darkness, and hoped she wouldn't have to wait long. Thankfully she didn't. A pair of footsteps sounded from above, and as they came closer, she heard Sally Ann asking, "Now that we've come to closure on the contract, when will I receive the funds for Sable's sale?"

"In about a month," Morse replied.

"That long?" Sally sounded angry as she snapped, "You said it would be no more than a week."

"War's on, Mrs. Fontaine. Financial transactions are getting harder and harder to execute."

Sally Ann had never been a patient woman and Sable could well imagine the sharp set of her hawklike features as she confessed, "The only reason I'm so anxious is because Carson is eager to leave."

Carson and Sally Ann had been married over thirty years. On the morning he'd left for the war, he'd assembled his slaves and family members to hear his last words. Mounted on his finest stallion and dressed in the trim gray uniform of the Confederacy, he'd jubilantly promised to be back in a few weeks, boasting it wouldn't take long to whip the North.

The boast had proven hollow. The weeks had lengthened into years. He'd returned eight months ago, one leg blown off by a Union shell. It was his deteriorating health that necessitated Sable's sale, or so Sally had claimed last evening. She'd heard about a clinic in New York that performed miracles on war-injured men, and she was determined to take him there.

Morse asked, "How's Carson feel about me looking after the place while you're gone?"

"He is resigned to leaving," she replied, then added tartly, "Damn that Lincoln! He ought to get on his knees and beg the forgiveness of every White woman in the South for what he's put us through. My sister in Vicksburg wrote me that food got so scarce during the siege, skinned rats were selling in the markets next to mule meat."

Sable shuddered as Sally continued, "Carson and I are both convinced our boys will rally and send the Yankees back to hell, but until then, Carson needs care. If I have to take him to a Yankee doctor, so be it. Once the South has won, we'll return here."

"How's he feel about selling Sable?"

Sally Ann was silent for so long, Sable thought she wouldn't reply. Finally she said, "He sees nothing wrong with it. She is a slave, after all. The funds from her sale will help us get North."

Sable had been curious about Carson Fontaine's role in her sale. Last night when she and Mavis sat in her room angrily denouncing Sally Ann's decision, Mavis had insisted Sally Ann had arranged the deal without Carson's knowledge. Sable had not been convinced.

Carson might have returned home from war bitter and crippled, but Sally Ann never made a decision without his direct approval. Granted, Carson had brought Sable to live in the house after her mother's death and as Sable grew older he'd allowed her to be educated right alongside Mavis. He'd even let her accompany the family to Europe five years ago as Mavis's personal servant when Mavis and Sanford took their wedding tour, and he had purchased Sable a whole new wardrobe for the trip. However, never once, in all her twenty-nine years, had he ever treated her or looked upon her as anything other than property; he was the master and Sable his slave.

Morse's voice brought Sable back to the present. "Mahti's so near dying now, I guess Carson feels he can ignore the curse."

Confused, Sable heard Sally Ann's shrill laugh. "Whatever do you mean?"

Sable knew that shrill note in her mistress's voice signaled either nervousness or flat-out lying.

"Come on now, Mrs. Fontaine," Morse drawled. "You and I have both heard the rumors."

Sally Ann replied haughtily, "I don't sully myself with rumors, sir."

Morse laughed softly. "So all that talk about Sable's mama and grandmama being queens isn't true?"

Queens?!

Sally Ann's reply sounded evasive. "I admit there were rumors of royal blood, but I never put any stock in them. Half the nigras in the South claim to be related to some jungle ruler in one way or another."

Sable, who had never heard any of this before, found the discussion riveting.

Morse sounded skeptical. "Then it's not true about Sable's ma killing herself in Carson's bed?"

Sable's body turned cold. This was by far the most startling piece of information she'd ever heard about her mother Azelia's death. Sable knew she'd died during an accident on Sable's third birthday, but little else. If what

Morse was saying was true, why hadn't Mahti revealed any of it to Sable before?

In reply to Morse's question about Azelia's death, Sally Ann answered in her frostiest voice, "Mr. Morse, you and I may be business associates, but I do not discuss my husband's whores with anyone. Good evening. Let me know when the funds arrive."

Sable heard the screen door slam and knew Morse had been left standing alone on the porch. Immediately afterward came the sound of his footsteps descending the front steps and heading down the walk. Once his carriage pulled away, Sable left her hiding place and went to the quarters in search of answers.

As she entered the small candlelit cabin, she was pleasantly surprised to find Mahti sitting up in bed. For the last few days, Mahti had been in a deep, deep sleep, a state she'd been falling into more and more often lately. Those who loved her best knew that one of these days her dark eyes would remain closed for eternity.

Now she was awake again, back from "talking with the ancestors" as she called the long slumbers. The brown-skinned woman seated near the bed was Vashti, the root woman and doctor for the quarters and Cindi's nana. Vashti and Mahti had been friends for many years.

Holding back her questions for a moment, Sable declared with a smile, "Mahti, you are going to live forever."

"Not if I can help it," she cackled, laughing. She'd lost her teeth long ago and whenever she laughed too hard, such as now, hacking coughs rattled her thin ebony frame. Vashti gave her a sip of water from a battered tin cup. The spasm eased and Mahti pointed at her old friend. "It's all Vashti's fault—her old potions are keeping me from going home."

Sable knelt beside the bed and kissed her aunt's wrinkled brown forehead. "We all want you to stay with us as long as you can. The sun shines brighter on my day, knowing you are here."

Mahti stared up at her, startled.

"What's the matter?" Sable asked.

For a long moment Mahti continued to gaze up at Sable. Then she gently grasped her arm, and Mahti's bony fingers squeezed her affectionately. "Someone said that exact same thing to me a long long time ago. To hear the words again from your lips jarred me a bit."

Sable started to ask Mahti who had said the words, but Mahti changed the subject. "How're things up at the house?"

Sable shrugged. "Nothing's changed."

Sable hesitated telling her aunt about her sale because of the adverse effect the news might have on her fragile health and because Sable had no solid plan for Mahti's future.

Mahti would not be fooled, however. "Something has indeed changed, has it not?"

Sable didn't know how or where to begin.

Mahti told her quietly, "I heard about the sale. Vashti told me. Your fate does not lie with him, however."

The words lifted Sable's spirit until Mahti added, "But your fates are intertwined—he will be the jackal and you the antelope until his death."

Sable felt the skin prickle on the back of her neck, though she did not understand what Mahti meant. Sable had learned at an early age that asking Mahti how she knew such things was akin to asking the wind why it blew. Mahti saw things others could not, felt things no one else could. She saw signs of fortune or disaster in the phases of the moon and the configuration of the stars. "The old ways still walk strongly within me," she would sometimes say, as if that were explanation enough. She represented not only the last of Sable's true female family but also the last link to the time of the Middle Passage and the first African ancestors forcibly brought to these shores. In Mahti lay all the wisdom and experience that had shaped the generations which followed, and when Mahti died, Sable knew she would carry the grief for the rest of her life.

"Mahti," she said, "I overheard Sally Ann and Morse talking about curses and queens. Morse said my mother killed herself in Carson Fontaine's bed. What were they talking about?"

"Things I have withheld from you."

"Why?"

Her reply was soft. "Because no child should carry such grief until she is strong enough to bear it."

Sable thought about that before saying, "I believe I am strong enough now."

Mahti took a moment to look deeply into Sable's river-green eyes before replying, "I believe you are, so let us start at the beginning."

The story began in Mother Africa.

"I had accompanied my aunt to a wedding celebration at a neighboring village. On the way home we were attacked by slavers. My aunt and the fifteen men who guarded her fought bravely. Seven of them gave their lives, but we were captured."

"Why did she have guards?"

"My mother's sister was both my aunt and my queen."

Sable stared in surprise. "Is this queen the woman Morse spoke of as being my grandmother?"

Mahti nodded and continued, "Those captured that day who did not die on the Middle Passage were sold to a man in Virginia named Bryce. Later, he said he knew from the moment he saw your grandmother in the slave market that she was someone special, simply by the way she carried herself. He purchased us and twenty other Africans who'd made the journey over in the belly of the same slaver. After he brought us all to his farm, he noticed that the other slaves did her work, that we deferred to her and bowed to her whenever she came near. He surmised that he'd purchased a great queen."

"What did he do?"

"He let her assume her natural place. You see there were a few other royals owned by masters in the region. Over time, these owners had learned that allowing royals or elected headmen to rule the captives made dealings with the African slaves easier, so Bryce followed their example."

Mahti took a sip of water before continuing. "My aunt was of mid-age when she was first brought to this country. Bryce treated her like the queen she was and never once approached her to breed her. He took care of her people, even taught us all to read. In exchange, she saw to it that his farms were productive and free of turmoil. We stayed with Bryce for almost ten years, then when he died, we were sold to a man in Maryland named Caufield."

Mahti's voice turned bitter. "Caufield did not respect your grandmother. One night, a few days after we arrived, he forced her to mate with him even though she swore she would kill herself afterward, and that he himself would follow her into death. Laughing, he did the deed anyway and months later, she gave birth to a female child, your mother Azelia. In our kingdom, the royal line runs through the woman, and a baby does not reach true life until the age of three years. On Azelia's third birthday, your grandmother placed the small queen in my care and kissed me good-bye. Her last words to me were, "The sun shines brighter on my day, knowing you are here."

Sable's heart seemed to stop. Those were the same words she'd said to Mahti only a moment ago.

As if she'd read Sable's mind, Mahti said, "Your words are a sign that she is near, and if she is near, it is time."

Sable had so many questions, she couldn't contain them all, but the one most prominent had to do with her grandmother's fate. "What happened to her?"

"Later that night, she took a skinning knife and went up to Caufield's bedroom. After preparing and cleansing herself, she drew the blade across each wrist. She let herself bleed to death atop his bed."

Sable felt her stomach roll.

In a firm angry voice Mahti said, "She was a queen, a royal, not a mare to be used by an illiterate barbarian, but she was avenged. The Society came for Caufield the next night."

"Who or what was that?"

"A group of African men who enforced the traditional spiritual laws. In our homeland they were a secret society and wore masks and robes designed to frighten. They were said to be the physical reincarnation of spirits. They would come in the middle of the night to remind you to stay on the right path."

"These societies existed here?"

"Oh yes. We were able to maintain many of our traditional ways for many years here. The maskers were one of our biggest secrets."

"Do these societies still exist?"

Mahti shrugged. "It is hard to know. There are very few of the Firsts still alive today."

"Did my mother know all these things?"

Mahti nodded. "Yes. Unlike you, she grew to womanhood knowing her history. I regret I didn't shield her as I did you."

"Why?"

"If I had, maybe she would have chosen a different path."

For a moment Mahti's memories seemed to take her away. Sable saw the sadness in her face as her great aunt reached out and caressed Sable's cheek. "We are getting ahead of ourselves. I was talking about Caufield, was I not?"

Sable nodded.

"The Society came for him in the middle of the night. I was a parlormaid for Caufield's wife at the time and she allowed me to sleep on the floor in her room. I awakened to the sound of her screams and saw five men in hideous, misshapen masks and red robes standing in the open doorway. They appeared to be taller than any men I'd ever seen, and they were holding the struggling Caufield by the arms. I knew right away what they represented and why they'd come. They began to speak, but just as at home, the masks were designed to alter the voices of the wearer, and so the speech came out distorted and fearsome. They told her they were taking her husband to be judged for crimes committed against the queen. They told her a similar fate would befall the remaining members of her family should any slave be punished for Caufield's taking.''

"Was he ever found?"

"Yes, the next morning. He'd been drawn and quartered. Mrs. Caufield never recovered. She sold every slave on the place the next day."

"And you were all sold to the Fontaines?"

"Yes, your mother was three years old when we arrived. Carson Fontaine was fifteen, nearly a man."

"So how did she die?"

"Just as your grandmother did. I warned Carson beforehand that Azelia was a royal, and of the fate he would reap should she be made to breed against her will, but like Caufield, he laughed. First Rhine was born and two years later, you. He stopped laughing the night he found her dead in his bed. She took her life just as the old queen had done."

"Why did she wait until after my birth?"

"Your brother Rhine was a male child. She needed a female heir for the royal line, so she waited for you."

An immense sadness welled up inside Sable. "What made Carson bring me into the house?"

"Guilt at first. I doubt he had any real feelings for Azelia, but remember, I told him what had happened to Caufield. After Azelia's death, he went up to Virginia where Mrs. Caufield was staying with her sister and talked to her. He returned home a bit more believing after that. He called all the slaves together and told them he would be bringing you into the house to live, and that you would learn all the things his daughter Mavis learned. He also promised you would never be sold.''

"Mrs. Caufield's story must have really frightened him.''

"I believe it did indeed. After he returned, he took me out of the field and made me overseer of the looms, but I told him at the time, the spirits didn't care how generous he'd become, he would still be punished for his crime against Azelia.''

"Is that the curse Morse spoke of?''

"I'm sure it is, but I didn't curse Carson. I simply told him the truth. Now that he has sold you, the time has come.''

"What time?''

"The time for you to begin your journey and for me to begin mine.''

Mahti began to cough and Vashti gave her another sip of water. When the spasm passed, she slumped back against the stuffed feedsacks bracing her in the bed. She appeared to be very tired. Her aged hand cupped Sable's cheek affectionately. "Vashti will tell you what you need to do. You and I will talk more tomorrow.''

Sable had no idea the talk would change her life forever.

The next night, Sable stood outside on the front walk watching the Fontaine mansion burn. The entire structure was engulfed, the flames dancing against the night sky. The blazing interior glowed with such a blinding light, it looked like a portal to hell. For Mahti it had served as a passageway home.

Vashti had awakened Sable less than an hour before and quietly instructed her to rouse Mavis and Sally Ann. She said Mahti wanted to speak with everyone outside as soon as possible.

Sable had little trouble getting Mavis to comply with Mahti's request. Upon hearing Sable's explanation, Ma-

vis took a light blanket, wrapped herself in it, and sleepily made her way downstairs.

Sally Ann proved more difficult. She snapped, "It's
the middle of the night, Sable. What could Mahti possibly want at this hour?"

"I'm not certain, but she's never given you anything
but loyalty all these years. Will you humor her, please,
just this once?"

At first Sable thought Sally Ann would refuse, but she
finally swung her legs over the bed, saying coolly, "Just
this once, Sable. And it better not take long."

"I'm certain it won't."

Carson Fontaine slept in the far wing. Since Vashti
had not given Sable instructions to rouse him, she simply
followed Sally Ann outdoors.

The first thing Sable noticed as she stepped outside
was the heavy scent of kerosene. She found the strong
scent puzzling, and looked around a moment hoping to
find the source but she became distracted by a small knot
of people assembled on the walk. On hand were most
of the remaining adult slaves. In their hands were
torches. Only then did she notice Mahti. Her great-aunt
stood off by herself, chanting softly yet audibly in the
language of her homeland. Sable had never before seen
the majestic red robe Mahti was wearing, or the heavy
gold jewelry around her wrists and throat.

Sally Ann called out angrily, "Mahti, why are we out
here?"

Vashti turned to her mistress and said in a firm but
low voice, "She needs silence to prepare."

It was the first time Vashti had ever spoken so sharply
to her mistress. As if stunned, Sally Ann didn't say another word.

While everyone stared enrapt, Mahti held her hands
up to the night sky. Seconds later, as if by command,
the moon came out from behind the clouds, bathing the
silent scene in an ethereal light.

Mavis slid up behind Sable and asked softly, "What is she doing?"

Sable shrugged, not taking her eyes off her aunt. In the moonlight, Mahti looked younger and stronger than she'd appeared in years.

In a loud voice Mahti called out, "The Queens are gathering. The time has come."

Sally Ann laughed. "I'm going back inside. I've had enough of this mumbo-jumbo."

Vashti took her by the arm. "You will stay. Watch and learn."

Mahti then began to recite a litany of names. A confused Sable looked to Vashti, who explained, "They are the names of the Old Queens. Out of respect she must summon them all."

When the naming ended a few moments later, the night was silent. Mahti stepped up onto the porch. Using what appeared to be a ladle, she dipped it into a weathered bucket at her feet and began tossing a liquid onto the porch and the dry, weed-filled grounds fronting the house. Chanting as she went, she seemed to be anointing the area around her. Once again the smell of kerosene filled Sable's nose, and a sliver of alarm gripped her.

Mahti tossed the ladle aside and took a moment to look out at the small assembled crowd before saying, "Vashti, the time has come."

Vashti took a torch from one of the slaves, and after walking up to the porch, placed it reverently in Mahti's hand. Once Vashti returned to her place beside Sable, Mahti touched the torch to the high weeds framing the steps. Flames leaped to life. She then touched the porch and the tall columns anchoring it. Fire appeared, climbing, seeking, spreading. A line of flame now stood between the house and the horrified onlookers. On the porch, behind the line, stood Mahti.

Looking directly into Sable's eyes, she spoke in a calm, clear voice. "I've given you all you'll need, my

Sable. The Old Queens send their love. They will protect you. Listen for them.''

Mahti touched the torch to the wood framing the door. Sable felt Mavis clutch her arm. "Father's still in there, Sable! Do something!"

Sally Ann tried to break away from Vashti's hold, but the old woman snapped, "Silly woman! It is his time to die, not yours."

A wall of fire separated Mahti and the burning house from those watching. The crackling flames had become a roaring conflagration.

"Someone do something!" Mavis screamed.

Mahti's voice rose on the night. "It is already done. If I burn in the Christian hell, so be it. What hell can be worse than slavery!"

Through the shimmering curtain of flame, Sable saw her aunt slowly remove the robe and jewelry. Nude now, Mahti began to walk farther inside the burning house. Not once did she look back to see the tears streaming down Sable's cheeks.

An hour had passed since then, and now Sable stood silently, watching the dying flames send Mahti home. Behind her Sally Ann sobbed softly. Carson had gone to his death, just as Mahti had promised. Sally and Mavis had lost husband and father, but Sable had lost the anchor of her whole world.

Grief wailed within Sable like a live beast, but because she'd been trained to hide her emotions, it did not show. She sat and kept vigil all night, long after a weeping Mavis had helped the broken down Sally Ann to the slave cabins to try and rest, long after the house had collapsed in on itself and the fire had died down to embers.

At dawn, Vashti came to Sable and said, "It is time for you to begin your journey."

Sable looked up with sad eyes.

Vashti held out an old canvas bag. "Mahti left you these things."

Sable took the offering and held it to her breast. She had no idea what the bag contained, but it had come from Mahti, and for now, that was enough.

"You must go now, Sable. Sally Ann has sent one of the children for Morse. You must be gone before they return."

Sable stood. She took a moment to give Vashti a hug of farewell and bask in the balm she received from the root woman's aged arms. As Vashti held the grieving Sable close, she whispered, "You have been raised to walk in both worlds, and the Queens will show you their purpose. Go with my love and with theirs."

Turning, Sable took a moment to commit to heart and mind the house's still smoldering remains, then she headed toward the road. Like her great-aunt Mahti, she did not look back.

Chapter 2

Staying off the road, Sable used the trees and thick underbrush lining the roadway to shield her passage. Thigh-high weeds snagged her skirts, and in some places she had to push aside low-hanging branches. The ground proved to be rocky and uneven as she crossed streams and followed the hilly terrain of the vast Fontaine land, but she kept pace, intent upon placing as much distance between herself and her past as possible.

Grief accompanied her like a companion, and on long, lonely stretches of the trek she let it have its head. At times she cried so hard, she couldn't see, and her heart ached as it never had before.

By the time the sun climbed directly overhead, she'd been walking for hours. Hot and weary, she finally surrendered, admitting the need for rest. She took a seat against the trunk of a sheltering tree, ate part of a yam she found wrapped in the canvas bag, then spent a moment surveying the other contents. There was a skin from which she took a small sip of water, a couple more yams, and at the bottom, a red kerchief that appeared to have something tied inside it. The red cloth had been of high quality at one time, but now looked old and frayed. As Sable untied the knots, the fabric fell away like dust, as if no one had opened the thing in many years. Inside lay a thin, elaborately carved gold bracelet. Its weight

22

made her guess it was very valuable. She wondered at its origins, and why Mahti had placed it in the bag.

A closer look at the bracelet's engravings revealed a delicately detailed moon, a sun, and a sprinkling of what appeared to be stars. The sensation of having seen the celestial pattern before rose sharply in her. Sable puzzled over the conundrum for a moment before she knew. Looking around to make certain she wasn't being observed, she raised her skirt and peered closely at the small design on her upper thigh. The two designs matched. She righted her skirt, then turned the bracelet over in her hand. Sable's skin carving had been done by Mahti, one week after Sable's first show of woman's blood. At the time, Mahti had explained it as tradition. Young women in her village were routinely given such decoration to enhance their beauty. Mahti's own ceremony had been performed after her enslavement in America. Two women servants of Sable's grandmother, the Old Queen, had presided over the ancient rite.

Sable turned the bracelet over again and wondered about its significance. Mahti had taken so many secrets home with her. Sable wished there'd been time to learn more. Grief began to rise in her again, but as if magically summoned, Mahti's parting words whispered clearly in Sable's mind, *I've given you all you'll need, my Sable.*

Sable drew a modicum of strength from the memory, and since she had no way of disputing the claim, she gathered up the bag and set out once more.

It came to her that maybe the bracelet would be safer hidden on her person than in the bag. Who knew what lay ahead? When Otis and Opal were planning their escape, they'd told her they were going to join the hundreds of other escapees who'd attached themselves to the Union army. That was Sable's goal too. But she was not so naive as to believe she would find the camps overnight or arrive there without incident. War was raging. Sherman's straggling troops, called "bummers" by the locals, were reportedly everywhere, stealing, poaching, and terrorizing. There were also hungry and desperate Confederate deserters trying to reach their homes. Sable looked around. Once again making sure she wasn't being watched, she cautiously raised her skirt and tied the bracelet into the frayed strings of her muslin drawers. She pulled the tapes tightly, then set out once more.

The road Sable was following led north to Atlanta. She'd traveled it many times with Mavis and Sally Ann. By carriage the journey took a full day. On foot, the trip would take infinitely longer, but the determined Sable walked on. Atlanta had fallen to the Union two weeks ago, on the first day of September. There were reports of many runaways who had joined the conquering Yankees. Sable had no way of knowing what she might find upon her arrival, but the prospect of an unknown freedom won hands down over the known reality of being a slave.

When dusk began to settle, she sought a place to sleep for the night. About a half mile further, she came upon the old Dresden place. The family had once been social acquaintances of the Fontaines. When the war broke out, Mr. Dresden, a teacher, had enlisted on the side of the Union. After his departure, his wife had been so ostracized and harassed by neighbors, she and the children had gone North to live with her mother. Last fall someone had set fire to the vacant house. Only a shell remained, but Sable hoped it would be safe enough for one night.

As she walked cautiously into the burned-out hulk, an old woman stepped out of the shadows and scared Sable half to death by saying, "I've been waiting for you."

Once Sable got over her initial fright, she studied the smiling, dark-skinned woman. The aged face was round and unremarkable, and a colorful bandanna covered her hair. The dark eyes holding Sable's were intelligent and powerful, eyes that reminded Sable of Mahti's.

"Who are you?" Sable asked.

"That was going to be my question to you, my dear, but introductions can wait. Come on now, I'll bet you're hungry."

Sable hesitated, trying to determine what to do, but the woman gave her such a commanding look that Sable followed without comment.

She led Sable outside and down into the Dresden cellar. Sable was surprised to see the stub of a candle and a mound of bedding on the earthen floor. Did the old woman live there?

As if having read Sable's mind, the woman offered, "I've been waiting for you for two days. I was just about to give up on you ever coming."

Confused to say the least, Sable asked once more, "Who are you?"

"Araminta is what my mama named me. Owner named me something else. The good Lord named me Moses. And you are?"

"Sable. Sable Fontaine. How could you have been waiting for me if you don't know me?"

"Dreamed about you."

Sable stared.

The old woman handed Sable a tin plate. On it was half a spitted rabbit, a helping of dandelion greens, and a slice of bread. "Here. Eat," she instructed. "We got a long walk tomorrow."

Sable was torn between wanting to devour the food and asking a dozen questions, but her starving stomach took priority over her curiosity.

Sable ate robustly but politely, and noticed that the woman watched her the whole time. "Something wrong?" Sable finally asked.

"Just admiring your manners. Raised in the house, I'll bet."

Sable nodded yes.

"Some of our folks'll resent you for that, but don't ever be ashamed of who you are. Can you read?"

"Yes, ma'am."

"That's a glorious thing, that reading. Hope I'll be able to one day."

"I could help you learn."

The woman's eyes shone as she replied, "You've a good heart, but I don't have time right now."

"Why not?"

"Have to take you to LeVeq."

"LeVeq?"

"Yep. Dreamed about that too."

Sable hadn't a clue as to whom this LeVeq might be. "Do you dream often?"

"Most of the time. A dream took me out of slavery."

"You're a runaway too, then?"

"Yep. Ran the first time when I was seven, but got so hungry I went back. Ran for good once I became a woman. My husband and brothers wouldn't go with me, so I went alone."

"You left your husband?"

"Had to. The good Lord needed me."

Sable did not know what to make of this mysterious new companion. "Are you from around here?"

"Nope, born in Maryland."

It astounded Sable to hear of a Black woman roaming so far from her home. "Why are you in Georgia?"

"Doing the work I was called to."

"Which is?"

Araminta smiled. "Freeing slaves."

Since Araminta told Sable it would be safer if they traveled at night, Sable spent that first night sleeping and regaining her strength; she spent the following morning listening to and marveling over the tales and adventures of the woman who'd taken her under her wing. Although the woman had originally introduced herself as Araminta, Sable learned that the rest of the world knew her as Harriet Tubman and that she was very famous. It seemed Mrs. Tubman stole slaves. Many slaves.

She explained to Sable that during her nineteen trips

into the South between 1849 and 1857, she'd led hundreds to freedom, including her aged parents, six brothers, their wives and fiancées, nieces and nephews. Although she'd been a slave when she married her husband, John Tubman, John had been free.

"We'd been married five years when my master died. Rumor had it that me and my brothers were going to be sold. A dream told me to run so we wouldn't be, but John chose staying put. So I ran alone. I went back to get him in '51, but he refused to see me."

"Why?"

"He'd taken another wife."

Sable's eyes widened.

"I was so angry and broken up inside, I wanted to storm right onto the place and confront him, and I didn't care if the master saw me and threw me back into slavery, if I could only give John a piece of my mind. But I came to my senses. You can't make a man love you, so—if he could do without me, I could sure do without him. Dropped him out of my heart then and there."

Sable sensed that the pain of the incident continued to linger in spite of Araminta's staunch stance.

"After that, I turned my life over to the Work."

Her "Work" entailed much more than encouraging slaves to leave their masters, Sable learned. Mrs. Tubman also did reconnaissance missions for the Union command, mainly the Second South Carolina Volunteers. "They're a Black brigade under Colonel James Montgomery," Araminta told her.

"You certainly don't look like a Union spy," Sable said with a smile.

Araminta grinned. "Sure don't. No one would suspect an old Black woman with a bandanna on her head to be scouting naval defenses or city fortifications. Who would believe I'd be behind enemy lines for the express purpose of gathering information on livestock, supplies, and rumors of troop movements?"

Sable had to agree. Araminta appeared aged and

harmless, not the kind of woman who always carried a pistol, or the kind who, on her treks north, threatened to shoot any man who faltered or whined about the hard journey.

She told Sable, "It's two things I got a right to and these are Liberty and Death. One or the other I mean to have. No one will take me back alive; I shall fight for my liberty, and when the time has come for me to go, the Lord will let them kill me."

They set out after dark. When Araminta instructed Sable to be quiet and sit still, Sable obeyed. When she asked Sable to stay behind and wait while she scouted ahead, pistol drawn, Sable did that also.

During the next day's daylight hours, they slept in the shell of a Yankee-burned mansion and headed out again as soon as dusk gave way to night. As dawn of the second day approached, Sable began to notice a change in the landscape. A dense forest had once covered this area but now, the land looked as if a giant had come through with a mighty scythe and cut down every tree. There were acres and acres of nothing but stumps for as far as the eye could see.

"General Sherman needed the wood," Araminta explained.

Sable marveled at the denuded land and her awe grew when she and her companion crossed what had once been one of the region's main railroad lines. The iron ties had been torn out of the rails and were now twisted macabrely around the trunks of the few trees that remained.

Araminta explained, "They're called Sherman's neckties. His men tear up the ties, then heat them in a pile. Once the ties are red hot, they're twisted around trees. Rebs can't use the ties or the railroad. Smart man, that General Sherman."

Sable could only stare in amazement.

They walked for four days, through burned-out battlefields filled with fresh graves, across land scarred by cannon fire and past abandoned fortifications. There were more Sherman neckties, and every now and then the bodies of soldiers in blue and gray who'd died alone and remained unburied.

Midnight of the fourth day found them crouched in the thick brush above the banks of the Ocmulgee River. It was a moonless night, and the surroundings were so silent, they could hear the water lapping softly against the embankment.

Whispering, Sable asked, "Why are we here?"

"To meet some friends," came Araminta's low reply.

Sable didn't see anyone. "Where?"

"Out there," Araminta answered, pointing at the dark river. "Let's see if they're at home."

Sable watched silently as Araminta struck a match on a flint and held the flame above her head. She waved it toward the river for only a second, then blew it out.

A few heartbeats later, an answering light appeared against the blackness. Araminta took Sable's hand. "Come, we must hurry."

Sable was surprised by the old woman's agility as they made their way quickly down the bank, but she was surprised even more to see six Black men propelling a raft silently toward them.

Araminta splashed out into the water to meet them, and Sable, faced with no other choice, did the same. Both women were helped aboard by strong arms.

"Take a seat, ladies," said a tall man. "We need to get across as quickly as possible."

Sable sat beside Araminta on the damp wood. The men dug their poles into the shallow water and turned the conveyance around. Sable had no idea where they were headed or who these men were, but she trusted Araminta and the Old Queens to keep her safe.

Up river, Major Raimond LeVeq of the Union army paced back and forth in front of his tent. Mrs. Tubman was a day late. If she didn't show up tonight, he and his small band of cavalry were going to have to push on without her, even though she might be carrying information vital to the Union command.

Not that she couldn't make her way back to the main camp on her own. Her reconnaisance and survivial skills were so legendary that the late abolitionist John Brown had dubbed her "the General." While in South Carolina with Colonel James Montgomery she'd headed a group of Black men who'd acted as the unit's scouts and spies. Montgomery, one of the Union army's best guerrilla fighters and foragers, had used her tips to mount raids in South Carolina, Florida, and Georgia. One of the most celebrated sorties had taken place near the Combahee River in June 1863. Not only had Montgomery and his eight hundred Black soldiers destroyed millions of dollars' worth of Confederate warehouses, cotton, and assorted other buildings, but Mrs. Tubman had led nearly eight hundred slaves to freedom that day. A front-page article in the *Boston Commonwealth*, printed a month later, had given her credit for guiding the soldiers, and noted that none of Montgomery's men received so much as a scratch.

Raimond hoped this delay didn't mean she'd been captured or injured.

Thinking about Mrs. Tubman's fate served another purpose. It took Raimond's mind off the heartbreaking news he'd received from home. His brother, Gerrold LeVeq, had been killed in a battle in Mississippi more than six weeks previously, but because of the war, Raimond hadn't received the letter from his grieving mother, Juliana, until two days ago, informing him of the death and subsequent funeral. Gerrold had been buried in the family plot outside their hometown of New Orleans. Had the news reached Raimond in a more timely manner, he might have been at his mother's side, consoling her, as his brother's casket was lowered into the earth. Raimond had loved Gerrold deeply, and his death left him stricken. Although he knew personal heartache had to be set aside during times of war, he found it impossible to keep the pain entirely at bay.

"Major?"

Raimond looked up to see his aide and friend, Andre Renaud. "The sentries say they've received a signal verifyng that Mrs. Tubman's on her way."

Raimond allowed himself a small smile. This was the best news he'd heard in days. "Good."

"Do you wish to head back tonight," Andre asked, "or shall we wait until morning?"

"Tonight."

Although Union forces now controlled most of the area surrounding Atlanta, the Rebs were not in full retreat. It had become a guerrilla war. Pockets of Confederate resisters, using hit-and-run tactics to harass Union camps and outposts, were beginning to drive Sherman to distraction. Raimond had no desire to tangle with the Rebs, mainly because the men assigned to this mission were as green as spring grass, newly mustered Black recruits who needed more training in weaponary and tactics before they could be called upon to defend themselves and those around them. "As soon as Mrs. Tubman arrives, escort her here, then have everyone move out. If we push it, we can make camp by dawn."

"I'll inform the sergeants they should begin preparations."

"*Merci*."

When the raft reached the shore, Sable waited while Araminta thanked the men, then both women waded ashore. The raft pushed silently off again. A quick scamper up the bank brought them to where a man wearing a blue uniform waited with a lantern. "Mrs. Tubman?" he asked.

"Yes, it's me."

"Welcome back, General. The major is waiting for you. Please follow me."

They fell in behind him, and Sable, surprised by the sight of a Black man in a uniform, said to Araminta, "I didn't know you were a general."

Araminta chuckled. "I wear many bandannas, child."

The soldier ushered them into a dimly lit tent. The man inside was dark-skinned and tower tall. The razor-thin beard highlighting his chiseled jaw set off a handsomeness that not even the shadows could mask.

Upon their entrance a smile creased his face. Hastening over, he grabbed Araminta in an affectionate hug that lifted her off her feet. Laughing, she cackled, "Put me down, you big bear. Old woman like me can't take all this."

He grinnned and set her on her feet. "I was beginning to worry about you. Where've you been?"

"Had to wait for Sable."

The man seemed to notice Sable's presence for the first time. He bowed. "*Pardonez-moi, mademoiselle.* In my zeal to greet an old friend I forgot my manners. I am Major Raimond LeVeq."

Even dressed in the ragged blue uniform, he was tall, gallant, and very overwhelming. "I'm Sable Fontaine."

"*Enchanté,* Sable Fontaine."

She sensed he was a man at ease with women. His coal-black eyes and dazzling French accent undoubtedly rendered most of them witless.

He turned his attention back to Araminta while Sable wondered why she'd been brought there. Araminta told LeVeq, "I need to pass my report on to General Sherman as soon as possible."

"I thought that might be the case, so we're pulling out as soon as we can."

"Good. I'll ride on ahead if you don't mind."

"No, I don't. I'll send a couple of men as escorts."

"Company is always welcome. Will you see to Sable?"

He turned back to her. "Of course."

"Get her a job clerking or something. She's real smart."

"I'll see what I can do."

Sable felt her chin rising of its own accord as their gazes held. "I prefer to go along with Araminta, if that's possible," she stated.

He shook his head. "It isn't. I can spare one horse, but not two. My men and I will see that you arrive safely."

Araminta interjected, "Then it's settled. Sable, I'll see you later today. Raimond, take good care of her. According to my dream, she'll be your reward."

"For what?"

"Just take care of her."

Before Sable or Raimond could question her further, she slipped out the tent's flap and was gone.

For a moment they just stood there, then Sable finally broke the awkward silence. "She sets great stock by her dreams, it seems."

"Yes, she does."

"Do you have any idea what she meant?"

"About your being my reward? No, but you're so beautiful, I'm interested in finding out."

He was a born charmer, she could already see that. "That's very flattering, but I'm not interested."

"No?" He folded his arms over his chest and surveyed her. "May I ask why not?"

"I'm here for freedom, not a dalliance with a man I don't know."

"How about a dalliance with a man you *do* know?"

She couldn't hide her smile. "No."

"Fair enough, but Araminta's dreams are very powerful. You may become my reward whether you like it or not."

Sable found fault with his logic, but not with his power to turn a woman's head. She tossed back saucily, "You are entirely too sure of yourself, Major. Certainly someone has pointed that out before."

"Never," he replied.

He had eyes that would make a woman surrender her soul. "So when are we leaving and where are we going?"

"I love a challenging woman."

Sable shook her head. "I'm not here to be a challenge."

"Just my reward."

"Rewards are earned."

"You doubt my worthiness?" he asked, his eyes sparkling with mirth.

"Just your faithfulness."

"To you I could be faithful."

"Lightning strikes those who lie, Major LeVeq."

Raimond laughed. "I am going to enjoy earning my reward, Miss Fontaine."

"You cannot earn what isn't offered."

"We'll see."

He escorted her from the tent. Their first argument began when Sable refused his offer to ride with him atop his beautiful stallion. "I can walk, Major."

Saddling his stallion, Raimond looked over at her standing beside the tent. The first thing he planned to do was find a replacement for that rag of a dress. She was too beautiful for such tattered attire. "Are you afraid of horses?"

"No."

"Then why won't you ride with me?"

"Because I don't know you well enough, Major."

"You're worried about your reputation?"

"Among other things, yes."

"It's a very long walk."

"Walking is all I've been doing for the past four days. I can make it."

"We must return to camp as quickly as possible. We can't do that if we have to match our pace to your walk."

"Why is speed so imperative?"

"These woods are full of Rebs and we're not looking for a fight."

Sable also had no desire to be caught up in a battle. She thought long and hard for an alternate solution to her dilemma, but could not come up with one. It came to her that riding with one of the other soldiers might prove better, but she didn't know any of them either. "I suppose I shall have to ride with you," she conceded.

"Excellent choice."

The horse was now saddled. Raimond mounted, then reached down to lift her up. When she was settled across the saddle in front of him, he told her, "You're going to have to lean back a bit, Miss Fontaine. I won't be able to see clearly with you sitting up as stiff as a fence post. I promise I won't bite unless asked."

Sable didn't reply to that last playful disclaimer. Instead she did as instructed and leaned back a bit so that his strong chest pressed against her shoulder and side.

"Comfortable?" he asked, looking down into her eyes.

"Not really, no, but I've no other choice, have I?"

"By now, most women would be melting in my arms."

"You remind me so much of my brother. Women come very easily to him too."

"And is that a bad thing?"

"For the women who are left in pieces, yes, it is a bad thing."

"Has a man ever left you in pieces?"

"No."

"And neither shall I."

He said no more as he urged the horse forward.

Raimond and his small band of fifteen cavalrymen were now gathered on the outskirts of the makeshift camp, ready to leave. Sable tried to ignore the curiosity she sensed in the other men as LeVeq introduced her as a friend of Mrs. Tubman. She knew that to them she looked more like a friend of the major, but no one expressed this thought, at least not within earshot.

As they set off down the road, Sable wondered where the Old Queens were leading her now. She was riding with a group of Yankees, and she didn't know whether to be elated or fearful. Since the beginning of the war, slaves had been told lurid tales about the Yankees. Owners like Sally Ann had gone out of their way to try to convince their slaves that the Yankees both consumed human flesh and committed such ghastly atrocities that no slave in his or her right mind would want to seek freedom. Sable didn't believe the tales, but she did feel apprehensive about crossing over into this new life.

"Where are we going?" she asked.

"A contraband camp up river."

"What's a contraband camp?"

"A place where escaped slaves can stay until the government decides what to do with them."

"I've heard about such encampments."

"They're overcrowded. There's sickness, little food. We're asking folks to go elsewhere if they can."

Sable wondered what he meant by "we." Although he had introduced himslef as a major, she doubted a man of the race would have anything to say about such matters. But then, she'd never been free before. Were such things possible? "How long have you been a major?" she asked.

"Since Lincoln opened the door for Black men to fight in '63."

"Where's home?"

"I was born in Haiti, but Louisiana's home."

She found that surprising.

"Where's home for you?" he asked.

"South of here," was all she'd admit.

She sensed him waiting for her to explain further, but when he didn't press she relaxed.

Sable had no idea she'd fallen asleep until she was shaken lightly awake. Disoriented and groggy, she opened her eyes. Her position atop the horse startled her just as much as LeVeq's smile did, but the memories soon slid back.

"*Bonjour,*" he said softly.

In the full light of dawn, he was even more handsome than he'd appeared previously. "Good morning," she answered sleepily. "Are we at the camp yet?"

"In another few minutes. I thought I'd give you the option of dismounting before we arrive, if you wish. I'm thinking about your reputation and all."

Sable had had no intention of falling asleep within his arms. "I must've been very tired. I'm sorry I fell asleep."

"No apology needed. I'm pleased you were so comfortable."

The road had become so narrow, they were riding single file. Sable looked up at the major and asked, "Can we stop for a moment? I need to . . ."

He searched her face and deduced her plight. "Of course."

She was glad she didn't have to explain fully. Having to voice the request had been embarrassing enough. In reponse to his shouted command, the line halted, and he veered his horse out of formation, carrying Sable into the dense trees bordering the road. He dismounted, then reached up, and after placing his sure hands around her waist, slowly eased her to the ground.

"I'll be right back," she promised, and hastened farther into the trees for privacy.

She took care of her needs, then returned. She felt much better as she repositioned herself, and he guided the horse back to the others.

"Better?" he asked as they got under way.

"Yes. Thank you."

Less than an hour later, the small company of Black cavalrymen crested a rise, and the sight of the vast encampment spread across the valley below them took Sable's breath away.

With a dignity that lent power to his words, her escort said, "Welcome to freedom, Miss Fontaine."

Filled with an emotion she couldn't name, Sable met his gaze. "Is this it?"

"Yes."

Sable realized there were tears standing in her eyes. *Freedom!* For three generations the women in her line had lived as captives, unable to breathe free, walk free, or live as they chose, but now the circle had been broken. She'd crossed over, and like Araminta, she vowed she'd die before they took her back. "I'd prefer to walk in on my own, if I might."

He nodded. Under the curious eyes of the others, Sable dismounted and began to walk slowly down the rise. She was vaguely aware of the rest of the mounted company passing her by as they rode pell-mell down the hill, their joy apparent, but she took her time. As she did, she turned her eyes up to the dawn sky and threw a kiss to Mahti and the Old Queens, thanking them for their protection and for sending Ararminta to be her guide to freedom.

The major had not exaggerated the camp's crowded conditions. Tents and wooden shacks covered the land for as far as she could see. There seemed to be hundreds of Black folks walking about, gathered around low-burning cook fires, seated in front of tents. Some were sitting silently while others conversed spiritedly. The smell of smoke and cooking food filled the early morning air. She heard babies crying and dogs barking. There were old women hawking eggs and livestock bawling from makeshift pens. She looked up to see the major mounted at her side and said happily, "I don't know whether to laugh or cry."

"Both, if they are with joy."

She liked him, she realized. Beneath his handsome playfulness was a man of depth and feeling. "Where do I go now?"

"With me to be processed."

Sable gave him such a skeptical look, his face brightened with a smile. "You doubt my intentions?"

Sable suspected he treated all women to his dazzling charm, making them feel as if they were the center of his world, but she saw no harm in basking in the attention for a short while. "I doubt your intentions, yes," she declared.

"Challenging, beautiful, *and* smart," he told her, his eyes shining with amusement. "Earning my reward may not be as easy as I first thought."

"Building snowmen for the devil may be easier."

He chuckled. "You are going to be worth more than gold, I'm thinking."

"Much more."

Their eyes held for a moment longer, and it seemed as if the world had ceased to turn.

Sable shook off the odd reverie. "Where does this processing take place?"

"At the big house in the center of camp." Raimond felt as if he'd just had roots worked on him. He swore he saw his future in her eyes.

She looked around. "Which direction?"

He pointed east. "About a half-mile that way."

The people in the camp flowed around them. Men tipped their hats to Sable as they passed. Others shook the mounted major's hand to welcome him back. She noted how he took time to reply to all the cries of "Good morning, Major" thrown his way, and to acknowledge everyone who approached him, from wizened elders and small children, to young women with flirting eyes. He appeared to be quite popular here. Although Sable would never admit it out loud, the respect he showed the residents and the respect they offered in return further enhanced his standing in her eyes. "Will I be able to find the processing station on my own?" she asked.

He shrugged. "Maybe, but this is a big place. It was once one of the largest plantations in the area, or so I've been told."

Sable knew she should probably distance herself from the French major. Who knew what could happen if she became susceptible to his charm? But she decided to accept his offer of help one last time. "I'll accept your escort, but I will not ride."

"Fair enough."

He set the black stallion's pace to match her steps, and they ventured into the camp.

On the way, he was greeted by more of the residents and many soldiers. Sable told him, "You seem to know everyone here."

"Just about."

"Do you hold a position of authority?"

"I suppose you could call it that. I'm in charge here."

Sable stopped in her tracks. "You're jesting."

He shook his head. "No, I'm the camp commander."

Sable's surprise lingered. "I knew the Yankees had some Black soldiers, but I never imagined they'd let men of the race be in charge of anything. Do you have real authority?"

"I have the authority to protect this camp and its residents against incursion, yes."

"I'm impressed, Major."

"I'm glad there's something about me that impresses you."

"Accustomed to impressing people, are you?"

"Women, yes."

She laughed. "Are all the men in Louisiana as "accustomed" as you?"

"My brothers and I are."

"Are there any women left unmoved once you and your brothers get through with them?"

"Hardly any."

"Well, then you should be glad we met."

"Why?"

"Because no man should get everything he desires."

"You're challenging me again," he cautioned.

Sable simply smiled and walked on.

Once they reached the original plantation house, with its tall white columns, Raimond urged her to let him take her inside so she could bypass the large crowd lined up outside. She politely declined. "No one will appreciate me going ahead of them. They look as if they've been here quite some time. I'll wait my turn."

"Challenging, beautiful, smart, *and* stubborn," he informed her. "Then I suppose I should go inside and get back to work. Will you at least come and clerk for me?"

Sable noticed the others in line listening to their conversation. "No," she replied. "I'll make my own way."

He did not look convinced, but Sable paid him no mind. Working for him would undoubtedly cause gossip, and she didn't need gossip trailing her to freedom. "Thank you for all your help, Major."

"My pleasure. I will see you again, I'm sure. *Au revoir, mademoiselle.*"

He turned the stallion around and rode off toward the back of the house. The sprawling structure reminded Sable of the Fontaines' white mansion. Thinking about them brought back the tragic memories of her last night there. Burying her grief over Mahti's death, she silently waited her turn.

At the front of the line Sable stepped up to the table in the parlor and faced the sour-faced Black soldier seated there. "Name?" he asked.

"Sable Fontaine."

"Were you a captive before coming here?"

"Yes."

"Are you carrying information the generals might be interested in?"

"What sort of information?"

"Troop movements, rumors, locations of supply depots."

"No."

He finally looked up. "Is there someplace else you can go?"

The question confused her. "I don't understand."

"Is there someplace else you can stay besides here in the camp?"

"No, why?"

"We've more runaways here than we can provide for," he stated bluntly. "People are sick and hungry. We're encouraging folks to go elsewhere."

"I've nowhere else to go."

He kept his face expressionless, but she sensed her answer had not pleased him when he said, "Everybody here works to earn his keep. How do you intend to feed yourself, Miss Fontaine?"

Sable had to admit she hadn't thought that far ahead. "Well, I don't know. What kind of work is there?"

"Do you have children?"

"No."

"That's something in your favor. Women on their own can take in sewing, rent themselves out to the locals, or find a protector."

Sable blinked at that last choice. Surely he wasn't encouraging her to become a woman of ill-repute!

"Are you a fancy girl?"

Sable blinked again. Did this man have any manners at all? Holding on to her patience, she replied stiffly, "No, I'm not a pleasure woman."

"Then I'm assuming from your speech and appearance that you were a house servant. Can you do anything?"

Sable took offense again. "It depends on what that means. Yes, I did serve in the house, but I'm sure I can contribute in some way. What needs to be done here?"

"Do you like laundry?"

She looked into his flashing eyes and replied truthfully, "Not particularly, no." As a ghost of a smile flitted across his full lips, she added, "But since I've admitted that, I assume that's where I'll be assigned."

"Correct. You'll find Mrs. Reese on the western edge of camp. Report there and she'll put you to work."

The man looked impatiently past her, then called out, "Next!"

Assuming she'd been dismissed, Sable turned on her heel and left.

Araminta was waiting outside, and Sable was certainly glad to see her. "Hello."

"Hello to you too, Sable. I see you made it here all right."

"Yes, thanks to you."

"Don't thank me. I just do what I'm called to do. You and the major get along?"

"For the most part, yes. Why?"

"Just curious."

Sable didn't believe that for a minute. She had the strong sense that Araminta was trying to play matchmaker. "Tell me about this dream you had."

"Let's get something to eat first. Hungry?"

"Extremely."

Araminta chuckled, then gestured. "This way."

As Sable followed her new friend through the crowded camp, she saw soldiers, both Black and White, dressed in the Union blue, driving wagons, patrolling, and practicing drills. "Seeing all these Black soldiers is still amazing to me," she said.

"They make you proud, don't they? There's almost two hundred thousand of them helping Mr. Lincoln win this war."

On the fringe of the main encampment, Araminta had erected a small camp that consisted of a small canvas tent and a cook fire. The women shared a breakfast of hardtack and coffee. Sable had never tasted hardtack before. The small, square Union staple was nothing more than hard, stale bread.

Araminta explained, "All the troops eat it. If you put it in your coffee, it'll soften up a bit."

Sable dunked an edge in the coffee and found it did help.

"The boys call them teeth dullers. Don't eat them at night though."

"Why not?"

"Can't see if there's worms in them. The boys call 'em worm castles too, just so you know."

Sable's eyes widened with alarm as she carefully surveyed the remaining portion in her hand.

Araminta chuckled.

Confident she hadn't consumed any worms, Sable said, "Now tell me about this dream you had about me."

"Not much to tell really. I had it about a year ago. I dreamed LeVeq and I were on one of his ships."

"The major owns ships?"

"Quite a few, but in the dream, the ship he and I were on was in the middle of a terrible storm. Lightning was flashing, and the waves were rising higher than our heads. Then came the biggest wave we'd seen and when it crashed onto the deck, it left a chest behind."

Sable's brows knitted in confusion. "A chest?"

"Yes, a big, old sea chest. The major finally got it open and you stepped out!"

"Me!"

"You. Of course I didn't know it was you at the time, but yes, Sable, you were in the chest."

"Was there anything else in it?"

"Yep. A bunch of babies. Brown ones, Black ones, gold ones. They came spilling out like a bunch of puppies."

Sable had never heard anything like this before in her life. "Babies?"

"Dozens of them."

Sable smiled and shook her head. "Was there anything else?"

"Yes, a thin gold bracelet."

Sable drew in a sharp breath.

"When the major placed it on your wrist, the sea calmed and the sun came out."

Sable didn't know what to think. Part of her wanted to show Araminta Mahti's bracelet to see if it matched the one in the dream. But did she really want to know? she asked herself. She answered with a resounding no! "How did you find me at the old Dresden place?"

"Funny thing. I had a dream about that same chest a few days before we met. It was sitting in front of a burning house, and I could hear something knocking around inside it. When I opened it, a golden bird flew out. I chased it for a long time, then finally caught it outside a house that looked a lot like the house where we met. When I got up that next morning, I set out to find that house. I had no idea where it was, or who or what I'd find there, but I knew something was waiting for me there.

"So you just up and went."

"Sure did. Glad I did too."

Sable smiled. She didn't know how much of this tale she believed, but she was glad Araminta had believed it, otherwise they probably would never have met. "Babies, huh?"

"Yep, babies."

Sable wondered if the dream meant she and the major were going to have children. She immediately decided that was something else she'd no desire to ask Araminta about. A change in topic seemed overdue. "Do you know why this is called a contraband camp?"

"It's the word everyone is using to describe the slaves who escape to the army. It was first applied to runaways in May of '61, when three male slaves deserted over to the Union forces stationed near Fortress Monroe, Virginia. The Union general Benjamin Butler took them in and let them stay."

"That was very fair-minded of him," Sable said.

"I agree, but a Confederate colonel arrived the following day waving a white flag of truce and demanding the return of his property."

"What did Butler do?"

"Declined. Told the Reb colonel that because the state of Virginia had chosen to withdraw from the Union, all property of any kind was subject to confiscation, as in any war. The three slaves were termed contraband of war and sent to work building a Union bakehouse."

"And that's where the phrase comes from?"

"Yep. The phrase became a popular one with the Northern press and soon came to be applied to all Blacks seeking safety behind Union lines."

"Interesting."

According to Araminta, by July 1861, General Butler and his troops had become a beacon of hope—almost a thousand new contrabands had sought safety behind Union lines at Fortress Monroe. When the first full year of the war ended, there were thousands of additional contrabands following the Union armies, camped outside Washington and in the tidewater regions of Virginia and South Carolina. To the west, camps formed in Union-held territory on the Mississippi.

Araminta said, "At first, Butler's decision to offer those slaves harbor didn't sit well with the Washington politicians. Up until then runaways had been returned to their masters."

Sable found that confusing. "It seems to me the Yankee politicians would have been better served by encouraging slaves to run, not returning them. After all, we slaves are—or shall I say were—the wheels on the Confederacy's war train."

"It took them a while before they finally figured that out."

Having been a slave, Sable knew that the enslaved population hauled supplies to the Confederate troops, worked in cotton factories and in munitions plants. In addition to mining gold in North Carolina, iron in Kentucky, and salt in Virginia, they built railroads, raised food, and fortified defenses around the cities. In fact, the Southern government thought its "property" so vital to its plans, slaves had been drafted into the war effort *before* the call went out for the White fathers and sons of the South to take up arms.

"So all of the escaped slaves are in these camps?" Sable asked.

"Not all, but many. Some are being relocated to what the Union's calling 'home farms.' They're given land and seed so they can support their families."

"Where's the government getting the land?"

"Most of it's confiscated Reb property."

"I'll wager the masters are real happy with that arrangement," Sable cracked sarcastically.

Araminta grinned.

When Araminta asked Sable how the processing had gone, Sable offered only that she'd been assigned to the laundry. Mrs. Tubman peered at her for a moment, then said, "I'd've thought you'd been put to work clerking or something."

"The laundry," Sable repeated emotionlessly.

"Well, I'll talk to the major about it later."

"No. The soldier was very specific. The laundry will be fine."

"Are you sure?"

Sable nodded. "I'm certain."

Araminta still looked puzzled, but said no more.

After breakfast, Araminta offered to show Sable the way to the laundry. They took a meandering route to give Sable a chance to see more of the camp that would serve as her new home. As they walked, Sable realized it was far larger and more crowded than she'd first thought. The tents were pitched so close together, one had to be careful to avoid stepping on bedding, tent poles, cooking fires, and small children. There were even more people than there were tents. Black people of all shades, ages, and sizes filled Sable's vision wherever she looked. Some women nodded greetings, which she returned generously, while others sized her up without smiling. There were men digging trenches, children playing happily, and areas that were roped off. Armed soldiers were stationed at the ropes as if guarding against something.

"Probably typhoid or measles," Araminta explained. "The area's quarantined."

"Are there doctors here?"

"Not nearly as many as we need. They put up a hospital of sorts in a house over behind the trees there, and the army does what it can, but the soldiers come first, as they should. I help out whenever I can. Once you get settled you might want to lend a hand too."

Sable thought she would, then considered the poor souls who were forced to live behind the ropes. It chilled her to think they'd come all this way to freedom, only to contract a disease that might well kill them. She offered a quick prayer for them before following Araminta deeper into the camp.

They passed a grove of trees where a woman sat surrounded by a large group of children and adults. She appeared to be showing them pages in a book. Araminta explained she was one of the Northern missionary women who'd come South to help in the camps. This particular woman ran one of the camp schools.

Araminta made a detour so Sable could see the vast gardens that had been planted. She also showed her the camp graveyard. It reminded Sable very much of the one at home. There were very few markers. Most of the spots were memorialized with objects last used by the person interred. Spread out on the ground were broken pieces of crockery, spoons, combs, and bits of colored glass. She saw pieces of fabric, and in one spot a beautiful quilt had been staked down. Near the quilt stood a small but exquisitely carved wooden idol. It had the look of the motherland and made Sable think of Mahti.

The laundry was set up on the banks of a fairly wide creek. According to Araminta, access to such fresh water was one of the reasons the camp had been settled here. Sable was led past huge cauldrons filled with boiling water and the silent, watching women tending them.

Yards and yards of rope had been strung between trees to form clotheslines. In spite of the still early hour, more than a few lines were already straining under the weight of bedding, army uniforms, union suits, and blankets. Sable smelled the lye and felt the heat coming off the vats, fed by stick fires underneath them. She watched a woman use a long length of wood to lift out a steaming mound of wash and transfer it to a neighboring vat to be rinsed.

This would be hard, grueling work, especially under a full sun. Sable silently and sarcastically thanked the processing soldier for the opportunity to work there.

Araminta turned Sable over to the head laundress, a kindly woman named Mrs. Reese, but before leaving she took Sable aside.

"I have to go do some looking around for the generals, and I don't know when I'll be back."

Sable tried not to let her disappointment show. "I'll never be able to thank you for what you've done."

"Sure you can. Just don't squander your freedom."

They shared a hug and Araminta smiled. "Stay on the path, Sable, and good things will happen."

She waved and was gone.

Mrs. Reese turned out to be a surprisingly optimistic woman. She was big and brown and had a sprinkling of freckles across her nose. To Sable's surprise she was not a runaway, but a free Black woman from Boston. "I own the biggest laundry in my part of town, and I wanted to come down here and help. When I arrived and explained what I could do, I thought General Sherman was going to kiss me, he was so happy."

"You came South to do laundry?"

"Yep. With me around, our boys can concentrate on whipping those Rebs instead of doing wash. Come on. I want you to meet the others."

The others turned out to be four women of varying sizes and hues. Some were older, some looked to be Sable's age, none looked overly friendly. Their names were Dorothy, Bridget, Paige, and Sookie. Only Bridget offered a smile.

Mrs. Reese then took Sable to a group of tents. "This is where you'll sleep. Had two girls run out on me, so you're in here with Sookie and Paige. It'll be kind of cozy, but it's better than being out in the open."

Inside the tent there were three pallets. Beside two of them were small bundles of clothing that Sable assumed belonged to her tent mates. Mrs. Reese pointed out the pallet on the far left as being Sable's, then escorted her back outside.

"First thing we need to do is get you cleaned up."

Sable could only agree. She hadn't bathed in quite some time, and her filthy clothing and dirty skin reflected it all too well.

"I had the troops rig me up a shower of sorts."

Sable studied the contraption. When the rope was pulled on an overhead bucket full of water, the bucket tipped and the water cascaded down in one fell swoop. The shower was housed in a listing wooden enclosure that offered a measure of privacy.

"You only get one bucket per wash."

Sable thought the shower was ingenious and couldn't wait to try it.

"Go ahead and wash. The water's going to be cold, but you'll get used to it. And you may as well toss that dress you're wearing onto the rag pile. I've got a few spares around. I'm sure I can find something that will fit. Use that sheet there to dry yourself. It's clean."

Sable was left to wash. She gasped as the bucket of icy water came down and rinsed her clean. She felt like a new woman.

Per Mrs. Reese's instructions, she dried herself with the rough cotton sheet. A knock sounded shortly thereafter, signaling the return of the laundress. Wrapped in the sheet, Sable cautiously cracked open the thin wood door and took the offered dress from Mrs. Reese's hand.

The common day dress, made of black and white checked gingham, was neither fashionable nor elegant, but it fit, as did the rough muslin drawers. Sable made a point of securing Mahti's bracelet to the strings of her drawers before pushing her bare feet into her worn slippers. Shoes were going to be a real need very soon. She doubted these would hold together much longer.

Mrs. Reese ushered Sable into her tent to finish acquainting her with her duties. "I'll pay you ten cents a day. The days you don't work, you don't get paid. Some of the girls have regular laundry customers, so make sure you don't horn in on somebody else's territory."

Sable nodded her understanding, then asked, "What about meals?"

"You can eat the army rations like everyone else here and take your chances with the salt horse or the lobcourse—"

"Salt horse?"

"It's army beef so full of salt you have to soak it in water for hours before you can eat it. Most times though, after it's soaked, you find it's so rancid you can't get near enough to eat it for the smell."

Sable's nose wrinkled. "What's lobcourse?"

"Soup. Made out of salt pork, hardtack, and anything else the army cooks can find to throw in the pot."

"Neither sounds very appetizing."

"They're not. I can cook for you if you'd like, but in exchange, I take twenty cents a week out of your pay. On Sundays you're on own. My food isn't fancy, but you won't starve like some folks here."

Since Sable was in no position to quibble, she agreed.

Chapter 3

Major Raimond LeVeq put down his pen and stretched wearily. He'd been doing paperwork for most of the day and was tired. Because no one in the local Union command had the time, or in some cases the desire, to deal with the ever increasing numbers of contrabands arriving daily, it had been left to him. He was in charge of what the army had loosely dubbed contraband liaison. General Benjamin Butler had recommended him for the post, and he now reported to Colonel John Eaton, tapped by Grant in 1862 to be superintendent of contraband for the Mississippi Valley.

Raimond had joined the fight as a member of the famed First Louisiana Native Guard, whose ranks were successors of the highly decorated regiment of free Blacks who had helped Andrew Jackson repel the British during the War of 1812. He'd been transferred to this Georgia camp less than a month ago. Helping contrabands bridge the transition to freedom had not been his reason for going to war, but he knew conditions here would be infinitely worse were he not present to help manage the chaos.

Raimond's aide, Andre Renaud, knocked on the partially open door. "May I come in?"

"If I say no, will you go away?"

"Probably not," the younger man admitted with a smile.

Raimond beckoned him to enter. Andre did, followed by a disgruntled-looking soldier.

Andre made the introductions. "Major, this is Private Dawson Marks. He beat up the sutler."

"Congratulations, soldier. I only wish I'd been there to lend my boot to him too."

Sutlers were one-man general stores, appointed by the government and contracted one to a regiment to sell supplies to the troops. Most were greedy bastards who took full advantage of their monopoly by selling necessities at prices far above the standard. Charlie Handler, the sutler there, sold butter for the outrageous price of one dollar a pound, and Mr. Borden's condensed milk for seventy-five cents a can. Only the six-for-a-quarter molasses cookies, a favorite of the Union troops, were reasonably affordable.

Raimond told the soldier, "Private Marks, in spite of how we all feel about the sutler, I have to put you on report."

"But he cheated me."

"Son, he cheats everyone. How much does he owe you?"

"Sixty cents."

"I'll see it's returned to you before the end of the day. In the meantime, you're assigned to stable-cleaning detail for the next two days. Dismissed."

The soldier saluted and left.

"Anyone else out there?" Raimond asked.

Andre nodded. "Reverend Peep."

Peep was a representative from one of the missionary societies that had been coordinating donations from the churches up North.

"Bring him in."

The Reverend Josiah Peep's kind heart was as large as his massive girth. Born in Virginia to a slave-owning family, he'd turned his back on that way of life and now devoted himself to his church and to helping the refugees. He entered carrying a large crate on his huge shoulder. "Afternoon, Major."

"Afternoon, Reverend. What can I do for you?"

"If you can stop these fool people from sending us worthless goods, I will put your name in my will."

He dumped the crate to the ground. It burst open and hammers spilled out onto the floor. "They sent us these this time around, Major. Last month it was horse bridles."

Raimond sighed tiredly. Hammers and horse bridles were certainly useful, but you couldn't sleep under them, nor could you feed them to hungry children.

"Tell your generals we need blankets and food," Peep demanded as he exited the office.

Raimond looked to Andre. "Anyone else?"

Andre shook his head.

"Good."

After Andre's departure, Raimond looked down at the hammers in the crate. He faced a dilemma shared by contraband camp commanders all over the South—too many people and not enough supplies. While some of the earlier camps established had been closed and their refugee populations moved to confiscated land, the numbers of confiscated and runaway slaves in many of the camps had climbed to critical levels. Where there had been only four hundred camped outside Washington in 1861, there were ten thousand a year later; an additional three thousand were camped across the river in Alexandria. Conditions ranged from tolerable to awful. Diseases such as diphtheria, typhoid, and measles found fertile ground among the weak and starving. Relief agencies run by both Blacks and Whites had stepped in to raise money and to distribute clothing, blankets and other goods, but there was never enough to go around. How the politicians planned to deal with the masses of former slaves when and if the war ended had not been clearly explained, but the size of the problem increased daily and Raimond did not believe it would simply solve itself.

He rubbed his weary eyes. He'd gotten no sleep last night, but his job didn't care. Every day the mountain of paperwork and problems grew higher, and the lines of new contrabands lengthened. Many had been following Sherman and his men for months and would probably continue to do so until the war ended, but the numbers of new arrivals were unprecedented.

He went over to the window and looked out. Below him were refugees lined up for processing. They'd been arriving twenty-four hours a day since the fall of Atlanta. There were men, women, grandparents, and babies. There were orphans, widows, and women of questionable character. Some had been brought in by troops and gunboats; others had simply walked in. To slaves all over the South, Mr. Lincoln's troops meant freedom, and contrary to the naysayers in the press and in Washington, Raimond knew that a majority of the freedmen were more than capable of successfully managing their own lives—if given the means and opportunity to do so.

From his own dealings here he knew that most of the contraband men were eager to work. They'd been hired by the army as teamsters, construction workers, and earth movers; some had even opted to don the Union blue and join one of the all Black regiments to help win the war. Every refugee in camp had come for freedom. Raimond shared their pride, but he was a man of action and adventure. He wasn't looking forward to spending many more days filling out papers and negotiating the complex army bureaucracy.

Black and White soldiers were being mustered here too. Many of the freedmen were choosing to wear the Union blue, but others were being forced by the army command to join the fight. They were being drilled, taught tactics, then sent off to war. Because slave owners forbade Blacks to handle firearms, most of the freedmen soldiers were hopeless on the firing range. They knew nothing about sights or triggers or the difference between a sixteen shot Henry and a musket. Some of the commanders were tolerant and patient, or as patient as men could be knowing that their green troops could be thrown into the fight at any time. Other officers, those with no patience and even less experience, tried to whip the recruits into shape with bullying and insults. When their soldiers proved unprepared for battle, the officers blamed the new Black soldiers rather than their own incompetence. Prejudice and incompetence tended to play havoc with Raimond's temper, so he made a point of staying away from the drill grounds as much as possible when such commanders were on site.

He hadn't had many problems with prejudice here lately, although that wasn't always the case. Many of the White soldiers had made it clear they were fighting for the Union and fourteeen dollars a day—not to free slaves. Raimond did not like the attitude, but tolerated it as long as the men were not disrespectful to his face, didn't countermand his orders or refuse to carry them out. Those who did were put in their place no matter what their rank. Raimond was a major in the U.S. Army, perhaps the only Black major outside the state of Louisiana. His grandfather and the other members of the Louisiana Native Guard, or the Corps' d'Afrique as they liked to call themselves, had saved Andrew Jackson at Chalmette during the 1812 war. Having been free all his life, and well educated, Raimond did not have the temperament to suffer quietly the slings and arrows of White soldiers who couldn't even read their own names.

Sable worked from sunup to sundown washing the clothes of soldiers, campers, and the garishly painted whores who made their living following the soldiers from post to post. It was bone-aching work. Even though it was nearing the end of September, the days were still hot enough to make standing over a boiling vat filled with lye, water, and laundry seem like a trip into perdition. The first night, her arms ached so badly from the strain of lifting her weight in wet laundry, she could barely raise her arms to feed herself. She was so stiff the next morning, she could hardly move. Her hands were red and chapped from the harsh soap, and she knew they would only get worse, but she did not complain; for the first time in her life she was earning a wage. Her success in this new, free world rested in her own lye-reddened hands. She'd promised Araminta she wouldn't squander her freedom, and she intended to keep that pledge. The sacrifices made by Mahti and the Old Queens also meant much to Sable, and she couldn't think of a better way to honor them than by working diligently and making her life count—as long as the work didn't kill her first.

She felt lucky to have a job. As the soldier who'd processed her had hinted, there were few opportunities for women here, and women with small children had even less choice. Only a few were lucky enough to find someone who'd watch over their offspring while they hired themselves out to the army or to the locals as laundresses, cooks, or seamstresses. Most were relegated to monotonous, uneventful days of waiting for their men to return.

None of the other women in Mrs. Reese's employ had offered Sable a hand in friendship, so during the day she kept pretty much to herself. At night, she lay on her threadbare pallet and remembered those she'd left behind. She wondered about Vashti and little Cindi, and most of all she wondered about her sister, Mavis. Would they ever see each other again? Sable missed her very much. Mahti too.

On the fifth morning in camp, Sable saw Major LeVeq approaching the laundry area with a bundle of clothes in his arms. Their paths hadn't crossed since the day she'd arrived. Seeing him now made her remember the teasing banter they'd shared and the sensation of falling asleep in his arms. His handsomeness hadn't diminished a bit—he was still tall, bearded, and dazzling.

He approached the laundress named Sookie, who looked as if she was going to swoon as he handed her his bundle. Sable wondered if it was considered an honor to do his laundry. The cow-eyed woman apparently thought so. Shaking her head at the silliness of some of her gender, Sable resumed stirring her vat of clothes.

The work took a great deal of effort. To move the long length of wood around in the clothes-choked vat took more strength than she'd initially guessed. She still found it nearly impossible to move all of the clothes from the washing vat to the rinsing vat in one load, but that didn't stop her from trying. Sable forced the long piece of wood deep into the boiling water and lifted as much of the load as she could. Her arm muscles bulging, she'd almost cleared the lip to complete the transfer when a familiar, accented voice behind her asked, "What in the world are you doing here?"

Raimond LeVeq's unexpected presence broke Sable's concentration, and the clothes fell back into the vat, sending up a small shower of scalding water.

Sable jumped out of harm's way, irritation on her face. "This is where I've been assigned."

Raimond stared at her ill-fitting dress and mud-caked shoes and said, "You would be more useful clerking."

"I'm fine here, Major."

She wasn't really, but she wanted no special treatment. Many of the single women had become whores in order to keep themselves afloat. Just this morning, she'd overheard the other laundresses talking about certain White officers who had harems of dark beauties at their beck and call. Sable did not want to make herself beholden to the major for any help he might throw her way.

To Raimond Sable was even more beautiful than the night they'd first met. Her mysterious eyes were as green as the sea. A sea-faring man, he'd sailed all over the world, and everything about her called to him like the bewitching song of a siren. In spite of her obvious mixed-race parentage, her rich dark hair knotted at her nape bore the wave and thickness of its African ancestry. One could also see her tribal roots in her proud nose and lush mouth. "You clean up well," he remarked.

"I'm glad you approve," she said, not missing the daggers being shot her way by the other women. She didn't want to draw their wrath. "I need to get back to work."

"Would you dine with me this evening?"

Sable looked up in surprise. "No."

"Why not?"

"Because I'm not here to be your dessert at the end of the day."

He chuckled. Although he found the wording of her refusal novel, he enjoyed the idea of her as a dessert. "I'll be on my best behavior."

"That's what I'm afraid of." She resumed stirring. "Now leave me before you get me in trouble with Mrs. Reese."

"As you wish, but I won't stop asking," he promised with glowing eyes.

"Go," she commanded, trying to hide her smile.

He bowed gracefully and departed.

As Raimond made his way back across camp, he smiled at the thought of the lovely Miss Fontaine. She had a spice and sass that seemed to breathe excitement back into his soul. The war, the refugees, and the untimely death of his brother Gerrold had stifled his usually exuberant approach to life. He'd seen more death than he cared to remember and more despair than the world should be able to hold. Men were dying, the country was torn apart, and his mother in New Orleans was having to sell her possessions piece by piece in order to eat. Over the past few weeks, he'd thought the sun would never shine inside him again, but Sable's presence seemed to be changing that. Yes, he'd had a few discreet liaisons during his time here, but they'd never been more than a mutual satisfaction of need. Sable Fontaine made his blood rise. The challenge of getting to know her better and maybe wooing her into his bed made him feel alive again.

That evening as Sable and the other women sat eating dinner outside Mrs. Reese's tent, Sookie, the young woman who'd been given the major's clothes to launder that morning, asked, "What did he say to you?"

Since Sable had never been included in the women's conversations before, it took her a moment to realize the question had been directed her way, and that Sookie was referring to the major. She shrugged. "Nothing." She went back to the beans on her plate, hoping that would be the end of it, but of course it was not.

Paige, Sookie's friend, added coolly, "He was down there an awful long time to be saying nothing."

In the silence that followed, Sable could see they wouldn't turn the topic loose until she'd answered, so she told them the truth. "He asked me to dine with him."

"See, I knew she was down there flirting," Sookie snapped. "So when are you going?"

Sable wiped her plate with the last of her stale bread. "I'm not."

They stared at her as if she'd just sprouted wings.

Bridget, who'd been quiet until then, asked, "You're joshing, right?"

Sable shook her head. "No."

"Can't you see how handsome he is?" Sookie questioned.

"Do you know how rich he is?" Paige put in.

Sable answered truthfully, "I don't care."

It was obviously not the answer the women had been expecting. Their stunned faces made her smile.

Bridget cracked, "There isn't a female in this camp who tells him no."

"Then I'll be good for him. No man should have everything he desires."

When several of the women shook their heads at her response she asked, "What's wrong?"

"You're just not who we expected," Sookie confessed.

"What did you expect?"

"Someone who couldn't pull her weight and would complain all the time."

"Why?"

"Because of the way you look and talk."

Sable appreciated their bluntness. She wondered how many others viewed her with the same jaundiced eye. The misconception that her light brown skin and refined speech automatically made her different irritated her. No matter what color or pedigree, a slave was still a slave.

Granted, there were those who'd taken advantage of their station as house slaves and lorded it over those who toiled in the fields; in fact, she'd known a few such irritating people on some of the plantations near her home. But house slaves came in all colors. There were those whose skin bore the paleness of miscegenation and others whose faces reflected the true skin tones of their African ancestors. Opal, the housekeeper on the Fontaine place, had never allowed any distinctions; no one lorded it over anyone. If anyone under her supervision did consider himself better, he knew to keep the attitude to himself.

"So you're really not going to have dinner with him?" Sookie asked in continuing disbelief.

"No."

They continued to shake their heads before turning the conversation to another topic.

To Sable's surprise, the next morning the other women began addressing her by her name instead of as "Hey you!" Bridget, who seemed to be the most friendly, called her Fontaine.

They showed her how to roast the green coffee beans

sold by the camp sutler, let her in on some of the camp gossip, and for the most part treated her as one of them. Their change in attitude made her wonder if last night's conversation had changed their opinion of her. Sable had always been straightforward, so she asked Dorothy, the oldest woman.

"Because you're one of us, no better, no worse. No airs, no complaining."

Sable accepted the plain-spoken explanation just as she accepted their newly offered friendship.

The next day brought more laundry and still more hard work. It also brought a lost child.

Sable spotted him on her way back from the privy. He was seated on the ground looking so sad, she stopped, then looked around to see if his parents were nearby. Seeing no one but the folks coming and going, she stooped and asked, "What's your name, little fellow?"

"Patrick."

Patrick looked to be no older than six or seven. "Where's your mama, Patrick?"

He began to cry silent tears. "Don't have one."

She felt her heart twist. "Do you have a pa?"

He shook his head.

She glanced around for someone to help and spied a few people looking on curiously, but no one stepped forward to express concern. Sable had to get back to her vat, but she balked at leaving the child alone. "Would you like to go with me and see if we can find someone to help you?"

He nodded and stood.

Sable took his small, dirty hand in hers. On their way back to the laundry, she learned that he'd come to the camp a few days ago with his Uncle Benjamin and a group of older men and boys, but he'd become separated. When Sable asked him if he would recognize his uncle or any of his companions if he saw them again, Patrick assured her he would.

The laundry ladies were moved by little Patrick's plight. When they learned he didn't remember when he'd last eaten, Mrs. Reese fed him, washed him up, and found him some clothes in her stash of left-behind items. By midday, he looked like a new little boy, but seemed no closer to being reunited with his uncle. Sable took it upon herself to locate him.

Mrs. Reese gave Sable permission to conduct a search, but reminded her she would lose half a day's pay. Sable agreed without complaint.

With Patrick in tow, Sable made her way through the camp. Everywhere they went she asked if anyone knew Patrick, or knew of someone who was trying to locate a child matching his description, but no one did. She did get a few promising leads, but none led to the boy's relative.

As dusk fell, they were still searching. Sable felt discouraged but didn't voice her feelings aloud so her young charge wouldn't lose hope. Someone told her of a place near the center of camp where people who'd become separated could leave word for their kin. The woman giving Sable the information wasn't sure where the posting place was located, but she had heard of its existence from another woman.

So Sable and Patrick set out once more. There were over a thousand people in the camp, and trying to reunite one little boy with his companions was proving harder than she'd imagined.

Conditions in the central camp were far more bleak than in the area surrounding the laundry. Sable had never seen so many people packed into one space. She could barely walk, nor could she turn around without bumping into someone. She must have apologized a score of times as she led Patrick through the thick throng. She saw runaways who had nothing but a thin blanket to protect them from the elements. There were families huddled together on the bare ground; people who looked unwell and destitute. She'd heard about the aid societies and the missionaries who'd come South to offer assistance, but they looked to be facing a monumental task. For every hale and hearty individual she passed, there were two or three who appeared frail and undernourished.

Finally, after many fits and starts, she found the place she'd been seeking. People in this part of the camp called it the Message Tree. Handwritten notes and letters were tacked onto a large piece of wood nailed between two stout trees. There were so many runaways trying to get a look, folks had formed a line. She and Patrick patiently waited their turn.

It was full dark by the time they neared the front of the line. Torches had been lit and posted. A tall muscular man ahead of them had tears in his eyes as he turned away from the board, clenching his fists in anger and frustration. As he made to pass Sable and head back toward the lights of the camp, his gaze met hers. He looked so distressed, she felt compelled to ask, "Can I help in some way?"

"Only if you can read."

"I can."

"My name is Avery Cole and I'm looking for my wife. I've been away a couple of weeks building bridges with General Sherman's engineers. We came back yesterday and I can't find her or my son."

The torches illuminated the distress on his face.

Sable looked down at Patrick, soundlessly asking if he knew the man, but the little boy shook his head no. "Why did you ask me if I could read, Mr. Cole? My name is Sable Fontaine, by the way."

"Nice to meet you. I asked because I need somebody to read this to me."

He placed his finger on a shadowy note on the board. "My wife can read, but I can only recognize my name. I know this is my name here, but what's the rest say? I've been down here three times today trying to make the letters talk to me, but I can't."

Sable saw that the message was indeed addressed to

Avery Cole, just as he'd suspected. "Is your wife's name Salome?"

"Yes!" he replied.

"Then yes, this message is for you. She says your son was ill and was seen by the army doctor. She'll come here each day at three in the afternoon to seek you out so the three of you can be reunited."

To Sable's surprise the man grabbed her and gave her a spine-cracking hug. "Thank you! Thank you. I don't know what I would have done, if it hadn't been for you."

Sable smiled. "You would have simply found someone else to help you."

He seemed to notice Patrick for the first time. "Is this your son?"

"No. This is Patrick. He got separated from his Uncle Benjamin and we're trying to find him."

Avery bent down and touched the child's head. "Poor little fellow. I'll ask around if you'd like."

"That would be very helpful, Mr. Cole. I work over at the laundry. You may send word to me there."

They shook hands. Cole thanked her again for her help, then walked off into the night.

Although Sable was happy about Mr. Cole's success, the board offered nothing in the way of clues for Patrick. No one had posted a notice about a missing boy matching his description. She and her new little friend were no closer to unraveling the mystery than they'd been earlier that day. They were also hungry, and since Sable had yet to complete her first full week of employment, she had no funds. She knew it was too late to get rations from the communal kitchen and doubted anyone in camp had food to hand out freely, but Patrick needed to eat. Looking around the dark camp, she also realized she had no idea how to get back to the river where she lived.

Patrick looked up at her and asked, "Are we lost?"

Sable did not lie. "Yep. But we're lost together, so if

you take care of me and I take care of you, we should
be all right.''

He gave her his first smile.

Sable smiled down in reply.

An hour later, Sable, more lost than she cared to admit, finally came across an area that seemed familiar.
She saw why when she spied the big white mansion that
served as the processing center and housed the army
command. Even at this late hour dozens of contrabands
stood waiting their turn to enter. Was the major inside?
she wondered.

Raimond had just returned from the makeshift showers behind the house and was toweling his head dry
when a knock sounded on the door. Scowling at the
interruption, he growled, ''What?'' His day was done.
Any problems would have to wait until morning.

The door opened and Andre appeared. ''Someone to
see you.''

The aide stepped aside to reveal Sable. Raimond's
eyes widened with surprise. ''Miss Fontaine.''

''Good evening, Major.''

He was shirtless and must have just come from bathing, Sable noted, because moisture still clung to his dark
torso and muscular arms. With Patrick in hand, she managed to pull her eyes away from his magnificent physique and say, ''I'm sorry if we've disturbed you.''

Raimond finally found his tongue. ''No apologies are
needed.'' He slipped on a clean blue shirt and gestured
her in to take a seat. ''Thank you, Andre.''

On the heels of Andre's departure, she asked, ''Do
you have something for a starving child to eat? He became separated from his companions and needs to be
fed.''

''I'm glad you came to me for help.''

''I'm assuming if you have enough food to invite me
to dine, you've enough to feed a small boy.''

She watched LeVeq assess her young charge before

hunkering down to Patrick's height "What's your name, son?"

Patrick volunteered his name. Under further questioning he told the major the same story he'd told Sable about becoming lost.

"Would you like something to eat?" Raimond asked.

"Is Sable going to eat too?"

The major gave her a questioning look, to which she replied, "Patrick, I don't know if he has enough to feed us both."

Patrick asked, "Is there some food for Sable to eat?"

Raimond smiled and nodded. "Come with me."

He ushered them outside and over to a large tent. "Welcome to my home."

The tent had few furnishings. There was a listing desk and an equally battered chair, a cot, and a big sea chest. The sight made her remember Araminta's dream. Sable quickly buried the memory.

There was a table on the far side of the tent. Atop it were some covered pots and dented pans. He lifted the lids to reveal the contents: chicken, collards, and yams. It was a veritable feast for someone who'd been eating nothing but Mrs. Reese's hash.

"We have the very resourceful Andre to thank for this," Raimond commented. "He found a woman in the area with a full cellar."

"I didn't think you Yankees allowed that."

He grinned. "You're right. How she kept her food out of the hands of the troops is a mystery to me, but she did, so I've hired her to cook for me."

Raimond withdrew a couple of tin plates from the chest. He fixed three plates and they all sat down on the tent's dirt floor to eat.

Raimond spent the meal watching Sable interact with the small child. It was apparent that they'd grown comfortable with each other over the course of the day. She seemed to like the boy and he her. "Do you have any children?" he asked.

"No. Do you?"

"No. I'd like some eventually though. I'll have to find a wife first, of course."

"What would you look for in a wife?"

He shrugged as he chewed. "Someone I wouldn't mind being with for the rest of my life, I suppose, though before the war, I never even considered marrying."

"Why not?"

He grinned. "Too many seas to sail and too many beautiful women to woo."

At least he's honest, she noted. "So what has changed your mind?"

"This war and all the death that has come with it. I want the blood and sacrifices of my parents and their parents before them to live on in my children and in the children my brothers will sire. I can't ensure that legacy if I don't marry."

Sable thought about Mahti and the other women in her ancestry. There would be no more queens, or so it appeared. Sable did not expect to marry, and if her brother Rhine never returned, the family line would end with her. "Gossip has it that you are very wealthy," she commented.

Raimond seemed to be assessing the intent behind her words. "Does the thought of my supposed wealth make me more desirable in your eyes?"

"No. I just imagine you would choose a wife from your own class."

"Not necessarily."

The intense interest in his gaze made her return her attention to her meal.

By the time they finished, Patrick was having a hard time keeping awake. Sable pulled him into her lap and he immediately fell fast asleep.

Raimond stood and held out his arms. "Hand him to me," he instructed softly. "We'll let him sleep on the cot."

Sable wondered about this show of chivalry, but handed the unconscious boy over to the major's gentle hold. He carried the sleeping Patrick over to his bed.

"Do you have any suggestions about what I should do about him?"

He covered the boy with a blanket and silently escorted her outside so they would not disturb the youngster's sleep.

"In the morning," he said, "I'll see if Andre has time to do some searching. Maybe he'll have better luck."

"Thank you."

"Just trying to earn my reward."

She grinned and looked away. She looked back up at him in the glow of the torches stuck in the ground outside the tent. He was a man of some prominence here. The idea of Blacks holding positions of authority was still new for a woman recently out of slavery. She realized she would be entering a whole new world as a free woman. "Where can folks go if they leave here?" she asked.

"Able-bodied men can join the fighting, work with the army engineers as laborers, or agree to a work contract on a federal plantation to grow cotton for the Union. Some of the Black regiments like the ones stationed here protect contraband settlements against raiding Reb guerrillas and marauding Union troops."

"Union troops?"

"Yes, they've been known to harass settlements like this one."

"What about the runaways who stay behind? What happens to them?"

"Some can't handle conditions here and return to their masters. Most are simply waiting for the government to settle on a policy that will offer them help so they can start their free lives."

Sable had no way of knowing whether the government would indeed step in, but everything she'd heard about Mr. Lincoln indicated he possessed compassion so she hoped he had a plan for the slaves he was setting free.

"Are you a runaway also?" she asked.

"No, I've been a free man all my life."

"*All* your life?"

He nodded.

The words surprised her because she'd never met anyone from the South who hadn't been born a slave. "What's it like to be free?"

Under the torches' flickering light, he shrugged. "It is not easy residing in a country that holds our race in such low esteem, but I am a man of the sea. I've seen too much of the world and accomplished too much to accept that I'm only three-fifths of a man."

"I went to Europe once. I thought the ocean would never end, but I loved being on the deck, especially at sunset and dawn. The smell of the sea, the wind in my face . . . If I were a man, I'd be a sailor."

He grinned. "It's hard work."

"I don't doubt that, but to be captain of one's own life, to come and go as you please—the work would be a minor thing."

At that instant he wished he was a genie so he could conjure them both a vessel to sail in around the world. He'd show her Egypt and Bahia, the Caribbean and Cathay. He wanted to watch her green eyes marvel as he steered her past waterfalls so spectacular the sight stole her breath, and through mountain channels with cliffs so high they kissed the sky.

Raimond shook himself. Whatever was the matter with him? He was waxing poetic over this contraband woman as if she were his own true love. He admitted being attracted to her, but his reactions reminded him of his best friend Galeno Vachon, and the way he'd once mooned over Hester Wyatt. La Petite Indigo, as Hester came to be known, had put Galeno through his paces before finally taking pity upon him and agreeing to become his wife. Raimond had found the sight of his invincible best friend reduced to pudding quite comical, though Galen had not appreciated the humor. If Raimond remembered correctly, Galen had voiced the hope that there would be a woman in Raimond's future who'd "stomp around inside his heart too." That had been nearly five years ago. So far no stomping had occurred.

"Do you always stare so, or is something the matter?" Sable asked. She'd become uncomfortable under his unwavering scrutiny.

"No, to both questions. Simply thinking back on an old friend. How'd you get to Europe?"

"I accompanied my half-sister Mavis on her wedding tour. I went as her servant."

"Did you get to see anything of the countries?"

"Very little outside the museums. Mavis insisted I be included on the museum outings because she and I have always enjoyed portraiture. We'd sometimes look through our tutor's books on the old Masters and concoct wild stories about their lives. Touring those museums changed my life."

"In what way?"

"I saw portraits and statues of people who looked like you and me. I'd never seen such a thing before. You've been free all of your life, so it's probably not surprising to you, but for me—I saw a vase in Greece with a White man on one side and a woman of the race on the other. Our guide said she was a Black princess named Lamia, and the man was the great god Zeus."

"Ah, Zeus and Lamia."

"You know the story?"

"Yes, my father was a seaman. I grew up on the tales he brought back from his world travels. Zeus loved the African princess very much."

"So much so that his wife, Hera, in a fit of jealous rage, made Lamia devour her own children, and then transformed her into a hideous monster."

"Did Mavis's family deal with you fairly?"

The change in conversation made Sable look up at

him. The genuine concern in his soft voice made it easy to answer truthfully. "Mavis and her brother Andrew did, but not their mother. She didn't care for me, but then I never cared for her either."

"But you care for the little boy in there." He gestured toward the tent.

"During the last few days, I've learned what it is to be alone in the world. It's scary enough for me, a woman full grown. It must be even more terrifying for a child." She spoke from her heart. "Thank you for feeding him."

He inclined his head. "My pleasure. The camp has a good number of orphans and lost children. Not all are fortunate enough to find someone to care for them."

"What happens to them?"

"The lucky ones are taken into another family. Some are left to fend for themselves and live on handouts or stolen goods. Others die from starvation or sickness."

Sable did not want that to happen to Patrick. He was too sweet a child.

Back in the tent, Sable watched him sleep. He looked as if he hadn't a care in the world. "I don't wish to disturb him, but we should be going. Mrs. Reese is probably wondering if she'll have to find a replacement to do my work tomorrow."

"You don't have to move him. There appears to be room for both of you on the cot. I can send Andre over to let her know what has happened and that you'll return later in the morning."

Sable shook her head. "I can't possibly impose. Besides, I've already forfeited half a day's wages. She won't be pleased to have me gone any longer than is necessary."

"Well, you certainly can't carry him all the way to the river, not at night. If you leave him here, I won't mind, but how will I explain your absence when he wakes up? He seems very attached to you."

Sable admitted he had a point. Patrick had been a very

scared and sad little boy when they'd met that morning. She didn't want him to suffer the same fear upon awaking and finding himself alone among strangers again. "And where will you sleep?" she asked.

"Outside beneath the stars. I'm accustomed to it."

Sable still had doubts about the offer. Suppose Mrs. Reese saw fit to discharge her for being unreliable? After all, she'd been on the job for less than a week. "I don't wish to lose my position, nor do I want to add to Patrick's anxiety."

"Stay then," Raimond implored softly. "I will speak to Mrs. Reese. If she's set upon replacing you, we'll simply find you employment elsewhere."

A final glance at Patrick sealed Sable's decision. "I'll stay with the boy."

Much later, as Sable and Patrick slept side by side on the old cot in the corner of the tent, Andre gave his report to Raimond outside. He'd spoken with Mrs. Reese. She would hold Sable's job for only one more day. After that there'd be no guarantee.

Raimond dismissed the man with his thanks. Raimond was pleased she'd not been discharged, but a selfish part of himself wanted to know more about the contraband with the sea-green eyes, and he could hardly do that if she were working the laundry detail on the far side of camp. Had she been discharged, he could have used his influence to secure her a position much closer, and in that way learn all he wanted at his leisure.

The next morning, Sable was pleased to learn she'd not been given the boot by Mrs. Reese. As she thanked Raimond for sending Andre to speak with her, Patrick awakened and gave her a sleepy smile. It lit up her heart, his smile. If she had to move heaven and earth she'd find a way to get him back where he belonged.

Raimond took the boy outside so he could satisfy his morning needs. While Sable sat on the cot awaiting their return, Andre entered carrying a tray filled with more dented pots and pans. He set it down, nodded, and exited.

Patrick ran in with the major growling and lumbering after him like a bear. He caught up with the boy and swept him into his strong arms. Patrick giggled with delight.

Breakfast consisted of eggs, ham, grits, and light, flaky biscuits.

"Where on earth did you get flour for biscuits?" Sable asked.

"My cook."

"We haven't been able to afford flour for years. It must have been very expensive."

He didn't answer. Instead he reached over and gave Patrick another helping of ham.

Sable felt as if she'd made some gaffe. Should she not have asked where the flour had come from?

Raimond finally explained, "War's on. Anything can be purchased if you know where to look and have the coin."

From his reaction, she thought it best that they discuss something else. The "something else" came with the entrance of the very efficient Andre. Trailing the aide was Avery Cole, the man she and Patrick had met last night at the Message Tree.

Raimond softly excused himself from the table and stood to greet them. Sable noticed Avery observing her before he quickly resettled his eyes on the major.

Andre said, "Major, this man wishes to speak with Miss Fontaine."

Raimond held her eyes for a moment, then turned back. "What about?"

Avery appeared very uncomfortable and Sable had no problem seeing why. The major's manner had cooled noticeably.

Avery replied with equal coolness. "I'd like to ask Miss Fontaine if she'd help a friend of mine."

Sable stood up. "Good morning, Avery. How may I help?"

"My friend Edward needs help writing a letter to his wife back home. I was wondering if you maybe have some time for him."

She nodded, then looked down at Patrick, wondering if she should take him with her.

"Leave the boy with me," Raimond instructed, still sizing up Avery. "I'll keep an eye on him until your return."

Sable asked Patrick if he minded staying with the major. He smiled at his tall new friend and said no. She thanked LeVeq and followed Avery out.

Avery escorted her to a tent not far away. Sable met Edward, who smiled and said, "Avery told me you were pretty, but he didn't say how pretty."

Sable accepted the compliment with a smile. Edward's letter took only a few moments. He dictated what he wanted to say and she put down the words. His wife couldn't read either, but she had a kind mistress who would read it to her. Sable addressed the letter per his instructions and handed it over. When she finished, some of the onlookers who had gathered to watch stepped forward and asked if she could write letters for them too.

Sable agreed. A couple of the men who were soldiers actually paid her three cents apiece for the letters she wrote. By noon she'd written almost fifteen letters for various individuals and had pocketed more than enough to make up for the money she'd lost by not doing laundry.

Today was the day Avery hoped to be reunited with his wife. He was very excited at the prospect of seeing her and his young son again, but he was enough of a gentleman to escort Sable back to the major's tent.

On the way there, he said, "You've found a good protector."

At Sable's look of confusion, he explained, "The major, he's a good man, I hear."

Sable laughed. "He isn't my protector. He's simply helping me find Patrick's family."

Avery didn't respond.

She peered into his face. "What?"

"Nothing. It's just . . . well, he seemed to be more than a good Samaritan, that's all."

"Why, because we were having breakfast? He was just making sure Patrick ate well, that's all."

A small smile crossed Avery's face, as if he knew something she did not, but he kept his thoughts to himself.

As they approached the tent, he said, "Here we are, safe and sound. Thanks again for all you've done. I can't wait to hold my wife and son. Good-bye, Miss Fontaine."

Sable echoed his farewell and entered the tent.

Inside she found only Andre.

He stood at her entrance. "The major and Patrick have gone to headquarters in Atlanta and should be returning later. He asked me to stop in and see if you need anything. Would you care for luncheon, Miss Fontaine?"

Sable chuckled at his formal manner. "No. Breakfast will hold me for most of the day, I'm sure."

He nodded his understanding.

"I'll wait to dine with Patrick and the major. Have you known the major long?"

"Most of my life."

"I see," she said. After Avery's startling comments, it might be prudent to know more about the free Black Frenchman, but if Andre Renaud had known Raimond LeVeq all his life, she doubted he would give her a true picture of his character.

She told Andre instead, "There's really nothing I need, so if you have things to do, feel free to go about them."

He bowed as gracefully as the major and departed.

LeVeq and Patrick returned less than thirty minutes

later, accompanied by a man Sable did not recognize, holding Patrick's hand. All three males appeared quite pleased with themselves.

The major made the introductions. "Miss Sable Fontaine, Mr. Benjamin Walls—Patrick's uncle. We found him working for a regiment in Atlanta."

Sable's dismay at the prospect of losing Patrick to his family caught her by surprise. Hoping her brittle smile hid her true feelings, she said, "Pleased to meet you, Mr. Walls."

"Are you the one who found Patrick?" he asked.

She nodded.

"Thank you so much. We were on a gunboat coming from downriver and when we docked and got off, Patrick was nowhere to be found. I was frantic, have been ever since. He's my baby sister's oldest boy. She died in childbirth about a year ago. I'm raising Patrick as my own."

He looked down at his nephew with unabashed love. "Next time we're traveling together I'll tie him to my belt. I couldn't bear losing him again."

Patrick had such joy in his face as he watched his uncle speaking, Sable knew the child had genuine feelings for his Uncle Benjamin too.

Still, it saddened her to lose him, even though she had no real claim and had known the boy only a short while. She would probably never see him again.

Ben Walls continued, "Thank you so much for caring for him. If you hadn't helped, I maybe never would have found him. Thank you."

Sable nodded. Patrick came over and gave her a big hug. A few moments later he and his uncle left.

The silence in the tent seemed to echo loudly once they were gone, and the tears standing in Sable's eyes made Raimond want to pull her into his arms and give her solace.

She stated softly, "He is better off with family."

"Yes, he is."

"I . . . need to go back to the laundry before Mrs. Reese thinks I've deserted her. Thank you for everything."

She dashed away her unshed tears and started toward the tent's open flap.

His voice stopped her. "You can still stay and have luncheon."

She shook her head no.

"Then come back for dinner."

Sable looked up into his concerned gaze. "I'll think about it."

As a slightly despondent Sable made her way back across camp, she gave the major's invitation little more than a fleeting thought. War was on. Next year at this time he wouldn't even remember her name.

Chapter 4

Mrs. Reese and the other laundresses greeted Sable's return warmly. Everyone was happy to hear Patrick had been reunited with his family, and once Sable finished the story, she dove back into her share of the work.

That evening, much to Sable's surprise, Avery Cole showed up to pay her a visit. With him were his wife Salome and his year-old son Avery the Younger.

Salome had tears in her eyes. "I'm so grateful to you, I can't find the words. If you hadn't been there to read my words to Avery . . ."

She gave Sable a long hug while Avery, holding the baby, looked on approvingly. Sable had tears in her own eyes too. The woman's sincerity touched her heart.

Avery said, "You know, I've been telling folks about you writing that letter for Edward and they all want to know if you'll do the same for them. There are a lot of people who'd write home if they had somebody to pen the letter. Do you think you could find the time?"

Sable thought it over. "I can, but it will have to be after I'm done with my day here."

"I'm sure that will suit them fine."

"All right then. Just have them meet me here at the end of the day and I'll do what I can."

Salome said, "You shouldn't do it for free though,

Sable. You will need every penny you can earn for your future.''

Sable agreed wholeheartedly. She decided the rate would be two pennies for composing and one for reading. Both Avery and Salome thought the rates were fair and promised to spread the word.

By week's end, Sable's writing and reading were proving almost as profitable as her laundry job. There were so many requests, Bridget and Mrs. Reese added their skills to the operation. One evening a soldier's request for a letter to his motherless son back home in Ohio made Sable think about Patrick as she lay on her cot that night. She'd been so busy juggling laundry and letter writing, she hadn't had an opportunity to inquire if he and his uncle were still in camp. Patrick's Uncle Benjamin appeared to genuinely care for the little boy, and she was certain Patrick would be well cared for.

She'd always had a soft spot for children. Were times and the world different, she might be married now with a passel of her own to love, but as it stood, slavery had robbed her of that hope. Although she was now free, she would be thirty years of age in November. By all accounts, that made her too old for a respectable man to marry and far beyond child-bearing years. Privately, she considered herself more than capable of loving a husband and bringing their children into the world, but having been a slave, she knew how powerful social constraints could be.

She shrugged off her melancholy and tried to sleep, but her snoring tent mates kept her awake. In another few weeks, she might save enough money to buy a tent of her own, but until then, she'd have to endure the communal living. Eventually she hoped to leave the camp and make her way North or South, or wherever the Old Queens led. Surely, now that slavery was in its death throes, there would be opportunities for a woman like her, who could teach, be a governess, or run a business like the free Blacks she'd met here. She'd even be a laundress if she had to, but she had to get out of the camp.

Her immediate objective lay in doing as much laundry as she could physically manage, then when her workday ended, she wrote and read dozens of letters for her fellow runaways. It seemed Avery had told the whole camp about her service. Just as during her last year as a Fontaine slave, she went to bed every night exhausted, but as the coins piled up, she was glad for the work—until the morning she awakened to find her tent mates gone and her small stash of savings missing. It took no scholar to put two and two together. Mrs. Reese was furious to learn she'd been employing thieves, but her anger couldn't restore Sable's money.

Mrs. Reese insisted Sable report the theft, so the following morning she found herself in line with many other contrabands outside the big white mansion. She hadn't seen the major in the weeks since Patrick's departure and found herself discreetly searching the premises for his handsome face. She saw many soldiers, both Black and White, but not Raimond LeVeq.

A large group of about twenty women and children were ahead of her in line. The soldier standing with them was explaining to the soldier doing the processing that the husbands of the women had been impressed by the Union army. Their commanding officer wanted the families to stay in the camps while their husbands fought the Rebs.

Such care had not always been extended, according to the rumors Sable had heard during her first days at the laundry. When the call went out from Washington in 1863 welcoming Black men into the fight, many Union commanders had been unconcerned about the fate of the family members left behind. There'd been tales of commanders forcibly turning away women and children to keep them from following their husbands. When the husbands began deserting to check on the welfare of their loved ones at home, the army reevaluated the situation and changed the policy. The Union needed the Black soldiers to fight, and they couldn't fight if they were worried about their kin.

When it became Sable's turn to approach the desk, her eyes widened with surprise at the sight of her brother Rhine seated behind one of the tables taking down reports. He wore a crisp, Union uniform, and when he looked up and saw her, his green eyes momentarily widened as well. He discreetly scratched his ivory cheek, an old signal between them that told Sable to approach him as if he were a stranger, even as her inner elation soared. He'd been gone for almost two years now, but there he sat, alive!

He wrote down all the information she could provide about the theft, and her description of the women, Sookie and Paige.

He then asked, "Will you be at the laundry this evening, in case I need more information?"

Sable looked into his oh-so-familiar eyes and replied, "Yes."

Although they weren't supposed to know each other, Sable dearly wanted to stay and talk. She wanted to ask him how he'd gotten there and where he'd been, and to tell him all that had happened to her since he'd left for the war, but when she glanced up, she saw that behind Rhine stood Raimond LeVeq. His dark and unfathomable eyes held hers, and everything seemed to go still for a moment. Not knowing what else to do, she nodded, and he inclined his head almost imperceptibly in kind. When he stepped over to the table and stood behind Rhine, she knew it would be best to save her questions for her brother until they were alone.

LeVeq leaned over Rhine's shoulder and read the report he'd written. He looked up. "It's good to see you again, Miss Fontaine. You've been robbed?"

"Yes."

She sensed Rhine's curiosity as he glanced between

the two of them. The major wanted her to retell the story of the theft, so she did.

He then asked, "Are you totally without funds?"

She nodded.

"I'll send Lieutenant Renaud to you later with some army scrip to tide you over until you are paid."

Sable could feel the eyes of the others in the room staring curiously, no doubt wondering what made her so special. Convinced the last thing she needed was gossip dogging her steps, she said, "Thank you, but that won't be necessary. Mrs. Reese will take care of my needs until I am paid again." She turned her attention back to Rhine. "Please contact me if anything arises."

Rhine nodded.

Sable walked toward the door, very aware that Major LeVeq's eyes were following her.

Rhine showed up after dinner that evening. Mrs. Reese raised an eyebrow at his presence until Sable explained he was the soldier looking into the theft.

Because Mrs. Reese hadn't found anyone to replace the women who'd run out on her, Sable had the tent to herself. With Mrs. Reese's approval, she escorted Rhine there. Once inside, they hugged each other tightly. Sable had missed him so intensely, and it felt so good to be held by someone who loved her, she had tears in her eyes when they finally eased apart.

"How in the world did you get here?" he asked.

Holding on to her own questions for now, she related the sad story of Mahti's fiery death and the events that had triggered it.

Rhine was livid. "Carson sold you? That bastard. Guess his slave-holding days are over now."

"I guess so," Sable echoed, though her heart still ached with the loss of Mahti. "What are you doing wearing Union colors? Where's Andrew?"

"Our illustrious half brother is by now in California. Once we made it through the first battle alive, Andrew had had enough. He said to hell with the South, freed me, and headed West.''

''So you joined up with one of the Black units?''

''No.''

He spoke the word so softly, Sable peered at him curiously. ''What's wrong?''

When he didn't immediately reply, her imagination ran wild. ''Oh Lord, Rhine, you're not a Reb spy, are you?''

He chuckled. ''No, Sable. I'm with one of the regiments that came in a few days ago.''

For a moment confusion held her. She'd heard nothing about a new unit of Black troops arriving in camp. The contrabands took such pride in their presence, any new Black units always caused a stir. She took a good look at her brother's uniform. Unlike the uniforms of the few Black troops she had seen, her brother's was the crisp, clean version worn by White soldiers. She gasped. ''Rhine, you're not passing as White, are you?''

He nodded.

''Why?''

''I'm tired, Sable. Just tired.''

''Tired of what?''

''Having no voice in my own life.''

''But Rhine, you're not White.''

''We both know that, but the army doesn't.''

Sable could only stare and ask again, ''But why?''

He shrugged. ''I'm not strong like you and Mahti. I can't stomach not being free to be who I am just because the law considers me less than a man.''

''So you're going to pass? What will that accomplish?''

''It will help me get what I want out of life. I'll have the freedom to choose what I want to do, where I want to go.''

''But slavery is almost dead. Everyone says so.''

''And afterward? Do you think the country is just going to embrace us? They hate us now and they'll hate us after slavery.''

"But you can't turn your back on who and what you are. What about Mahti, our mother? Have you forgotten the sacrifices they made?''

"Yes, and as I said, I'm not that strong. You know I've always sought the easiest road, and besides, I've had plenty of practice passing. Andrew let me do it all the time.''

Sable simply could not believe her ears. And yes, he had passed before. The first time she'd realized he could do it successfully had been on one of her first trips to Atlanta. She couldn't have been more than eight or nine summers, which made Rhine ten or eleven. That evening, Andrew decided to go downstairs ahead of everyone else and order the family's dinner at the hotel's restaurant. As a slave, Rhine should have been eating in the kitchen with Sable and the slaves of the other guests, but Carson Fontaine found Andrew and Rhine seated together in the fancy eating room, drinking lemonade. Rather than cause a scene, Carson held his tongue and let Andrew and the ivory skinned, green-eyed Rhine have their fun. When they returned home, Rhine received the worst whipping of his life. Carson personally laid the strap across his back and did not let up until Rhine promised he'd never pass as White ever again. It was obvious now that neither Rhine nor Andrew had kept the promise.

"Rhine, you can't do this.''

"Sure I can, Sabe. After the war, I'll probably follow Andrew West, or maybe I'll settle in Canada, but I'm done suffering for no reason.''

"You're the only person I have left in this world, yet you would leave me too?''

He stared into her eyes. "You know how much I love you, but yes.''

The pain in her heart made her close her eyes tight.

He spoke with the earnestness that had always been a

part of his nature. "You and I have never been free, and I refuse to wait and have my freedom grudgingly handed over by believers in a Constitution that counts me as three-fifths a man."

Sable looked up at her brother. He'd taught her to climb trees, to fish, and to read. He'd been her hero, her bane, and her dancing partner at the county's annual slave ball. That he could just walk away from the race, and her, brought tears to her eyes.

"Don't cry, Sabe. You're a queen. Queens don't cry."

She stiffened with surprise. "You know about the queens?"

"Yes, Mahti told me their story the night before Andrew and I went off to fight. She wanted me to know in case something happened to her."

"Then if you know the tales, how can you do this?"

"Because I have the blood of queens in my veins too. I refuse to grovel for the rest of my days."

"But Rhine—"

He shook his head, and his voice sounded sad. "No more, Sable. My mind's made up. You can't change it."

"So will I ever see you again, hear from you again?"

"My unit's scheduled to be here for another few days. After that we're marching to South Carolina. Only the queens know if you'll ever hear from me again, but I'll always carry you and Mahti in my heart. Always."

She wrapped her arms fiercely around his waist, and he held her tight as they both wept.

The next morning Rhine brought her his laundry. She still found it hard to accept the path he'd chosen, but it pleased her to have him near for the time being. Mrs. Reese, always happy for new business, greeted him with a smile and asked if there'd been any progress on finding the two thieves. When he told her nothing had turned up so far, she went about her day. Sable knew Rhine wanted to keep their relationship secret so she didn't tell

Mrs. Reese the truth. She had introduced him as Sergeant Rhine Clark, not as Rhine Clark Fontaine.

Rhine insisted upon paying Sable for doing his laundry, which she thought only fair. He then asked about Otis and Opal.

"They ran away about six weeks before I did," Sable replied. "I thought maybe they'd come to this camp, but so far I've not seen them."

Thinking about the Fontaine housekeeper and her husband made a long-forgotten memory rise. She asked her brother, "Remember the time she caught us snitching those tea cakes she'd made for Silly Ann's Christmas tea?"

Rhine grinned. "Do I? Andrew must've eaten a dozen before she caught us. Not only did we have to wash every window in the house. We couldn't sit for a week."

Sable laughed. "I can still hear her and Silly Ann yelling at us."

They were still laughing when the major strolled up, carrying a few shirts. Upon seeing the two of them together he paused, and Sable wondered why he looked so displeased. His disgruntled expression suggested he would move on to another woman, but much to her dismay, he came to her station.

"Good morning, Miss Fontaine."

Uncertain of his mood, Sable nodded in response. "Major."

Rhine saluted. "Good morning, Major."

He returned both the salute and the greeting. "Good morning, Sergeant. Here to avail yourself of Miss Fontaine's services?"

Was it her imagination, or did the major seem to be intimating she might be offering more than laundry service?

Apparently her brother felt the same sting, because he looked LeVeq in the eye and said coolly, "If you mean am I here to have my wash done, yes sir, I am."

The major looked over at the large pile of wash awaiting Sable's attention and replied smoothly, "Alas, Miss Fontaine seems to be a bit behind. Maybe you should see one of the other laundresses."

"I made my arrangements last night, sir."

Rhine had always possessed a quick mind, but the major didn't seem to appreciate it. "When last night?"

"Last evening when I came over to followup on her report of the theft, sir."

"Well, soldier, I outrank you. Find someone else to wash your drawers."

Sable's mouth fell open in astonishment. Of all the arrogant, high-handed . . . She gritted her teeth. "Major, his coin is as good as yours, and he was here first. *You* find someone else."

She was certain LeVeq was not accustomed to being spoken to in such a manner, but she really didn't care. How dare he act so rude! Ignoring him, she told her brother, "Sergeant, please, hand me your things."

Tight-lipped, Rhine complied, and she placed his bundle atop the pile of items to be washed. "I'll have these for you tomorrow."

She then looked at LeVeq and asked, "Are you still here?"

His eyes sparkled dangerously. "Yes, Miss Fontaine, I am." And while still holding her eyes he said to Rhine, "Sergeant, you've conducted your business. Don't you have a detail this morning?"

"Yes, sir, I do."

"Then be on your way."

Rhine looked to Sable, only to have the officer add warningly, "Now, soldier."

Rhine saluted angrily. "Yes, sir!"

He turned crisply and headed back toward the main camp.

Watching him leave, Sable was furious. "You are possibly the most arrogant man I've ever met."

"*Merci beaucoup, mademoiselle*," he replied and bowed.

Irate, Sable snatched the pile of laundry from his hand. "Be gone. I'll have these done tomorrow. Send an aide to retrieve them."

"And miss the opportunity to watch your eyes flash like a storm at sea? No, *I* will be back to retrieve them. *Au revoir*, Miss Fontaine."

As he marched away, Bridget sidled over. "You really don't like him, do you?"

Shooting daggers at his back, Sable confessed, "At this moment, no. Not at all."

Back near his tent, Raimond was angrily tossing darts at a board set up on a tree and thinking, How dare that little contraband take up with another man! He'd seen how she'd smiled up into the soldier's eyes, her face filled with a warmth he'd yet to have directed his way. He was not accustomed to being either ignored or verbally flayed by a woman he desired. He walked over to the board and snatched the darts free, retreated a few paces, and began hurling them again.

In the midst of his bad mood, Andre Renaud walked up, eyed the darts sticking haphazardly out of the board, and drawled dryly, "I assume you are not trying to hit the mark?"

"Shut up, Renaud."

Andre raised an eyebrow. "What gator bit your nose?"

Raimond flung another dart. "A green-eyed one named Sable Fontaine." A whistling dart struck nowhere near the center.

"Ah," Andre replied sagely. "It seems there *is* one woman in the world immune to the charms of the eldest son of the house of LeVeq."

Raimond's eyes flashed like an angry god's.

"This will definitely go into my next letter to Galeno," Andre added.

"If you reveal even a sniff of this to Galeno, I will personally toss you into the nearest privy."

"He will enjoy hearing of it."

"Don't you have some duties to attend?"

"No sir, everything is under control."

"Then go and see what you can find out about a White soldier named Rhine Clark. He seems to be paying Miss Fontaine a bit of attention."

"Is he a rival for your lovely contraband's affections?"

"Just do as I asked, Andre."

"The answer must be yes. I believe Galeno is going to fall out of his chair laughing when he reads about this."

Raimond turned on Andre with yet another malevolent look, and a grinning Andre said, "I'm going, I'm going."

After Andre's departure, Raimond snatched the darts from the target and took them back inside the tent. Sable Fontaine had him in knots—not only had she not returned for dinner the evening after finding Patrick's kin, but she seemed no more interested in him than she'd been the first night they'd met. He had never confronted such a situation before. Didn't this contraband know the LeVeq charm had dazzled women all over the world? Didn't she know that whenever he pulled into port, no matter where, no matter what hour, women flocked to him like birds to corn? They all wanted to be with him, to share his bed, to bask in his smile. Being around Sable Fontaine was definitely a humbling experience, especially coupled with the evidence that she might be keeping time with another man. What was wrong with her? Had his physical attributes suddenly changed? Had he awakened this morning as ugly and misshapen as Shakespeare's Caliban? He didn't understand any of it, and her even less.

Andre returned later that evening with a report on Rhine Clark. He had just opened his mouth to speak when Sable came barreling into the tent. She angrily and forcefully threw Raimond's clean but wet shirts against his chest and sailed out. An astonished Raimond met the equally astonished eyes of Andre, who, on the heels of her startling appearance and exit, burst into laughter. Growling, Raimond went after her.

Sable was hurrying as fast as her legs could carry her. All day long, the more she'd thought about the major's behavior that morning, the madder she'd gotten. How dare he intimate that she was offering more than laundry! Her original intent had been to return his shirts and give His Royal Arrogantness a good piece of her mind, but by the time she'd marched across camp to his tent, she'd worked up so much indignation that throwing his shirts at him had been by far the safer option. A minute alone with him and she might have done him bodily harm.

Sable marched past many familiar faces as she went. They all looked at her a bit strangely, but she didn't stop.

She also didn't get very far.

She had no idea he'd followed her until he tackled her from behind and threw her over his shoulder. Her yells of outrage, her kicks and flailings, were all ignored as he clamped a big arm across the back of her knees and proceeded to carry her through camp like a sack of meal.

"Put me down, you insufferable Frenchman!"

"Or what? You'll hit me with more wet shirts?" He did not break his stride. "Quit squirming before I drop you on your head."

Many camp dwellers stopped in their tracks to view the determined major carrying the boisterous and fuming laundress over his shoulder. Some even clapped—mostly men. When Raimond passed Avery standing in front of his tent, an upside-down Sable demanded that Avery do something. He only grinned.

Once back in his tent, Raimond turned to Andre,

who'd followed them, and said, "Miss Fontaine will be staying for dinner."

"I will not! Put me down!"

Raimond ignored her outburst. "Make the arrangements, Andre."

"Stay where you are Andre! The only thing I will be having for dinner is his head! Release me this instant!"

"Go, Andre."

Grinning Andre saluted and left to do his major's bidding.

Raimond eased her feet to the ground and beheld the absolute fury in her eyes.

"Who is your commanding officer?" she demanded.

Raimond scratched his head. "Actually, I don't have one."

"There has to be someone to whom I can report this outrage."

Chuckling at her angry indignation, he bowed elegantly. "I apologize if my methods were a bit unorthodox."

"A bit! Do you know how much gossip you've created, carrying me through camp like a sack of yams?"

He poured a cup of water from a pitcher. "Refreshment?"

"Charm does not become you."

As Raimond drank, he watched her over the cup and wondered if this was how Galeno had become enraptured with his wife, Hester. Had he experienced this same, nearly overwhelming urge to take on the challenge of winning her for his own?

Sable wanted to box his ears. For the first time in her life she wished she were a male so she could order him to choose a weapon and meet her at dawn. He was far too handsome for his own good, and even in the throes of wanting to feed his liver to a hog, she couldn't deny how he affected her. She didn't want to be attracted to him in any fashion, but it appeared she was. Still, she would continue to fight it, because she knew instinctively that for Raimond LeVeq women were dessert, and dessert was probably his favorite meal.

"Mrs. Reese is expecting me back," she informed him.

"I'll escort you there after we've eaten."

"I'm not staying. Not even a man as arrogant as you can make me eat against my will."

"How old are you, Sable?"

The abrupt change in subject threw her. "I'll be thirty years of age in November."

"Are you a virgin?"

Her eyes widened. "That, sir, is none of your business!"

"Never mind, I already know the answer."

Sable felt his allure slowly softening her will in spite of this impossible situation.

"I will send Andre around to Mrs. Reese to offer an acceptable explanation for your delay."

"I'm going to lose my job because of you."

"No, you won't." But he did wonder how much longer he could beat back the urge to kiss her. He could only guess at the passion she kept chained within her. "I claim dinner tonight as payment for my assistance in returning young Patrick back to his kin."

"You would bring an innocent child into this?"

"We French have few scruples."

"Arrogant and unscrupulous," she said, arms folded across her chest.

He gave another ironic bow.

She couldn't help it, a grin peeped out. How did one defend oneself against such a man? "All right, you win. I do owe you—but only dinner. I will not be dessert."

He nodded and toasted her with his tin cup.

"After this, my debt is paid. In full."

He simply smiled.

Raimond found it oddly pleasing that she'd finally relented. Patrick had been his last card. Playing it had won him an evening he was quite looking forward to. He didn't think Patrick would mind.

When they moved to the table, the major helped her with her chair as if they were dining in a castle instead of an army tent. The lamps were turned low to beat back the encroaching darkness, making the surroundings shadowy and intimate. Sable tried to behave as if she'd experienced such a rendezvous many times, but the reality was, in all her thirty years, she'd never dined alone with a man.

Although she was doing a good job of masking it, Raimond sensed her unease. Before he could ask about it, the ever efficient Lieutenant Renaud entered with their meal. He left them a roasted chicken, potatoes, collards, more glorious biscuits, and a bottle of wine.

After Andre withdrew, Sable looked at the food and wondered what this man really wanted from her. She considered the question appropriate. After all, she knew next to nothing about him except that he was kind to lost boys and had let her sleep in his arms. She decided she needed to set the ledger straight once more before the meal began. "I'm serious about not being your dessert at the end of this meal."

In the middle of pouring a glass of wine, Raimond paused and glanced into her exotic eyes. He shook his head and chuckled. "Miss Fontaine, you will not have to be dessert. However . . ." He took a moment to pour her a glass of wine as well. "If I wanted you for dessert, I'd have you for dessert. And trust me, you would be willing."

Sable's heart pounded as it never had before.

"Shall we eat now?" he asked.

Sable nodded.

As the meal progressed she became more and more aware of him: the way he held his tableware, the way his eyes held hers over the glass as he drank his wine. She'd never had much experience with spirits either and found the taste rather unpleasant.

"Don't you like the wine?" he asked.

"Not really. I suppose the taste is something one acquires?"

"Yes."

To Raimond, she still appeared damn uncomfortable. "Is something the matter, Miss Fontaine?"

"Truthfully? I've never dined alone with a man."

"I see."

Raimond felt an inner pleasure rise in response to her words. Admittedly, being the first man to share this experience with her massaged his male pride. He wondered what other experiences he might introduce her to—besides the obvious, of course. And that path interested him more and more. He found the interest a bit surprising since he usually prefered the darker roses of the race. He'd grown up among the free Black elite of Louisiana, where most of the heralded beauties had skin of *cafe au lait,* mirroring their mixed African, Spanish, French, and English heritage. They were ofttimes so fair, they were forced by law to don colorful head wraps to distinguish themselves from the Caucasian women of the city. God forbid some local merchant should embarrass himself by mistaking a Black woman for White and treating her with respect. Raimond had had many liaisons with the fair-skinned beauties back home, but after becoming a man of the sea he'd come to favor the magic of their darker sisters. Now he'd become attracted to this bronze-skinned contraband with sea-green eyes and he could not place his finger on exactly why.

"You're staring again," she pointed out.

He inclined his head gracefully. "My apologies."

Raimond sipped a bit of the wine, then set the glass down. The faded black and white gingham dress did not do justice to her loveliness, but even in rags, she was beautiful. He doubted she could be coaxed into sharing his bed tonight, but the idea of her being dessert sometime in the near future thrilled him enormously.

They finished the meal in silence—Raimond looking

at her like a tiger preparing to pounce, and Sable lying to herself about how much he affected her.

She did not want to like this man, not in the way a woman liked a man. He was too handsome, too arrogant, and he knew it all too well. But her likes and dislikes didn't seem to matter. All that mattered appeared to be this uncharacteristic nervousness and the steady beating of her heart.

She tumbled from her reverie when he asked, "Did Sergeant Clark uncover anything about the theft?"

"No."

"The two of you appeared to be having a good time when I walked up this morning."

"He's very charming."

"You're aware that the army frowns on White soldiers mixing with contraband women?"

"I never knew doing laundry constituted mixing," she replied frankly, holding his eyes. "White soldiers bring us laundry all the time." She wondered what it was about Rhine that had raised LeVeq's cockles. "Do you not like him because he is White?"

"Who says I don't like him?"

"You weren't exactly polite this morning."

"The color of his skin makes me no never mind."

"Then what is it?"

He smiled as he drained the last of his wine. "You don't know?"

She shook her head.

"It's called jealousy, Sable. Pure, green-eyed jealousy."

She found this all too confusing. "You've nothing to be jealous of."

"Ah, but I do. I'm jealous of the way you were looking at him when I walked up."

Sable wondered if he'd had too much wine because she had absolutely no idea what he was talking about.

He continued. "For lack of a better word, you had

what I would describe as love on your face. You practically glowed with it."

"You believe I'm in love with Sergeant Clark?"

"Do you deny it?"

Sable wondered how long she could hold on to her laughter. "No, I don't deny it."

Evidently she hadn't done a good job of masking the humor sparkling in her eyes because he asked, "What is so funny?"

"Nothing," she lied. "I'm simply listening."

"Then if you don't deny it, I will have to kill him."

Sable burst into laughter.

Had she become deranged? Raimond wondered. Threats of death did not usually elicit such a response.

Sable picked up her cotton napkin and wiped tears of mirth from the corners of her eyes. "Where do you find hats large enough to fit over that swelled French head of yours? Kill him indeed. He's my brother, you ninny."

Raimond's eyes widened. *Her brother!*

Sable shook her head. Men.

"Why didn't you inform me earlier?"

"It was none of your concern."

"Your brother."

"Yes, my brother."

Her brother, Raimond thought, relieved. He'd been running around half-cocked over her damn brother. He felt like a fool, but the elation made him want to turn flips.

Although Sable hadn't intended to reveal her true ties to Rhine, she thought it best that the major know. She didn't want him giving Rhine a hard time for no reason.

Raimond looked into her eyes. "Has he always passed?"

"No. That's a choice he settled upon recently."

"Is he planning on staying White?"

"Yes. He says he's tired of carrying the cross we slaves have had to bear."

Raimond observed her closed face over the candles

atop the table. "How do you feel about it?"

"I don't like it, but it's his life. I love him very much. He and I are the last of my mother's line. When he leaves, I'll have no one."

Although Raimond's father had been lost at sea when Raimond was twelve, he'd grown to adulthood surrounded by a large, loving and extremely noisy family. He had a beautiful and vibrant mother, Juliana, and four remaining younger brothers. He could only imagine how bleak life would have been without them. This woman had no one.

"What happened to your mother?" he asked.

"She took her own life rather than be forced to breed again."

Raimond sensed her pain. "How old were you?"

"Three, according to my aunt."

"And this aunt?"

"Dead also."

Raimond considered his mother, Juliana, and how she'd raised him and his brothers. "A woman alone in the world must be strong."

"I am strong. My mother and grandmothers were queens."

Raimond didn't doubt the claim for a moment. It had nothing to do with the way she looked, but with the strong and confident way in which she carried herself. Her lineage might also account for her sometimes blunt speech and impertinent behavior.

"A contraband queen," he mused aloud.

"A queen with no subjects and no lands."

"But her first courtier."

Sable fought the effect of his words, reminding herself he couldn't possibly be attracted to her in any meaningful way. "I believe I'm a bit past the age of courtiers."

He shrugged. "I don't share that opinion, but since you are the queen . . ."

She decided to change the subject. "What did you do before joining the war?"

"I was a partner in a shipping firm. A close friend handled the business end and I commanded the ships."

"How much of the world have you seen?"

"Most of it. Sailing is my life."

She heard the passion in his voice, and wondered if she would ever find something in this new, free life that would fill her with the same intensity.

Judging from the subdued sounds coming from outside the tent Sable could tell the hour had grown late. The camp was a bedlam of activity during the day, but as night took hold, much of the hustle and bustle eased. "I should be going."

Raimond had no desire to relinquish her company. "Rhine's an odd name."

"You're trying to stall me."

"I know. Indulge me."

She smiled and shook her head. "Aunt Mahti said he was named for the Rhine river, where he was conceived. Carson Fontaine and his wife Sally Ann, were on their European wedding tour at the time. My mother was brought along as Sally's servant."

"They were on their wedding tour?"

"Yes, Rhine and the Fontaines' son Andrew are only two weeks apart in age. Andrew's sister Mavis and I were born six minutes apart. My mother nursed us both."

"What happened to Mavis?"

The question made memories of the night Sable had left home flare to life, bringing grief and sadness. "I wish I knew." She shook off her despondency and remembered the lateness of the hour. "I really must be going. Thank you for dinner."

She stood.

"Stay awhile longer."

"No. Some people already believe you're my protector."

"Really?"

Sable swore he looked pleased. "Avery does, for one,

and your performance this evening will only fuel more rumors.''

''You don't approve, I take it?''

''No.''

''Why not?'' he asked, pouring himself more wine, then taking a swallow.

''Well, let me think. I doubt I'd grow accustomed to being referred to as the major's green-eyed whore,'' she said easily.

Raimond choked on the wine. Once he was able to breathe again, he assessed her with his dark eyes. He knew then and there that he wanted this woman in his bed. Only there would he be fully able to sample her fire and spirit. He'd never liked his women passive. ''The only thing I enjoy more than a challenge is a challenge tossed down by a woman,'' he said.

''I'm not challenging you.''

''Ah, but you are . . . among other things, you're challenging me to kiss you and find out if your lips are as ripe as they appear.''

Sable brought a hand to her mouth.

He flashed a dazzling smile.

She hastily put the hand down. ''A gentleman would never speak that way.''

''I'm not a gentleman, Miss Fontaine. It says so in the Constitution.''

She sat back down.

''You shouldn't look so shocked. You've probably had any number of suitors over the years.''

''I've had none.''

''You're a very beautiful woman.''

''A very beautiful *slave*. The Fontaines never let anyone court me, nor was I allowed to have a beau from the fields.''

''Why not?''

''I've no idea. Maybe it had something to do with my mother, or maybe it was purely out of spite. As I said before, his wife and I couldn't abide one another.''

"Well, it's far too late for you to be out wandering around in the dark. There are probably many who've no idea I'm your protector and would do you harm."

"You are not my protector."

He sipped his wine and remained silent.

"I don't need a protector."

His eyes flashed amusement.

"I may need a protector to keep you at bay, but that is all."

He toasted her with his glass. "Beautiful *and* astute."

She couldn't hide her grin.

"That being the case," he went on, "we will make a pact. You may return to Mrs. Reese's, but I will escort you."

"No."

"Yes. Now come," he said, standing.

"Do you always decide what is best for others?"

"Habit. I have four younger brothers, so indulge me."

"And if I choose not to?"

"There's always dessert . . ."

Sable stood.

Outside, the night air was chilly. She pulled her shawl tighter and tried not to be affected by the man at her side or the moonlight bathing his tall, bearded handsomeness.

Looking down at her, he said, "You know, if we were in Louisiana I would court you, Sable."

"If we were in Louisiana, you wouldn't pay me a minute of attention."

He grinned in the dark. She was as hard as a Brazil nut. "Why do you say that?"

"Because you don't impress me as a man who courts women. Men like you simply beckon and the women trip over each other to do your bidding. You and my brother are very much alike."

He grinned. "I admit that is sometimes true. But you I would court."

Sable rolled her eyes.

They walked the remainder of the way in silence. Raimond realized he enjoyed their parrying and wanted more. As they approached the creek which led to the laundry, he asked, "Would you walk down by the water with me for a bit?"

She chuckled. "No. I have to get up very early and I need my sleep."

Raimond found himself wondering how it would feel to awaken with her at his side, to touch her softy and rouse her with his kiss. "You are very hard on this poor Frenchman."

"Only because you warrant it. Undoubtedly you get your own way far more often than is healthy."

As he looked down into her smiling eyes, he placed a hand beneath her golden chin and raised it. She supposed she could have stomped on his foot or kicked him in the knee to stop the slow, sweet kiss that followed, but she did not. Instead she let him have his way, and he took a leisurely advantage that left her with her eyes closed and her knees weak.

Finally, her eyes opened and she whispered, "You're fairly good at this . . ."

He smiled. "I'm fairly good at most things."

"Your hats must explode quite regularly."

He chuckled. "Let's get you home."

The effect of his kiss stayed with her as their walk ended outside her tent. She hadn't intended for him to know his kiss had moved her, but she'd been so dazzled the words had come out before she could snatch them back. Mrs. Reese and the others were already asleep, so Sable kept her voice low. "Thank you for dinner."

"My pleasure."

"Good night."

Raimond picked up her hand before she could enter the tent. "Will you walk with me again?"

Sable sensed she was being drawn in by his spell. "When?"

"Now. An hour from now. You choose."

"We agreed my debt would be paid after tonight."

"Again you are making this very hard for me."

She smiled. "Courting a queen should never be easy. Good night, Major."

She squeezed his hand gently and went inside.

Chapter 5

A s she entered the tent, Sable heard, "You're back awfully late."

The voice belonged to Bridget McKinney. The sight of her sitting up on one of the pallets took Sable by surprise. The tiny stub of a candle burning on a large rock barely illuminated the tent's interior. "What are you doing here?"

"Mrs. Reese found replacements for Sookie and Paige. I asked if I could move in here with you. Dorothy snores like a train. Do you mind?"

Sable and Bridget had gotten along fairly well since Sable's initial arrival, so she replied truthfully, "No, I don't mind. Paige and Sookie snored something fierce too."

Bridget smiled in the darkness, then asked, "Where do you think those two disappeared to?"

Sable shrugged. "So far, the army's not been able to find out anything. I doubt the theft's a priority though. It isn't as if General Sherman can call a halt to the war just to search them out. How well did you know them?"

"Not as well as I thought, I guess. I never pegged them as thieves."

"Neither did I."

Sable yawned sleepily.

"Are you usually out so late?"

Sable's lingering memories of the major's kiss made her smile as she took off her shawl and sat down on her pallet. "No. Tonight was an exception."

"I'm guessing you like him a lot better tonight than you did this morning," Bridget teased.

"I agreed to dinner to pay him back for helping with Patrick."

"Uh huh. Rumor has it he's sweet on you."

"The rumor's wrong."

"Heard he carried you through camp. That rumor wrong too?"

Sable tried to hide her grin. "No."

"So, how was dinner?"

"Fine."

"He kiss you?"

"Bridget McKinney, you are the nosiest woman I know."

"Answer the question, Fontaine. Did he?"

"Yes."

Bridget hooted so loudly, Sable scolded, "You're going to bring Mrs. Reese down on our heads if you don't hush!"

"Is he a good kisser?"

Sable shrugged. "How would I know? I've never been kissed before."

"You are too innocent to be alive, Fontaine. Are you sure you've never been kissed?"

"Why would I lie about something like that?"

"Women do it all the time. You, though, I believe."

"Thank you, I think. I take it you've been kissed."

Bridget grinned. "More times than there are stars in the sky."

Sable raised a doubtful eyebrow.

Bridget chuckled and confessed, "I think I'm going to like having you as a tent mate." She pulled the blankets up over her head. "Good night, Fontaine."

"Good night, Bridget."

* * *

The two women became fast friends over the next few days. Bridget had a past that set her apart from anyone Sable had ever known.

"I owned a bordello. You do know what that is, don't you, Fontaine?"

Speechless, Sable nodded as she hung wet wash on the lines set up among the trees.

"Had a small place about thirty-five miles outside Atlanta. After the Yankees burned me out, I came here."

Sable knew about the havoc caused by the Union's conquering armies. There'd been lootings, burnings, and rapes perpetrated on both races. But Sable had never heard of a Black woman owning a bordello.

"My master owned the place originally. When he died he willed it and me to his eldest son. Because the son's young wife succumbed to the vapors anytime anyone even mentioned the business her husband had inherited, I ran the place and he pocketed the profits."

Sable could only stare. Everyone in the South knew that not all slaves worked on cotton plantations. Many captives held positions in the cities and countryside as clerks, foundry workers, miners, and seamstress apprentices. Some went to sea with their masters on merchant vessels, while others accompanied wagon trains going West. One, like the famous slave York, owned by William Clark, traveled West as a member of the Lewis and Clark party and proved to be a valuable member of the expedition. But a bordello?

"Why do you find that so surprising?" Bridget asked. "If we can manage diners and dress shops, surely managing a place that caters to a man's intimate needs is not so far-fetched."

Sable supposed she was right.

"Want to change your mind about sharing the tent with me now that you know?"

"No, but at the bordello, were you . . . I mean, did you . . ."

"Was I on the menu? Yes. Not so much toward the

end though. I was more valuable to the business sitting upright and going over the books than I was working on my back.''

Sable's eyes widened.

Bridget shook her head. ''Fontaine, before our association ends, you're going to learn more than you probably ever imagined about many things, but they will serve you well.'' Sagely, she added, ''Especially if you're being pursued by that devil of a Major. Man like him needs a woman.''

''I'm a woman,'' Sable replied, taking mock offense.

''No, you're not, but you will be when I'm done with you.''

That night as they lay atop their pallets, shivering in the fall air beneath thin blankets, Bridget went on with her story. ''As I said, the son's new wife was appalled by the idea of her husband owning a bordello and she wanted it and me promptly sold.''

''So what did you do?''

''I seduced him so he wouldn't.''

Sable was speechless yet again. She and Mavis had discussed many things as they lay in bed at night, but Sable had never been party to a discussion as eye-opening as this one.

Amused, Bridget reminisced, ''He came into the office one morning and there I was, a nude daughter of Africa lounging temptingly in a large tub of scented bathwater. I thought his eyes were going to pop from his head.''

Sable's felt as if her own were threatening to do the same.

''Before midday, I had convinced him I was a sorceress of unimaginable delights. And for a man raised in the backwaters of Georgia it didn't take all that much.''

Sable wanted to know what ''unimaginable delights'' entailed, but she didn't have the nerve to ask.

''We moved the tryst to my suite upstairs and he sent

a note around to his wife saying he'd been called to Atlanta on business. I delighted him for three days, after which I became his mistress. He was so enamored, he gave me my free papers for Christmas.''

"Did you love him?"

"Of course not, Fontaine. For me it was strictly a business transaction. I'd've seduced Lincoln himself to stave off being sold again.''

"How any times were you sold before the bordello?"

"Three. The first time I was too young to remember. Second time I was twelve.''

"To whom?"

"A gambler named Robert Braggs. Traveled all over the South with him until I was nearly sixteen. He was killed in a knife fight in Atlanta and I was sold on the block at auction along with two other whores he owned. I wound up at the bordello. I've no idea what happened to them.''

The institution of slavery had ripped apart lives for nearly two centuries. Sable wondered if any of the lost relatives, acquaintances and friends could ever be reunited after its death.

Changing the subject, Bridget said proudly, "I found me a beau today. Name's Randoph Baker.''

"Who is he?"

"A White and married soldier.''

"What? Bridget—"

"I know, I know. No lecturing, please, but I have to get out of this camp, and he's going to be my ticket.''

"Why him?"

"I'll let you know soon.''

Wondering what her friend had planned made Sable shake her head at Bridget's machinations.

The next evening, Rhine came to pick up the last of his laundry and say good-bye. Sable understood she couldn't change the course he'd chosen for himself, but she would never stop wondering about his fate, or loving him.

They were alone in Sable's tent. Bridget had gone off to keep an assignation with her new beau, and her absence gave the siblings one last time to be together.

"I want you to look at something before you go," Sable said. She quickly turned her back and lifted her dress to get at the gold bracelet she'd found in Mahti's bag after the fire. She handed it to him.

He smiled sadly. "It belonged to the Old Queen. Mother wore it too until she died. Mahti showed it to me the night she told me about them."

When he handed it back, Sable peered at it again. "I suppose it's very valuable?"

"I'm certain it is."

"Do you have any idea what the symbols mean?"

"They were the Old Queen's personal spirits. She looked to them for wisdom and guidance. Evidently, that bracelet was the only piece of jewelry she was allowed to keep after her capture. Mahti said the master sold the rest."

"The symbols match my skin markings."

"Each queen wore similar patterns. If you ever return to the motherland, those markings will confirm your birthright."

Sable could not envision doing so. After all, she knew nothing about the world the Firsts had come from, nor could she speak the language. Even though she hoped one day to go there and walk the soil as a tribute to Mahti, a feeling deep in her soul told her her destiny lay here, in this land where she'd been born. The Firsts had sacrificed much to transform America into the nation it had become; for their labor and blood they were owed something.

She peered up at her brother's ivory face and swore she would never forgive herself if she cried. "You're pulling out at dawn?"

He nodded.

As they stood staring into each other's eyes, the pleasure and pain they'd shared as brother and sister filled them both. No parting words were spoken. They were both aware that this might be the last time they would ever see each other, and no words could express the depth of that sadness.

Rhine pulled her close and squeezed her tight. Sable embraced him with the same ferocity. He kissed her forehead, eased away.

He did not look back.

It was now early October. Since Sable's arrival she'd found employment, friends like Bridget, Avery's small family, and the many folks she wrote letters for, but she'd also found sadness in the loss of her brother Rhine. He hadn't written and Sable did not expect he would.

There seemed to be no end to the stream of refugees seeking shelter in the camp. The numbers had climbed to well over a thousand in spite of those leaving daily and the many deaths of the ill and feeble. Rumor had it the camp would close soon because a Union victory appeared imminent, but rumors flowed like water in the place Sable now called home, and most folks preferred to just wait and see.

That morning Sable went out to her laundry vat, only to be told by Mrs. Reese to report immediately to the camp's hospital. A large contingent of wounded Black soldiers had arrived less than an hour ago, and Mrs. Tubman and the doctors needed assistance from as many volunteers as could be mustered. Sable had had no idea Araminta had returned, but she and Bridget quickly made their way to the war-scarred mansion that was serving as the army hospital.

The field outside was a scene of chaos. Injured men lay everywhere: on the bare ground, atop litters, and propped against trees. Their faces and uniforms were darkened by powder and blood. As Sable approached, she saw more of the wounded being assisted from wagons and carts. The moans of men who'd yet to receive care punctuated the air, while men who were already bandaged and hobbling on makeshift canes and crutches administered what help they could to their fallen friends. Sable saw women weeping over men so badly hurt she could hear their breath rattling in their lungs as she passed by, and she saw men who were simply sitting, their eyes focused on a horror only they could see.

Inside, injured men screamed while surgeons and corpsmen rushed here and there. The thick, hot air reeked of blood and death. She and Bridget were almost bowled over by men toting more injured soldiers on litters. They stood there paralyzed looking over the chaos until Araminta appeared. Her face was grim. "Sable, over there, and do exactly what the doctor tells you. Bridget, come this way."

Sable hurried over to the table and stood next to a gray-haired man in a blood-covered apron. He held a saw in his hand. He looked Sable up and down. "What's your name?"

"Sable Fontaine."

"I'm Dr. Gaddis and this here is Private Scott."

Private Scott was the young soldier lying atop the bloody tarp covering the table. His brown face was covered with sweat and powder. He appeared to be in much pain, but managed to say, "How do, Miss Fontaine."

"Hello, Private."

Two other soldiers stood around the makeshift bed. Sable returned their grim nods of greeting, all the while wondering what type of assistance the surgeon needed.

He told her, "Miss Fontaine, I want you to hold Private Scott's hand as tight as you can and tell him all about yourself. Okay?"

Sable was confused but nodded agreeably. She held the young man's hand tightly in her own, but as she leaned over to speak, she saw the surgeon place the saw against the young man's leg and the other two men hold him down tightly. The implication almost made her faint away. The surgeon placed a hunk of wood between the soldier's teeth and told him to bite down hard. Gathering herself, knowing she would be of no use to anyone if she swooned, she fought to think of something pleasant to say about herself but couldn't, so she sang, the only song she could think of—"When This Cruel War Is Over," one of the most popular songs of the war.

As the saw began its slow, deliberate slide across the mangled limb, the young soldier's face bulged with pain. Sable buried her horror deep inside and sang, never taking her eyes from the soldier's own, never crying out when his hand squeezed tightly enough to shatter the bones in her fingers. The grating sound of the saw slicing through bone and sinew made her stomach roil. Sweat rolled down young Scott's face as if he'd been drenched by rain. Blessedly he passed out about midway through, but Sable held on to his hand until the leg was lifted away.

It was the first of many "capital" operations, as amputations were called, that she participated in that day. The surgeon Gaddis went about the business emotionlessly but efficiently. When one of the doctors handed her an amputated limb and told her how and where to dispose of it, she fought down her panic and went to handle the task. The severed limbs were placed outside in a cellar-sized pit dug into the yard. She placed the lifeless flesh atop the many others on the pile, then hurried back inside. By the end of the afternoon, she had made her seventh trip to the fly-covered pile, and unable to fight off the nausea any longer, she went off into the trees to be sick.

When she finally raised her head, she found Raimond LeVeq at her side. Concern lined his face as he handed her a canteen. She rinsed her mouth with water, then dropped onto a nearby crate, trying to pull her world back into place. "Have you been inside?" she asked.

"Yes. I've been trying to get the names of the men who've died. Their families need to be told. Are you better?"

Sable nodded. "Yes, and I must return. The doctors are waiting."

He waved her back to her seat. "Take a minute to clear your head. The doctors said you performed well in there. They've requested you be transferred to their staff, if you're agreeable."

She studied him for a moment.

"You'll be on the army payroll," he continued. "The compensation is only a few cents more than your pay from Mrs. Reese and the hours will be longer."

She chuckled in spite of the awful day. "If you're attempting to make it sound *un*appealing, Major, you're succeeding."

His smile was soft. "That isn't my intent. I just want you to be aware of what to expect. Do you want to think it over?"

"No. I'm agreeable to whatever aids freedom."

"Are you certain?"

"I am."

The decision to move to the hospital felt right. Sable wanted to aid the fight. She couldn't pick up a gun and affect the war's outcome in that way, but she could assist the men who were in need of healing. No one had to tell her that memories of the death and gore she'd experienced today, and would experience in the days to come would become a part of her soul. She already knew that. "I've never witnessed such hurt and pain," she said. "Where are these men from?"

"They're a local contraband regiment. They've been in the war only a few months and were rebuilding a rail line about fifty miles from here when they ran into some retreating Rebs. They were outnumbered two to one and sustained significant losses, but they fought bravely. When the commanding officer was killed, one of the sergeants took his place, leading the battle."

"Some of them will not see morning."

He nodded in sober agreement.

Turning her thoughts away from the brave men who

were dying, she asked several practical questions regarding her new status. "Will it be necessary to find new lodgings now that I no longer work for Mrs. Reese?"

"I'm afraid so. The surgeons will want you close by. Mrs. Tubman has quarters not far from here. She's offered to put you up for as long as necessary."

Sable stood. "I must return. Thank you for the respite."

"My pleasure. I'll see you later."

As she hurried back, he watched her go.

Sable spent the next four days assisting the surgeons with more "capital" operations, and attending enough resectionings and wound repairs to last a lifetime. She watched doctors remove huge pieces of soft lead embedded in the flesh of one soldier, and held the hand of man who had to have half his jaw removed, without benefit of ether because the surgeons were afraid he'd choke to death on his own blood. Her respect for Dr. Gaddis grew with each passing day as she watched him wrangle with painful decisions. Should he amputate to save a life, knowing the soldier would be affected forever by the loss of the limb, or should he leave the limb and pray the man would recover? Some did. Many others did not.

One of those who didn't was her first patient, Private Scott. Three days after the loss of his leg, infection set in. He died the next morning. One of the recovering soldiers who'd known Scott since childhood asked if Sable would break the news to Scott's wife, Helen. She'd been trailing his regiment since his induction and was camped out in the trees surrounding the hospital, awaiting her husband's fate. Upon learning the news, the woman wept. Sadly, Sable found she could not. Her emotions had been scorched away the moment the surgeon removed Scott's leg. All the blood and death in the days that followed had left her numb inside.

Bridget had not been able to stomach the infirmary's gory conditions and had not returned after the first day. But Sable stayed. She put in eighteen- and nineteen-hour days, aiding the doctors, staunching wounds, and maintaining a pleasant face for those men who were healing.

She had no idea her presence in the ward had been particularly noticed until a man on his way back to the front lines stopped beside her as he was leaving.

"Thank you, Miss Fontaine."

"You're welcome."

She did not expect him to say more, so when she looked up from the ward rosters she was going over to see him still standing there, she gave him a tired smile and asked, "Is there something else, Sergeant?"

"Yes, ma'am, just this. You've been very kind to all of us here, and I just want to say that knowing you'd be there when I opened my eyes each morning gave me a reason to want to wake up."

Sable inclined her head in thanks. "I am proud to assist such gallant men, Sergeant."

He saluted her crisply, then headed out to the wagons that would take him back to the war.

Sable could do nothing to soothe the ache in her heart brought on by Rhine's departure, but helping the soldiers allowed her to place the events of her own life in proper perspective. How could she mope about her situation when she met men who would live the rest of their days with missing limbs? Her self-pity took a backseat to patients who were so injured, there was nothing Dr. Gaddis or anyone else could do but give them whiskey to dull the pain and pray the good Lord took them home soon. Her own miseries seemed minuscule when she watched Araminta try to bring down a man's fever with nothing to aid her but ice, herbs, and prayer because the Black units were ofttimes the last to receive medical supplies.

On the morning of Sable's fifth day in the wards, she fell asleep in a chair, and Dr. Gaddis shook her awake.

"Go home to bed, Sable."

Mumbling sleepily, she came awake slowly, rubbing her weary eyes. She was seated at the bedside of a man who'd been brought in the night before. The surgeons had taken his right arm and been worried he would not survive the night. She'd stayed on the off chance he would awaken and need aid, and to ward off the flies. Unless the nasty little insects were constantly fanned away, they swarmed over the bed-bound patients. She'd not realized she'd fallen asleep. "I'm fine, Dr. Gaddis. How's our patient?"

"He's sleeping easily, which is more than I can say for you. Go home, or do I have to find Mrs. Tubman?"

Even exhausted, Sable knew a serious threat when she heard one. "Okay, I'm going, but I'll be back in a few hours."

"No, Miss Fontaine. I don't want to see your lovely face for at least twenty-four hours. And that's an order."

Tired but smiling, Sable gave him as crisp a salute as she could muster, and left the premises.

She was back six hours later. Her sleep had been neither restful nor sound. She'd tossed and turned on the borrowed cot in Araminta's quarters, unable to shake the tension of the past few days. When Dr. Gaddis happened upon her spoon feeding one of the wounded soldiers whose hands were bandaged because of severe burns, he didn't fuss or threaten her with Araminta's wrath. He simply shook his head at her stubborn devotion and continued his rounds.

Sable learned much in those first few days, not only about the care of the injured but also about herself. She was forced to call upon a strength and fearlessness she'd never known she possessed. Now, after all she'd seen and done, she felt confident she could take on any challenge, even the challenge of living in a free world.

On her seventh day in the wards, she was making up one of the spare cots when she noticed Andre Renaud handing the doctor more of the paperwork the army required. The sight of him reminded her she'd not encountered the major in what seemed a long time.

Renaud explained the major's absence. "He's gone to accept delivery of a large number of contrabands. He'll be back in four or five days."

"I see." Sable hoped he would be safe.

"He has instructed me to inform you that I am at your disposal should the need for assistance arise."

Renaud's formal speech and manner always made her smile. "Thank you, Lieutenant Renaud. I doubt I'll need you, but I'll keep the offer in mind. My regards to the major."

He bowed. "Until later, Miss Fontaine."

Four days later, a very weary Raimond finally made it back to his tent around midnight and fell upon the cot like a dead man. He was desperate for a way to be relieved of this duty as contraband liaison. Now that the war seemed to be moving toward a Union victory, he wanted to be in the thick of the fight, not stuck here enforcing silly regulations.

Raimond and a small contingent of soldiers had been sent South to escort to the camp a group of thirty-five former slaves whose plantation had been confiscated by the federal government. No one had told Raimond that the army command had promised the people they could bring along their livestock. During the three-day journey, he'd had to contend with chickens, hogs, and an old milk cow that died on the way. Both contrabands and animals were now being processed and given a place to bed down. He just hoped one of the hogs didn't wind up on a soldier's spit.

He admittedly took a certain pride in a job well done, but for a man of action, the inactivity he'd faced these past few months had begun to wear on him It outweighed all the stellar reviews handed down by his superiors in Washington. His was one of the few camps still operating, and despite the army's attempts to settle the contrabands elsewhere, they were still arriving in droves. Their fate and that of all the other slaves still being held captive in the South had become a volatile national issue.

Lincoln's pocket veto of the Wade-Davis bill that past July had put Congress and the President at odds on both emancipation and the reconstruction of the Southern states. Lincoln had vetoed the bill, saying the pending Thirteenth Amendment was the only way constitutionally to abolish slavery. To invoke the emancipation by statute as the Wade-Davis bill wanted would have been, in Lincoln's opinion, a ''fatal admission'' that the states still at war with the Union had seceded legitimately. He also had doubts about the procedures mandated by the congressional bill to readmit the rebelling states back into the Union. He wanted flexibility if and when the war ended and refused to be held to one method of restoration.

The inability of those in Washington to come to agreement did nothing to clear the muddy waters surrounding the contrabands. The infighting in the Republican Party over the issues of reconstruction and emancipation had left many believing Lincoln would not be renominated. There hadn't been a renomination of an incumbent president since 1840 and no incumbent had been reelected since 1832. Still, Northern Blacks had no doubt about whom to throw their weight behind. The Great Emancipator won hands down over the Democratic choice of the former commanding officer of the Union's Army of the Potomac, General George B. Mc-Clellan, a man who had publicly doubted the value of adding Black soldiers to the fight and had returned fugitive slaves to their owners. Lincoln was not perfect. Black leaders found great fault with his fence-straddling ways on issues such as allowing Blacks to fight, and universal emancipation for *all* slaves, not just those held in the states at war. But under his leadership progress had been made, and the Black population continued to offer its full support.

Raimond's musings were interrupted by the entrance of Andre Renaud, who saluted and said, "I don't mean to disturb you. Just wanted to say welcome back."

Raimond sat up. "I'd be lying if I said it's good to be back, so I'll just say thanks."

Andre smiled.

"Anything happen I should know about?" Raimond asked.

"The new major arrived for those troops brought into the hospital last week. Name's Major Claude Borden. He should be wearing gray, not blue."

Raimond knew that meant the major harbored attitudes that were more in line with those of the secessionists.

"He's done nothing but berate the men since he arrived. He doesn't know any of them by name, yet called them a bunch of slackers and layabouts, accused them of getting their colonel killed."

Raimond shook his head and pressed his hands against his burning eyes. "See what you can find out about him."

"Already have. Here's the file."

Andre placed it atop the table as Raimond asked, "Anything else I need know?"

"Well, Miss Fontaine is still working with the surgeons over at the hospital."

"How's she doing?"

"Fine, but she appears to be very tired. The doctors say she works as hard as they do."

"Have you been keeping an eye on her as I asked?"

"When I've been able to, yes. She's moved in with Mrs. Tubman. All the men in the hospital think highly of her. She sends you her regards."

"Oh, really?"

"I think she was just making pleasant conversation."

"Don't toy with me, Andre. What exactly did she say?"

"She asked why she hadn't seen you and I told her

you'd gone to pick up a group of contraband."

"And what did she say?"

"She said, 'I see.' "

"Just, 'I see'?"

"And 'Send him my regards.' "

"That was it?"

"I'm afraid so. Don't look so disappointed. She might not have asked after you at all."

"Go away and let me sleep."

Grinning, Andre saluted and departed.

Raimond lay on his cot in the dark, an image of Sable floating in his mind. He'd missed their verbal jousting during his absence, and he thought about her more often than he cared to admit. How had she taken her brother's departure? According to what she'd revealed, Rhine represented the last of her family. His departure left her alone in the world. To be without family was a loss Raimond could not conceive. He and his five brothers had all gone to war, and the fight for freedom had cost one of them his life. They would all feel Gerrold's loss for the rest of their days. Each night he prayed for the safety of his other four brothers.

But Sable had no one to pray for her. He realized he wanted to see for himself how she was faring, and he wanted to see her now. His weariness seemed to vanish as he got up, dressed, and headed over to the hospital.

It was a warm, moonlit night, and he found her sitting on the porch with Araminta, rolling bandages. "Evening, ladies."

Both women looked up, and Sable felt a warmth spread over her as his gaze met hers. She'd missed him, she realized.

"Welcome back, Major," Araminta said. "What brings you out on this beautiful night?"

"I thought I'd come and visit the two prettiest women in camp."

"Your lies are almost as handsome as you are," Araminta cracked. "Everybody knows who you've really come to see—so, Sable, set those bandages back in the basket and go take a walk in the moonlight. I can handle things here.''

"Araminta, there are patients to see—''

"Quit fooling around, girl. Life is too short. Go.''

Mrs. Tubman's tone and the commanding look on her face made it plain she was not offering Sable a choice. And because Sable had been raised by Mahti and Opal never to question her elders, she did as she was told.

Her walk with the major began in silence. Ignoring the way he made her feel was impossible. Her heart had begun pounding from the moment he'd stepped onto the porch, and it hadn't slowed. She paid no attention to the little voice inside her that kept saying he would leave her in pieces. She preferred to listen to Araminta—life was indeed too short.

"That's a beautiful moon,'' she said. It hung fat and low in the sky. The light it cast was so bright they had no trouble seeing the path. The stars were out too, and she imagined the Old Queens were looking down on her from their heavenly perch.

"Indeed it is.''

"Where are we going?''

"To a place where we can enjoy the moon and I can enjoy your company.''

That someplace turned out to be up a tall tree.

Sable stared in amazement at a treehouse nestled in the high branches. "Up there?''

"Yes. Do you know how to climb?''

"As well as I can breathe.''

"Well, lead us up, Your Majesty. The rope ladder's right here.''

It took them only a few minutes in the bright darkness to execute the climb up the trunk to a wooden platform, and immediately, Sable understood why he'd wanted to come. She could see for miles, and the glowing moon seemed close enough to touch. "Did you build this?''

"No," he replied. "Sherman's engineers built it as a lookout tower."

It was just a wooden platform—no walls, no roof. There were branches below the platform but nothing above except the black, star-studded sky.

Sable glanced over at him and found him watching her. Though the night prevented her from seeing the true message in his eyes, she sensed his restlessness, his desire.

He said, "I suppose I should have waited until morning to see you, Sable, but I couldn't force myself. How have you been faring in my absence?"

She didn't know what to say to his first statement, but she had no problem responding to his question. "I'm spending most of my time at the hospital, as you probably know." Her voice became distant as she looked out over the night. "It's grueling, wrenching work. I've had to force myself to bury my feelings in order to aid the surgeons and the men. I've become so adept at it, I can assist in the removal of a young man's leg without a flinch."

She looked back at him over her shoulder. "Can a person be dead inside and remain alive?" she asked bleakly.

He stepped closer and held her tight.

"It has been so awful," she whispered against his chest as she clung to him. The memories of all the death and gore she'd experienced welled up, making her remember horrors she'd rather forget.

Raimond squeezed tighter and kissed her brow. This part of her life would remain with her until the grave, just as it would for everyone else touched by the war. He had his own demons to exorcise, demons brought on by the battles he'd particpated in, the men he'd killed for freedom, and the deaths of friends and family members now buried. But he held on to her, letting her draw from his strength and seek solace against his heart.

Sable didn't want him ever to let her go. No place

seemed safer. She felt protected, sheltered, impervious to further hurt. "Can we live up here and never go down?" she asked, leaning back so she could see his shadowy face.

"Whatever you wish."

She gave him a bittersweet smile, then tenderly touched her hand to his bearded cheek. "Thank you for holding me. You probably think I'm a weak and silly female, but I'm not. Life seems to be careening around me, and I—"

He took her hand and kissed her palm. "No explanations are necessary," he assured her quietly. "Even queens need to be held now and again."

She dropped her eyes for a moment and then smiled. "You've earned a reward tonight, Major."

"Have I now?" he asked, grinnning.

"Yes."

Crooking a finger, she beckoned him down. When he complied, she raised herself on her toes, kissed him softly, then slowly drew away.

"That's not nearly a large enough boon, Your Majesty."

Feigning offense, she put a hand on her hip. "You dare ask your queen for more?"

He slid a finger slowly over her lips and replied huskily, "I dare." Then, using the same slow finger, traced the satiny edge of her jaw and the soft skin beneath her chin. "I dare, because my queen needs solace, gentleness, and only I can make her come alive again," he whispered in a tone ripe with heat and promise. "Let me banish your dragons for at least this one night." He gently lifted her chin to search her shadowed eyes. "May I?"

Heart beating fast, she nodded, and her eyes closed as he brushed his lips across her own. The searingly sweet contact made her melt and lose touch with everything but him.

"You're so lovely," he whispered in a voice as soft as the wind rustling the trees.

Her lips parted and he nibbled her bottom lip. Sensations began to rise, as faint as the light from a distant star at first, but with each passionate draw upon her lips they grew stronger. He slid a hand to the nape of her neck and deepened both the kiss and their embrace— inviting her, bewitching her with his lulling power. She had no defense against him. Only being held by him in this thrilling way mattered. Her emotions had been drained by events at the hospital, but his fiery kisses were making her feel again, just as he'd promised.

When his hand began to roam ever so gently over the back of her dress, the heat in his palms seeped through to her skin, warming the new woman blossoming within. He lowered his kisses to her jaw and throat, and her soft gasp of pleasure mingled with the whispers of the trees. Hands as gentle as the night mapped her waist and shoulders, then slid over the buds of her breasts, making them tighten with flaring arousal.

She was indeed feeling. His kisses and caresses were opening the window on a previously unknown world, a world ruled by sensation. No man had ever cupped her breasts or filled his strong hands with her hips. Her hands had never journeyed over a man's powerful back or up his arms as they held her close. Standing with him under the black velvet sky filled her with a recklessness and daring she thought she'd left behind in her youth. She wanted to touch him and be touched in return; she wanted to be shown what passion was really all about. Employing some of the tricks she'd heard about from Bridget, Sable slid the tip of her tongue over the warm corner of his mouth and shuddered pleasurably as his tongue mimicked the move. She kissed him fully, sensually, wanting him to be as affected as she was by this interlude under the stars.

Sensations flared as he lowered his head and tenderly nipped her breast through the thin gingham dress. Her head fell back, and she arched against the strong arm bracing her as he treated the other nipple to the same thrilling caress. Moans slid from her lips and heat welled inside her as the play intensified. The silent suckling set off sharp shards of response so vivid and lush, she thought her whole body would melt.

"Does this please Your Majesty?" he asked huskily, while his fingers toyed with the pebble-hard points.

"Yes," she whispered. "Yes." Her nipples were pleased, ripe and full. Her lips were kiss swollen, and desire had given birth to a soft, rhythmic pulsing between her thighs. She didn't want it to stop—any of it. Not the way his mouth teased her breasts, or the dangerous sensation of his warm hands sliding possessively over her hips. His heated kisses were making her lose sight of who and where she was, but she didn't care. Life was too short.

Raimond wanted nothing more than to strip away the ugly gown and explore her fully. The sweet fire he tasted in her lips had him as hard as he'd ever been. Passion spurred him to woo her, touch her, lay her down on the wooden platform and let the night wind join him as he spread kisses over every bared inch of her golden skin. Her full breasts burned his palms, and her sweet sighs of pleasure as he suckled her again made him want to take her to the heights. But he had to get her back to the hospital. Maybe next time, he would free her to his glowing eyes and sensuous touches, and show her the path to *le petit morte*. "We need to get back before Araminta sends out a search party . . ."

The words had to be the most disappointing ones Sable had heard all day, but she knew he was right. Duty took precedence over her wish to remain in his arms.

Raimond touched his lips to hers and slid a parting caress over her curves. "There will be other nights . . . I promise."

"I will hold you to that promise," she whispered softly.

They climbed down the rope ladder and retraced their steps to the hospital. When they were almost there, he pulled her back into the shadows and took a moment to give her a dazzling, knee-melting kiss of farewell. As he slowly broke the seal of their lips, it took her a few moments to find herself in the foggy state of desire left in the wake of the kiss, and only then could she open her eyes. She looked up at him standing there so handsome and tall and said, "You could have any woman in this camp. Why me?"

"Because you're the only one I desire."

Early the next morning, Sable received a visit from Avery Cole. She knew him fairly well by now, but not since the first night they'd met had she seen him look so visibly upset. She ushered him outside onto the hospital's porch so their conversation wouldn't disturb the men in the ward. "Whatever is the matter, Avery?"

"There's a man asking after a green-eyed slave woman named Sable Fontaine."

Sable felt her heart go cold. "What does he look like?"

Avery described a man who could only be Henry Morse.

Sable's chin rose. "It sounds like the man I was supposed to be sold to. Is he still here?"

"Yep. Says he's going to the head army man to get help locating you."

"Well, I'm not going back, so he might as well go on home."

Avery shook his head. "He didn't look the type to give up easy. I heard he wasn't real respectful when asking after you, so as far as I know, no one told him anything."

Sable was grateful for that. "Was he alone?"

"They said he had a woman with him. His wife?"

Sable shrugged. She hoped the woman would turn out

to be Mavis. Sable wanted to give her the news about Andrew.

"I've good news too, though. Me and the family are going North. Salome's been helping one of the missionary societies distribute clothing, and the missionary has found a church in Rhode Island to sponsor us. We leave in the next few days."

Sable inwardly flinched at the prospect of yet another loss, but she replied sincerely, "That is good news."

Avery seemed to be speaking from the heart when he said, "Sable, Salome and I will never forget you. Salome's going to have a baby next spring. If it's a girl, we already plan to name her Sable, after you."

Sable had tears in her eyes.

Avery had wet eyes too. "You take care of yourself, now. And remember, that man can't take you back unless you want to go. You're free."

Sable nodded and watched as another person she had feelings for turned away and walked out of her life.

Later that morning, as Sable sat at the bedside of a soldier who wanted a letter written, she looked up to see Henry Morse stride in. At his side was Major Borden, the new commanding officer. He'd been nothing but rude and uncivil in his dealings with the Blacks around him, and how on earth he'd ever been assigned to a command in the United States Colored Troops was anyone's guess. Sable had yet to hear a kind word from his lips. The army command had relegated his new unit to rebuilding roads and guarding railroads. Although Sable didn't want to see his men thrust back into the war, she and everyone else wished him someplace else.

As the two men wove their way among the cots, Sable had no doubt about whom they'd come to see. Avery's warning had been a timely one. Morse's triumphant eyes held her own, and Sable heard Mahti's warning echo inside: *He will be the jackal and you the antelope until his death.*

Major Borden stopped beside Sable and asked Morse, "Is she the one?"

Morse smiled down at Sable. "Sure is, Major."

"Then she's all yours. Last thing we need around here is a murderess."

Sable's eyes widened. Murderess! A buzz went through the fifteen men in the ward.

"Who is it I've supposedly murdered, Mr. Morse?"

"Your daddy, Carson Fontaine, and I'm taking you back."

Sable shook her head. "No, you aren't. I didn't murder Carson Fontaine and you know it."

"We'll let the authorities decide. Gather up your things and let's go."

Sable didn't move.

Dr. Gaddis happened into the ward. He looked over at the two men grouped around Sable, saw the anger in her face, and asked, "What's going on here?"

Borden replied, "Just a contraband going back to be questioned about a murder."

Gaddis came closer. "Murder?" Wide-eyed, he looked first at Sable and then at Borden. "You must be joking. I don't believe Miss Fontaine is capable of such an act."

"Thank you, Dr. Gaddis."

"Does he have a warrant for her arrest?" the doctor asked the major.

"Nope, he don't need one. I'm authorizing her transfer to the civilian authorities."

"Like hell you are," snapped a new voice. Araminta marched over from her seat at a soldier's bedside.

Morse stared at her as if she were a plant that had suddenly spoken. "This is not your concern, Auntie. I'd advise you to stay out of the affairs of your betters."

Araminta blinked and snarled at the dark-eyed Morse, "My betters!"

Some of the men in the ward began to voice their disapproval. The tension was palpable.

Sable told Borden, "Why don't we step outside, Major. The men are becoming upset."

He inclined his head and gestured for her to lead the way. Araminta and the doctor started forward also, but Borden said, "Doctor, don't you have patients to see?"

"Yes, but . . ."

"Then see to them."

The doctor appeared reluctant, but Borden snapped, "That's an order!"

Dr. Gaddis's eyes brushed Sable's before he strode away.

Borden then turned to Araminta. "I already warned you once, Auntie. This doesn't concern you. Now get!"

"Oh, I'm going to get, all right," she promised, her dark eyes flashing.

Araminta strode angrily out the door.

"Now, Mr. Morse," Major Borden said, "you may take her, and good riddance."

"No, he may not."

Sable turned toward the familiar voice of Raimond LeVeq. Beside him stood an angry Andre Renaud and an even angrier Araminta.

Borden looked over at the tall dark-skinned major and snapped, "Don't you people understand English? This has nothing to do with you."

Raimond viewed his adversary coldly. "And you are . . . ?"

The shorter major drew himself up importantly. "Major Claude Borden. United States Army."

Raimond nodded in Morse's direction. "And you?"

"Henry Morse, her owner. And I have the papers to prove it."

Raimond didn't even a glance at the sheaf of documents Morse waved in his hand. "This is Union territory, Mr. Morse. No one here is owned by anyone."

Borden stood slack-jawed. "What are you called, soldier boy?"

"Major Raimond LeVeq. Contraband liaison. United States Army."

Borden's eyes popped in their sockets.

Raimond had dealt with men like Morse and Borden all his life, men who cared not a whit that he was educated, articulate, and could trace his family back from Haiti to the Moors of Spain. These were men who acted as if they'd been handed a document from God confirming their superiority based on the lack of color in their skin. Raimond took a perverse pleasure in cutting them down to size.

"So," Raimond said smoothly. "Now that we have established our identities, what seems to be the problem?"

Sable thought Araminta looked more than pleased now that the red-faced Borden had been put in his place, but she was certain Morse hadn't any idea whom he was up against.

Borden answered Raimond's question by saying arrogantly, "I've given Mr. Morse here permission to take that contraband back to be questioned by the local sheriff."

"On what grounds?"

"She's a murderess."

"That isn't true, and Morse knows it."

Borden chuckled. "Of course she's going to lie. Most jigs would, but it don't matter, she's going."

"By whose authority?"

"Mine."

It became so still it seemed as if the world had suddenly stopped.

"You have no authority here."

"Says who?"

"Says me, Major. This is my camp, and we do not return contrabands to their masters. Ever."

"That girl killed her own daddy," Borden accused, turning a mean eye on Sable.

"She says she didn't."

"So it's her word against his?"

"Yes."

"And you'd take her word against mine?" Morse demanded, amazed. "Since when is the word of a slave worth anything?"

"Since the day I arrived at this camp, Mr. Morse."

Morse appeared outraged. Now he knew that Major LeVeq was unlike any Black man he'd ever encountered. He turned to Borden. "I can't believe you're going to allow this buck to have the final say. Is this how you Yankees run things?"

"Yes, it is," Raimond offered before Borden could reply. "Unless I receive a message from General Sherman himself, Miss Fontaine stays. And unless you have other legitimate business to discuss, Mr. Morse, I suggest you leave the grounds."

"This is not the end."

"Yes, it is. Lieutenant Renaud, please escort Mr. Morse off Union property."

Andre gestured forward with his rifle. Morse stopped before Sable and told her, "He can't protect you forever."

Andre prodded him in the spine with the rifle to hurry his exit.

After Morse's departure, Major Borden turned to Raimond. "How dare you undermine my directives."

"This discussion is over, Major Borden. If you have a complaint, write to Washington."

He turned to the many soldiers who'd gathered in support of Sable and directed them back to whatever they'd been doing. They all complied, but they went away with proud smiles on their faces and a story they would tell their grandchildren about the brave Major LeVeq and how he'd saved Sable Fontaine from her former master.

Chapter 6

After the yard cleared and Borden stormed away, Sable walked over to the tall, bearded major. "Thank you. I've never had a champion before."

"Glad to be of service. Was there a murder?"

Put so directly, the question made her wonder for a moment if he'd believed Morse's claims. "Yes."

"Your father?"

She nodded.

"Were you involved?"

"I was present, but I didn't cause his death."

"If those two go to my superior officers, I want to be able to argue the truth so I'll need to hear your side of the story."

"Then ask me to eat dinner with you."

Raimond's face showed his surprise. "You're asking to dine with me?"

"I thought it might be nice to share your company and to tell you the story too. Is that too forward?"

"No, no," he reassured her. "I find it amazing, is all. I don't have to beg or slay a dragon in exchange?"

"You already have," she replied softly. "And you were very timely."

"I was already on my way over to see you when I ran into Mrs. Tubman. She was very upset and said you needed help."

"And I did."

"Do you really wish to spend the evening with me?"

"Why do you find that so hard to believe? I thought we had a wonderful time last night."

"I shall come for you at dusk."

"I'll be ready."

He bowed gracefully and was gone.

Araminta, who'd been standing off to the side observing, walked over to Sable. "He's going to be all you'll ever need."

"For what?"

"For life."

Sable turned and stared. "What do you mean?"

"Just keep on living, Sable, and you'll see."

As the day continued, none of the men in the ward mentioned the morning's incident and Sable mentally thanked them for respecting her privacy.

No one respected the afternoon's lunch fare, however. On the tin plates handed out to the soldiers were portions of what the army called dessicated vegetables. The troops thought the word "desecrated" described the vegetable more accurately. The compressed, dried cakes of mixed vegetables were rationed to each soldier in a piece that weighed about an ounce. Once the little cake was soaked in water or wine, it swelled to an amazing size, revealing tasteless layers of cabbage, sliced carrot, turnips, an occasional onion, and any other vegetable the makers had found to include.

Next to the desecrated vegetables were pieces of what the men called "embalmed" beef—their name for the tinned meat supplied to the Union by the meat-packing houses of Chicago. Sable decided she wasn't hungry.

She was quite hungry by the time dusk fell though. Araminta had taken a group of children out on an herb hunt and hadn't returned, so Sable had the little tent to herself. She used the makeshift shower behind the hospital to wash herself clean, then took a moment to run a comb and brush through her unruly dark hair. She refashioned the thick length into a knot on the nape of her neck and pinned it down. She didn't have to spend any time debating her wardrobe; she possessed only two dresses, and both were bloodstained and old. The one she had on, a very washed out, navy-blue shirtwaist and skirt, also bore the dust and dirt of the day. She gave the skirts a shake, brushed off the shirtfront, and that was that. If the major wanted a perfumed woman in silk and satin, he'd have to wait until he returned to Louisiana.

To her complete surprise, he rode up on the beautiful black stallion they'd shared on her first arrival in camp. "He's truly a magnificent animal," she said.

"I've had him since he was a colt. Sable, meet Pegasus."

"Hello, Pegasus," she said with a curtsy.

The horse gave her a stately bow in return, and she laughed in surprise. "He's trained?"

"To ride into the jaws of death, if need be," Raimond bragged, patting the animal's powerful neck. "We are here to carry you off. Are you still willing?"

"I am."

"Then let's get you aboard."

He maneuvered the horse to her side, then reached down and lifted her effortlessly. She settled before him in the saddle. "Very gallant, Sir Knight."

"Only the best for my queen."

His whispered words and the glint in his dark eyes set her heart to pounding, making her confess unintentionally, "You're very overwhelming, Major."

"So are you, Your Majesty, so turn around before I kiss you."

She dropped her head with a smile of embarrassment and did as she was told.

The tender threat stayed with her as they rode through the camp under the watchful, knowing eyes of the residents. The sight of her riding away with the major would undoubtedly cause talk and speculation for weeks to come, but Sable wouldn't worry about that, not now. Thinking about being kissed by him and the passion they'd shared in the treetops gave her more than enough to dwell upon.

The pale light of the rising moon partially illuminated the landscape and the empty road ahead of them as they left the camp. Raimond's solid presence behind her was potent, vital, and as impossible to ignore as the sheltering circle of his arms as he guided the reins. She felt as if they were lovers bound for a midnight tryst.

They stopped a ways down the road before a burned-out mansion illuminated by torches stuck in the ground. The once grand house looked as if it had been brought down by cannon fire. The roof was gone, and the remaining outer walls stood ragged in the soft light. Raimond guided Pegasus up the weed-choked walk. As they approached, Sable saw two armed soldiers standing guard on the porch.

"What is this place?" she asked.

"Our dining salon."

Skeptical, Sable looked around. "And the men?"

"Security detail. There are renegade Rebs running loose in the area. They hit a camp south of here a few days ago. Reports have them heading north. The soldiers are here to keep an eye out."

"We could have eaten at camp, then."

"I know, but what would have been the fun in that?"

"You like danger, Major." She spoke it as fact, not a question.

"Sometimes. Sometimes for the fun of it, other times because it is necessary."

"Into which category does tonight fall?"

"Both. I wouldn't intentionally expose you to danger, but I wanted us to have some privacy. Do you approve?"

"Yes, I think I do."

He dismounted and held out his hands. He gently grasped her by the waist, then slowly, very slowly, brought her to the ground. She drew in a shaky breath as the heat of their bodies mingled. Attempting to draw a steady breath became even more difficult as he traced his finger across her cheek.

"Come," he whispeed.

Sable placed her hand in his, and feeling recklessness return, let him usher her inside.

He guided her on a torchlit journey through the debris-strewn house and up an iron staircase to the second floor. One of the inner rooms was ablaze with additional torches. The wavering light illuminated a central table covered with a beautiful white cloth. Sable stared amazed at the gleaming crystal and the shining porcelain plates. Sparkling silver serving dishes lay covered and waiting. Sable didn't know what to say. For the past week she'd waded in blood and watched men die. Before coming to the camp, she'd had to work from sunup to sundown just to survive. She couldn't remember the last time she'd experienced beauty of any kind.

"It's lovely," she whispered.

He raised her hand to his lips and gently kissed the tips of her fingers. "You deserve a bit of beauty in your life."

Tucking her hand back into his own, he guided her to the table and politely helped her with her seat while cautioning, "One leg of the chair is shorter than the other, so be careful."

Sable sat gingerly until she was certain the chair would support her weight. He sat opposite her on a chair with no back.

"Who do I have to thank for this lovely table besides you?"

"Our precious cook, and the ever resourceful Renaud."

"Please do thank them for me."

"I will."

Raimond looked across the table at his companion and wished he were home in Louisiana so he could entertain her royally. Broken chairs and a room with no roof were far below his usual standard. Were they back home, she would be draped in a beautiful gown, her skin perfumed, her neck adorned with jewels. They would leisurely sample the most succulent dishes his cook had to offer, and he would feed them to her one by one. He—

"You're staring again, Major."

He shook himself. "It's begun to be habit, I'm thinking. My apologies."

"None needed. It doesn't really bother me. It's simply hard to know what you're thinking, and I wonder if I have said or done something to offend you."

"Never. It's my own preoccupation with you."

"More flattery?"

"More truth."

"Truth or not, it's good to hear."

"Shall we dine?"

"As long as there's no skillygalee or lobcourse beneath the covers."

Skillygalee was a Union specialty made from hardtack soaked in water and fried in pork grease. In the mornings the crackling scent of it filled the camp's air.

Raimond smiled. "It's a wonder our soldiers have the strength to fight at all, considering what they're forced to eat. No, there'll be no skillygalee or lobcourse tonight."

"Bless you."

Under the covered dishes were savory potatoes and a sweet, well-prepared fish. Accompanying them were more of the wonderful biscuits and slices of pound cake.

To Sable, who'd been subjected to the camp's spare diet, all the offerings tasted heavenly. "Is it wrong to wish to eat this well all the time?"

"When the war ends I will treat you to the most fabulous meals you can imagine."

"With or without desecrated vegetables?"

He grinned. "Without, certainly."

"Then I shall hold you to that promise too, even if it takes me a decade to find you again."

"It shouldn't be that hard. Especially if you will agree to what I have planned."

"Which is?"

"To send you home to my mother in Louisiana until the Rebs surrender."

Sable struggled to hide her consternation. "Why?"

"So you will be safe."

She looked around the torchlit room. "Do you come here often?"

"Only occasionally. This is where I retreat when I need a respite from the camp. You aren't going to answer me?"

"The house must have been lovely at one time."

"I'm sure it was. The iron staircase reminds me of my mother's house. Sable?"

"Do you think the South will ever be restored?"

"You can't put off answering forever."

She supposed he was right, so she looked across the candles and into his waiting eyes and replied, "Major, I am flattered by your offer, but no."

"Why not?"

"I can't impose on your mother that way. Whatever would she think of me, arriving on her doorstep like a foundling?"

"She would welcome you and care for you until my return."

"And then?"

"I will set you up in rooms so that I may visit you whenever I wish. We'd have to agree that you would see me exclusively."

"Uh huh." She studied him before asking with amusement, "You simply assume I would say yes to being your mistress?"

"Why, of course."

She shook her head. "Major, Major, Major. Having so many women at your disposal for so many years has definitely been unhealthy for you. I have no desire to be your mistress or anyone else's."

"Why not?"

Sable pretended to think deeply. "Well, let's see. I've been a slave for thirty years, subject to the whims of whoever owned me. Why in heaven would I trade my newly found freedom for a different kind of enslavement?"

Her reply seemed to surprise him. "I never viewed it that way," Raimond confessed grudgingly.

"I know. The females in your life must spoil you terribly."

He chuckled as he drained his cup. "You're a hard woman, my queen."

"And you are a very tempting man, Sir Knight. Too tempting, I think."

He lowered his cup and offered sincerely, "Good, then maybe there is hope for me yet."

The air surrounding them seemed to have warmed. She found her attention settling on his full lips. The memory of the kisses they'd shared reawakened her senses. "I do enjoy your kisses though."

"Do you?" he asked in a voice as soft as the star-studded night.

"Yes, I do."

"Then come here. Let's see if you like this one . . ."

The invitation touched her like heat. Her heart began a quick cadence as she set aside her silverware and napkin. She stood on trembling legs and took the few steps necessary to place her at his side. She only wished she could stop shaking.

Still seated, Raimond reached out and lightly traced her mouth, filling her with a sweet need. The first kiss was soft, gentle. His warm, knowing lips seemed to be learning her all over again, exploring her, tempting her to join him in a kiss that promised more. Tiny licks of his tongue sparked against the corners of her mouth, and her lips parted like African blooms.

"I enjoy your kisses too . . ." he breathed. Placing a possessive hand at the small of her back, he brought her closer, deepening the kiss. He held her like a lover, his manhood pulsing in response to her passionate sweetness. Her mouth, as potent as Spanish wine, wove a spell that bound them together. Virgin or not, she must be his here, now.

He eased her down into his lap, his mouth continuing to seek, moving to the shell of her ear and to the curling hair at her temple. His hand began to trace circles over her back, and he felt her trembling response against his palm. "I would never enslave you, *bijou*. Never."

Sable knew the whispered French word *bijou* meant "jewel." And that was how she felt seated atop his thighs, like a finely treasured jewel. She guessed he employed this potent mix of words and kisses all the time, and she now understood why females adored him so. The idea that she was probably only one of hundreds of women he'd had just this way cooled some of her ardor and made her slowly break the kiss so she could catch her breath.

Raimond assumed he had overwhelmed her, so he contented himself with tracing the skin over her jaw while waiting for her to gather herself. He'd thought he would be content with just touching her, but now knew it would not be enough. Fueled by the need for her, he pressed fleeting kisses against her jaw, brow, and temple, silently pleasuring her in this leisurely way.

"I can't think clearly," she confessed in a hush.

"It is only fair, *bien-aimé*. I've been unable to think clearly since the day we met . . ."

He slowly recaptured her lips; this kiss pulsed with power. Lacking defenses against him, Sable willingly surrendered once again.

When he finally drew away, she swore the room was spinning. Her nostrils were flared, her lips parted, and he was smiling down at her like the proverbial satisfied tiger.

Looking up into his handsome face, she confessed without shame, "I see why the women throw themselves in your path."

He responded with a chuckle. "Finally you give me the proper respect. I should kiss you more often."

In fact, he did just that, making the room spin even more, then eased his lips slowly and reluctantly from hers. "Now you can go finish your cake."

A bedazzled Sable returned to her seat and ate her pound cake under the close scrutiny of his glowing tiger's eyes. Every time their gazes locked, her newly awakened passion pulsed unashamedly. Being here with him made her think about Bridget and all the wild and scandalous talks they'd had about men and how to be a sorceress of unimaginable delights. She could tell by his kisses that LeVeq was a man of experience. He could undoubtedly teach her much about the passion that Bridget called a necessary element in the lives of men and women—were Sable of a mind to be taught. She thought she might be. She doubted she would ever find a man to court her as heatedly as the major, regardless of his intentions, and she knew without being told that a woman's memories of a passionate encounter with a man like him would last a lifetime. After she'd faced the harsh realities of survival these past few years, a part of her welcomed such a memory.

She finished the dessert, left him at the table, and walked over to the edge of the room. The outer wall stood no longer, enabling her to look out over the black surroundings. She decided she needed to tell him the story of Mahti's death before the evening advanced any further. He'd expressed an interest in hearing the story behind Morse's charges, and now seemed as good a time as any. Looking back over her shoulder at him still seated at the table, she asked, "Will you come sit with me? I've a story to tell."

He nodded and moved to her side.

She sat down and let her legs dangle over the floor's

edge. He followed suit, pleased that she apparently had no fear of her precarious perch.

"It began a long time ago . . ."

She told him the story of the Old Queen and the circumstances surrounding her death. Next came the tale of her mother, Azelia, and her tragic ending. Sable then chronicled her own story, telling him how she'd been slated to be sold and of Mahti's demise. "She walked into the fire and never looked back . . ."

"Carson Fontaine was the only person still in the house?"

"Yes."

Pain and grief rose within Sable as fresh as if Mahti's death had happened yesterday. She wondered if the ache would ever heal. "Morse has wanted to own me for a long time. I was about fourteen summers when he first tried to buy me. Back then he was the son of a dirt-poor hog farmer, and Carson Fontaine laughed at the offer. But Henry Morse has grown very wealthy scavenging off the war, and the respectable families now invite him into their homes. He cornered me in the kitchen at Sally Ann's last New Year's party in '62 when he was so drunk, he could hardly stand. He kept spouting foul and crude suggestions about how I might help him usher in the new year and then he attempted to show me how. If Otis the houseman hadn't happened in and threatened him with a buggy whip, I believe he would have done me harm."

Raimond wanted Morse dead, on the spot, but kept his thoughts to himself.

"You loved Mahti very much, it seems."

"Yes, I did. Even though Carson took me into the house, Mahti raised me. She even named me, she said. Named me Sable, hoping my skin would darken up."

Raimond smiled.

Sable smiled too. "Of course it didn't. Now, with Rhine gone, I've no one left."

The night breeze teased the candles, making them flicker.

"Have you accepted your brother's decision?"

"I'm handling it a bit better now than I did initially. I finally realized that there isn't anything I can do. I'll always wonder about him and I'll always love him, but he's chosen his path."

Raimond heard the sadness in her tone. As always, he wanted to give her comfort.

She added softly, "I learned this morning that Avery and his family are leaving also. They're being sponsored by a church in Rhode Island. I'd hoped to know them longer."

"People will always ebb and flow through your life."

"I know, but life seemed so much more settled before the war. Folks had friends, acquaintances—now nothing seems permanent anymore. I keep telling myself it's a good thing, slavery is dying after all, but I must admit, I don't know if I can bear to lose someone else I care about."

He draped his arm across her shoulders and coaxed her closer. Smiling at his understanding, she placed her head on his comforting chest and savored being held. "Being with the men at the hospital gives me other things to think about besides my own misery. I can't very well feel sorry for myself after witnessing their sufferings. My broken heart seems such a small thing in comparison to men who'll have to live out their lives with one leg or no arms."

Talking about the men sent her thoughts back to this morning's altercation. "Major Borden was not real pleased with you today."

"Good, because I'm not real pleased with him either."

"Why in the world would he be assigned to Black troops?"

"Because his past record makes him unfit to command anywhere else."

She drew back. "What do you mean?"

"He's fouled up every White command he's ever been involved in, according to the reports Andre received. There are also whispers that he embezzled unit funds."

"Then why hasn't he been discharged?"

"Because his father is a very influential politician in Washington. Rather than send him home in disgrace, and embarrass his powerful family, army command reassigned him to the United States Colored Troops. They seem to feel he can't foul up an assignment that only involves rebuilding railroads."

"He has little respect for the race."

"You're being far too kind, Sable. The man's as bigoted as a Reb. Mrs. Tubman told me about the disrespectful way he spoke to her."

"He was very rude, but you set him right." She looked up into his eyes and added seriously, "We made an enemy today. I could see it in his face."

"I agree."

"Do you believe he will make trouble?"

"I'd be very surprised if he didn't. That's another reason why I want to send you to my mother. If you aren't here, you won't have to worry about him."

She placed her hand against his bearded cheek. "Once again, the answer is no. But thank you."

"You're very stubborn, Your Majesty."

"Most queens are."

He turned her palm to his lips and pressed a soft kiss there. "I won't bring the subject up again."

"Bless you."

The stars were now out in full force. Sable looked up at them overhead and said, "If I were your mistress, do you know the very first thing I'd want you to teach me?"

Raimond could not believe she'd asked such a question. "What?"

"The names of all the stars and how to be guided by them when I'm sailing the world."

"Oh."

She looked his way. "Is something wrong?"

He started to lie, then decided not to. "Not really. I just assumed you meant something different."

"Something a bit more carnal, I'm guessing?"

He chuckled.

"Men," she declared sagely. "What is your ship named?"

"Are you sure there's not something else you need my tutoring in?"

"No, you handsome devil. What's the name of your ship?"

He leaned over and kissed her soundly. In the hazy aftermath, Sable heard him whisper the name *Andromeda*.

Somehow she managed to ask, "After the constellation?"

"Yes, and because Andromeda was an Ethiopian princess."

Sable straightened. "Really?"

"Really. She and Perseus became lovers after he rescued her. She bore his children, but I don't believe he ever married her."

"I've read that myth many times. I never knew she was an African."

"The name Andromeda means captive princess."

"I'm impressed by your knowledge, Sir Knight."

"And here you thought I knew only about women."

"I never said that. But it is apparent that you are very learned in that area."

"No one has ever complained."

"And I will not be the first," she tossed back saucily.

"I could kiss you until dawn and still not be satisfied."

Sable blinked at his blunt speech, even as the heat of

his words made her senses simmer. "And I'm of a mind
to let you have your way."

"You banter well for such an innocent," he whispered, tracing her beautiful full mouth with a long dark
finger.

"Blame it on Bridget," Sable replied, trembling under the intensity in his gaze. "She's taken it upon herself
to lecture me on all I'll need to know to be a real
woman . . ."

He kissed her then, a real man kissing a real woman,
and Sable's passion swam up to meet his own. He pulled
her closer and she rose to her knees to keep from losing
his kiss. His hand began lazily to slide her skirt against
her thighs, then circle higher to her hip. Heat rose like
a fever on her skin. He brushed his mouth against hers.
"*Bijou* . . . If I don't see you safely home right now, you
aren't going to have a stitch of clothing on . . ."

"Then I suppose you should take me home," she replied breathlessly. The heated promise in his warning set
off a delicious thrill.

As Raimond anchored his hand in her tumbling hair
so he could enjoy her even more, he wanted to kick
himself for being such a gentleman, but he knew she
deserved better than to lose her innocence on the floor
of a burned-out mansion. He helped himself to a few
more long tastes of her sweet lips, all the while wondering when he'd become so damn noble.

Finally he drew away and took her home.

The next morning after sharing a breakfast of bully
soup and coffee with Araminta, Sable headed across the
yard to the hospital. The sight of a White woman riding
in that direction atop an old mule made her pause. The
rider's features became more distinct as she neared, and
recognition made Sable's heart stop, then pump furiously. "Oh, my Lord! Mavis!"

Sable took off at a run, screaming her sister's name.
Mavis jumped off the mule and ran to meet her. They

collided with such force they almost knocked themselves to the ground, but they were so busy laughing and crying, neither cared.

Mavis gushed through her happy tears, "Oh, Sable, I'm so glad you're okay."

Sable hugged her sister with all her might. "I've been so worried."

When they were finally able to turn each other loose, Sable confessed truthfully, "I've missed you, Mavis."

"And I you."

"Are you well?"

Mavis sighed. "I suppose I should be thankful I still have my health, but things aren't well back home. Mama and I are living in the quarters. They're the only structures still standing, and we've no place else to go."

"What happened to Cindi and Vashti?"

"They disappeared the day after you did. I've no idea where they went."

Sable prayed they were safe.

Mavis added softly, "The others left with some Yankees a few days ago."

"How's your mother?"

"Remarkably well, all things considered."

Mavis's voice was so thick with sarcasm, Sable felt compelled to say, "Explain."

"She and Morse are marrying on Sunday."

"What?!"

Mavis nodded. "Sunday. Daddy's probably spinning in his grave."

The idea of Sally Ann Fontaine marrying Henry Morse certainly knocked Sable for a loop.

Mavis explained further. "She really believes he's in love with her, but it's the land he wants. He's been courting her since the day after the fire. I tried to get her to sell it to him because the land isn't worth a thing if there's no one to work it, but he has her convinced he can restore her and the plantation to glory."

"Morse was here yesterday."

"I know, I came with him. He and Mama had the idea I could make you come back. She's going to be furious when he returns empty-handed. She holds you responsible for what Mahti did."

Sable looked into Mavis's eyes and asked bluntly, "Do you?"

Mavis shook her head. "I loved my daddy very much, Sable. I know you didn't have the feelings for him that I had, but the fire was Mahti's doing not yours. I can't hate you for something you had no hand in."

"So do you hate Mahti?"

Mavis's voice quieted almost to a whisper. "I don't want to, but yes, I do. My father's dead because of her."

Sable knew that debating the point would serve nothing. They had each lost someone very important to her. Although she and Mavis had been together most of their lives, race would always make them see and interpret certain situations differently. "So what are you going to do?"

"I've no idea. On the ride here with Morse yesterday, I decided I wasn't going back. I'm so tired of listening to Mama rant and rave about the changes the war's brought. It isn't my fault she can't have new dresses or hats or that her hairdresser was burned out by the Yankees. I want her to sell the place to Morse and just leave, but she won't hear of it. She says she was born in Georgia and she's going to die in Georgia."

Mavis had always been thin, but now she appeared gaunt. Her usually sunny face bore lines of fatigue and hunger. The dress she was wearing had been purchased five years ago on a shopping trip to Atlanta. "Have you eaten this morning?"

Mavis shook her head.

"There's bully soup left, if you'd care for some."

"What in heaven's name is bully soup?"

"Hot cereal made out of cornmeal and hardtack. It's boiled in water, wine, and ginger. The Union troops eat it."

"Is it any good?"

"It beats starving."

"Then yes, I'll have some."

Sable fetched Mavis a bowl of the cereal from the pot on the cook fire outside the ward, and while Mavis ate silently, Sable sat at her side. "Rhine was here a few weeks ago."

Mavis's head snapped up. "Was Andrew with him?"

"No, he's out West."

"Out West. What happened to his commission?"

Sable shrugged. "I've no idea, but right after the first battle, Andrew freed Rhine and headed off to California."

"So he deserted."

"It appears so."

"Well, good. Andrew never wanted to go to war in the first place. A pretty girl and a good bottle of bourbon were all he ever wanted out of life. Did Rhine say he was well?"

"Last he saw him he was."

Sable didn't tell Mavis about the path Rhine had chosen for his own life.

Mavis finished off her bully soup and set the bowl aside. "So where are you going from here, Sable?"

"Eventually North, I hope. What about you?"

"I've no idea, really. I thought about going up to Philadelphia. Mama has a sister there, maybe she'll take me in."

"Do you have funds?"

"No."

Sable reached into the bosom of her dress and unpinned a small cloth wallet. Since the theft, she'd kept her money hidden on her person. "Take this. It isn't much, but it will tide you over."

"Sable, no. I can't take your money."

"Why not? Regardless of everything that has happened, Mavis, we are still and will always be sisters. I refuse to let you starve."

"No."

"Take the money, Mavis, or do you want to live with Sally Ann and Morse for the rest of your life?"

Mavis shook her head. "No—but what about you?"

"I have a job, Mavis, I can make more money. I cannot make another sister."

Looking very reluctant, Mavis held out her hand, and Sable placed the wallet in it.

Mavis had tears in her eyes as they shared another hug. "I love you, Sable."

"And I you. Now find somebody heading North and get going before Morse tries to drag you back as well."

"Will we ever see each other again?"

"Pray we do, Mavis. Pray we do."

As Mavis rode away on the mule, Araminta peered into Sable's teary green eyes. "Who was that?"

"My sister, Mavis. She has no place to go and no money. I gave her all I had."

Araminta placed her arm around Sable and hugged her tight. "You've a good heart, child."

Bridget stopped by the hospital around midday. She found Sable out back hanging freshly washed sheets on a line to dry.

"So, Fontaine, how did your tryst with the major go last evening?"

"It was not a tryst."

"It would have been, had you been me. Haven't you been listening to anything I've tried to teach you these last few weeks?" she teased.

"I have, but the major is a gentleman."

"Sometimes being a gentleman is not all it's cracked up to be, believe me."

"I'm sure you're correct, but we had a good time nonetheless."

"Kisses?"

"Yes, as a matter of fact."

"You're smiling, Fontaine. There must have been lots

of kisses. Maybe there's hope for you after all.''

"How'd you know I spent the evening with him?''

"Riding through camp with him on a black stallion is not a very discreet mode of travel. The entire camp is gossiping about the two of you.''

That was not what Sable wanted to hear.

"Well, at least they aren't talking about me being a murderess.''

"Oh, that's being discussed too. You really need to be thinking about leaving here, Fontaine—major or no major. That sharecropper Morse and his Reb friend Major Borden won't let this rest. I'm guessing neither one has ever had to take orders from a man of the race, and it didn't go down well.''

"The major expects them to cause trouble.''

"All the more reason for you to leave.''

"That's easier said than done, especially with no funds.''

"What happened to your money? You haven't been robbed again, have you?''

"No, I gave it all to my sister, Mavis, this morning.''

"All of it?"

Sable nodded.

"Fontaine, what were you thinking?''

"She's my sister, Bridget. I couldn't let her starve. Besides, I'll be paid soon.''

"Says who?''

"I'm on the army's payroll now—''

"And you'll be lucky to see what you're owed before the new year arrives. The Yankees are notorious for paying their soldiers when they get around to it.''

Sable had to admit she had heard many of the men grousing about the length of time between payments, but Mavis had needed her help. Sable did not regret offering it. "What happened to your own plans for leaving? Wasn't Randolph supposed to be your ticket out?''

"He still may be. He's hinting about leaving sometime early next week.''

"Is he being transferred?"

"No, he's going to desert."

"Desert?" Sable whispered, looking around to make certain they weren't being overheard.

Bridget nodded. "He's tired of war, and he misses his wife and daughter. When he goes, he's promised to take me along."

"How's he going to get through the lines?"

Bridget shrugged. "I've no idea and I haven't asked. All I care about is leaving here. He can handle the details. Do you want to tag along?"

"Maybe."

Sable thought about never seeing the major again, and a chill grabbed her heart.

"Well, I'll look in on you later in the week and let you know if he's set on his plan," Bridget said. "You're going to need money though, Fontaine. Find some. Borrow it or steal it if you have to."

"I doubt I'll have to go that far, Bridget."

"You never know. Now give me a hug and I'll see you later."

They shared a quick, tight embrace.

As Bridget strode off across the yard, Sable called out, "Tell Mrs. Reese I said hello!"

Bridget turned and waved. "I will!"

Sable went back to hanging up sheets and thinking about leaving the camp. Common sense told her to give serious thought to Bridget's invitation. Going North was Sable's ultimate goal, and right now, she had no way to get there. Could she leave LeVeq? Although he'd stolen her heart, she knew she must. For all his gallant courting, he would be heading back to Louisiana after the war, and once there, he'd pick a wife from the wealthy daughters of his elite class. In a year's time, she doubted he would even remember her name.

Certainly he would never know she loved him, because she had no intention of telling him.

Chapter 7

"**H**ow many more?" Raimond asked Andre as he scribbled his signature on yet another camp document. It seemed as if he'd been signing duty rosters, supply requisitions, and field reports all day.

"Only five more."

Raimond growled. He detested paperwork.

Andre placed another sheaf under Raimond's pen and waited for him to sign it before giving him another. "I'd've thought you'd be in a better mood after your evening with Miss Fontaine."

Raimond did not comment.

"You didn't have a good time?"

"Yes, I had a good time."

"Then why the growling?"

"Let's just say I'd hoped for a *better* time, but my conscience reared its head."

"Your conscience? You have a conscience?"

"Evidently I do, and I'm still trying to decide whether I'm proud of it or not."

"Galeno is going to laugh himself sick."

Raimond glared.

"He is, you know."

"Don't talk to me about Galeno. If he hadn't wished this on me, none of it would be happening."

"Wished what?"

153

"That one day a woman would come along and put me through the same paces La Petite Indigo put him through."

"And the lovely Mademoiselle Fontaine has made Galeno's wish come true."

"Are we finished here?" Raimond snapped.

"Nope, two more."

Raimond signed them and Andre placed the documents in his ledger. "You know, if it's any consolation, I believe your mother would genuinely like Miss Fontaine," Andre observed.

"I believe so too, but Sable wanted no part of my plan to send her to Louisiana."

"Really, why not?"

"She asked me why in heaven would she trade her newfound freedom for another type of slavery by becoming my mistress."

"She has a point."

Raimond glared again.

"She does, there's no sense in lying about it," Andre continued. "I can't remember a woman ever turning you down this way, though. It appears to be rather painful."

"Don't you have work to do, someplace else?"

Andre saluted. "I will leave you to your misery."

He gathered up the remaining papers and headed toward the tent opening, whistling cheerily.

Raimond sat brooding and silent in the tent. He couldn't remember ever wanting a woman as badly as he wanted Sable Fontaine. After returning her to camp last evening, he'd been hard pressed to let her go. He'd ached to make love to her in as many ways as one night could hold. He wanted more of her kisses, more of her soft sighs. He wanted to brand her with the full extent of his sensual expertise so that she would remember him for the rest of her life.

But he hadn't, and because of their flirtation with passion he'd gone to bed as hard as a railroad tie and had awakened this morning in the same state. Would having her finally put an end to his obsessive desire, or would it only increase? Who ever would have thought he'd hesitate to consummate a relationship with a beautiful and desirable woman because of a conscience he never knew he possessed?

When he and Galeno had spent their university years in Paris, they'd sampled the courtesans as freely as they had the wines. Perfumed and provocative women with names like Yvette, Simone, and Gabrielle had tutored them in the sensual arts, showing them the many and varied roads to a woman's pleasure. In the years since then, he'd had the daughters of counts, court officials, ministers, and escaped slaves. He'd made love in haystacks, perfumed boudoirs, and stately gardens, and never once had his conscience bothered him. Never.

So why now? Raimond took pride in loving a willing woman to the fullest. Had he been with someone other than Sable last night, he doubted there would have been any hesitation; he would have stripped her slowly and taken her right there on the floor beneath the torchlights. But it had been Sable, and as he'd told himself last night, she deserved better. For reasons he had yet to untangle, he didn't wish to be remembered as the man she'd made love to on the sooty floor of a burned-out mansion.

He did want her to be his mistress, however, and although he understood why she didn't embrace the idea, being turned down flat did not sit well with him. The charm of the eldest son of the house of LeVeq was legendary, yet with Sable he felt like a destitute little boy standing outside a sweet shop with his face pressed longingly against the glass.

Raimond rubbed his hands over his weary eyes, and vowing to set aside all thoughts of Sable, began to go over the day's reports.

Union troops had forced most of the Rebels back into Alabama after the fall of Atlanta, but they hadn't been polite enough to stay there. By now Rebels under the command of Sherman's old adversaries Hood, Forrest, and Wheeler had become a major annoyance for Sherman. Their hit-and-run attacks on Union-held roads, railroads, and cities were forcing the general to waste valuable time recapturing territory he'd already taken. Tired of chasing the Rebs back and forth, Sherman now proposed to ignore them altogether. He intended to leave a few regiments behind to hold Atlanta while he and the bulk of his men pushed through to the sea, thereby effectively cutting the Confederacy in two and giving Grant a chance to march right up to General Lee's backside.

Raimond had thought the plan made sense when the general had briefed him and the other officers back in late September, but Sherman had had trouble selling the idea to the President and to Grant. He'd gone to Washington to plead his case in person, and had returned this morning with their approval. He and his army would be moving right after Election Day. The report on Raimond's desk gave the date as the fifteenth of November, less than two weeks away.

Raimond looked over the roster of the troops who would be staying behind and his face soured at the sight of Major Claude Borden's name. Raimond had hoped he'd be among those leaving.

The next report on his desk dealt with a request from Grant that soldiers from the state of Indiana be allowed to return home so they could vote on Tuesday, November 8. Nineteen states were allowing their resident soldiers to vote in the field; Indiana was not one of them. The Republicans considered Indiana crucial in next week's election so army commanders were being asked to help the President's reelection by giving these men speedy furloughs.

The last report of note concerned the Davis Bend plantation, located about twenty-five miles south of Vicksburg. Before the war it had been owned by Jefferson Davis's brother, Joseph, but after the fall of the Mississippi Valley, it had become a Union spoil. Grant

had thought the fertile land an ideal place to settle contrabands, and this past April the land had been leased
to seventy-five free Black heads of households, represent-
ing a total population of about six hundred former slaves.
They were leased plots as small as one acre and as large
as one hundred. As with all the new home farms, the
government provided rations and teams of mules and
horses to get them started as farmers, with the understanding that the debts would be paid from the profits
of the crops planted.

The report Raimond was reading had been forwarded
to all Union commanders, informing them that the ex-
periment had been a great success. Not only had the
lessees planted their crops, sold them, and repaid the
government, but most of the free Black farmers had also
turned a profit. In one case more than a thousand dollars
had been cleared. Many attributed the success of this
particular group of freedmen to the attitude of their former master, Joseph Davis, who'd been known to en-
courage enterprise and self-respect among his slaves.
Raimond attributed the success to the determination of
the former slaves themselves, who were handling their
own business transactions, setting up their own court
procedures, and enforcing their own laws.

News of the success at Davis Bend filled him with
pride. He hoped the Northern press would pick up on
the story, counter balancing clamorings of the "Know-
Nothings" across the country who believed the Black
population of the South could never provide for itself.
They believed the race was intellectually inferior and
predisposed toward laziness. Never mind that Black
hands and backs had built every major city in the South,
laid hundreds of thousands of miles of railroad tracks,
and worked in all kinds of occupations. Never mind that
before the war, slave labor had made the American
South one of the wealthiest regions on earth. Many people in the North and South were convinced Blacks would

never work when freed, not without the lash across their backs to prod them on.

But Davis Bend spoke for itself.

Another success story came from a colony on Roanoke Island where contrabands had leased the land and built 591 houses. The land value had increased almost forty-fold by the time they celebrated their first year of freedom.

All over the South, contrabands were staking their claim to a better life. Many were leasing the very land they'd worked as slaves. Others leased wherever they could, whatever they could. Land ownership coupled with an education were the chief goals of a free man, and thousands were working toward those ends. Now that the freedmen could own their cabins and were not as crowded as they'd been during slavery, the cabins were being fixed up and whitewashed. Wells were sunk, crops planted. If the freedmen were given the chance to compete on an equal footing with their former masters, Raimond envisioned great success, not only for the freedmen and women, but for the country as well.

He slid the reports aside and searched through the clutter for his marriage ledger. Once a month, the army sent a chaplain to conduct marriages, and today was the day. The first marriage day had occurred about a week after the camp was established, when there were so many couples wanting to tie the knot, the chaplain had married them en masse—191 in the first hour alone. Raimond had no idea what the numbers would be today, but overseeing the ceremonies was one of the few duties here he genuinely enjoyed. It had touched his heart to see the love in the eyes of a former slave couple who'd been together for fifty years but been denied the right to marry, or to hear the story of a man who'd walked from plantation to plantation looking for the wife who'd been sold away from him decades ago. A report out of a Vicksburg camp had counted more than three thousand marriages conducted over an eight-month period. Five hundred, or one-sixth, of those couples had been forcibly separated by slavery.

Sable hurried to finish the last of her hospital paperwork so she could head off to the wedding festivities. She'd not been at camp for the last marriage day, but she was looking forward to what Bridget described as a "good ol' time." According to her, in the evening after the ceremonies, there would be fiddlers, dancing, and much socializing. Sable was looking forward to seeing Major LeVeq. Every time she thought back on last night's dinner, the memory of the sensation of being in his arms rose vividly. He'd left her breathless. She'd never known kisses could be so moving or that being held against him would leave her feeling so singed. Thankfully he'd remained clear-headed enough to prevent passion from totally possessing her; otherwise the evening might have turned out quite differently.

The crowd was already thick by the time Sable made her way from the hospital to the area near the Message Tree where the ceremonies would be held. It appeared as if every contraband in camp had come, and she saw many familiar faces as she stood on tiptoe in an effort to locate Bridget. She waved and called out hellos to those she knew and asked if anyone had seen her friend. A few said they had, but no one could offer a definite location, so Sable gave up for the time being.

There appeared to be quite a few couples waiting to be married by the chaplain. Some of the men were soldiers who looked smart in their starched blue uniforms. Many of the women were being married in the only dress they owned, but it didn't seem to matter. The love on their faces mirrored the true measure of their wealth. The couples were old and young. Many had been together for as long as Sable had been alive, while others had met and fallen in love there in the camp. In the years before the war a few of the masters back home had permitted their slaves to marry, but Carson Fontaine had not been one of them.

The chaplain was a young, redheaded man from Boston named Charles Drayer. He and Sable had talked many times over at the hospital. His family were staunch abolitionists from Boston.

The tall, bearded LeVeq stood next to the shorter chaplin, and the sight of him filled her eyes. He seemed to sense her interest, because he turned from speaking with the chaplain, looked out into the crowd, and met her gaze. The world seemed to stand still. He nodded and as she nodded in return, the intensity of his gaze heightened the pace of her breathing and made her lips part unconsciously. Once again she felt singed.

Sable didn't realize Bridget had sidled near until she heard, "He truly is a gorgeous man, isn't he?"

Sable grinned at Bridget, then directed her eyes back to the man in question. "Yes, he truly is."

Sable wanted to talk with Bridget about his desire to make her his mistress, but with the crowd pressed so tightly, she decided to wait for a more private moment.

Bridget kept hopping up and down trying to see over the heads blocking their view. "I can't see a damn thing. Come on, let's look for a better spot."

She and Sable worked their way over to a place with fewer tall people, then watched as the first couple came to stand before the chaplain. Thirteen couples were waiting in line, and both Sable and Bridget beamed upon seeing Avery and his wife, Salome, among them.

"I thought they were leaving," Sable said as Avery recited his vows loud enough for all the world to hear.

"The church in Rhode Island wouldn't sponsor them until they were married. They'll be leaving tomorrow."

Sable's heart swelled with pride as Salome, holding the infant Avery the Younger, spoke her pledge too.

A few more couples stepped up and were married, then came the curious sight of a man who stood before the chaplain with two women.

His name was Hiram Geerson and the two women were the two different wives he'd had under slavery. Neither woman appeared pleased to be there. He looked sheepish. His dilemma revolved around which one to marry.

"Well," said Chaplain Drayer, "which one do you wish to marry?"

"Both," came Hiram's reply, and everyone laughed.

Smiling, the chaplain shook his head. "The law says you can have only one wife."

"How am I supposed to decide?"

The chaplain shrugged. Several members of the crowd called out to suggest Hiram flip a coin or have the women draw straws. Arms crossed, both women shifted impatiently.

Finally the chaplain asked, "Which woman has borne you the most children?"

Hiram pointed to the woman on the left.

"Then she's the one you should marry."

The woman who'd lost Hiram asked pointedly, "And what of *my* children? Who will provide for them?"

Out of the crowd rang a loud voice, "I will, if you'll have me."

Everyone laughed, thinking it was a joke, until a man who rivaled Raimond LeVeq in both size and good looks stepped forward. The woman appeared as surprised as everyone else. "But you don't know me and I don't know you," she countered.

"You're right. My name is Levi Bond. I've a job and some land not far from here and I need a woman to help make it a home. Your younguns will be welcome. Will you have me?"

She looked up at the chaplain, who appeared quite pleased with the outcome, then back at the tall waiting man. Tears in her eyes, she nodded yes.

Shouts of approval rang out from the crowd. The new couple got in line behind Hiram to await their turn to become husband and wife.

When the ceremonies ended some time later, the crowd began drifting away. Some came forward to congratulate the newlyweds. Sable and Bridget hugged both Avery and Salome, then wished them well on tomorrow's journey North.

Bridget headed back toward the laundry, promising to come and get Sable later so they could attend the evening's celebrations.

Sable started out for the hospital, only to have the major fall in beside her. "Hello, Miss Fontaine."

"Major."

"May I have the pleasure of your company this evening?"

She paused to look up into his playful eyes. "I'd enjoy that."

"Good, then I will come by the hospital later."

Sable knew she was staring at him, but couldn't seem to stop herself.

He told her boldly, "If there weren't a hundred pairs of eyes watching, I'd kiss you right here."

"And I'd let you," she countered softly.

He bowed and departed.

True to his word, he came for her at the end of her shift. He held her hand as they walked together in the November moonlight toward the bonfires, where the revelry was already well underway. "You're the first man I've ever walked with in the moonlight," she said.

"I still find that hard to believe."

"It's the truth. I was sweet on a young coachman a few years ago and I'm fairly certain he returned my feelings. He'd promised to dance with me at the quarter's New Year's gathering, but Sally Ann wouldn't let me attend. I spent the whole evening serving cake and tea to her friends."

"Whatever happened to him?"

She shrugged. "Later that spring his master moved to Texas. I never saw him again."

Sable and Raimond reached the festivities just in time

to catch the end of the broom jumping. Broom jumping was a parlor game of sorts. The idea was to see who would wear the pants in the household of the newly-weds—the new husband or the new wife. The broom was held about a foot above the ground and it had to be jumped backward without being touched. The person who cleared the broom would be the boss.

Sable laughed as the man Levi Bond got his big boots tangled in the broom and crashed to the ground. His smiling wife waited until the broom was held aloft again, then raised her skirts and jumped over it as neat as a cricket.

Her feat was met by laughter and applause. Several folks told Levi he wouldn't be able to leave the house without his new wife's approval after the way she'd sailed over that broom, but Levi just laughed. To Sable he appeared more than pleased with his choice of a mate.

As she and the major strolled off, Sable said, "I wonder if Levi and his wife will be happy together."

"Time will tell, but he's a good man to take on an unknown woman and her children."

Sable thought so too.

"Hungry?" he asked.

She nodded.

"There's a reception being held for the soldiers who were married. Would you like to attend?"

"How fancy is it?"

"Pretty fancy."

Sable looked down at her scuffed and muddy army boots, her stained and ragged black and white checked dress, and said, "Maybe I'll decline. I wouldn't want my appearance to reflect poorly upon you."

"You will be the most beautiful woman there."

"Not in these clothes."

"How about I go inside and steal a couple of plates? We can eat elsewhere."

"That would be better," she confessed, glad for his understanding.

"Then that's what we'll do."

The reception was being held in the large tent that usually served as the soldiers' dining hall. Outside, waiting for the major to return, Sable tapped her toe to the lively fiddle music and listened to the happy chatter of the party goers. The smell of the pig roasting nearby made her stomach growl.

"Well, if it isn't the murderess."

Out of the darkness stepped Major Borden.

Sable didn't acknowledge him with more than a leveling look before turning away.

Borden stepped closer. "Your jig major embarrassed me yesterday, but he'll get his and so will you."

Sable remained silent.

"In fact, I'm working on it right now, missy."

At that moment Raimond stepped up to them. "Working on what, Major Borden—bad manners? A gentleman does not accost a lady in the dark."

"You got a real foreign way of talking, LeVeq. Where're you from?"

"New Orleans."

"Oh, you're one of those French jigs."

Raimond didn't bat an eye. "Haitian, actually. My ancestors helped kick the French out of Haiti and save Andrew Jackson from the English in 1812. What were your people doing in those days?"

"Owning slaves."

"Just as I suspected. Well, know this," he said, and his voice softened with warning, "if you try to compromise Miss Fontaine or her freedom, you will have me to answer to."

Not even the dark could mask the surprise in Borden's eyes. He finally sputtered, "How dare you threaten me!"

"That wasn't a threat, Major," Raimond replied smoothly, "that was a promise. Now, Miss Fontaine and I are going to find a quiet spot to eat our dinner. Have a good evening."

Sable walked away feeling as stunned as Borden undoubtedly did. Having been a slave all her life, she'd never heard a man of the race speak so forcefully before. "Won't you get in trouble threatening him that way?"

"Probably. But he'll think twice about causing you harm."

"What will happen if he reports you?"

"In a fair world, it would be my word against his, but since fairness is as fickle as the wind in this country, I would probably be booted out."

"You don't seem concerned."

He shrugged. "If I'm booted out, so be it. All I want to do is return to the sea anyway, so they'd actually be doing me a favor."

"But what if charges are leveled? Couldn't you be imprisoned?"

"Only if they can find me. I've friends and family all over the world who'll harbor me, and I can conduct my shipping business from Quebec or Martinique just as easily if I have to leave the country."

Sable shook her head.

"What's the matter?"

"You do enjoy danger, don't you?"

He grinned, but did not answer.

They returned near his tent to eat. The bonfire outside provided both heat and light as they sat under the stars.

As Sable ate the roast pig, potatoes and collards, she thought about the confrontation with Borden. "Would you really leave the country?" she asked.

"If it became necessary, yes. Seamen are citizens of the world. There are very few ports where I could not find a home."

"It must be wonderful to have such freedom."

"Yes, it is. When the war is done, we can sail the world together and you'll experience it for yourself."

"Is that another veiled invitation to be your mistress?"

"Of course not," he lied baldly.

They shared a smile and finished their meal outside under the November moon.

The wind started to pick up as the moon rose, but the fiddlers and the revelry could still be heard in the distance.

"Chilly?" he asked.

"A bit," she confessed, pulling her frayed shawl tighter.

"Then come sit beside me so I can warm you."

"You make that sound so innocent."

"It is. I'm a gentleman if nothing else. It pains me to see a young woman shivering in the night air."

"Uh huh."

But she went over to where he sat anyway.

He placed an arm around her shoulders and cuddled her close. "Better now?"

Sable reveled in the solid feel of him and confessed, "Yes."

The first kiss came not more than a heartbeat later, and she reveled in it also. He moved his hand to the back of her head and deepened the kiss until her world became hazy. "You're supposed to be offering me warmth," she whispered.

Nibbling her bottom lip, he replied, "I am . . . Can't you feel it?"

Yes, she could, and it was the most delicious warmth she'd ever experienced. She could also feel the gentle but lightning-charged explorations of his tongue and the heated pressure of his hand on her ribs.

"Let's go inside," he whispered, but didn't stop his kisses. They stood, kissed their way out of the wind and into the tent. Passion climbed as they entered the quiet shadows only to be interrupted by someone clearing his throat.

They both looked up to see Andre Renaud outlined against the tent's opening.

Embarrassment heated Sable's cheeks as she stood in the major's arms.

Raimond was just plain mad. "What?"

Clearly uncomfortable to be interrupting them, the glower on the major's face not making it any easier for him, Andre stammered, "My apologies, but, uh, in the hubbub of tonight, Mrs. Fogel wasn't paid."

Sable had no idea who Mrs. Fogel was.

"Hurry up," Raimond growled.

Sable watched as Andre went to the big sea chest beside the cot.

"Mrs. Fogel is our cook," Raimond explained. "She prepared the meal for us last evening and for the soldiers who were married today."

"Is she the one who makes those heavenly biscuits?"

"One and the same."

Andre seemed to be having trouble with the lock and key.

"What the hell are you doing, Renaud?"

"It won't open. I told you you needed to have this lock replaced."

Raimond stormed over and managed to open the rusty-looking padlock, but once it came open the key would not come free. "I'll have someone fix it soon. Here."

He tossed Andre a small bag that appeared to be made of black velvet. Andre caught it, shook out a few coins, and handed the bag back.

Andre stood and bowed in Sable's direction. "My apologies again, Miss Fontaine."

"Just go, Andre," Raimond said impatiently.

He did.

Raimond pulled her back into his arms. "Now, where were we?"

"You growled at him like an old bear."

"It's what old bears do when they're interrupted in the middle of eating their honey."

"You shouldn't growl at Andre, he's just doing his job, isn't he?"

"Do you wish to be kissed or to spend the time discussing Andre?"

"You need to exercise more patience."

"If I do, will I get more kisses?"

"You're shameless."

"You don't know the half of it, *bien-amié*."

"That means 'sweetheart,' doesn't it?"

"Yes, it does."

Although Sable felt certain the endearment was one he employed often, it nonetheless gave her a thrill because she'd never been called sweetheart by any man before.

He asked, "How much French do you understand?"

"Quite a bit actually. Mavis's tutor thought the world rose and set with the French, so we were forced to learn whether we cared to or not."

"Any other languages?"

"A smattering of Spanish, German, and Latin."

"So you are as educated as you are beautiful?"

"I am educated, but the beauty, that is debatable."

He stroked her cheek. "No, *bijou*, it is fact."

The tone of his voice told her he intended to kiss her again and he did, slowly, thoroughly, completely.

Soon his hands were sliding circles over her back, and the kisses became more fervent, more dizzying. She felt as if she were melting inside and out. His touch set her aflame. She dropped her head back, and he placed sweet, fiery kisses on her throat, her jaw. When his hand came up and cupped her breast, the intensity made her moan softly. She knew she should not let him take such bold liberties, but she couldn't find the words or the will to break the spell.

He spoke against her ear, "Do you know how much I want to make you mine?"

Sable wanted to be his, wanted to know what it meant to be consumed by passion.

"Were you mine, I'd make love to you before the fire and watch the flames reflect against your skin . . ."

His words conjured up such sensuous pictures in her mind, she trembled in response.

"I'd spend hours scenting your skin with the finest perfumes my gold could buy . . . Then I'd kiss you here . . ." he promised as his lips closed over her nipple through the thin material of her ragged dress. "And here . . ." he added, moving his caress to her other breast. Sable moaned and arched as her nipple peaked within his warm mouth.

"I'd kiss all of you, *bijou*, all of you."

Sable wasn't sure how long she could remain standing. His lips were magicians, his hands tempters. She and Bridget had talked about being rendered insane by passion, but Sable was only now beginning to understand just how overwhelming being with a man could be. His heated words were enough to put her in a spiral; were he to touch her as he wished, she knew she would ignite and burn. Her nipples were hard and yearning, and parts of her body she never knew could be set afire were blazing under his sensual tutoring. Taking her cue from him, she ran her hands over the strong lines of his back and arms and nibbled his full bottom lip.

The sound of gunshots startled them both. Raimond backed away and moved quickly to the tent's open flap. He heard the return fire of Union rifles, women screaming, men shouting.

"What's happening?" Sable cried.

"I don't know. Stay here until I get back."

He grabbed up his gun and ran out.

Sable began to pace anxiously. The sound of shots became louder as more guns joined in. What in heaven's name could be happening? A heartbeat later, Bridget ran in. "Oh Lord, thank goodness I found you. The camp's under attack. We have to leave. Right now."

"Under attack by whom?"

"Reb cavalry. Come on."

Bridget grabbed Sable's arm, but she pulled away. "No, the major wants me to wait."

"Fontaine, you don't have time. Borden's looking for you. He has Morse with him."

"But—"

Into the tent rushed a White soldier Sable did not recognize. "Come on Bridget!" he snapped.

"Fontaine, this is Randolph Baker," Bridget said. "He's one of Sherman's aides. Tell her what you told me."

"I heard Morse and Borden talking last night. They made a deal. Morse gave Borden gold on the understanding that you'd be turned over to him. Borden says he has Sherman's approval to do so."

"No!" Sable couldn't believe it.

Outside, the guns were still reverberating and chaotic cries filled the night air.

"I want to wait for the major."

"Dammit, Fontaine, he can't help you. He's being brought up on charges for threatening Borden. Randolph handled the papers less than an hour ago. Do you have any money?"

"No." Sable was beginning to catch Bridget's fear. Having been a slave, she began to question whether a man of the race could indeed protect her from such powerful enemies, but she'd die before she was taken back.

Bridget said hastily, "You'll need money, Fontaine. Does he keep any here?"

Sable remembered the bag in the chest. "Yes, but I don't want to steal from him."

"Fontaine, do you want to go back on the block?"

That prospect sealed her decision. She had to flee. She ran to the chest beside Raimond's cot and prayed he would understand. The broken lock gave her immediate access to the small velvet bag. She emptied out a handful of coins but Bridget said, "Take it all, you'll need it to get North."

Sable swallowed her guilt and did as she was told. At the last minute, she turned her back and untied the gold bracelet from her drawers. She put it inside the bag, then placed the bag back in the chest. She looked up to see Randolph Baker rifling through the papers on the major's makeshift desk.

"What are you doing?" she asked.

"Looking for passes so we can get through the lines." He snatched up some papers and slipped them inside his coat. Just as he did, the major returned. Sable opened her mouth to greet him only to see Baker slip up behind him and bludgeon him in the back of the head with the butt end of his rifle. LeVeq's surprise mirrored Sable's own as he dropped to the ground like a stone.

Sable ran to him, screaming to Baker, "Why did you do that?" She quickly checked Raimond for injuries. He appeared to be breathing, but was out cold. "Why?!" she snapped again.

Bridget explained. "Randolph is deserting, Sable. He can't risk being seen."

"Bridget, he could have killed him!"

Baker knelt at Raimond's side and placed his head against his chest. "He's still breathing, let's go!"

Still on her knees beside him, Sable was torn between wanting to escape and wanting to aid the man she loved.

"Come on, Fontaine!" Bridget implored. "Come on!"

Sable's vow not to return to slavery overrode all else. She took a moment to kiss Raimond softly and whisper, "I'm sorry," before she followed Bridget's hasty retreat.

Chapter 8

Boston, 1865

Sable looked out at the gray March day and yearned for the balmy winters of Georgia. Boston's frigid temperatures made her wonder if she would ever be warm again. Her employer, Mrs. Jackson, assured her spring would come, but the knee-high snow presently blanketing the street made Sable seriously doubt the claim.

She'd been in Massachusetts since late November. The hasty flight she'd taken from Georgia with Bridget and Randolph Baker had culminated here after nearly a month of walking, taking trains, and hitching rides with others fleeing the war. More than once, to her absolute surprise, Baker had donned a Confederate uniform to cross disputed territory, and Bridget and Sable had posed as his slaves. At the time Sable wouldn't have cared if he'd posed as Mr. Lincoln himself if it helped her escape reenslavement.

Raimond LeVeq still weighed heavily on her mind. Every time she thought back, the memory of him lying prone and still on the tent's dirt floor tore at her heart. What must he think of her? Or did he even think of her at all? She'd vowed to return the money she'd stolen from him, though she had no idea how she would find him to do so.

Upon their arrival in Boston, Baker had gone on to his family upstate, leaving Bridget and Sable alone in a city where neither woman knew a soul. Bridget's desire to establish herself as quickly as possible sent her in search of a brothel that would take her on. Sable had no such aspirations. She gave Bridget a hug and a vow to remain in touch, then set out to find a more traditional way to make a living.

For the first week or so, she stayed in the basement of one of the Black churches, using the name Elizabeth Clark just in case Morse had trailed her North. Like most refugees she was provided a cot on which to sleep, a few changes of used clothing and a hot meal once a day. Some of the church ladies were generous enough to help her learn a bit about the city, and in exchange Sable helped them with the makeshift school they'd organized by teaching reading and sums to some of the local children. When Sable politely asked if they knew anyone who might employ her, they directed her to a semi-invalid member of the congregation, an elderly woman named Verena Jackson. Mrs. Jackson, a leading member of Boston's Black elite, needed a companion. At the initial interview Sable and Mrs. Jackson got along so well that less than three weeks after coming to Boston, Sable had a job. Her duties included reading to the nearly blind woman and seeing to her needs.

Mrs. Jackson, a native of Louisiana, was not well. She'd come North thirty years ago upon marrying her second husband and she would soon be seventy. Her advanced age and Boston's cold weather had taken their toll on her health. In the spring, war or no war, Mrs. Jackson was determined to return South. The feisty old lady vowed not to be buried where it snowed.

Mrs. Jackson hadn't been feeling well for the past few days. As a precaution, Sable had sent one of the neighborhood children around with a note to the doctor. He was presently examining the elderly woman. His footsteps entering the parlor drew Sable from her reverie.

"Miss Clark, Mrs. Jackson is resting quietly now. She should stay in bed for the next few days."

Sable chuckled. "Who's going to tell her that, you or me?"

The kindly old doctor smiled in reply. "Certainly not me."

They both knew how stubborn she could sometimes be.

"She insists upon going to hear Mr. Douglass speak tomorrow," Sable said.

"Well, she can't. You tell her. At least she'll listen to you."

"Only sometimes," Sable reminded him.

"She *never* listens to me. Hasn't for the fifteen years I've known her."

"Maybe the freezing temperatures will deter her, though I wouldn't count on it."

"Is she still set upon going South?"

"Soon as Lee surrenders, she says. I haven't been able to dissuade her."

"The journey may kill her."

"I know, but she is determined. Is her cough a sign of something more serious?"

Sable had grown very fond of Verena in the short time they'd been together.

"Just congestion from her cold. I left a draught on her nightstand."

"Thank you, Dr. Ellis."

"You're welcome. So, have you thought about that proposal I put to you?"

Dr. Ellis had been trying to match Sable with his youngest son since the day she and the doctor had first met.

He added, "I'd be real proud to call you an Ellis, Miss Clark."

"I'm flattered, Dr. Ellis, but I'm not looking for a

beau. I'd like to settle into my position first. Please don't be offended. If your son is as fine a gentleman as you are, I'm sure I'll be pleased to meet him someday soon."

"Just thought I'd ask, no offense taken."

Sable escorted him to the door. He tipped his hat and headed down the snowy walk.

Mrs. Jackson was sitting up in bed when Sable came up to check on her. "That ol' sawbones wants me to stay in bed, doesn't he?"

"Yes, he does."

"And what do you think?"

"I think you should follow his advice."

Verena snorted. "What time is Fred Douglass speaking tomorrow?"

"It doesn't matter. You aren't going."

Verena slumped back against the pillows like a sullen child. "You're as bad as Ellis."

"And you are going to get wrinkles, pouting that way."

Verena grinned. "Wrinkles? I've more wrinkles now than a dried apple."

"But you're much prettier."

Verena shook her head. "I do adore you, Elizabeth. Those other two girls I hired before you shook in their boots every time I so much as looked at them. You've a backbone, child. I like that."

"I like you too, Mrs. Jackson. How about I read the paper to you for a while, then fix us some luncheon?"

"You have a deal, miss. First, though, is that ol' sawbones Ellis still trying to get you yoked to that varmint son of his?"

Sable couldn't hide her grin. "He did mention his son today, yes."

"Well, the minute you see him, start running. He's handsome but he's a cad. Some young ladies see his smile and forget you're not supposed to let a man sample the milk until he buys the cow, if you get my meaning."

"I do."

Sable thought back on the handsome Raimond LeVeq and his devastating smile. Shaking off the sadness, she asked, "Shall I read the papers now?"

"By all means."

When Sable first began her job as Mrs. Jackson's companion, the papers were filled with reports of Sherman's remarkable march to the sea. After pulling out of Atlanta on the fifteenth of November, he and his sixty-two thousand men headed south to conquer Savannah, 285 miles away. Although Wheeler's Rebs destroyed bridges, toppled trees in their path and mined the roads, their actions did little to slow Sherman's daunting twelve-mile-a-day pace. His men spread out like locusts over the land, foraging for food and destroying everything of military value to the South, and anything they could not eat. They stole from farms, homesteads, and slave cabins; they made Sherman neckties out of the railroads, burned cotton, encouraged slaves to run, and generally caused hell for the people of Georgia. But Sherman's men weren't the only ones plaguing the citizens of the state. Deserters from Wheeler's own cavalry were just as lawless. Their actions caused one Southern newspaper to angrily conclude, "I don't think the Yankees are any worse than our own army."

On December 10, the ten thousand Confederate soldiers defending the city of Savannah fled rather than be trapped inside the city by the men in Union blue. General Sherman sent President Lincoln a telegram that read: "I beg to present to you, as a Christmas gift, the city of Savannah, with 150 heavy guns and about 2,500 bales of cotton." Marching into the city with Sherman and his troops on that triumphant day were his corps of Black teamsters, Black laborers, and the ten thousand contrabands who'd trailed him from Atlanta.

Like most members of the race, Sable and Verena were always eager for news of the 180,000 Black soldiers and the 30,000 Black naval men who were fighting the war. The United States Colored Troops comprised

120 infantry regiments, twelve heavy artillery regiments, ten light artillery batteries and seven cavalry regiments. Black troops guarded Confederate soldiers in places like Point Lookout, Maryland, and Rock Island, Illinois. They fought against small bands of guerrillas, protected contrabands growing Union cotton, and did not desert as often as their White counterparts despite impressment, unequal treatment and pay, and the threat of being captured and sold into slavery.

Sable was elated to read that the first soldiers to enter the conquered city of Charleston on February 18 were the Black Twenty-first United States Colored Troop, and two companies of the Fifty-fourth Massachusetts. The article she read to Mrs. Jackson went on to say that following the Fifty-fourth were men of the old Third and Fourth South Carolina regiments, many of whom had been among the city's eighteen thousand resident slaves when the war began.

Before coming North she'd had no idea so many Black men were in the war. Each day as newspaper reports of their accomplishments filed in, she felt more and more proud. Their bravery and courage during battles at such places as Miliken's Bend, Fort Pillow, Battery Wagner, and Olustee showed a previously doubting country that, yes, they were men.

And because of their bravery the country began to change. On January 31, 1865, the House of Representatives passed the unprecedented Thirteenth Amendment. Unlike the Emancipation Proclamation of 1863, which abolished slavery only in those states at war with the Union, the new amendment outlawed slavery everywhere in the United States. The next day, February 1, Senator Charles Sumner sponsored a Black Boston lawyer named John Rock for the right to practice law before the Supreme Court. He was the first man of the race to be afforded such a distinction. Eight years earlier, in the case of *Dred Scott v. Sanders*, the Court had denied that Blacks were even citizens.

Then, on March 4, 1865, Frederick Douglass was invited to President Lincoln's second inaugural reception. It was the first time a member of the race had been invited to a White House social function. Blacks were now being allowed to sit in the galleries of Congress and to testify as witnesses in federal courts. Segregation had been outlawed on the streetcars in Washington, D.C., and members of the race were no longer barred by statute from carrying the United States mail.

Positive change seemed to be occurring all over the country, but for Robert E. Lee and the Confederacy events had taken a turn for the worse. According to newspaper reports, his army had been reduced to thirty-five thousand men. The South had no money to pay them and no food to feed them as a result of Sherman's punishing push through Georgia and South Carolina. The end seemed near.

Sable and everyone else in the North celebrated April 3 when Union troops took Richmond, the Confederate capital. The first Union troops to enter the city were the all Black, Fifth Massachusetts Cavalry, commanded by Charles Francis Adams, grandson of former President John Quincy Adams. The Black citizens of the city greeted the liberating Black cavalry with deafening cheers.

On April 6, 1865, three Union corps captured six thousand members of Lee's army, and by the tenth of April, the first war between the American states was over. The nation's joy was short-lived; four days later, President Lincoln was assassinated by a man the papers described as the sad, mad, bad John Wilkes Booth.

Late April 16, Sable and Verena arrived in Washington by train. Because of the tremendous crowds it was hard to find a hack to rent at the train station, but after a few unsuccessful attempts Sable was finally able to secure one. The Black driver helped them with their small valises, then got them under way.

Sable saw hundreds of people on the journey to the center of the city. Most were walking the same route as their carriage and all appeared as somber as she herself felt. Church bells clanged mournfully and office buildings and storefronts were draped in black. Because of the vast numbers of folks keeping vigil outside the White House, it was impossible for their driver to get them any closer than a few blocks away. After paying his fare, Sable took Verena's arm to give her support and the two women blended into the crowd as it moved quietly up the avenue.

Everyone appeared to have taken the death hard, Black people in particular. Lincoln had been the President of the United States, but to the Blacks of the nation, he'd been Moses, Father, the Great Liberator. He'd formed the United States Colored Troops, emancipated three and half million slaves, and now he lay dead.

The cold rain continued to fall. Sable's clothing had soaked through hours ago, but like everyone else she paid the drizzle no mind. Hymns were sung, prayers were offered. Later that afternoon the White House doors were opened to the public. Sable, Verena, and nearly twenty-five thousand others were allowed to file past the body as it lay in state in the East Room.

The next day, a funeral service was conducted inside the White House and the crowd of sixty thousand lining the streets watched with heavy hearts as the black hearse bearing Lincoln's body slowly made its way to the Capitol rotunda, a mile away. The large procession trailing the hearse marched solemnly to the beat of muffled drums and the dirge bells of the regimental bands of cavalry, artillery and marine units.

Leading the slow-paced cortege was a Black regiment, marching with their guns reversed. A city procession followed. Thousands of Blacks joined in, including the entire membership of the Baltimore Conference of the American Methodist Episcopal Church, which had convened its annual meeting only a few days before. They marched under a banner that read: "We mourn our loss."

On Friday, April 21, the funeral cortege pulled out of Washington at eight in the morning. The journey to Lincoln's home state of Illinois took his body to such cities as Philadelphia, where reportedly more than three hundred thousand people were waiting, and to New York, where about two thousand Blacks, many of them wearing Union uniforms, were among the crowd that marched in the civic procession from City Hall to the Hudson River Station.

Blacks in the South grieved also. All three thousand Black residents of the city of Michelville wore crepe on their arms until April 30. Charleston's Zion church stayed draped in black for a year.

When Lincoln was buried on May 4, Sable thought a reporter for the *Harper's Weekly* summed up the feelings of the race best when he wrote, "His death burdened every black with a personal sense of loss . . ."

Not since the death of John Brown had the race grieved so deeply.

By the end of May, Verena and Sable were making final preparations for their long-anticipated relocation to New Orleans. As the day of departure approached, Mrs. Jackson took on an inner glow. She seemed lively and energetic. She fussed less and smiled more, making Sable believe that maybe the move was not such a bad idea after all.

After a grueling cross-country trip by both rail and coach, they arrived on the doorstep of their new house in early June. On the journey through New Orleans, refugees and soldiers clogged the streets. The hired driver had to stop their coach more than once to let the foot traffic pass. She saw hundreds of dust-covered women, men, and children making their way down the crowded streets, carrying their meager possessions in their arms and on their backs. She saw old men pushing handcarts piled with bundled goods, and barefoot children sitting

on the walks alone. There were people hawking vegetables, fish, and fruit.

Like the rest of the country, Sable knew that many of
the freedmen now had no place to go. Had she not escaped to Boston, she'd be one of those trudging through
the streets, displaced by freedom.

Seeing the refugees made her think back to the army
camp and the people she'd met there. Where were they
all now? she wondered—Avery and Salome, Araminta,
the soldiers at the hospital. And where was Raimond?
He made his home here in this city. Would their paths
ever cross? She hoped they would. Guilt had been plaguing her since the day of her escape. She owed him not
only money, but also an explanation.

By mid-June, Sable and Mrs. Jackson were comfort-
ably ensconced in their small cottage. The structure re-
sembled many others in the city's south ward, with
beautiful iron grillwork on the balcony. Thanks to the
kindness of her neighbors, Sable had learned where to
market and how to get Mrs. Jackson to St. Louis Cathedral, where she and most of the other French speaking
Black Catholic citizens went for Sunday Mass.

After church one Sunday, Mrs. Jackson happened
upon a friend she hadn't seen since leaving New Orleans. She introduced Sable.

"Elizabeth Clark, I want you to meet a dear friend,
Juliana LeVeq."

Sable's eyes widened. Could she be a member of Raimond's family? The short, dark-skinned woman's eyes
sparkled with warmth as she said, "I am pleased to meet
you, Elizabeth. Thank you so much for bringing Verena
home to us. Let me introduce my son, Beau."

Beauregard LeVeq was as handsome as his mother
was beautiful. Tall, with sandy brown skin, he bowed
over her hand like a courtier. The bow instantly reminded her of Raimond, and her heart began to pound.
She managed to say, "Pleased to meet you, Mr.
LeVeq."

"Call me Beau, please, mademoiselle."

Beau's manner definitely reminded her of Raimond. Thinking back, she remembered him mentioning four younger brothers. Could Beau possibly be one of them? Like Raimond, Beau had a handsomeness that was positively overwhelming, but it didn't touch her with the intensity of the major's charm.

Still looking into Sable's eyes, Beau said, "Mother, maybe you would like to invite Mademoiselle Clark and Madame Jackson to the rally tonight."

"What rally?" Sable asked. She sensed his interest in her as surely as she felt the sunshine beaming down on them.

"We are rallying to demand something be done about the freedmen's plight," Juliana LeVeq explained. "Hundreds are arriving in the city daily, and no provisions have been made for their welfare. We have not an inch of space left in our churches and shelters to house them. Many of the refugees want to work but are being denied free access to jobs. Roving bands of white toughs are robbing them. There are even reports of refugees being killed for merely saying they are free. The situation is critical, and no one seems to have the authority to do anything about it."

Beau told Sable and Verena, "Mother is on every committee in town and adds her name to every new one that is formed. Attempting to keep up with her can be very tiring, Mademoiselle Clark, so be warned."

Sable admired women of action. She wouldn't care to spend her life doing nothing but shopping, entertaining, and going to balls, as some of the women she'd met here were wont to do. "Do you need volunteers to work with the children?" she asked.

"Heavens, yes," Juliana exclaimed. "We need teachers, folks to write North for aid. We could use a thousand spellers—"

"Where can I sign on?"

Juliana smiled. "I'll send a coach for you tonight and we'll talk further, agreed?"

Sable nodded. "Agreed."

Juliana then turned to Verena. "My apologies. I suppose I should have asked you if I may have Elizabeth. After all, you are her employer."

Verena waved her off. "Elizabeth's evenings are her own. I'm honored you would invite her along. As for me, I'm too old to fight. I came to New Orleans to die, and I intend to enjoy myself by doing absolutely nothing until the time comes."

"She's going to outlive us all," Sable countered drolly.

Everyone laughed, and shortly thereafter they said their good-byes.

Beau kissed Sable's hand once again. "It has been a pleasure to meet you, Mademoiselle Clark. I hope to see you this evening."

"It has been a pleasure meeting you also."

After he and his mother walked off to their coach, Sable helped Verena to their own rented hack.

While Sable worried over how to approach Mrs. LeVeq with questions about her possible ties to Raimond, Verena said sagely, "That Beau is a very handsome man. You might want to set your cap after him. Even a half-blind old woman like me could see he was bowled over by my lovely Elizabeth."

"You are not to play matchmaker, Verena." If Raimond and Beau were indeed siblings, she saw no future in any dealings with Beau.

But Verena pretended she hadn't heard a word. "Looks just like his father. Juliana has four—or is it five sons? I can't remember. It might even be six. Whatever the number they're all as handsome as a sunset."

"Do you know her husband?" Sable asked as the hack started up the street.

"I did, but he's been dead many years now."

"So she is a widow."

"Unless she has remarried during my years in Boston. Beau looks just like his late papa. You'd do well to travel under her wing. She is well known and was wealthy at one time. If anyone can find you a suitable husband, it will be Juliana."

"I don't need a suitable husband, Mrs. Jackson," Sable protested.

"So you keep saying, but suppose I die, what then? You have no family and no one to care for you. Times are too chaotic to try and make your way alone. Didn't you hear Juliana talking about all the problems?"

"Yes, I did."

"Those will be your problems if we don't find you someone."

"Finding someone is not my priority right now, Verena."

"Well, it should be."

Smiling at Verena's singlemindedness, Sable shook her head and sat back to watch the city go by.

That evening, Juliana's coach arrived promptly at eight. As Sable stepped into it, she beheld the sight of Juliana on one seat and four handsome, grinning young men squeezed onto the other. She recognized Beau, but not the others.

Juliana explained, "Elizabeth, my sons. Beau, you've met. Beside him are Archer, Drake, and Phillipe."

They all greeted her at once and Sable nodded back, although she felt a bit confused.

"They all wanted to meet you," Juliana informed her dryly.

Sable took a seat beside Juliana. The son named Archer drawled, "You weren't lying, Beau. She is beautiful."

Embarrassed, Sable had no idea what to say, but she prayed they would reach the rally soon.

"Where are you from, Elizabeth?" asked dark-eyed

Drake. His eyes matched his skin. Of the three brothers, he favored their mother most of all.

"Georgia," she replied. She saw no reason to lie because she doubted they could link her to her real self, given such limited information.

Archer, never taking his eyes off Sable, replied, "His Highness was stationed there for a time."

Sable wondered whom he meant.

Juliana came to her rescue once again. "He's talking about his eldest brother, Raimond. It's how they refer to him when they are being sarcastic. He's in the Sea Islands presently. I expect him home within the month."

Sable felt her world briefly totter. So these people were his family. The enormity of the realization made her both elated and afraid. She wanted to blurt out the whole tale, but she didn't know any of them well enough yet to make such a confession. What would they think of her if they found out her true past? She decided to bide her time, and keep her secret until Raimond returned.

The rally took place in one of the city's Black churches. Speaker after speaker came to the pulpit to denounce the government for not offering a hand to the freedman. There was talk of a group of prominent men going to see Congress to ensure that their concerns were heard. Freedmen were then asked to step up and tell their stories. Most related tragic tales similar to the ones Juliana had mentioned that morning outside the church. They spoke of being beaten by angry former masters and being thrown off plantations for refusing to sign contracts that gave them only a tiny share of any profits a former master made from their labor. One man stood up and related how he and a group of men had set out for Shreveport to find work, only to be set upon by thugs who swore to kill any Blacks who called themselves free. The thugs stole their horses and money, then set all their belongings on fire.

In the end, petitions were passed around for everyone

to sign. The leaders vowed to take them to army representatives the next morning.

For the next two weeks, Sable spent all her free evenings helping on Juliana's many committees. She wrote letters to the Northern aid societies on behalf of the crowded schools, asking for teachers, clothing, and supplies. She took baskets of food to church basements and wherever else refugees were being housed. There was sewing to do and blankets to distribute. Many a dawn found Sable having worked the night through, but she dismissed her weariness. She was a freed woman too, and were it not for the guidance of the Old Queens, she could be the one in need.

Sable especially enjoyed the company of Juliana's sons, even if it did appear they were competing for her attention. Archer, who owned a hotel and one of the best restaurants in town, escorted her to the market; Beau, the artisan, took her to the theater, where Blacks had box seats on the second tier. Drake, a builder and architect, took her on a tour of the city. And she had a chance to view Congo Square and other landmarks with Phillipe, a merchant seaman.

The brothers brought Sable flowers, candy, and oranges. They were so competitive she started keeping a tally of where she went and with which brother, so she could not be accused of playing favorites. Juliana commented one evening that her sons reminded her of a litter of puppies all vying to be the one Sable picked to take home.

In truth, Sable didn't want to take any of them home. Although she had come to care for them all, her heart was already taken. Drake was funny, Archer was smart, and Beau and Phillipe were two of the handsomest men in the city, but they did not move her, not the way their brother had.

Raimond LeVeq finally arrived in New Orleans during the first week of July. Juliana was so glad to see him walk in the door that for a moment, she could do nothing but stand there, feast her eyes on him, and allow silent tears to fall down her cheeks. As tears of joy welled in his own eyes, Raimond held his arms open, and she ran to be enfolded. He held her tight, as tight as he could because he loved her and had missed her so much.

Once they could bear to part, Juliana, wiping away her happy tears, took him by the hand and led him into the salon. Raimond looked around the fondly remembered room and was disturbed to see that many paintings and other fine pieces of art were missing. Most of the furniture was gone too. His mother had been collecting beautiful things all her life. Knowing she'd had to sell many of her adored possessions in order to eat made him vow to restore as much of her way of life as he could. As dire as her circumstances must have been, she'd never once written to any of her sons to complain. Even now, dressed in an old gown that would have once been relegated to the rag pile, she stood proud and erect.

"It's so good to have you home, my son."

"It's good to be here. How are you?"

"I am fine."

"And the Brats?"

She chuckled. "Your brothers are fine as well. They are all out at the moment, no doubt over at the church competing for the affections of a lovely young woman named Elizabeth Clark."

"All of them?" he asked surprised.

"They're acting like puppies in a box. You should see them."

"The woman is enjoying all the attention, I assume."

"No, she isn't. To be truthful, she finds their suits embarrassing."

"So would I."

They both laughed, but Raimond saw sadness in his mother's eyes. "I'm sorry I wasn't here when you buried Gerrold."

Juliana had explained the circumstances surrounding his brother's death in the belated letter she'd sent last August. Gerrold had received a fatal ball to the chest while trying to bring the body of a dead comrade back from behind enemy lines.

Juliana stared off a moment, then said in a voice thick with grief, "His captain said the Rebs wouldn't let them retrieve his body for three days. Every time I close my eyes, I see him lying there alone."

Raimond held his mother while she cried. She was not prone to emotional displays, but she loved her sons as much as she loved life. To lose one had been akin to losing a part of her heart. Raimond knew how much she hurt because his grief was just as great.

Juliana said, "We were worried about Ginette for a while. I seriously thought she would do herself harm. Her parents are thinking of sending her back to Martinique, hoping it will revive her spirit."

Gerrold's fiancée, Ginette, had been a friend of the family all her life. She and Gerrold had loved each other very much. "I'll stop in and see her in a few days," Raimond promised.

"She'd like that, I'm sure."

Raimond spent the next half-hour telling her of his work with the contraband towns being established in the Carolina Sea Islands, and of the hopes and dreams of the former slaves who'd been settled there. "How're things here?" he finally asked.

"Property values have plummeted. Credit is almost nonexistent, and when the Yankees took over in '62, after the Battle of New Orleans, they burned the property of everyone, no matter the race."

One of the properties torched had been Raimond's shipyard. Luckily, he'd had the good sense to send his merchant fleet south to relatives in Cuba just before the Union navy came calling, and by so doing had safeguarded his future. It had not been enough, though. He and his friend and business partner, Galeno Vachon, had lost a fortune in lumber, warehouses and goods. They had funds stashed in banks in major cities all over the world, but not even they could easily absorb such monumental losses.

"Everyone I know is living hand to mouth," Juliana confessed. "At one time the free Black families here owned millions of dollars in property and businesses, but now many of us are no better off than the freedmen."

Juliana had always been an astute businesswoman, but not even she could turn a profit without money to make initial investments.

"How much have you lost?" Raimond asked.

"Nearly everything. What the Yankees didn't burn, they confiscated, and taxes are outrageous. Oh, there's money in Paris and Havana, but it will take time to find a bank here with the means to secure it. To right the family ship, I'll need a large infusion of funds, preferably gold, as quickly as possible. Property can be picked up for a song right now, if you can sing the tune."

Raimond had a sizable estate awaiting him in Havana from Juliana's paternal grandfather, an old pirate comrade of the notorious Lafitte. The old man had been very generous in his will, but the conditions under which the property could be accessed had not been to Raimond's liking. Now, because he knew how hard his mother had been struggling to keep her head above water, he'd made arrangements to fulfill the conditions of the will.

"In about ten days your accounts should be full again, Mama."

Juliana's face showed her consternation. "What do you mean?"

"I mean, I've made arrangements so you will have the funds you need."

Juliana knew her eldest son well, and when he wouldn't meet her eyes, she realized something was amiss. "What have you done, Raimond?"

"Nothing that I did not think over long and hard."

"Tell me."

When he did, his mother could only stare.

"You will have to marry to gain that inheritance!" his mother exclaimed.

"I know, Mama, but we all need it."

"No. I will find another way. I cannot let you do this."

"It is already done. I signed the papers and the first installment is right here."

He dumped a bag of gold coins onto a small decorative table.

Juliana's eyes widened with amazement, but she shook her head again. "This is not right, Raimond, and I will not take it."

"Mother, think how much good you can do if you invest this gold wisely. Think of the money you can lend to the businesses struggling to get back on their feet. Think about the Brats and the losses they've incurred. According to the barrister, the second installment will be mine when your first grandchild is born."

His mother continued to shake her head. "Raimond, who on earth are you going to marry?"

"I've no idea, but I'm sure you will find an appropriate candidate."

"Me?"

"Yes, Mama. You. I've neither the time nor the inclination. Let me know what day and time to show up at the church. I don't wish to know anything about her either. Let me be surprised."

Juliana appeared stunned. "Raimond, this is not a decision I should make for you."

"Who better? I've no plans to love this woman, just to marry her and get her with child so that we may receive the second installment of the old pirate's money."

"What has made you so unfeeling all of a sudden? You've always loved and respected women."

"The war. It affected us all."

Juliana didn't know this cold, distant side of her eldest son. "Raimond—"

"Mama, find me a wife so that we all may go on with our lives. Let her know I don't plan on giving up my mistress, however, and that I'll have little time for social gaieties. There's much to do in the city, and I don't plan on spending my time composing sonnets."

Juliana's face and voice turned flat. "Will you eventually tell me who she is?"

Raimond didn't know what she meant. "Tell you about whom?"

"The woman who broke your heart."

For a moment he didn't answer. He searched her wise eyes, then confessed with a bow, "You know me too well."

"I've been around you a long time."

Memories of Sable rose in his mind, bringing back the times they'd shared. In a distant voice he said, "I was in love for the first time in my life."

Juliana stared at him in surprise. "Raimond LeVeq, my eldest son, in love?"

He chuckled softly. "Yes."

"What happened?"

"She left me. Afterward, I learned she was not the sweet innocent I thought her to be."

"Is there any chance you may find her again?"

"I don't wish to find her, Mama. I've no desire to risk betrayal twice."

"And this is why you don't care whom you marry?"

"Exactly. I'll never give my heart to a woman again."

"You were hurt so much?"

"Yes. She's why I went to the Sea Islands. Building houses and planting crops with the freedmen gave me something to do besides think and dream about her." Seeing Juliana's concerned face, he smiled. "It's all right, Mama. I'm fine now, so find me a wife and let's see if we can't get the house of LeVeq sailing under full steam again.''

On the fifteenth of July, Mrs. Verena Jackson died and was buried as she'd wished—in a city with no snow. Sable had gone into Verena's room to bring her breakfast and found her lying in bed with a look of profound peace on her face. At first, Sable thought she was simply sleeping, but death had claimed her in the night. Thankfully, Sable was able to call upon Juliana's help in making funeral arrangements.

On the way back to Mrs. Jackson's apartments from the cemetery, Sable sat beside Juliana in the coach and pondered her immediate future. Just as Verena had predicted, Sable had been left with no one. Being alone had become a familiar refrain in her life since Mahti's death, but that did not make her heart any more immune to the hurt and loneliness. She supposed she could look for a new post, but most folks she knew there had barely enough money to spare for bread, let alone the means to hire a companion. There were opportunities in the city to assist the freedman, but trying to wangle a paying job from the army or the government agencies would take too long for her needs.

She heard Juliana say, ''Verena was a good woman.''

Sable nodded in solemn agreement. Her employer had been kind and fair. She'd even left Sable a small pension. The house would have to be sold as soon as possible. ''She wanted me to find a husband before she died. Said I needed someone to look after me in these chaotic times.''

''Matchmaking seemed to be her calling in life. I met my second husband at one of her balls.''

''Really?''

''Yes, indeed. We had twelve good years together before the sea claimed him.''

''You must have loved him very much,'' Sable said quietly.

"I did."

There was silence in the coach as they both mulled over their own private thoughts, then Juliana asked, "What will you do now, Elizabeth?"

Sable shrugged. "Try and find work, I suppose. I've not many options."

"Well, I have a suggestion you may wish to consider. How would you like to be my first and only daughter-in-law?"

Sable went stone still.

"My eldest son, Raimond, needs to marry as soon as possible, and he has left the choice of the young woman to me. He's marrying to fulfill the conditions of my late grandfather's will, so the family can access the funds we need to get back on our feet. It also stipulates that a child must be born by the end of the marriage's second year."

Sable blinked.

"Of course the two of you have never met and the Brats will probably pout for a week because you won't have married one of them, but I believe you and my eldest will suit each other very well."

Sable didn't know whether to laugh or faint.

"Now, to be truthful, he plans to keep his mistress, but over time, I see him abandoning that position, especially once he sees how beautiful you are."

Juliana stopped speaking and peered into Sable's face. "Elizabeth, you look pale. I shouldn't have sprung this on you in this manner. What am I thinking? We just buried Verena."

"It—it isn't that." Sable decided the truth needed to be told before Juliana went any further. "Juliana, I do know your son."

Juliana cocked her head. "Really? I didn't know you'd been introduced. Were you with one of the Brats at the time?"

Sable shook her head. "No. I met him at a camp in Georgia."

Juliana's eyes widened in surprise. "Oh my. Go on."

"He and I parted rather . . . abruptly. I had to leave, and—I took some money from him went I left."

"How much?"

"Quite a bit, I'm afraid. I intend to pay it all back. I even have a few coins saved."

"Is Elizabeth Clark your true name?"

The abrupt question took Sable by surprise, but she confessed, "No, it's Sable. Sable Fontaine."

Juliana had a mysterious smile on her face as she settled back against the seat. "To be truthful, you never impressed me as an Elizabeth. The name Sable suits you much better." Juliana searched Sable's eyes. "Did you love my son?"

Sable hesitated a moment as she tried to determine Juliana's motive. "Why do you ask?"

"My own motherly curiosity. Humor me, please."

Sable nodded. "I believe I did."

"Why did you need the money?"

"To come North. My old master threatened to reenslave me, so I ran."

"Raimond came home a few days ago."

Sable turned her eyes to the window and stared out at the passing street as her heart opened up and memories of him spilled out. "How is he?"

"He appears well."

"He will not wish to marry me."

"You sound so certain."

Sable turned back to her. "I am. As much as I would be honored to be your daughter-in-law, I doubt Raimond will go along. You'll have to find someone else."

Juliana patted her hand sympathetically. "Okay, we will leave that subject alone for now and turn to something more pertinent. Where will you live now that Verena is gone?"

"I don't know."

"I've plenty of room. You're welcome to stay with me."

The idea was tempting; by week's end Sable would have no home. "I will have to face Raimond eventually, won't I?"

"Yes, you will."

"Ideally, I would arrange to pay him back as much of the debt as I can now, then move to another city."

"I don't agree with the moving part—my sons and I care for you a great deal—but if that's what you wish . . ."

It wasn't really, but what she wished could never be granted. "Your offer is very generous, Juliana. May I mull it over for a few days while I tidy up Verena's affairs?"

"Of course, dear. Take as much time as you need."

Sable spent the rest of the day wrestling with the idea of Raimond marrying another woman. Admittedly, it was not something she wished for, but she had no power to prevent it. Dreams of him had followed her from the camp to Boston and now here. What a muddle. The only way out would be to arrange to pay back the debt and then relocate to another city where she wouldn't be tortured by the sight of Raimond and his new wife. With all the obstacles facing former slaves, she knew it would be difficult starting over somewhere else, but there seemed to be no other solution.

A few days later, as Raimond and Juliana toured the damaged city in search of viable property to buy, he told her about his new plan to work for the Freedmen's Bureau. "There are very few Black agents, but I doubt they'll turn me down. With all the experience I gained working as an agent in the Sea Islands, I'd think they'll be glad to have my help."

"The Rebels are moving back into positions of power, even in the bureau," said Juliana. "Getting them to hire you may not be as easy as you imagine."

The Freedmen's Bureau, formally called the Bureau of Refugees, Freedmen, and Abandonded Land, had first been proposed back in 1863 to deal with the many up-rooted slaves and White citizens of the South. After many debates over which government agency would oversee the bureau, the War Department had won out and opened the first offices this past March.

"I don't know how they operate here," Raimond said, "but in the Carolinas we were given a year's mandate. I doubt it will be enough. There are too many freedmen and not enough bureau agents or resources."

In addition to helping the former slaves make the transition to freedom, the bureau distributed food and helped with the building and acquisiton of freedmen schools, hospitals, and churches. It was also the only place where Blacks could file complaints against employers and former masters who'd hired and then cheated them, or report those who'd terrorized them or kidnapped their children.

Raimond stopped the coach in front of the warehouse. He'd had his eye on this particular place since before the war, but the owner had refused to sell. The government had it on the rolls as abandoned, and it was easy to see why.

He and Juliana got out and walked around the tottering structure. The fire damage was extensive.

"It'll cost us a fortune to restore it," Juliana pointed out.

Raimond tended to agree, but it was near the site where he planned to rebuild his shipyard. It would make sense to have a warehouse close by. "Maybe the Brats would like to share some of the expenses. They'd all be welcome to use the facility once it's rebuilt."

"I like the location," Juliana admitted. "But how much structural damage is there?"

Raimond could not tell. Many of the warehouses had sustained shell damage from Yankee warships during the battle of '63. "Maybe Drake should take a look. He should be able to determine whether it's worth pursuing

or not. If it isn't salvageable, I say we buy the lot and
put up our own building.''

They agreed, then walked back to the carriage. ''Have
you visited your brothers since coming home?''

''Not yet.''

He'd been back less than a week, but he'd been avoid-
ing the reunion, mainly because seeing them all would
make him remember Gerrold. He had not come to terms
with his brother's death. ''Seeing them will remind me
how much I miss him.''

He didn't have to explain to Juliana whom he meant.

''We all miss him, Raimond. You and Gerrold were
the eldest, and the Brats worshipped you. But they need
you in their lives so that they can heal too.''

Raimond turned to his mother. ''You're right as always, Mama.''

He helped her into the open carriage and took up the
reins. ''Have you found me a wife?''

''As a matter of fact, I think I have.''

He looked at her in amused surprise. ''Really?''

''Yes. I decided it might be best if it's someone you
already know.''

He shrugged. ''I've no preference either way. Just
make sure she's someone you like, as the two of you
will undoubtedly be spending time together.''

With a mysterious smile, Juliana LeVeq settled back
against the seat and let her son drive her home.

Chapter 9

By week's end, Sable had disposed of the last of Verena's affairs, sold the little house, and decided to accept Juliana's offer of a place to stay. "This is only temporary," Sable vowed.

Juliana nodded her understanding and led Sable up the wrought-iron staircase to the second floor. "I thought I'd put you in here."

She opened the door and ushered Sable into a large suite. The verandah doors stood open, letting the sun stream in. There was a large canopied bed in the otherwise empty room, but the sense of the previous owner remained strong. "This was Raimond's room, wasn't it?" Sable said.

Juliana nodded, then stepped in further. "He has his own apartments across town now. I doubt he'll mind if you stay here."

Sable looked at the woman who wanted to be her mother-in-law and asked, "Juliana LeVeq, what are you about?"

Juliana pointed to herself. "Me? Absolutely nothing. I just want you to be comfortable while you're here."

Sable didn't believe her for a moment.

As Sable walked over to see the view from the open doors, Juliana said, "The Brats are coming to dinner tonight. Will you join us?"

"Juliana, I don't wish to impose while I'm here."

"Nonsense. Join us. Six o'clock. Don't be late."

She sailed out, leaving Sable to settle into her new room.

That evening, Sable enjoyed a lively dinner with Juliana and the Brats. Once the meal was finished, Juliana ushered everyone into the parlor, saying, "There's something I wish to discuss."

Since the lack of furniture made seating limited, Sable settled on one of the two chairs while the Brats stood.

Juliana looked around at the faces of her sons, then at Sable, before announcing, "I've invited Elizabeth to marry into our family."

Shocked, Sable remained speechless, but the LeVeq brothers immediately broke into a jubilant celebration, elbowing one another and patting one another on the back.

Beau asked confidently, "Which one of us is it going to be?"

"Yes," Phillipe added eagerly. "Which one has Elizabeth decided upon?"

"None of you," Juliana replied.

"What?" they all shouted in unison.

"What do you mean, none of us?" Beau exclaimed.

"Just what I said. None of you. I've asked Elizabeth to wed Raimond."

"What?" they shouted again.

"With all due respect, Mother," Archer stated, "have you lost your mind? He hasn't a faithful bone in his body."

"Hear hear," Drake chimed in.

Soon the room was filled with the din of four brothers explaining why Raimond didn't deserve to marry the lovely Elizabeth, most having to do with his lack of fidelity and his well-documented apetite for beautiful women.

"I am aware of Raimond's past, but he loves her," Juliana explained simply.

Silence.

"That isn't possible," Phillipe finally said, his voice cracking.

The Brats turned to Sable, as if seeking an explanation, but she was still staring at Juliana as if Mrs. LeVeq had indeed lost her mind. "Juliana, why would you fabricate such a falsehood?" she exclaimed.

"It isn't a falsehood, my dear. Raimond does love you."

Sable's eyes widenend. *That isn't possible*, she told herself.

Archer stated confusedly, "But they've never met. How can he be in love with her?"

"They met during the war."

Then the brothers understood, and each responded with a few audible sighs of resignation.

"Why does he always get the prize?" Drake complained. "Next time, I want to be the firstborn."

The others laughed.

Sable still couldn't believe Juliana was continuing to pursue this futile quest. "Raimond is not going to want to marry me, Juliana. I explained that."

"I listened to your explanation, but I believe the two of you can get past your differences and be happy."

"Raimond in love," Drake drawled. "I don't believe it."

"Neither do I," chimed in Archer. "Are you certain, Mama?"

She nodded. "A mother knows."

Sable still needed a lot more convincing. She knew Raimond had harbored some tender feelings for her back at the camp, but love? Juliana must be mistaken.

Juliana went on. "Since your brother has left it to me to find him a wife, I choose Sable."

"Who's Sable?" asked Beau.

"I am," Sable confessed sheepishly. She'd told so many half-truths these past few months, she wouldn't blame them if they showed her the door and demanded she never return. "My real name is Sable Fontaine."

She then told them the story of how she'd met Raimond and the circumstances that had prompted the theft.

Drake said, "Let me get this straight. You stole Raimond's purse, and now Mother wants the two of you to marry?"

Archer added confidently, "I think you're investing in a losing propostition, Mama."

"I don't," Juliana replied.

Still confused, Sable asked, "But why me, Juliana? Surely one of the daughters of your friends would make a more suitable wife. I'm a freed woman."

"I know that, dear, and I also know you have spirit and determination. You're the type of woman I envision my Raimond marrying, not some addle-brained child who'll spend her day shopping and visiting the hairdresser. Raimond needs someone who will give as good as she gets, and not be put off by his challenging ways. And he loves you. What more can a mother-in-law ask?"

"You keep saying that," Beau pointed out, "but what will His Highness do when Elizabeth—I'm sorry, Sable—walks down the aisle and he realizes who she is?"

"Probably kill us all," Phillipe threw in knowingly. "Or maybe he won't since we'll be in church."

"I say we hide her until the morning of the wedding," Archer said. "I want to see the surprise on his face."

"I say we don't," Sable countered. "I will not marry your brother without his knowing that I'm the candidate."

Juliana smiled. "You've agreed then?"

Caught momentarily off guard, Sable stammered, "Well, no. I—I don't know what I'm saying."

"Say yes," Juliana implored.

Sable knew she had to be insane to do this, but she'd been moved by Juliana's words. Although Mrs. LeVeq had never gone into detail, Sable knew how desperately the family needed Raimond to marry so they could begin using the inheritance to repair their lives. They needed her. And in reality, she needed them. The idea of having a family tempted her mightily. By agreeing to Juliana's proposal, Sable would instantly acquire four charming brothers, a mother-in-law she adored, and a whole passel of relatives residing both here and abroad. Moreover, she'd gain a home, something she'd never had before. She looked around at the four young men who'd treated her so gallantly since her arrival. The last thing she wanted was her marriage to their brother to jeopardize their friendship.

"If I do marry Raimond, will we remain friends?"

At first no one replied, then Drake drawled, "We should torture her, you know."

"You're right," Archer agreed. "Make her wait a week before we give our blessing."

But both men had smiles on their handsome faces, as did everyone else in the room.

Juliana had the widest smile of all. "So do you agree?"

Sable nodded. "If Raimond will have me, I agree."

But she didn't believe he would.

The next evening Sable paced the floor of the salon. Her stomach was in knots and she felt a headache coming on. In a few minutes Raimond would walk through the door, and they would confront each other for the first time since the camp. She did not expect the meeting to go smoothly. In fact, she doubted he would stay for more than a few seconds upon finding her there. He'd probably denounce her and angrily declare his opposition to her as his mother's choice for a bride.

So Sable was bracing herself for the worst; she didn't believe he would agree to be her husband under any conditions.

She stopped pacing when she heard the door handle being turned. The sound seemed to echo loudly in the nearly empty room. Juliana entered and Sable relaxed at the sight of her kind face, but the tension returned as Juliana said, "He'll be right in. Are you ready?"

"No," Sable stated truthfully.

"Don't worry. Everything will be fine."

Juliana stepped out of the doorway, and Sable heard her call to him.

Raimond LeVeq, dressed in a well-tailored suit, entered the room. He was as tall and as handsome as he'd ever been, and Sable's knees weakened for just a moment.

Their eyes met. His widened and then blazed with anger. "What the hell is she doing here?"

Juliana ignored the question, saying instead, "Sable Fontaine, my son Raimond. I believe the two of you know each other. Say hello, Sable."

"Hello, Major."

Raimond had never thought to hear those words from her lips ever again. A boiling cauldron of warring emotions filled him as he took in the green eyes and the golden face that had plagued his dreams. He wanted to rail at her even as he longed to pull her into his arms, but he held himself in check, viewing her coldly. "Miss Fontaine. Once again, what is she doing here?"

Juliana replied, "Raimond, you may vent your wrath on me later, but the two of you have unsettled business."

Looking into his wintry eyes, Sable sensed she'd been right; he'd never agree to their marriage, and as a consequence, she sought to bring this reunion to a close as quickly and as painlessly as possible. "Your mother wants us to marry."

Raimond turned a curious eye on Juliana standing by the door. "Is that correct?"

Juliana nodded. "Yes, she is my choice."

In a voice as cold as his eyes, he looked down at Sable and said, "Then you shall have your wish."

Sable gasped in surprise and consternation.

"Leave us, Mother, if you please."

Sable beat down the panic she felt as Juliana complied, leaving them alone.

As silence resettled over the room, Sable wanted to run. She wanted to hike up her skirts and flee as fast as her legs would carry her, but she stood, chin raised, like a queen poised for battle.

He began, "I never thought I'd see you again."

"I did leave abruptly."

His smile did not reach his eyes. " 'Abruptly' is an apropos way to describe it, I suppose. Where'd you go?"

"North—with Bridget and Randolph Baker."

"Is he the one who hit me over the head?"

Consumed with guilt, she whispered, "Yes."

Raimond could not believe it. The betraying beauty whose traitorous kisses had haunted him since the night she'd left was being presented to him like a gift on Christmas morning. "Does my mother know about your past?"

"She knows I'm a contraband."

"Does she know you're also a thief?"

Sable flinched at the harsh description. "Yes, I told her the truth."

"The real truth or *your* truth?"

Sable knew he had reason to be angry, but she didn't care for his contempt. "They are the same," came her tight response.

His mocking eyes told her he didn't believe a word.

His attitude made her wonder whether he would change his mind even if he did learn why she'd stolen his money. The man whose kisses had inflamed her during those warm Georgia nights did not seem to exist any longer. She pushed aside that small sadness and asked, "So, will you turn me over to the authorities for theft?"

"No, but I do want to know how you managed to wheedle your way into my family's good graces."

"I did not wheedle," she replied tartly, then as patiently as possible, she told him how she'd met Verena

Jackson in Boston and eventually come to New Orleans.
"I met your mother quite by accident."

His manner did not change, making it impossible to
tell what he thought about the tale, but Sable decided
his opinion didn't much matter to her. "I'd like to pay
you back as much as I can. I have a small cache of coins
I've been saving—"

"I don't want them."

"Then what do you want?"

"What my mother has already given me. You."

"But you don't wish to marry me."

"No. I don't wish to marry anyone, but you will do."

"You intend to punish me, then?"

"No, I intend to take you as my wife. Once you are
with child, my formal duties toward you as a husband
will cease. Of course, I will provide you and the *bébé*
with whatever you require, but you and I will lead separate lives."

"It sounds very bleak."

"For you it undoubtedly will be."

She found his manner so arrogant and insulting, she
was tempted to marry him out of spite. "Then why wed
at all?" she asked.

"Because my mother has sacrificed enough. The war
has destroyed her way of life and taken the life of her
second son. I'd marry Medusa herself if it would make
her happy."

Sable observed him closely. Only a fool would believe marriage to him could evolve into a love match,
but she had hoped for companionship and, yes, affection,
given time to work out the problems between them.
Now, according to Raimond, there would be neither.
Common sense told her that regardless of their personal
difficulties, the life he'd pledged to provide for her and
her babies would far surpass the alternative of having to
scratch out an existence in the streets. So why was she
so despondent? The answer lay in her heart; she'd fallen

in love with him during those warm Georgia nights, and
in spite of everything, she loved him still.

"So, knowing how I stand, are you still willing?" he
asked.

Sable's chin rose. "Yes. Your mother has been very
kind to me. Like you, I would marry the devil himself
to make her happy."

"Then we have an agreement."

"Yes."

A few nights later, moving with careful control, Sable
removed her expensive gloves and borrowed jewelry and
placed them onto the small vanity table. She had never
been so angry.

Tonight had been a disaster. Juliana had invited a
small group of friends and family to an engagement
party to celebrate the upcoming nuptials. Everyone had
shown up—except the groom. He'd sent a note around
to his mother at the end of the evening expressing his
regrets. There'd been no explanation, just his apology.
Juliana had vowed to kill him on sight.

Sable took off her beautiful dress and draped it over
a chair. Had he humiliated her intentionally? Had he
purposely left her open to the gossip and veiled innuen-
dos flying all over town? Did she know that there were
already more than a few women who'd come up to her
in the markets and shops and announced to her face that
she had no business marrying into the house of LeVeq?
His absence tonight would only add fuel to the fire.

Sable plopped down onto her bed. Thank heavens for
her new brothers. They'd danced with her, fetched her
refreshments, and generally helped her meet each new
guest with a smile. She'd heard more than one man
promise to bring her Raimond's head on a platter for
making her endure such a humiliating evening, and right
now she wanted not only his head, but both arms as well.

*   *   *

Mounted on Pegasus, Raimond held up his hand and the other mounted men in his small party came to a halt. The plantation they'd come to visit lay up ahead. The owner, undoubtedly asleep at this late hour, had been stealing Black children for weeks and making them work his land. Although the parents had been begging the Freedmen's Bureau to intervene, neither the agents nor the army had seemed inclined to get involved. When Raimond was finally able to bring the matter to the attention of a captain who seemed to care, he'd lacked the authority to send in troops. Angry over the official lack of concern and faced with no alternative, Raimond had mustered up his own troops for the purpose. All were Civil War veterans, and all were committed to making certain the freedoms won by the war were not denied to those who'd been freed.

"All right," Raimond said quietly. "Three of us will take the front. You two enter through the back. Make certain you're masked."

Following Raimond's lead, the five men placed black hoods over their heads and rode slowly toward the large, dilapidated plantation house. Masking their identities was essential if they wanted to save themselves and their families from retribution.

They had no trouble entering the place. There were at least fifteen children of varying ages asleep on the floor of the front room. Raimond and his men stepped quietly over them, not wanting to awaken them until matters with the owner were settled.

The owner, a pale, portly man named Dillard Huckleby, lay asleep in his bed. Raimond firmly placed the business end of his rifle against Huckleby's nose and barked, "Wake up, Huckleby!"

The man roused as one of Raimond's companions lit a lamp. Huckleby's eyes widened in panic upon viewing the masked intruders. "All of my gold's in the bank," he volunteered hastily. "I've nothing valuable here in the house, I swear."

"We're not here for money," Raimond said. "Tell me about those children sleeping on the floor in your front room."

Huckleby began to sweat. "Uh, they work for me. They're orphans, for the most part. Law says they have to work."

And indeed it did. In an effort to control the freedmen and their movements, some communities had passed statutes making it illegal for any freedman to be unemployed. Many of the jobless were being forced to sign work contracts with their former masters that bound them to their employer for life. Children, a prime source of cheap labor, were being kidnapped from the streets with frightening regularity.

"We're here to take the children back to their parents."

"You can't do that! I've got papers for them—legal papers—that they all read and signed."

"Did they now?" Raimond asked skeptically.

"Yes," Huckleby vowed.

"I don't believe you. I'm guessing there isn't a child out there that can read more than his name, if that. If it wouldn't be a waste of cartridges I'd shoot you right here for all the grief you've put their parents through."

Still pressing the gun against Huckleby's bulbous nose, Raimond instructed his friends to start waking the childen.

As they departed, Huckleby snapped, "You can't do this! Them pickaninnies are mine! I'll have the authorities on you!"

"Only if I leave you alive."

Huckleby's eyes widened, and sweat dripped down his face.

"Now, you're going to stop preying on people's children or we'll be back, and when we do, we'll be less inclined to talk, if you get my meaning."

Huckleby did, and his expression said he didn't like it.

"Good night, Mr. Huckleby. I advise you to wait in here until we're gone."

As Raimond turned to depart, Huckleby filled the air with smoldering invectives aimed at Raimond and his bunch of "gun-totin' nigras," but Raimond paid him no mind.

He and his men roused the children, and after calming their fears, quickly led them out into the night where a wagon waited to transport them.

It was nearly dawn by the time Raimond and his men returned to the city. They dropped the true orphans off at one of the church shelters. The other children, whose parents had been asked to wait at the Freedmen's Bureau office, were ecstatic to be reunited with their families.

All in all, it had been a worthy endeavor. Raimond just hoped his mother would agree when he apologized later today. Sable, no doubt furious, would probably assume he'd missed the gala on purpose. Let her think it; he didn't care. She was a Jezebel and a traitor, and he should be turning her over to the authorities for her betrayal back at the camp—a betrayal that might have cost Union lives. He had no business marrying her, that was certain, but he couldn't resist the temptation to claim her, bed her . . . She was a fire in his blood, and he was no more immune to her now than he'd been months ago at the Union camp.

When he explained his absence to his mother, Juliana was indeed understanding—still angry but understanding.

Raimond asked, "Shall I find Sable and offer my apologies in person?"

"She isn't here. Archer took her shopping."

"My brothers seem to be quite taken with my little bride."

"They adore her, and all of them have a bone to pick with you over last night also."

"She didn't become hysterical when I didn't show, did she?"

"Has she ever impressed you as being prone to hysteria?"

He had to adimit she never had. "No."

"Then you have your answer. She performed admirably considering the distressing circumstances."

Raimond felt guilt rise, but it faded when he reminded himself that those children had had to come first. "Suppose I buy her a bauble. Will she forgive me then?"

"Save that sort of thing for your mistress."

"Ouch, Mama. I have apologized for standing her up."

"And luckily you had a good reason. Now, truthfully, how angry are you with me over thrusting Sable back into your life?"

"I won't lie and say I'm pleased." Raimond didn't trust Sable a bit, but his mother seemed set upon having her as the mother of her grandchildren, and who was he to argue over an issue that seemed to make the lovely Juliana so happy? However, should Sable ever bring shame to the house of LeVeq, he swore she would rue the day she'd ever come to New Orleans.

"Will you be able to see it through?" his mother asked.

"Since my heart won't be involved, I see no reason why not. You seem to care for her a great deal, and that's what matters to me. A potential *grandmere* should like the woman who'll birth her *grandbébés.*"

"And I do. In spite of the difficulties keeping the two of you apart, I care deeply for her."

"Then that's all that's required. When is the wedding date again?"

Juliana looked so appalled at his forgetfulness, he couldn't hold back his chuckles. "I'm only teasing, Mama. I know that it is in three days at eleven."

"You do plan to attend?"

"Yes."

"Good. I will see you then."

Raimond gave her a peck on her dark cheek and went on his way.

Sable awakened the morning of her wedding to a day of sunshine and blue skies. She hadn't slept more than a wink last night. Such a beautiful day did much to soothe her nerves, but she still wondered if she'd lost her mind by agreeing to marry Raimond LeVeq.

According to the schedule Juliana had set down on paper yesterday, the hairdressers would arrive first, followed by the seamstress who'd designed her dress. Sable forced herself to drink some of the coffee and eat a bit of the toast on her breakfast tray. The butterflies in her stomach wouldn't let her consume more, but the hectic morning passed by in such a daze, Sable was on her way to the church before she knew it.

Across town, Raimond awakened to find his brothers Archer and Drake seated in his room. "What the hell are you two doing here?" he demanded sleepily. Even half-awake he could see that they were dressed formally.

"Making certain you arrive at the church," Drake replied.

"On time," drawled Archer. "So get up."

"I don't need nursemaids, especially ones as ugly as you two."

Raimond swung his big body from beneath the sheets. Seeing them first thing this morning did not help his aching head. Their yammering didn't make them much welcome either.

"I can get to the church on my own," Raimond declared.

They didn't move. It was obvious they hadn't any idea how much cognac he'd consumed last night in order to work up the courage to go through with this madness today. What had he been thinking to agree to something so outrageous? Sable Fontaine was a thief and a traitor. Why in the world had he agreed to marry her? *Because now that you've found her, you want to keep her. For-ever,* said a sage voice inside his pounding head. Rai-mond ignored the voice and blamed it on the cognac. "Tell Mama I'll be there directly."

"Is he deaf?" Archer asked his brother Drake.

"Advanced age does that."

Raimond shot them a malevolent look.

Archer drawled, "Save that face for someone who cares, big brother. Mother wants us to *bring* you to the church. And Drake and I are here to carry out her or-ders."

"If you two don't get out of my house—"

"Maybe *you* prefer to tangle with the lovely Juliana," Drake said, "but *I* do not. So, if we have to tie you up and toss you into a bag, you are coming with us."

Archer smiled. "Very succinctly put, my brother."

Raimond growled at their antics. "All right, all right. Wait downstairs. I'll be with you as soon as I'm washed and dressed."

As they moved to leave, Drake boasted, "We really could have tied you up and tossed you in a bag, had we cared to."

Raimond pointed to the door. "Out."

In a church anteroom, Juliana spent a few minutes fussing with Sable's hair and dress before finally step-ping back and saying, "You look beautiful, my dear."

Sable felt beautiful. The white dress with its yards of silk was easily the most lavish garment she'd ever worn. The hairdressers had swept her hair back, then braided and twisted it elegantly. Soft wispy curls had been left at her temples.

Juliana adjusted the veil fashioned from sheer pol-ished silk. "Raimond will be dazzled in spite of him-self."

Sable doubted that, but she hoped he would at least be civil.

A beaming Juliana stepped back and said happily,

"This will be a memorable event in the house of LeVeq. Thank you for coming into our lives."

Sable gave her a tight hug. "I'm not sure Raimond would agree with that, but thank you for taking me in." Then she asked, "The groom is in attendance?"

"Yes. Drake and Archer escorted him in a little while ago. He did not wish to wrangle with me, not today."

Juliana gave Sable's hand one last squeeze, then slipped out to take her seat with the guests. Alone now, Sable thanked the Old Queens for their guidance and love and asked for their continuing care. The organ sounded, her signal. Swallowing her fear and unease, she drew in a steadying breath, gathered up her skirts and small bouquet, and began the long walk down the aisle.

The St. Louis Cathedral was filled with more people than Sable could have imagined. Her approach signaled the guests to rise. The veil made her feel as if she were floating inside a sheltering cloud. From behind it she could see the smiling faces of her new brothers and mother-in-law, and the many acquaintances she'd made during her committee work. Their presence did much to allay her fears.

Walking slowly down the white runner, Sable finally turned her eyes to the altar. There he stood, as handsome and as cold as he'd been since the day they were reunited. The closer her steps took her, the tighter her throat became. Her heart was pounding so loudly, she was certain the guests could hear it plainly. Every fiber of her being screamed she should turn tail and run. Surely Juliana could find someone else to marry her eldest son. But Sable's feet kept propelling her forward.

The veil created a barrier between them as she joined him at the altar. He gazed down, then gestured for her hand. Shaking, Sable slipped her cold fingers into his and he sheltered them in his warm grip. Sable dearly wanted to stop shaking, but could not. She assumed he could feel it because he looked down at her with those icy eyes and asked, "Are you unwell?"

She shook her head and turned her attention to the priest.

Raimond recited his vows in a strong voice. She whispered her replies. By the time the service ended and the priest declared them man and wife, Sable was so overwrought she could hardly breathe. She steeled herself as he prepared to raise the veil.

He lifted the silk slowly, almost reverently. Sable could not control her trembling. She'd done him a wrong back there in the camp and he had every right to denounce her publicly and turn her over to the authorities to be jailed. His features were stony.

Chin raised, she whispered, "If you plan to denounce me, do so now. I am ready."

A slow smile swept his full lips, a smile that did not warm his icy eyes. "That would be the easy way out for you, *n'est-ce pas?*" He paused, then slowly traced his fingertip over the satiny rise of her golden cheek. "I believe I can come up with a more creative solution . . ."

His touch spread fire, and Sable fought to draw a steady breath. "What do you intend?"

In the softest of tones he replied, "To show my mother and her guests how pleased I am to have you as my wife."

That said, he gently raised her chin, and Sable looked up into his dangerous tiger eyes. "We are going to play at love, you and I. I am going to be your courtier, and you, my Jezebel, will be my shy virgin queen . . . at least for today . . ."

To the guests in the church pews, Raimond appeared to be conversing tenderly with his new bride. No one could hear his whispered words or her hushed replies, but the passionate way he stroked her cheek, then lightly traced her mouth, convinced more than a few mamas that Raymond LeVeq was genuinely taken with this penniless bride. All hope for their own daughters to marry successfully now lay with Juliana's remaining sons.

Sable's rational self recognized Raimond's posturing

for what it was, but her sensual self was unable to distinguish his tender pretense from reality. His whispered words and fleeting touches made it impossible to remain indifferent to him. How on earth would she survive this day? "Please, you and I need to talk privately," she pleaded.

He offered her another cold smile. "Oh, don't worry, we will."

Sable moved as if in a dream as he took her hand and led her from the church. Guests lined the walk and their shouted well wishes hastened their journey to the waiting closed carriage. Raimond opened the door, and she hitched up yards of silk and took a seat inside. As soon as he was settled on the opposite bench the coach pulled away.

The thick silence did nothing to calm Sable's frayed nerves, nor did his unwavering stare. Beneath his icy control, he appeared furious with her.

The carriage finally came to a stop in front of Juliana's large home. Thanks to funds from the old pirate, the house was already being restored to its prewar splendor. The reception and wedding dinner would be held inside and out on the grounds.

Raimond said, "The guests will expect me to be affectionate with you."

Sable swallowed.

"So I will be."

He slowly eased to the edge of the bench.

Sable knew it had to be her imagination but the coach's interior seemed to grow smaller, so much smaller she could feel the heat of their bodies mingling. He leaned over, further closing the distance between them, and slid a strong finger over her parted lips. "If I remember correctly, your kisses were sweet . . . That will make playing this game less of a chore. Do you think you can play along?"

Part of her yearned to play any game he wished, but

she knew he'd have complete control over her if she succumbed without a fight.

He whispered softly, "What will you do when I kiss you like this . . . ?"

He kissed her so gently her mind began to spin.

"Or . . . like this . . ."

He brushed his lips across her own for a long, trembling moment until hers parted welcomingly.

Sable whispered back, "Then I suppose I shall have to respond like this . . ."

She kissed him just long enough to remind him of the taste of her kiss, then gently teased her tongue against the corner of his mouth. "Will that convince them, do you think?"

Sable swore she saw a smile slide into his eyes, but it disappeared quickly. Two could play at this game, she told herself. If he planned on making her melt, she'd make certain he paid the same dazzling price.

"The guests are waiting," she informed him.

Raimond ran his eyes over her lush mouth and saw in her eyes the lingering remnants of the desire he'd coaxed to life with his kisses. Beneath all that white silk was a woman made for seductive games. He looked forward to what promised to be an intriguing afternoon . . . and evening.

"I'll be at your side the whole time, so don't think you can flee," he warned.

"It never crossed my mind."

Inside he took her hand and led her through the throng. Many people offered their congratulations, which she accepted with as true a smile as she could muster. Eventually they found the stunningly dressed Juliana and Drake.

Juliana observed them shrewdly. "You two didn't fight on the way here, did you?"

Raimond shook his head. "No, Mama."

"Good, then smile. You too, Sable."

Chagrinned by Juliana's sunny optimism, Sable smiled.

"She's much more beautiful when she smiles, don't you think so, Raimond?"

His voice was deep and even "Yes, she is."

Sable met his gaze, and a part of her wished he truly meant the words.

Drake drawled, "Treat her right, brother, or we will have to kill you."

Raimond chuckled. "So you keep telling me." He then added, "Don't worry."

Over the course of the afternoon, his cold eyes met Sable's often—whether he was across the room or perched on the arm of a divan inches away. She read aloofness and anger there, but she also read a passion so strong and undisguised it seemed to reach out and stroke her. Her nipples responded by slowly hardening beneath her gown, her lips parted of their own accord, and on more than one occasion she had to turn away from his knowing, tigerlike smile.

The wedding dinner following the reception was an intimate affair attended only by family and dear friends. Afterward they stayed around the long table to enjoy coffee, cognac, and one another's company.

Sable's husband had discarded his wedding coat and sat with his arm draped across the back of her chair. He was in a deep discussion with an uncle over the plausibility of forming freedmen co-ops. Every now and then his warm hand strayed to her neck and gently stroked her, seemingly unconsciously. The sweet shock of his featherlike touch made Sable pause in the middle of what she'd been saying to Juliana seated across the table.

Raimond appeared not to realize the effect he was having on his new bride, but Sable assumed it was all part of his game. She gently placed her hand atop his to stop his languid caresses and tried to drag her mind back to her conversation with Juliana.

"I'm sorry, Juliana, I seem to have lost my train of thought."

"No apologies needed, my dear. Raimond, behave yourself."

Raimond turned to his mother in confusion. "What am I doing?"

"No need to torture us," Archer stated.

Phillipe added, "We're already jealous enough as it is."

Raimond still looked confused, so Drake drawled, "You're stroking your wife, Raimond."

A small smile of understanding finally curved his lips. "Sorry," he said directly into Sable's eyes, but in direct contradiction, he leaned over and kissed her slowly and sweetly until she saw stars. Then he went back to the conversation on co-ops. Reeling, she wanted to sock him.

Raimond had had no idea he'd been touching her honey-gold skin until his mother had brought it to his attention. He'd given Sable the kiss to pay her back for being so damn bewitching. He'd expected to be repelled by her presence, knowing her true nature, but his unquenched desire had sprung to life hard and true from the moment he first saw her in his mother's parlor. Instead of being repelled, he was hard as iron and angry with himself because of it.

It had been a long, emotionally tiring day. As the cigar smoke thickened and the talk and cognac continued to flow, Sable yawned discreetly behind her hand. Nervous jitters had kept her from sleeping last night, but tonight she envisioned no such difficulties. Who knew? Maybe she would awaken in the morning to find it had all been a dream.

As if he had heard her thoughts, Raimond turned from his conversation with his uncle and held her eyes. For a moment he said nothing aloud, but his dark gaze, alternately dangerous and desirous, made her heart begin to pound. He leaned over and whispered in her ear, "It's time for us to retire, my queen. The night is still young . . ."

The heat in his voice sapped the last of her strength. She'd survived the day, but doubted her luck would hold. As her part of this arranged union, she'd agreed to have his child. She knew of only one way in which that could be achieved.

They did not linger over their good-byes. She shared a tight hug with a teary-eyed Juliana, and the brothers raised their glasses in salute as Raimond led her out the door.

A carriage and driver stood waiting. On the dark ride through the city, Sable was silent and off balance. She felt him watching her from the opposite seat, but he seemed content to be silent. The urge to explain the reasons for her flight from the camp become overwhelming, but he didn't appear to care about hearing her side.

She asked instead, "Where are we going?"

"To a house I purchased a few days ago."

"Is that where I'll live?"

"Yes. I'll keep my own apartment across town."

Sable knew from their earlier conversation that she would not be sharing his life, so why did hearing it again now create a tiny ache in her heart?

The large, sprawling house lay in shadows as they entered. Only a few candles had been left burning on the main floor. He took her by the hand and led her up the stairs to a room ablaze with light. Shimmering candlelight undulated over the furnishings, particularly a large net-shrouded four-poster bed dominating the far wall. The verandah doors were opened to let in the breeze and the stars. Near them had been placed one of the largest bathing tubs Sable had ever seen.

She turned from her visual tour to find him staring at her. Once again she read desire in his eyes. Not certain how to proceed, she asked, "Am I supposed to remove my clothing now?"

"No. When the time comes, I will remove it."

Sable fought to keep her breathing even but did a poor job. Her previous impression of him as a tiger couldn't be more true. He'd lured her into his lair, and she was as mesmerized by his powerful presence as she was wary of it.

Raimond gently placed his hand beneath her chin and lifted her eyes to his. He ran his gaze slowly over the face that had floated through his dreams since last November and said honestly, "Sable, no matter how angry I am with you, I will never, ever take you in anger. Never. We can fight tomorrow, but this is our wedding night, and I wish to make love to you as I would a true wife."

His words touched her with such sweet force, she felt tears well in her eyes.

"Don't cry," he whispered. The sight of her tears twisted his heart and made him place short, soothing kisses against both damp eyes. Not even his anger could mask how good it felt to have her near again.

"I'm not crying," she replied softly. "We queens know that crying alters nothing."

Short, sweet kisses were now falling on her cheeks, her eyebrows, her jaw. She drew in sharp, soft breaths as he brushed his lips across the lobes of her ears and then her parted mouth.

Raimond wanted her. He knew she was a Jezebel, but he craved nothing more than to taste her fully and without inhibition. Her traitorous lips were lush and sweet, even sweeter than he remembered. The sultriness shining behind her proper, well-mannered facade called to him with the mind numbing song of a siren. Although he'd originally planned to seduce her out of vengeance, he'd become ensnared in his own net.

And for now, he didn't care. The touch, taste, and scent of her overrode his original purpose; all his desire centered on making love to her until dawn.

Sable trembled as he slowly turned her and began to undo the long line of hooks down the back of her dress.

He had a sure, deft touch that signaled his familiarity with the task and soon had the dress open wide enough for her to feel the night air mingling with the long, lingering brushes of his lips across her neck and the skin above her silk shift.

As he continued to press his lips against her awakening skin, his expert hands slid slowly around her breasts, cupping them, stroking the already ripened buds until she closed her eyes. When the sweet conquest continued, her head dropped back and a small moan escaped her parted lips. He leaned down to recapture her mouth while his hand continued to make her nipples ache. She turned to him to savor more of his kisses and desire flared higher as he undid the dress past her waist. She drew in a soft breath as his palms slid her silk drawers over her hips. His touch warmed her, tempted her to open herself to him.

As he pulled the long-sleeved dress down her arms, Sable reluctantly broke the kiss, but because he wouldn't stop pressing his heated lips against the crowns of her breasts and the pulse point at the base of her throat, it took more time than it might have to free her arms and step out of the gown. Once she did, he kicked it gently aside, and stood looking down at her with his hungry tiger's eyes.

Raimond eased down one side of her shift and feasted his eyes on her lush golden breast. He reached out to stroke it but stopped as he caught sight of what appeared to be a star carved across the skin. "Who did this to you?"

"My aunt."

Sable waited for his reaction to the knowledge that his wife's skin bore the symbolic markings of the Firsts. Since she'd always thought the work beautiful it had never crossed her mind until now that a husband might not agree.

"How extensive is it?"

"Not very. I've some moons on my upper thigh and a sun on each hip."

Raimond's manhood flared at the idea of slowly exploring her until he learned every intimate part of her. "Let me see . . ."

Sable swallowed her self-consciousness and removed her camisole. He brought one of the fat candles over and set it down close. The sputtering light revealed the delicately carved moons that were splayed like jewels across her breasts just above the dark nipples. His glowing eyes made her nipples tighten in response.

He filled his hand with her honey-gold breasts and his nostrils with the scent of her neck. The markings on her drew him like a spell. He slowly placed his lips against her shoulders and slid a whispering finger over the moons cresting her breasts. On his world travels he'd seen many forms of ritual marking, but Sable's was unlike any design he had ever seen.

"Do you know what any of it means?"

She doubted her ability to answer his question in the face of his distracting lips and wandering hands, but she managed to say, "Some of it has to do with my grandmother's tribe."

He took her nipple between love-gentled teeth. Her choked cry of response floated on the room's silence. As he moved his attentions to the moon adorning the other breast, she found it hard to stand without swaying. He suckled her deliciously, languidly. He slid his hand into her drawers and wantonly explored her virgin's heat. Using his tongue to trace the golden undercurve of her breasts, his hand continued to cup, stroke, and slide over her silken hips and thighs.

He picked her up and carried her to the bed, and his commanding presence took her breath away. Never in her life had she imagined being so overwhelmed by a man, or by his ability to bring her pleasure. He set her down on the large mattress as if she were the most precious possession on earth, and for this one night Sable didn't mind pretending she was. He'd opened passion's treasure chest and gifted her with kisses and caresses she was certain she'd never experience with any other man.

Holding her eyes, he removed her stockings and untied her drawers. His gaze was so fiery she expected flames to encircle the bed. Leaning back on her arms, she lifted a bit so the garment could be eased away, and a breath later she was nude. He was seated on the edge of the bed beside her. Under the flickering light of a lone candle, he slowly traced the aureole of one sable tipped breast with a feather-light touch, first one way and then the other until she arched her back sinuously in response. He rewarded her by lightly circling his tongue around the yearning, straining bud before suckling her wholly. She moaned from the rising intensity and he treated her other breast to the same erotic sampling, leaving it damp and throbbing in the candlelight.

Raimond found her too magnificent to resist. She was a Jezebel with satin breasts and a mouth created by the gods. He eased her to lie flat, and her golden skin drew him to taste, savor, and caress. His roaming hand found the thin line of moon and stars banding her left thigh. Its beauty left him in awe. Bending down, he greeted each tiny symbol with a deep kiss, then placed another on her navel. He felt her trembling beneath his roaming mouth, heard her halting breath when his hand explored the silken hair below. He found her damp and sweetly flowing. Watching desire bloom on her face, he slowly and intimately circled her heat. The sight of her rising so shamelessly to his hand fired his desire even higher. He continued to play, stroking, teasing, and tempting her to enjoy the pleasure of his touch.

And Sable did enjoy it—each and every nuance of his vast expertise—so much so that when he slid a bold finger over her swollen gate, the sensation made her hips rise and a moan slip from between her lips. He plied the small jewel until the sounds she made became a song in the night, and release crackled over her like lightning.

When she finally regained enough sanity to open her eyes, his bearded face was above her looking down. She reached up to stroke his cheek and he turned her palm to his lips. She realized she knew very little about this man she'd married, the man she loved, but the thought soon fled as his lips found her wrist. He blazed a trail from it back to her mouth and the loving began again.

He kissed her eyes and nose, her lips and chin. He kissed his way down the front plane of her body, using his hands to keep her breasts ripe and hard, then pulled away and stood.

Raimond took a moment to remove his clothing, then as nude as the good Lord made him, he joined her on the bed. He kissed her gently, coaxingly, thoroughly.

Sable thought him the most beautifully made man she'd ever seen, and she used her hands to tell him so. She'd lost her modesty about the male form during her stint at the camp hospital, where she'd viewed far more of the male anatomy than was proper, but she'd never seen a man whose physique made her hands yearn to explore. The dark muscles of his arms seemed to be fashioned for her to caress. His shoulders and collarbone conformed perfectly to her kiss. She'd always enjoyed his kisses, and tonight she couldn't seem to get enough.

Raimond reacted to her hot, seeking mouth like any other male. He gathered her close and lost himself in the feel of her softness melting against his strength. He slid his hand up her luscious behind and discovered yet another set of carvings. He rolled her onto her stomach to get a better view of the two sunbursts adorning a golden bottom he couldn't help but squeeze. He kissed each sun with the passion of a lover and the reverence of a knight, while his hand played brazenly. She reacted to his touch by turning to seek his kiss, and he gave her what she craved.

Unable to break the kiss, he eased her again onto her back. Skimming his hands down her thighs, he gently parted her and as slowly as he could manage, eased his manhood home.

"Am I hurting you?" he asked, kissing her ear softly as he moved gently within her.

Sable wanted to say no, but the joining was more painful than she'd anticipated. Still, the slow, lulling rhythm was as impossible to resist as the distracting spell of his kisses and hands.

"Relax, *ma reine* ..." he breathed against her ear. "Let me teach you ..."

And soon, because of his patient and fiery tutelage, she was no longer filled with pain, no longer tense with anxiety. His distracting hands and fabled kisses filled her instead with his virile male heat.

Raimond found her so beautifully responsive, he burned to ride her like a stormy sea, but because she was new to this and to him, he kept his movements slow, as slow as his near-bursting desire would allow. Maintaining the pace became difficult, however, as she began to rise and fall to his thrusts. Soon, they were in the midst of the whirlwind. Her sharp cries of response mingled with his hoarse cries of pleasure. He filled his hands with her sunburst hips and stroked her as possessively as he'd ever dreamed.

Sable met every stroke with a fierce and possessive wildness of her own. She wanted to brand him and be branded in return, but release claimed her and the world exploded and she was swept away.

Raimond watched *le petite morte* tear through her body, and the sight set off his own roaring release. Increasing his thrusts, he rode the storm of love to its tempestuous conclusion.

Under the light of the lone and now dying candle the newlywed couple returned to an awareness of their separate selves like castaways washed upon the shore. Just before Sable fell asleep, she felt Raimond pull her close, kiss her softly, and whisper, "*Bonne nuit, bijou.*"

That last part must have been a dream, she decided, because she knew he'd never call her his jewel again— not in reality.

Chapter 10

The next morning, Sable awakened still close to Raimond's side. She looked up to find him watching her. Innocent though she'd been, she knew last night had been extraordinary. She sensed that he too had been touched by their passion.

"Well?" she offered. She had no idea how to approach him in the fresh light of a new day.

"Well, what?" he responded, all the while wanting to pull her atop him so he could kiss her lips and fill his hands with her sunburst bottom. He resisted the urge, telling himself he had no plan to become entrapped by his thieving wife.

"What happens now, is what I'm asking," she explained quietly.

Unable to resist touching her any longer, Raimond ran his finger gently down the curve of her spine. "You'll return to my mother's home until this house is ready, and I will go back to my own world."

He cupped her bottom and traced the small raised sunbursts. "How old were you when this was done?"

Sable forced herself to move away from his too tempting touch. Sitting up, she dragged a sheet across her nakedness. "I was twelve, thirteen." Until their relationship became clearer, she would not succumb to his

227

seductive play. "It was part of my great-aunt's traditions."

"Was it painful?"

"No. Vashti, our root woman, gave me something to drink that numbed my skin and made me feel like I was part of the clouds. When the marks began healing they burned like the dickens. I think they're very beautiful."

Gazing into her eyes, he agreed, "Very beautiful."

Looking away lest she be snared, Sable added, "Sally Ann didn't think so. She called them heathen jungle carvings. She just about fainted when my sister Mavis asked to have her skin marked too. Sally Ann got so mad she banned us from going to see Mahti for a month."

"I'll bet you went anyway."

Sable smiled. "As a matter of fact, I did." She observed him seated across the bed and said truthfully, "I didn't know Baker intended to hurt you."

"I'm sure you didn't. You and your accomplices planned on stealing Sherman's papers and disappearing into the night."

Sable stared at him. "What papers?"

"Oh, come on, Sable, playing the innocent is fine in bed, but don't take me for a fool."

"I've no idea what you're talking about."

And she truthfully did not.

"Be glad you changed your name to Elizabeth Clark, because if the army had found you, you and eventually your friends would've been tried for treason."

Her eyes widened. "Treason?"

"That's what it's called when you work for the enemy."

"Are you saying they thought we were Rebel spies?"

"Weren't you?"

"Of course not! Don't be ridiculous!"

"Where's Baker now?"

"Still in Massachusetts, I assume."

"Who else was involved besides you?"

"I wasn't involved in anything other than the theft from your chest, and I already told you that Bridget came North with us."

Sable studied him closely. He actually believed she was a traitor! No wonder he acted so thunderous all the time. "I had nothing to do with the general's papers."

"I don't believe you."

She now had her answer to the question as to whether he would change his mind upon hearing the truth. She set aside the hurt and with a raised chin replied, "Whether you believe me or not, I was not involved."

"You stole from me."

"I'm an ex-slave, Raimond. I was afraid."

"Of what?"

"Being reenslaved. I know you said you would protect me, but never in life have I seen a man of the race win a battle against a man like Morse. When Bridget told me Baker overheard Morse and Major Borden making a deal to send me back, what was I supposed to do? I'm sorry I stole your gold, but I saw no other solution."

"You could have waited for my return. Had you asked, I would have given you the gold."

"There wasn't time." The set of his face told her he didn't believe a word. "I'm sorry you don't believe me," she whispered.

"I am too."

With the past standing between them like an impenetrable wall, Sable slid from the bed to get dressed. Her eyes strayed over small spots of blood on the sheet, proof of her deflowering, but she did not dwell upon them. Because she had no other clothes, she slipped back into the gown she'd been married in. She wished she could wash but doubted he'd want her there any longer than necessary. The contract had been fulfilled, the marriage consummated. Now he would return to his mistress and his own life and she would try to carve out a niche of her own while waiting to see if last night's loving had produced a child.

Raimond came up behind her and fastened the hooks of her dress. He hadn't planned on ending the morning this way, but it had. He waited while she ran one of his brushes through her hair and braided it at her nape. She faced him then as bold and as proud as one of the Old Queens. "I will wait for you downstairs."

But she didn't wait.

When he came downstairs with the intention of escorting her back across the city, he found she'd already gone.

Juliana appeared surprised to see Sable at her door, but per Sable's request, she paid off the hack waiting in front of the house and joined her in the study.

"Whatever has happened?" Juliana asked, closing the study door. "Where's Raimond?"

"Still at the house, I suppose. He's convinced I was a Rebel spy."

"What?!"

Sable waited until her astounded mother-in-law took a seat before explaining as best she could what Raimond had revealed.

"No wonder he's so distressed," Juliana said softly.

Sable nodded. "I understand now too, but how will I ever convince him of the truth?"

"In your own way and and in your own time. You love him, he loves you. Raimond has broken female hearts all over the world. Now the shoe is on the other foot, and he's finding the fit very tight, that's all."

Sable found that theory hard to swallow. "If he was in love, Juliana, which I doubt, he is no longer, especially not if he believes I betrayed him in such a vile way."

"Once he takes the time to hear your words in his heart, he'll change his mind. Faced with the prospect of becoming a slave, who among us can honestly say what we would or would not do to stay free?"

Sable thanked the Old Queens for pairing her with

such a wise woman. "So do you have any advice?"

"No, but I do know that because you were the one to break my eldest son's heart, you are the one who must mend it. Whether he admits it or not, beneath all his mistrust and anger, he loves you."

"I still think you're wrong, Juliana."

"Mothers are always correct. Wait until you have your own children, you'll see. Now, it appears you could use a bit of buoying. How about we draw you a nice hot bath? You can soak away the despairs of the past, take to bed for a while, and awake a new woman."

Sable thought the idea a grand one.

For the next two weeks, Sable threw herself into her new life as the wife of Raimond LeVeq. She worked at the new schools for the freedmen in various churches throughout the city, went shopping with Archer for the extensive new wardrobe Juliana insisted she have, and spent the evenings sitting around the table with Juliana and her brothers-in-law. There were at least two brothers present at each evening meal, and when they weren't poking fun at one another, they were usually discussing politics and the future of the country. One subject they avoided was Raimond. From his siblings and others around town Sable knew that he was hard at work with the Freedmen's Bureau, but she hadn't seen him since their passionate wedding night. She made a conscious effort not to think about him but with little success.

One afternoon as she and Juliana sat writing letters requesting yet more aid for their causes, Sable asked a question that had been on her mind for some time. "Why doesn't Raimond favor any of his brothers?"

Juliana looked up. "He and the Brats had different fathers."

"Ah."

"My parents married me off very young to a handsome man in Port-au-Prince. I was in love, or so I thought. He was wealthy, the eldest son of a powerful count, and I was certain I would be with him for the rest of my life.''

''What happened?''

''On my wedding night I learned he enjoyed inflicting pain. For him, pain was pleasure. I went to my parents the next day, but they refused to take me in. A contract had been signed. He was my husband. My parents and the church said I had to stay.''

Sable realized that Juliana had experienced her own form of slavery.

''Raimond was born during that first year. I ran away eight months later, not knowing I was carrying Gerrold. I knew my family would be furious and would try and bring me back, so I went to the one person they feared most—my pirate grandfather in Havana. He gave me a place to live, and most of all protection. We were with him for almost a decade, the two oldest boys and I. Since I'd always been good with numbers, he made me his bookkeeper. Everything I know to this day about finance and acquiring real estate I learned from him, practicing with his gold. He was a very wealthy man when he died, and since I'd been saving and investing right alongside him, I was a very wealthy woman.''

''What happened to your husband?''

''He died about five years after I ran away. From syphilis. I didn't grieve.''

''How long was it before you married again?''

''Two years after the old pirate died. Raimond was nearly twelve and Gerrold a year younger when François LeVeq blew into my life like an ocean gale. I never thought I'd be able to love again, but to him I gave not only my love but my soul. When the sea took him in our twelfth year together, had I not had the boys I would have walked into the sea to join him. I loved him that much. His best friend, Henri, saw me through most of my early pain. Henri kept me focused on the needs of my sons, kept reminding me that they'd lost their father too, and needed me to be strong. Henri and I shared a mutual grief for many, many years.''

''Where is Henri now?''

''In Paris, but due back any day now. You will enjoy him.''

Sable noted the glow in Juliana's eyes when she spoke of Henri, but she kept the observation to herself.

That evening after her bath, Sable sat alone in Raimond's old room, nude beneath a loosely tied jade-green wrapper. She took a moment to inspect the new garments that had been delivered by the seamstress earlier in the day. The armoires were already stuffed, yet Juliana and Archer kept fitting her for more clothes. Sable had grown up owning no more than two dresses at a time, and she didn't know whether to be delighted by all the beautiful things she now possessed or appalled by the excess.

She took down a gold ball gown. Walking over to the standing mirror, she held the expensive gown against herself to see how it might look. She fingered the sleeves, peered at the stitches in the hem. Hearing the doorknob turn, she looked up.

It was Raimond. She beat down her happiness upon seeing him again, knowing happy feelings had no place in this marriage; he didn't want her or trust her, he'd made that quite clear.

Determined to maintain her distance, Sable rehung the gown, saying, ''Good evening, Raimond.''

He closed the door behind him and entered, filling her senses with his presence. ''Good evening. More clothes?''

''I keep telling your mother I have enough, but she and Archer refuse to listen.''

''Archer?''

''Yes, your brother has excellent taste. He chooses the fabric, tells me which designs will be flattering, et voila, on to the next shop.''

''My brother has been dressing you?''

"Yes. The shop girls say his mistress is one of the best-gowned women in the city."

Raimond wondered why he suddenly felt the urge to throttle Archer.

"Is there a problem?" she asked.

"No. I'd no idea Archer had so much time on his hands, is all."

"He's been very helpful."

There was an awkward silence while she waited for him to state his business. When he didn't, she fished for conversation. "Your mother didn't think you'd mind me using your old rooms."

"She is correct."

He peered around. She'd redone the room a bit.

"I changed some things."

A few of the older chairs had been reupholstered, and she'd replaced the heavy window drapes with fabrics in lighter, softer colors. To Raimond it appeared to be a woman's quarters now. "I approve, though your own house will be ready soon."

"There is no hurry. I am content here."

Raimond was not content. From the moment he'd walked into the room, the urge to pull her into his arms had been battling against his defenses. For the last two weeks she'd occupied his every waking thought and every nocturnal dream. Exacting revenge no longer seemed paramount. Making love to her did. He could plainly see she had nothing on beneath the thin summer wrapper, and the thought of opening it and feasting on the sunbursts and stars within brought his manhood throbbing to life. Maybe if he allowed himself one more taste of her, he could cure himself of this thundering need and get on with his life.

Sable could see the intense desire brimming in his eyes. Even though she'd vowed to remain aloof, his smoldering gaze touched her in all the places he'd touched the last time they'd made love. In spite of the problems keeping them apart, neither of them seemed able to mask feelings. It gave her hope. If she could feed his desire, maybe acrimony and mistrust could be burned away by the heat of passion. What would happen if she purposefully set out to seduce her husband? "Did you come to visit for a reason?" she asked him, meeting his gaze.

"I came by to check on you."

His presence alone could make her melt like butter on a hot stove. "I haven't run off with Juliana's silver, if that's your concern."

"There was that, but I really came to see how you're settling in."

"I'm fine."

He was dressed for going out. The tailored dark suit fit his masculine form flawlessly. The white shirt appeared snowy against his dark skin. She wondered how he would be spending the evening, and with whom. Pride kept her from asking.

Raimond couldn't tear his thoughts away from making love to her again. The bare skin beneath her robe wouldn't let him dwell on anything else. "Are you always nude in the evenings?"

"Do you wish me to be?"

Raimond's manhood surged as if it had been caressed. Her eyes were fearless.

"You're very provocative, *ma reine.*"

"Being provocative will intrigue you, Raimond. Being meek will not."

Raimond's hands ached to open her gown and caress the warm beauty it shielded. "Most men want their women meek."

Sable felt her nipples blossoming in response to the heat rising between them in the quiet candlelight. "But you don't."

"Are you certain you know what I want?"

Once again she flashed fearless eyes. "That you are here offers a clue . . ."

He grinned. "You play this game well."

He came over to where she stood in front of the low vanity table and raised her chin so he could commit her beauty to memory.

She told him softly, "I will not share you with a mistress, Raimond."

He ran his thumb over her sultry bottom lip, so maddeningly slow that her eyes slid closed.

"Why not?" he whispered.

Then bending down, he touched his lips to hers in a fleeting but fiery kiss.

After he drew back, Sable could do nothing but float on the sweetness for a few moments. Finally she found the words to reply, "I am a queen and queens do not share ... ohhh ..."

His mouth had captured her nipple through the thin jade gown. The staggering teasing continued until she groaned with pleasure.

"Does Her Highness approve of this?"

He untied the wrapper and slid his warm palms over the already hardened buds of her breasts. They throbbed blissfully in response to the seductive circles he made while he kissed the pulsing point at the base of her throat. "Tell me, Your Majesty ... do you approve?"

Her breasts were fairly singing under his potent mouth and hands. When he moved to drink from the arched column of her throat, they were left bereft, aching and damp. He teased kisses over her parted lips, and his hands slid down over her flaring hips, rubbing the sunbursts languidly.

He cupped her hips, letting her feel the singeing heat of his hot palms, then the thin cotton moving shamelessly and wantonly over the backs of her thighs and hips. He teased her brazenly, deliciously, filling her with such heated delight, she parted her legs so he could play as he pleased.

Raimond dallied leisurely, expertly. Unable to resist, he bent so his lips could sensually ply a sable-tipped breast. He savored the feel of the hard bud as much as he did the damp, swollen gate of her core. The feel of her passion flowing so freely around his touch made his manhood surge with need.

"Lean back, *bijou* . . ." he instructed huskily.

Hazy with passion, Sable braced herself against the edge of the vanity table. As she did, he whispered hot, moan-evoking kisses over the points of her breasts and her fluttering throat. Using his palms to lead the way, he let his lips meander down the front plane of her soft body, worshipping as he went. Kneeling now, he curved his hands down her waist, and his tongue flicked over the small nook of her navel. Sable arched to the sparkling feel of it and of his palms sliding up and down her legs.

His hand drifted lower, over her hair, and slowly unveiled the jewel it sheltered. Her supporting arms trembled as he coaxed his queen to surrender her temple, tempted her to let him enter. His touch wielded such sultry magic that when his fingers found her fully, her body tightened and she crooned aloud. She didn't care how brazen she appeared or how scandalously her legs were parted, she just didn't want this to end.

Raimond knew he would never forget this encounter. The sight of the pleasure blooming on her face and the honey flowing between her golden thighs would be seared in his memory for all time. He placed a tender kiss against the marks banding her upper thigh, then drew his finger over the small, swollen jewel. The courtesans of Paris had taught him well; he knew that circles were best and that varying the pressure and rhythm could unlock a woman's soul. He also knew something else . . .

Filling his hands with her silken hips, he brought her forward.

Sable was so buffeted by the intensity, she had no time to be shocked. Nothing in life had ever prepared her for such a tribute. All she could do was ride the storm and let him have his way. He parted her, loved her. He treated himself to such a slow, erotic feast, it didn't take long for *le petite morte* to crackle over her and tear his name hoarsely from her throat.

As she lay against the vanity, throbbing and pulsing, he began to undress. Raimond didn't care about the engagement he had tonight. He wanted his wife and he wanted her now.

Sable sighed pleasurably as he entered her a moment later. The lulling pace of his rhythmic invitation pressed her bottom against the edge of the vanity, and she winced. He must have seen her small show of pain because he lifted her clear and she instinctively locked her legs around his dark waist.

They never made it to the bed. Raimond loved her there, standing in the middle of the room. With her pulsing so tightly around him, he fought off his own release. He wanted to enjoy her a bit longer, wanted to stroke her until she gasped his name, wanted to see if he could take her to the pinnacle again.

Sable fed on his raw male power; each blissful thrust increased her need. She lifted slightly for his kiss, then dropped her head back as the pace increased. She felt boneless in the large, strong hands guiding her hips so deliciously. He drew her back and forth, letting her savor the ride.

Raimond knew he couldn't last much longer. When he felt her tighten in the beginning throes of release, his tenuous hold on his own satisfaction came crashing down. Gripping her hips possessively, he poured out his soul with a loud growl.

They made love again and again until the wee hours, and afterward, lying in bed too sated to move, he placed a good-night kiss on her forehead. In response, a very sleepy Sable snuggled close to his side and said as she drifted off, ''See, you don't really need a mistress.''

Raimond wondered what she'd say if he told her he'd had no appetite for his mistress since his return to Louisiana. Instead, he grinned and pulled her close. "Go to sleep, Your Majesty."

So she did.

A few hours later, Raimond slipped from the bed that still sheltered his sleeping wife and dressed in silence. He'd come here last evening just to see how she was faring, not to make love to her until dawn. She was entirely too bewitching for her own good, he noted with irritation as he searched the floor for the trousers he'd discarded so hastily. He found them lying near the vanity table. Seeing the very prominent wrinkles did not help his mood, but he dragged them on.

As he did up the placket, he wondered how in the world he would explain to his mistress, Muriel, why he'd missed her birthday party last night. Muriel had been very understanding so far about his lack of interest in her since his return home. He doubted she'd continue to be so understanding upon learning she'd been stood up because he couldn't resist his satin-skinned wife. Last night his mistress had been the very last thing on his mind. Only Sable, beautiful, seductive Sable, with her sunburst hips and her moon-marked breasts had ruled his thoughts. Just thinking about her—them—made him hard all over again. By all rights he should have turned her over to the authorities the moment he saw her. Instead he'd made love to her with all the passionate abandon of a man who'd been celibate for decades.

And he wanted still more. He hadn't gotten nearly enough of her kisses, but even as he continued to desire her, a small voice kept reminding him that she'd betrayed him and the Union. Luckily, one of Randolph Baker's contacts, a well-known Confederate provocateur, had been intercepted outside Richmond, and the papers outlining Sherman's plans for Savannah had been found in his inside pocket. The man had confessed to having gotten the papers from Baker, but he'd refused to say anything else. He was subsequently jailed, but Baker couldn't be found; Baker was not his true name, the army had discovered. According to the records, the real Randolph Baker of Boston had died at Little Round Top.

Raimond looked over at his sleeping wife. Had she really been involved with the spies, or had she been a victim of circumstances beyond her control, as she claimed? He didn't know the answer, and last night he hadn't cared.

He'd cared that night back at the camp, though. After being slugged from behind by Baker, he'd come to on the dirt floor with a very worried Andre kneeling beside him. After helping Raimond to the cot, Andre had looked through the rifled chest, found the coin bag empty and the slim gold bracelet. Placing the bracelet on the cot at Raimond's side, Andre had moved to the papers strewn all over the desk. He'd determined that five signed passes and the briefing papers on Sherman's November 15 march toward Savannah were missing. The announcement had worsened Raimond's already splitting head, and he'd known he had to report the matter.

He wasn't able to do so until days later. The Rebel attack on the camp that night had kept everyone too busy battling the mounted guerrilla force, putting out fires, and burying the dead. He rode into Atlanta at the first opportunity to file his report with army command. While there, he was informed that because of the extensive damage the camp had received, the government planned to close it down. Less than a week after Sable's betrayal, Raimond, Araminta, and Andre had reined their horses east and headed for the Sea Islands of South Carolina.

He'd stayed there helping the freedmen build houses and plant cotton until he'd come home this summer. Sable had been the last person he'd expected to find here, under his mother's roof.

After pulling on his wrinkled shirt and coat, Raimond moved soundlessly back over to the bed where Sable slept unawares. Part of him wanted to strip and climb back beneath the sheets so he could be there when she awakened, but the rational side of himself demanded he maintain his distance.

He couldn't leave without placing a parting kiss on her cheek. Then he withdrew, left the room, and quietly closed the door behind him.

Downstairs, he found his mother seated on the porch drinking her morning *cafe au lait*. She took in his rumpled clothing, but didn't remark upon it. She said instead, "Good morning, Raimond. Would you care for coffee?"

"Good morning, Mama. No, I must get back."

Before he could say anything else, Archer's coach pulled up. The sight of his brother increased Raimond's irritation.

As Archer stepped onto the porch, he took one look at Raimond's wrinkled suit and asked with a raised eyebrow, "What dustbin did you sleep in last night, big brother?"

"I'm going to ignore you, brat—except to say, stay the hell away from my wife."

"You have a wife—oh yes, Sable, the wife you seem determined to ignore."

Archer went over and kissed his mother's cheek. He poured himself some coffee.

Raimond said, "No more shopping."

"On the days she wants to go shopping, who's going to take her?"

"I will."

Archer started to laugh. Seeing the disapproval on his mother's face, he controlled himself, but he couldn't keep from commenting, "Raimond, you can't dress *yourself*, let alone a beautiful woman. That suit is a sterling example."

"Shall I wrinkle you the same way?" Raimond countered. "I'm spoiling for a fight this morning."

Philippe was halfway up the walk before anyone noticed. He'd evidently heard Raimond's threat because he drawled, "If I'd known he'd be here throwing his weight around, I'd have stayed home."

Ignoring Raimond's glare, he went over to his mother and kissed her cheek. "Good morning, Mama. May I have some coffee? What's big brother raging about now? Good Lord, man, where'd you sleep last night? Look at his suit."

Trying to keep a straight face, Juliana poured Philippe coffee.

Archer volunteered an answer to the first of Phillipe's questions, "He doesn't want me to take Sable shopping anymore."

"Who's going to do it? Him?"

"My sentiments exactly," Archer pointed out.

Over his cup, Phillipe asked "I suppose you're going to forbid me from taking her to the baseball game on Saturday. She enjoys baseball, Raimond. Did you know that?"

"Dammit, we've been married less than a month."

"And in those few weeks, you've seen her how many times? Mother said Sable arrived back here in a hired hack the morning after the wedding night. What's wrong with you? I've seen you treat tavern girls better."

Raimond rubbed his hands over his weary eyes. "It's very complicated."

Archer drawled, "Uh huh. If you don't want her, say so. The Brats and I will draw straws."

"More than likely pistols," Phillipe countered dryly.

Raimond's eyes narrowed, but his brothers ignored him.

"We missed you at Muriel's last night," Philippe observed. "Where were you?"

"None of your damn business."

"You missed your mistress's birthday party?" Archer asked, surprised. "On behalf of Sable, I say splendid."

Raimond looked up to see Sable standing in the doorway. She had on the same jade-green wrapper he'd taken off her last night, and his manhood began to pulse with a strong and familiar beat. He wondered how much she'd heard. "Good morning, Sable."

"Raimond."

The silence on the porch grew thick.

Speaking as if they were alone she said, "I heard voices, but I assumed you were gone. You left your watch."

She held it out on her palm.

He took it and placed it in his coat pocket.

Sable ignored the knowing grins on the faces of Archer and Philippe, and instead told her husband softly, "Oh, and Raimond, tell your mistress I apologize for causing you to miss her birthday party last evening. I'll try not to let it happen again . . ."

She turned and walked back inside, mesmerizing him with the sultry sway of her hips.

Her sarcasm was not lost on anyone on the porch, nor was her challenge.

Archer tossed out, "I think she just declared war."

Still afire with the memory of their lovemaking, Raimond said, "I think you may be right."

That afternoon, after leaving the Freedmen's Bureau for the day, Raimond knocked lightly at Muriel's door. She opened it with an unreadable look on her face, then stepped back so he could enter.

"I owe you an apology for last night, so here I am. I apologize."

Muriel was as darkly beautiful as she was tall. She and Raimond had begun their liaison before the war. She was intelligent, well read, and often put up with him when no one else would.

"How angry are you?" he asked

"Not very much, truthfully."

He was certain she read the surprise on his face. "Truly?"

"Truly," she said, showing him into the small flat he'd been leasing for her for nearly four years. "I was a bit put out when you didn't arrive, but I'm a realist, Rai.''

He took a seat. "Which means?"

"Do you realize we've not made love since you came back from the war?"

It was the truth and Raimond felt almost guilty about it.

"No need for guilt," she said, correctly reading him. "We had some good times together, you and I."

Due to the demands of soldiering and the upheavals of war, he'd been able to see her only twice since 1863. When he'd returned home for good last month, the spark had not been there. At first he'd blamed it on the natural progression of things—it was simply time for him to move on—but now he had to admit there'd been more involved. Bittersweet memories of the Sable he'd met at the camp had left a lasting impression that made him immune to all other women.

There was silence for a moment before Muriel said, "I hear she is very beautiful."

Raimond knew better than to pretend he didn't know who she meant. He owed her the truth. "Yes, she is."

"I've lost you to her, haven't I?"

"Part of me wants to deny it."

"But you cannot."

"No, I can't."

She went and stood by the window. "I've met a man who wants to take me to Port-au-Prince. I told him yes."

"When will you leave?"

"In five days."

"Where shall I forward your settlement?"

She shook her head. "That isn't necessary. You've been more than generous over the years, and I've accumulated a sizable nest egg." She paused for a moment, then said, "Rai?"

He looked into her eyes. "Yes?"

"Promise me you will be as generous and loving with her as you've been to me."

He was not surprised by her words. She'd always possessed a kind heart. "I promise."

"Good. Now, get out of my house before I start to bawl."

With a bittersweet smile, Raimond LeVeq stood, bowed, and exited.

Chapter 11

That evening, Drake and Beau came to dine with Juliana and Sable. Everyone had just sat down at the gleaming table when Raimond walked in. "Good evening."

A surprised Juliana said, "Good evening to you too. Have you come to join us?"

"I thought I might."

Sable too was surprised by his unprecedented appearance. He'd never dined with them before. She moved her chair to make room for a place beside her. Juliana fetched him a plate from the new china cabinet.

Sable was unsure how to act with him so near. The tender and passionate man in her bedroom seemed to bear little resemblance to the formal, unapproachable man she encountered elsewhere. She decided she would simply follow his lead.

Over the course of the meal, they discussed the ongoing restoration of the house and its furnishings, and Juliana's desire to hire a new staff of servants. "I've been doing my own cooking since '63, and truthfully, I'm tired of it," she confessed.

"Mama, I hear Little Reba's back in the city," Drake said.

"Maxi's niece is here?" Juliana exclaimed. "Is she employed?"

"I'm not certain, but I can find out."

"Oh, do, that would be an answer to my prayers."

"Who's Little Reba?" Sable asked.

"The niece of one of Mama's very good friends, Maxi," Beau explained. "Little Reba moved to Michigan before the war to live with her aunt, who is the cook for Raimond's best friend Galeno Vachon."

"And like her Aunt Maxi, Reba's calling is cooking," Juliana added. "If Reba agrees to come and work for me, I'll never have to eat my own food again."

Talk then shifted to Raimond's work with the Freedmen's Bureau.

"It isn't going well," he stated. "For every good agent, there are three who have only the interests of the former masters in mind. They couldn't care less about the job they're supposed to be doing."

"Aren't there laws governing the bureaus?" Juliana asked.

"Yes, but they vary from state to state, so there's no set rule for how the agents are to proceed. In some places, such as here in Louisiana, there are superintendents who are doing their best to help the freedman. In other places, agents have been accused of striking and kicking refugees, and letting planters run off their new Black employees when pay day comes. According to many reports, embezzlement is rampant."

Drake asked, "What is this I hear about Reverend Benjamin Randolph signing on as an agent? I met him during the war when he was the chaplain for the Twenty-seventh USCT."

Raimond replied, "He's trying to get a post, but not many Blacks are being asked to come on board. You'd think they'd hire him immediately. The man's well educated, an Oberlin graduate. He even said he'd work for free as long as they place him where he can help best."

It didn't make much sense to Sable that the Freedmen's Bureau refused to hire a man like the Reverend Randolph. The talents of educated Blacks from the north and south were invaluable in aiding the former slaves. Freedmen schools were opening all over the South, in billiard parlors, warehouses, and abandoned boxcars, and many educated Blacks were needed as teachers.

Sable also knew that the involvement of free Blacks served to defuse the ofttimes heated debate being waged over whether free Blacks should ally themselves with the freedmen. Some of the free elite in places like New Orleans, Mobile, and Charleston were refusing to send their children to the freedmen schools and were publicly disassociating themselves from both the freedmen and their causes. According to what she'd learned from the city's aid workers, the *New Orleans L'Union*, a thrice weekly newspaper published by the free Black brothers Louis-Charles and Jean-Baptiste Roundanez, once re- flected these same sentiments. When the newspaper was founded in 1862, its editorials, published in French, ad- vocated granting suffrage and civil rights to property- owning free Blacks only. They saw no benefit in being linked to the masses of uneducated Blacks out in the countryside.

Sable understood their thinking even if she did not agree with it. Before the war, free Blacks owned nearly fifteen million dollars' worth of property in New Orleans alone. Many were slave owners, a fact she found star- tling. Some had been landowners for generations and been educated in Spain and France. When war broke out, the freeing of the slaves affected their incomes and traditions too. Some free Blacks fought for the Confed- eracy and supported it financially. Bernard Soulie, a wealthy business associate of Juliana, had personally loaned the Confederacy ten thousand dollars.

Since the end of the war, the elitist stance supported by men like the Roundanez brothers had changed dra- matically, mainly because the country was refusing to differentiate between the Blacks. The fates of the free and recently freed were entwined whether folks liked it or not, and neither side would be able to enjoy the rights promised by the Constitution without the help and support of the other. The abolitionist and poet Ralph Waldo Emerson called liberty a "slow fruit," and Sable had to agree.

After dinner, Raimond surprised Sable again by asking her if she'd like to take a stroll outside with him. Still uncertain of his mood, she searched his eyes, trying to glean his intent before admitting, "I'd enjoy that."

He helped her rise and the two excused themselves from Juliana, Drake, and Beau. They walked out to the moonlit grounds behind the house and over to the small gazebo that had been erected by some of Drake's workers only a few days ago.

Raimond peered up at the beams of the open air structure. "I'm glad Drake built Mama a new one. The old one was falling apart."

"How long had it been standing?"

"My stepfather built it for her during their first year together. I remember them spending many an evening out here after dinner."

"I get the impression they loved each other very much."

"Yes, they did."

Considering all the difficulties she and Raimond seemed to be having, Sable did not expect she'd ever know a love so strong. "Why did you ask me out here?" she asked quietly.

"I don't know," he confessed. "Maybe to tell you that my mistress and I have parted, or maybe just to have you near. I don't know."

He was standing with his back to her, silhouetted against the moonlight and looking as if he were standing on the deck of one of his ships.

"Have you really parted from her?" Sable asked.

"Yes. I haven't shared her bed since I returned home. It seems I've developed a craving for moons and sunbursts."

Although Sable found the news thrilling she did wonder what it all meant in terms of their marriage. "Does this mean you've changed your opinion of me?"

"No, I still don't trust you, but you're like a siren. The more I try and stay away, the more I want you in my arms."

He turned and looked at her. Even in the dark she sensed his conflicted feelings and overwhelming desire. He told her, "Come, I'll walk you back to the house."

Sable spent the next day as she did most days lately, combing the city for orphans in need of rescuing. The city authorities estimated that at least twenty thousand freedmen would be added to the local population by year's end, many of them children. She found them on the steps of churches, in doorways, rooting through the refuse behind restaurants and hotels, and wandering aimlessly. A few had been separated from their families, and Sable's heart always filled with joy when they were reunited with their relatives. Others, truly orphaned, had no one to feed them, love them, or protect them from the city's lawless elements. There was no one to keep them from the clutches of disreputable planters who were using the new statutes forbidding unemployment to force them into reenslavement.

The children she rescued from the streets were usually given over to the care of the Sisters of the Holy Family, a Black Catholic order in the 700 block of Orleans Street. According to the story the sisters told Sable, Catholic convents were once closed to free Blacks, but in 1842 a free woman of color named Henriette Delille, with help from a White woman named Marie Jean Aliquot, managed to get an order sanctioned and affiliated. Delille and Aliquot were soon joined by two other free women who'd also dreamed of serving God by being nuns, Juliette Gaudin and Josephine Charles. Using a building donated by a Delille relative, the nuns opened a school, a church, and an orphanage.

Another New Orleans charity helping destitute children was the Institution Catholique des Orphelins Indigents. Money for its establishment had been donated by Madame Marie-Justine Couvenant. She'd come to Louisiana as a slave, but died a very wealthy woman in 1837. In her will she authorized money for a school for children of color, but White protests prevented her wishes from being implemented. It took the financial muscle of free Black philanthropists like Aristide Mary and other powerful members of the community to finally get the will probated. In 1847, ten years after her death, Madame Couvenant's dream became a reality.

The charity workers had lovingly dubbed Sable *Madame D'Orphelins* for her tireless work on behalf of the orphans. Shop owners were now holding on to the children they found, keeping them put until she could retrieve them on her rounds. They also alerted her to any who might have come begging in their stores but run off. Freedmen stopped her on the streets to ask after missing children, and she scoured the Black newspapers, especially the local *La Tribune*, for notices posted by parents looking for lost little ones.

Sable's own experiences made her highly sensitive to the children who had no one. She continued to carry Mahti and her brother Rhine in her heart, but thanked the Old Queens every morning for the loving members of the house of LeVeq.

She didn't know whom to thank for Raimond, however. Knowing he no longer kept a mistress made her smile. Even as Sable and her driver prowled the streets in their search for children in need, her last passionate encounter with her husband still played vividly in her mind. She'd thought nothing could surpass the pleasure she'd experienced on their wedding night, but she'd been proven wrong. Just thinking about how scandalously she'd enjoyed herself made her desire rise. His touch left her so enthralled and throbbing, she wished to be a real queen so she could demand he make love to her whenever she commanded. Raimond was not the type of man to be commanded, however, and she doubted she would be attracted to him if he were. Still, he awakened a need within her that yearned to be satisfied by him and him alone.

Across town, Raimond sat on the new loveseat he'd purchased for Sable and wondered if getting drunk would make him feel better. He'd spent most of the morning dealing with the freedmen at the bureau, but not even their pressing needs could clear her face from his mind. Sable had him so tied up in knots he didn't know how to proceed. Deciding to see if cognac would lighten his despondent mood, he took the crystal decanter from the sideboard. Before he could retrieve a glass, however, he heard a carriage pull up outside and went to the front door. Upon seeing Galeno Vachon descending regally from the rented hack, Raimond grinned broadly. His smile widened further at the sight of Galeno's lovely wife, Hester.

Raimond set the decanter aside and rushed out to greet them. After sharing tight hugs and spirited slaps on the back with his two friends, he ushered them into his home.

The first words out of Hester's mouth were, "Where are your facilities?"

"She's carrying again," Galen announced proudly.

Raimond hastily pointed the way and Hester took off.

Raimond added up the number of Galen's children as they took a seat. "This will be the fourth?"

"Correct. Another little dragon for Maxi and Mama Frances to spoil."

"As if you won't also." Raimond chuckled. Maxi was Galen's cook. Frances was Hester's mother. "I was there when Francine was born, remember? You carried that baby around for hours at a time. Wouldn't let me hold her until she was almost a week old.''

"A father's first child is always special. Besides, I was afraid you would drop her.''

Raimond snorted with comic outrage. Hester returned in the middle of their playful ribbing. "Are you two cubs at it already?''

Galen gently squeezed his wife's shoulders as she seated herself by his side. "Better now?''

"Infinitely.'' She sighed with pleasure. "What were you laughing about?''

Raimond supplied the answer. "How possessive Galen was with Francine when she was first born.''

Hester grinned. "He did go a bit over the top, didn't he? He wouldn't even let *me* hold her at first. Maxi had to remind him that babies needed their mamas for feeding if for nothing else and he very reluctantly handed her over. He was a bit better with the other two girls, but not much.''

Lord, it was good to see them again, Raimond thought. Although Galeno had been born in New Orleans, he now called Michigan home. The two men had known each other since childhood. During the volatile abolitionist years they'd been part of the Underground Railroad, leading runaways North. Furious slave owners had issued warrants for their arrest for what were termed "crimes against the South,'' and the bounty offered had made each men worth his weight in gold to the feral bands of slave catchers roaming the North. In fact, had it not been for slave catchers, Galeno and Hester might never have met. She'd hidden him in her cellar after he'd received a severe beating from a group of the mercenary predators, and by the time he'd recovered enough to be taken home by Raimond and the Brats, he'd fallen in love.

"What brings the two of you down here?'' Raimond asked.

"You,'' Hester said. "Your mother wrote us of your marriage. I'm very offended that we weren't invited.''

"For you to have arrived here so quickly, she must have written to you the moment the engagement was agreed upon."

"Yes, she did, and we immediately booked passage south."

Raimond owed his mother thanks for bringing about this reunion, but he wondered how much of the story she'd revealed.

Hester must have seen the emotions playing over his face because she asked, "What's the matter?"

Galeno leaned forward. "Why so glum? Don't tell me the bride looks like a bear."

Raimond glared.

Galeno grinned. "I'll take that glare to mean she does not. So what's the matter?"

Hester asked warningly, "Raimond, you didn't get some poor freedman's daughter with child and *have* to marry, did you? Juliana wrote that she was a former slave."

"She also said you are in love, Rai," Galeno added.

The glare darkened even further.

Galeno observed the man whom he loved like a brother and began to laugh. "You *are* in love, aren't you? *Petite*, look at his face. How miserable are you?"

Raimond didn't answer.

"Does she hate the ground you walk on? Is it unrequited love?"

Hester looked to her husband. "Stop it, Galen."

"Oh, no. Not after the way he dragged me through the mud over you. This is choice. Tell me the story, Rai, or so help me, I'll go right to Juliana and ask her. She'll tell me."

Raimond knew he'd receive little sympathy for his plight from Galeno, but he trusted him with his life. Even though Galeno was having fun at Raimond's expense, Raimond valued his advice almost as much as his friendship.

So he told the tale, starting with his initial meeting

with Sable and finishing with the wedding and his parting from Muriel.

Hester stared, her dark eyes wide. "You have given up your mistress for a woman who may or may not have been a Rebel spy?"

Galeno couldn't seem to help himself. He was laughing so hard, he almost rolled off the divan.

Hester, doing her best to hold in her own laughter, smacked her husband across his knee. "Now stop, Galen. This is serious." She turned back to a scowling Raimond. "When can I meet her?"

"Now seems as good a time as any. I vowed to stay away from her, but I can't do it."

Galeno howled.

Raimond looked to his laughing friend, who now had tears of mirth sliding down his ivory cheeks. "With any luck, he'll laugh himself to death on the ride over. Come on, Hester. I'll escort you to the coach."

When Sable returned to Juliana's it was past dark. She'd spent the last part of the day over in Freetown, a growing city of shacks and tents across the river. A child she'd been searching for all day had reportedly been seen there, but after asking around for nearly two hours, Sable and her driver had given up. The muddy grounds of Freetown had left her hem and shoes covered with mud. Having to crawl into an abandoned boxcar that the orphans sometimes used for quarters had ruined the dress she was wearing for anything but gardening. At the time, Sable hadn't cared about appearances; finding the child, a small girl, had been her only priority, but now, seeing the many carriages parked in front of the house, her husband's among them, Sable almost wished she'd had a more sedate day.

The house was filled with people. Seated around the parlor were Juliana, all her sons except Archer, and a man and a woman Sable did not recognize. The atmosphere seemed so festive, Sable fought to remember if today was the birthday of someone in the family, or if Juliana had mentioned a gathering that morning. Had her preoccupation with the passionate night she'd spent with Raimond made her forget?

Juliana's voice rang out, "Ah, here she is, everyone."

Sable stepped further into the parlor. Her eyes immediately sought her husband's. He took in her muddy appearance and, smiling, shook his head.

Beau, standing with a glass of cognac in his hand, asked, "Where on earth have you been, little sister? Digging for gold?"

The other Brats were soon suggesting other scenarios to explain her bedraggled state, each more ridiculous than the last. Well accustomed by now to their wry humor, Sable poured herself a glass of lemonade and said, "You're all wrong. I was playing in a boxcar over in Freetown."

"Looking for more children?" Juliana asked solemnly.

Sable nodded.

Juliana took Sable's dirty hand in her own. "You'll be blessed for all you're doing. Come, let's introduce you to some old and dear friends. Raimond."

Raimond set his glass down and damned himself for loving this woman. Even covered with mud, she made his heart pound. "Sable, I want you to meet Galeno Vachon and his wife, Hester. This is my wife, Sable."

Hester held out a black-gloved hand. "I'm glad to meet you, Sable."

"As am I you."

Galeno bowed over her own hand and kissed it. "I am truly pleased to meet my dream come true."

Confused, Sable looked to Hester, who replied, "Pay him no mind. Finding Raimond married has left him a bit delirious."

Galeno then asked, "Lovely lady, would you care to dine with us this evening?"

Sable looked to Raimond, who replied, "The decision

is yours. I'd like a chance to see them, but if the day has been a long one for you, tomorrow will do just as well.''

"Dinner sounds fine," Sable replied. "Let me wash up and I'll be right down.''

Upstairs in her room, Sable hastily stripped down to her underwear. She was washing her soiled face and hands when Raimond entered.

Her heart picked up its pace at the sight of him, making her wonder if he would have that same effect on her for the rest of her days. "I'm certain your mother taught you to knock first," she said.

"She did.''

He closed the door behind him and stepped into the room. As always, his presence filled the space, making Sable remember how thoroughly she'd been loved. "If you've come to rush me along, I'm truly moving as fast as I'm able.''

"No, I came to say you don't have to come if you don't wish to.''

"Do you want me to stay here?" she asked quietly. She knew her heart would break if he said yes, but her face remained unreadable.

"No. I want you to know my friends." His small confession took her somewhat by surprise.

"Where are we going?" she asked, trying not to be affected by his smoldering gaze. She needed to know what to wear.

Raimond gazed openly at her soft curves clad in nothing but a camisole and drawers. "Archer's place, I believe.''

Sable went over to the armoire and took down a simple but elegant gown. As she put it on she confessed, "I do wish I had time to bathe. I'd love a real bath after such a day.''

"I'll give you one when we return.''

Desire flashed over Sable, sharp and hot.

"Hurry and dress now. I'll wait downstairs."

As he left, she was still reeling.

The dining room in Archer's hotel served excellent food and was one of the most popular and fashionable free Black eateries in town. Because of its reputation, it never lacked for patrons, and tonight was no exception. Knowing the owner helped, and they were given a table in one of the back rooms.

They spent the evening laughing, talking, and reminiscing. Sable found she liked Hester very much. She enjoyed Galeno's company also. It was apparent that the Vachons were still very much in love after six years of marriage and three children. They had a way of looking at each other that made Sable envious. With Raimond's mistrust hanging over her own marriage like a threatening cloud, she doubted they would ever achieve such closeness.

As the waiter removed the dinner dishes, he told Sable, "Monsieur Roundanez wishes to send you dessert."

Raimond swiveled around in his seat until he could see the newspaperman across the room. Louis-Charles nodded politely. Raimond offered a terse nod in reply before turning back to his wife. "Why is he buying you dessert?"

"It's his way of thanking me for working with the children. He buys me dessert at least three times a week."

Raimond glowered.

Sable chose to overlook her shocked husband and the now laughing Galeno Vachon, and replied to the waiter's question. "Yes, George, I'll have my dessert."

George smiled. "Yes, madame."

After George had taken orders for coffee and dessert from everyone else at the table, Raimond asked her, "You know the waiters by name?"

"Yes. I eat luncheon here with Archer most days. This *is* your brother's restaurant, Raimond."

Raimond looked over at Louis-Charles Roundanez once again. Roundanez grinned and Raimond smiled falsely in reply. He turned back to his wife, wondering why he was so irritated all of a sudden. He knew she worked tirelessly on behalf of the orphans, but he'd no idea she'd made so many friend in the community or become such a regular public presence. What else did he not know about his wife?

George wheeled in dessert, coffee, and cognac. He placed slices of pecan pie in front of Raimond, Galeno, and Hester, but Sable received something else entirely.

"Sable, what is that?" Hester asked. "It looks wonderful."

George volunteered the answer. "The chef calls it Strawberries du Sable, after madame."

Stunned, Raimond asked, "You have a signature dessert?"

"It isn't something I asked for, but yes. The chef created it one day, and Archer named it for me because he knows how much I love strawberries."

Raimond could feel how tight his jaw had become. He took a deep breath in an attempt to relax. It would not do to fly into a jealous rage; Sable would undoubtedly consider him insane, and Galeno would laugh so hard they'd have to cart him away. He found Hester watching him intently, knowingly, as if she could see into his heart.

Yes, he was jealous, jealous of everyone Sable had ever spoken to or blessed with her smile. He wanted to storm over and demand Roundanez never buy his wife dessert again. He wanted to punch the chef, and Archer too. In less than two months she'd become so well known and loved, men were buying her dishes of strawberries topped with golden meringue, and he hadn't known a damn thing about it!

Raimond was beset by such a storm of emotions, he felt in desperate need of fresh air. He stood abruptly and excused himself from the table.

Sable watched him walk stiffly away. She had no idea what he was about, but she assumed his agitation stemmed from her. She looked to his friends, hoping her disappointment didn't show, and asked Hester about her three daughters. As Hester began naming them, Galeno excused himself and went in pursuit of Raimond.

Alone at the table, Sable and Hester sat quietly for a few moments, each preoccupied with her own thoughts, then Hester asked Sable quietly, "You love him very much, don't you?"

Sable offered up a bittersweet smile. "Is it that obvious?"

Hester nodded.

"I'd hoped to hide it."

"Why?"

"Because he doesn't love me, and probably never will." She then added, "Since our husbands are such close friends, I assume he has told you the story of our past?"

"Yes."

"And that he believes I was involved in the theft of General Sherman's papers?"

"Were you?"

"No."

Sable sensed Hester believed her, but she didn't reply. Instead, Hester said softly, "Raimond loves you very much also."

Sable smiled wanly. "Even though it's not true, it *is* nice to hear."

"I'm being truthful, Sable. I haven't known him for as long as Galen has, but I know Raimond LeVeq in ways Galen does not. Did I mention he's the godfather of all my girls?"

"All of them?"

"Yes, and I refuse to have anyone else as godfather. Should anything happen to Galeno or me, I know Raimond will see that my babies lack for nothing, that he'll love them as fiercely as if they were his own."

"How long have they known each other?"

"Since they were boys here in New Orleans. Before the war they were conductors on the Underground Railroad and led many slaves North. My Galen went by the dashing name of the Black Daniel to mask his true identity. He and Raimond had very large bounties on their heads for what was known as 'crimes against the South.' "

Sable was impressed. "He's never told me about that part of his life."

"Of course they are both prone to exaggeration, but they were very serious about the roles they played in freedom. I'm certain Raimond would tell you his stories if you asked."

"I don't know," Sable said, looking doubtful. "I wonder if we'll ever be as at ease with one another as you and Galen seem to be. If there were a way to bring Baker here and make him tell Raimond my story, I would."

"But right now you can't, so let love build the trust you two need instead. My pride was the obstacle that kept Galeno and me apart, but his love made me set it aside, just as love will make Raimond set aside his mistrust."

"I'd like to believe that."

"Then do. He stomped out of here because he's jealous of all the attention people are showering on you. He's in love. Build on that. Seduce him in a dark carriage—that always works with Galeno. Tempt him, make him so wild for you that he thinks of nothing but you. Both of our men are very—shall we say—talented in the bedroom, but they are also very playful, like tiger cubs or puppies. Play with him. Galeno and I make mudpies."

"Mudpies!"

"Yes. I'd never made them before Galen showed me how. Now making mudpies is a very important part of our marriage."

Sable echoed, "Mudpies."

"Yep," Hester summed up proudly.

"When we make mudpies we leave the worries of the day behind. We play, talk, even argue on occasion, but it has become our special time to be close and alone with each other."

They were interrupted by the newspaperman Roundanez, who'd come over to meet Sable's guest. She introduced him to Hester, and both ladies invited him to sit and chat.

Outside, Raimond pulled in deep draws of the night air and wondered what the hell was wrong with him. Roundanez was a friend, Archer was his brother, yet he was so jealous of both men he could hardly see.

Galeno walked up to him and in all seriousness asked, "Are you ill, *mon frere*?"

"No. I am losing my mind."

"Love will do that to you."

Raimond sighed with impatience. "Has a man ever sent your wife dessert?"

Galeno chuckled. "Not and lived, no."

Raimond knew Galeno didn't really mean that, but he allowed himself a small smile. "This is absolutely maddening. Just looking at her makes me ache."

"She's your wife, Rai. She's supposed to turn you inside out. I don't know why you're struggling to keep her at bay—she's intelligent, beautiful. It's apparent she loves you, so what is your problem?"

"Can I trust her?"

"Oh."

Silence settled as both men stood in the darkness.

Galeno finally said, "Personally, after being with her tonight, I can't picture her as anything other than a victim of circumstance."

"And if she wasn't?"

"Then she'll break your heart."

"Exactly."

The two had been through a lot together, but love was proving to be a far more treacherous journey than any of their previous adventures. "So is this how you felt when you were pursuing Hester?"

"Yes, and as I remember you weren't very sympathetic."

"My deepest and most sincere apologies. I had no idea."

Galeno grinned. "So what are you going to do about the lovely Sable?"

"Surrender. It's all I can do, truthfully. I just pray I don't discover later that I'm mated to a black widow."

Galeno patted him on the back. "Everything will work out. You'll see."

Before they could head back inside, Archer walked up to them and drawled dryly, "While you two old goats are out here debating Lord knows what, the wolves are inside circling your ladies like spring lambs."

Raimond looked over at Galeno. "How about we vow that he'll be next?"

"Next what?" Archer asked.

"Next to be impaled on Cupid's arrow."

Archer started laughing. "Oh, no. There isn't a woman alive who can make me give up my mistresses. One of my lovelies works roots, and she makes certain I stay immune."

"Out of the mouths of babes—" Galeno said.

Raimond added, "And brats. Let's go clear the wolves from the pasture."

Archer's description proved to be accurate. Hovering around the table were most of the eligible and in some cases not so eligible men in the room. Since Archer's restaurant catered only to the wealthy and powerful members of the elite, the wolves were prominent citizens. There was the newspaperman Louis-Charles Roundanez, of course, and next to him, the Bazile brothers, Albert and John, joint owners of the largest and most profitable cigar-making business in New Orleans. Also

competing for the ladies' attention were Jacques La-
Motte, an architect making a small fortune helping to
rebuild the city; pharmacist Joseph Bowman; and an intense young man Raimond did not know.

"Gentlemen, may we rejoin our wives?" Raimond's
polite but firmly spoken request parted them like the Red
Sea.

"Thank you."

As Raimond and Galeno took their respective seats,
the pharmacist Joseph Bowman said, "Good to see you
out and about, LeVeq. We were beginning to wonder if
you were really married to our lovely Sable. We rarely
see the two of you together."

Raimond assessed the tall, thin man before replying,
"That's a perception I will certainly remedy from now
on."

Sable looked up from the young poet kneeling so de-
votedly at her side and assessed her husband. He was
still tense with suppressed emotion, but now there was
a hot light in his eyes, a flame that singed her in places
only he had touched.

The other men took turns expressing their pleasure at
seeing Raimond again. Most knew Galeno also and
shook his hand to welcome him home. After offering
their good-nights, they drifted back to their own tables—
all except the young man still kneeling at Sable's side.
He was scribbling hastily on scraps of paper and handing
them to Sable to read.

Raimond watched and waited for a few moments, but
when Sable's attention continued to be monopolized, he
called softly to her, "*Ma reine . . .* "

She looked up immediately. He'd never addressed her
as "my queen" in public before, and it made her a bit
breathless.

"Who is he?"

The young man stood and declared, "I am Gaspar
Cadet, and I am in love with your wife. A woman as

fine as Labelle Sable has no business being with a husband as inattentive as you, monsieur."

Sable gasped. "Gaspar!"

He cut her off. "No, Sable, he doesn't deserve you. Choose your weapon."

Galen had begun laughing about halfway through Gaspar's impassioned soliloquy and by now he had tears in his eyes.

Hester appeared to be as shocked as Sable.

Raimond took in the poet's earnest young face and without raising his voice said, "I advise you to take your pencils—and your papers—and leave before I stand up. Because if I get up, you will need something far more dangerous than a weapon to keep me from tossing you out in the streets on your arse."

Gaspar's eyes widened. He was obviously beginning to understand that the man he'd challenged so flippantly was truly dangerous, because he didn't utter another word. Instead, he bowed in Sable's direction and hastily made his retreat.

Galeno used his napkin to dry his eyes. "This has been the best trip we've taken in a long while, *petite*. When's the second act, Rai?"

Raimond could only smile in response to his friend's enthusiasm. He then asked his wife, "Where in the world did you meet Gaspar the Brave?"

"At the orphanage my first day there. I had no idea he harbored such strong feelings for me."

"Poets are often impassioned," Hester offered.

"Well, his impassioned plea almost got him hurt," Raimond cracked. "Choose your weapon, indeed. Do you believe that, Galeno?"

Galeno began chuckling again. "The look on your face was priceless, *mon frere*, priceless."

Raimond ignored that and turned to his golden wife. "How many more court jesters am I going to have to banish before my throne is secure, Sable?"

Unable to resist teasing, she drawled, "Hundreds."

He grinned. "What was he scribbling?"

"Love poems."

"Let's hear one," Raimond invited.

"Are you sure? I wouldn't want poor Gaspar to be hung by his toes."

"I promise to control myself."

Sable picked up one of Gaspar's scraps and read: "Thy beauty blinds my soul. I am breathless at the sight of thee, staggered by thy smile; come with me to paradise and I will treasure thee as mine."

"I think that's beautiful, even if the meter is a bit off," Hester said, breaking the silence. She turned to Galeno. "Why don't you ever write me love poems?"

"Because you prefer mudpies . . ."

"How right you are, forgive me."

Sable, sensing the desire sparking between the Vachons, asked Raimond, "Do you want me to read another?"

"No." Raimond had no desire to hear another man's words echoing the feelings in his own heart.

The evening eventually drew to a close, and tight farewell hugs were exchanged by both couples. Since Galeno and Hester were guests of Archer's hotel, they had to go no farther than the stairs to reach their suite of rooms. They were going to be in Louisiana for at least another week, and the Vachons and the LeVeqs vowed to get together again the next day.

Chapter 12

Riding home in a hack they had hailed outside Archer's hotel, Sable glanced over at her silent husband and considered the advice Hester had given her. Sable had to admit that seducing him had already crossed her mind once before—but on that particular night, she'd wound up being seduced instead. Not that she had any complaints—he could seduce her any time he desired, a small voice crooned inside. Sable put away her yearnings, chastising herself for being such a wanton, and settled in for the return to Juliana's.

But it appeared they were headed elsewhere. She knew the city well by now, and when the driver did not turn onto the street he should have taken, she asked her husband, "Where are we going?"

"I promised you a bath," he replied in a voice that stroked her senses. "Remember?"

Yes, she did, and sudden anticipation dissolved her into a puddle right there on the seat.

He slid a finger over the soft rise of her cheek. "Our marriage has gotten off to a good start in some ways . . . and in other ways it hasn't, mainly due to the past— would you agree?"

"Yes."

"You fascinate me in the bedroom, Sable, but I want us to share more than that."

His eyes were difficult to read in the shadows, but she sensed his sincerity. "What are you saying?"

"That I wish to come home to you in the evenings, have meals with you, be there in the morning when you rise."

"What about Randolph Baker?"

"The past is behind us."

She searched his face. "Then you believe I wasn't involved?" It was a question she needed to hear him answer truthfully.

But he seemed to be more interested in something else as he touched his mouth to hers, just lightly enough to pique her interest too. He answered her softly, "What I believe about the past has no bearing on our future."

"But it will, if it remains between us."

"It is no longer an issue with me . . ."

His words faded as he brushed his lips against her ear. As the opening notes of desire floated through her blood like an elusive melody, she accused him, less firmly than she'd intended, "You're trying to distract me . . ."

His lips journeyed across the scented skin of her neck. "Who . . . me?"

"Yes, you . . ."

His hands were wandering leisurely, his warm lips doing the same. "Why would I want to distract you, *bijou* . . . ?"

"Because you don't wish to discuss . . . oooh . . ."

His mouth had encircled her nipple through the fabric of her dress and he teased it just long enough to elicit her response before moving to its twin. As her senses began to tingle and her heart pounded, he asked huskily, "Why in the world would I care to discuss a Reb turncoat when I can discuss how well your breasts fill my hands . . ."

Sable thanked heaven for the sheltering canopy of the carriage as he eased aside the bodice of her gown and filled his palms with her bared, dark-tipped golden flesh.

His tongue *discussed* while she *purred*. He made certain each peak had an opportunity to beg and throb before he rose to kiss her parted lips. His hand slid possessively up beneath her gown, mapping her thighs, caressing the band of moons, then drifting to her center.

She arched to the hot, sweet magic. She wanted to scold him for being so commandingly arrogant, but couldn't call up the words.

There were no words needed—just croons, sighs, and moans as he lingered over her bared breasts, dallied at the gates of her temple, and set off such a whirlwind of sensations she didn't want to leave the coach ever.

But the coach had stopped in front of the small mansion he'd purchased for her, and they had to get out.

"Come on . . ." he whispered against her lips, righting her dress,

Sable wasn't aware of leaving the coach. She was barely aware of standing dazed, passion throbbing like a drumbeat between her pulsing thighs, while he paid the driver.

Raimond scooped her up and carried her to the porch. Once inside, he set her on her feet and recaptured her lips. Their journey up the stairs was interrupted by kissing, touching, and the slow, sure pleasure of his hands guiding her dress up to her waist. The same hands moved bewitchingly over her bottom, then expertly undid the strings of her drawers. She barely noticed as the garment fluttered away. The touch of his bare hands fondling her so erotically made her cry out.

"I can't wait, *ma reine* . . . " he breathed thickly. The interlude in the coach had left them both near to bursting.

So they made love there, on the stairs, bathed by the moonlight streaming in through the still open front door.

Sable didn't get her promised bath until late the next morning. He treated her to a passionate mix of bathing and *discussion* that seduced her into climbing desire's heights once again. He carried her wet body out onto the verandah and had her stretch out on a quilt under the warming rays of the Louisiana sun. As she lay there, ripe, damp, and breathless, he sensually used a towel and his lips to dry the dark, straining buds of her breasts before transferring his dazzling ministrations to the swollen, sensitive bud between her thighs. Only after she was rendered twisting and mindless did he fill her with the iron of his own pulsing need, and love her until release shattered them both.

Hunger made Sable rise later that afternoon. While Raimond slept on, she eased from the bed and padded nude from their room to see what there was to eat. On the way down the stairs she found her drawers, her dress, and his trousers. She also found three buttons that had once been attached to his shirt. Remembering how they'd come unattached made the heat of embarrassment warm her cheeks. She retrieved them and placed them in his pants pocket. Last night, in her eagerness to caress his bare skin, she'd sent the buttons flying free. He hadn't minded, just as she hadn't minded the large rent he'd put in the front of her thin camisole in his own lustful eagerness.

The buttons and her torn camisole were a measure of how strong their passion had been. As she continued down the stairs, she smilingly envisioned a future filled with popped buttons and scandalously torn underthings.

Downstairs, she was struck by the wealth of furniture now filling the rooms. There were paintings, beautiful upholstered divans and chairs, and a gleaming new desk in the study. She had no idea when Raimond had added all the furnishings, but each piece showed his excellent taste.

On a counter in the kitchen stood a beautiful crystal decanter half-filled with an amber liquid that appeared to be cognac, but there was no food in the cupboards. Not even a carrot. Not even a spoon, she realized, conducting a further investigation of the drawers and bins in the spacious room.

"Pretty empty, huh?"

She was startled by the sight of Raimond framed in the doorway, wearing a black silk dressing gown.

"Good morning," she said, enjoying the idea of having him around.

"Nice attire," he said, indicating her nudity.

She spun around as if showing off a new gown. "It's all the rage, you know."

He grinned, feeling his manhood leap with appreciation at the sight of her all nude and golden. The thought of making love to her again tempted him mightily. "I suggest you find something to put on over your fashionable attire unless you wish to be in need of another bath, Your Majesty."

She stood a moment as if mulling over the proposition, then replied slyly, "This counter appears fairly solid . . . are we allowed to make love in the kitchen?"

Raimond's manhood surged to full life beneath his robe.

She walked over to the table in the center of the room, blinding him with the sight of her moons and sunbursts as she passed provocatively. "Or . . . here, maybe . . . ?"

Raimond chuckled, his tiger eyes blazing. "You are very playful, *ma reine* . . . "

"Being playful will intrigue you as much as being provocative, Raimond."

It was a reference to the conversation they'd had the night he'd missed Muriel's birthday party.

"You are correct," he affirmed while making a mental note to take her on the counter at the first opportunity. "However, my voracious *bijou d'or*, a man, unlike a woman, needs time to recover after such . . . extensive activity."

"Oh."

Raimond shook his head. Virgins. No, he corrected himself, former virgins. "So go and put on some clothes. Later, if you're good, I'll show you the table, the counter, and probably that bench over there too."

Sable executed an exaggerated pout.

He laughed aloud. "After all the love I bestowed on you, how dare you pout. Upstairs, shameless woman. Look in the armoire for something to wear, and don't come back unless you're covered."

Grinning saucily, she left to do her husband's bidding.

She returned to the kitchen wearing one of his robes. It was so voluminous, she could have made a dress and two blouses out of the material flowing around her bare feet. "Is this better?" she asked.

"Much."

"Good. Now explain to me why there's nothing in your pantry."

He shrugged. "There's been no need. I only sleep here. I've been taking my meals at Archer's place."

"Do you ever plan on doing something besides sleep here?"

"I don't know, I'll have to ask my wife."

Sable smiled.

"I sold my apartments in town," he told her. "This is where we'll be living from now on. Just so you know."

"And if I choose to live elsewhere, my arrogant knight?"

"Then expect me to lock you in my tower until you surrender."

"That doesn't sound too terribly awful. In fact, I may enjoy being locked up in your tower."

He shook his head at her provocative and playful green eyes.

They decided to go to Juliana's to eat. Sable had no alternative but to put on the same dress she'd worn last night. She prayed the Brats were off attending to business so she wouldn't be subjected to their ribbing.

Her prayers were denied. In fact, all of Juliana's sons were in attendance, enjoying a late luncheon. Sable did not know the handsome, gray-haired gentleman seated at Juliana's side.

As soon as Sable and Raimond entered the dining

room, Archer took one look at Sable's wrinkled dress and cracked, "Now it appears big brother has her sleeping in dustbins with him."

Sable cut him a grin. "Archer, it is terribly impolite to bring up a lady's disheveled appearance."

Phillipe countered, "There's disheveled and then there's *disheveled*. Sweet sister, that dress looks as if it spent the night under a bed."

"Almost," Raimond replied meaningfully.

"Raimond!" Shocked and a bit embarrassed, Sable looked askance at her husband.

Grinning innocently, he asked, "If it wasn't under the bed, where was it?"

Her eyes widened and she punched him in his well-muscled arm. "Stop it," she demanded, scandalized.

The brothers were all chuckling.

Before things got any more out of hand, Juliana said, "Sable, I want you to meet Henri Vincent, an old and dear friend."

Sable wondered if anyone else could see how Juliana was glowing. "I'm pleased to meet you, *monsieur*."

"*Enchanté*," he replied, rising to his feet.

Sable watched as he and Raimond embraced each other with genuine emotion. It was easy to see the two men shared a special bond. Sable knew from her talks with Juliana that Henri had helped her when her beloved François died, and that he'd been a substitute father to her sons. Raimond and Gerrold had been in their early twenties the year François died, but the Brats had ranged in ages from Phillipe's seven to Archer's eleven, and Henri's presence had meant a lot to them.

"Henri's birthday is a few days away and I'm going to have a ball in his honor," Juliana declared.

The tall, handsome Henri looked at Juliana affectionately but countered, "Ana, that isn't necessary."

"Yes, it is. I told you long ago that on your sixtieth we would celebrate, and the year is here."

Beau said, "*Oncle* Henri, you know once she has set

her mind, not even the angels can change it, so you may as well surrender.''

''I am well aware of her determination. It was one of the things your father loved most about her.''

Sable watched the silent interplay between Juliana and Henri and wondered if anyone else in the room realized the two were in love.

She asked Raimond about it later that evening as Raimond drove his carriage over to Archer's hotel to pick up the Vachons for a night at the theater.

He responded by saying, ''Mama in love with Henri? You think so?''

''Yes, I do.''

''Well, I share your opinion. I believe they've been in love for years but haven't acted upon it out of respect for François's memory.''

''I don't mean to be disrespectful, but François's death occurred many years ago. Your mother deserves some happiness.''

''I agree.''

After retrieving the Vachons, the two couples journeyed through the congested streets to the Orleans Theater. On the program tonight would be the noted Northern poet Louise DeMortie and the Black composer Edmund Dede, whose symphonic arrangements were especially adored by the citizens in his hometown of New Orleans.

The couples took their seats among the other elegantly attired members of the crowd. Most in attendance were the French Creole and free Black elite, though Sable did see a few soldiers and some missionaries who'd come South to help the freedmen. She also saw more than a few hostile eyes cutting her way.

Hester must have noticed them too because she leaned over and said quietly, ''You and I are probably the two most despised women here.''

''I know why the daggers are coming my way—I'm

reviled for marrying above my head—but what bone do they have to pick with you?"

"The same. I am married to Galeno and they are not."

Sable caught the eye of a particularly hostile older woman who'd accosted Sable at the market one morning. "See that old bat over there?"

Hester did.

"Her name's Heloise Trudeau. She told me to my face that I had absolutely no business marrying into the house of LeVeq. She said slaves belong in the shacks in Freetown, not in the ballrooms of their betters."

"Oh, really. She had Raimond picked out for her own daughter, I'm guessing."

"Yes."

"Well, I'm treated no better. I met Galen's set for the first time when his grandmother Vada died back in '59. Some of the people were pleasant, but many were as cold as Michigan in January. Galen promised me we'd have very few dealings with them from then on, and he's kept that promise. I avoid them whenever possible."

"I lack that luxury. I live here."

The lights went down, curtailing further conversation.

The performances were magnificent, and afterward many in the crowd retired to Archer's restaurant for sustenance and socializing. Upon securing a table for their wives, Raimond and Galeno spent a good portion of the evening engaged in debating the topic on everyone's lips, Louisiana's political situation.

The most intriguing bit of new news had to do with a convention being proposed for early fall. It would reportedly bring together native White radicals and influential members of the free elite. The purpose: to affiliate Blacks with the Republican Party. The convention was being promoted in part by the former editor of the now defunct *L'Union*, Louis-Charles Roundanez, and his new publishing partner Jean-Charles Houzeau, a Belgian-born aristocrat and astronomer whose radical politics had cost him his job at the Belgian Royal Observatory in 1849. The two men were now publishing a newspaper called *La Tribune de la Nouvelle Orleans*, more commonly known as the *Tribune*, the first and only Black daily in the nation. Unlike *L'Union* which had spoken mainly for the French-speaking, free Black Catholic interests of New Orleans, the *Tribune* was published in both French and English. It also took a wider view and attempted to tie the fates of the freed and the free together. The new paper had been widely embraced by White radical elements in Louisiana state politics and by Blacks of all classes. Its editorials called for suffrage for all men of color, equality, and desegregation of the state's schools and New Orleans's streetcars. It also called for clear laws to govern the division of Union-confiscated plantation land among the freedmen.

When Raimond and Galeno finally made their way back to their table, they found their wives surrounded by admirers, and seemingly involved in a serious discussion. Raimond heard Sable declare to someone, "Sir, you are an idiot."

A few chuckles rose from the crowd. The recipient of Sable's comment, a thin young Black man in a cleric's collar, appeared stunned. "Madame LeVeq, surely you agree that education is essential. You yourself are an enlightened woman."

"Yes, I am, and I agree education is essential to our race. However, I take issue with Northern Gideonites who wish to replace our preachers and our teachers with men handpicked by themselves."

"But we are well trained and I am ordained. We came down here to help these unfortunate souls."

"And we unfortunate souls are truly grateful, but you can't mandate how people worship."

"But the preachers here are ignorant."

Sable said coolly, "In some parts of the South those same men preached the Word in the quarters when it was against the law to do so. They may lack your extensive training, Brother Julius, but many are eloquent and all are committed. How many of the freedmen preachers have you met?''

"Enough to know that they should be replaced. Condoning and encouraging all that shouting and yelling and jumping up and down is not the way to conduct a service to Him.''

"We unfortunate souls are tasting freedom for the first time in generations, Brother Julius,'' Hester told him. "If folks want to praise Him by standing on their heads, who are you to say it's wrong?''

He hastily turned away from Hester's condemning eyes and said to Sable, "Madame LeVeq, I conducted a service on Sunday at one of those tent churches. My service was both saintly and dignified. In response they called it boring and mocked me as a Presbyterian.''

Sable tried to hide her smile. "Then find a congregation that will appreciate your saintly dignity, and leave other folks be.'' She turned to her adoring male crowd and asked, "Wouldn't you agree, gentlemen?''

Raimond noted that not a single man protested, but then, they would have agreed that the moon consisted of cheese if she'd asked.

Unfortunately, the young cleric didn't have enough sense to lick his wounds and retire. "Fine. I'd like your opinion on this then. I heard a so-called preacher open the service by asking his followers to 'tumble with him through the third chapter of John'! What does that mean?''

"Did you ask him?''

"Of course not!''

Hester asked, "How on earth are you going to learn enough about the freedman to be of any help if you don't ask?''

Both women waited for an answer.

When he gave none, Sable spoke to him honestly. "Brother Julius, you are an intelligent and educated

member of the race and therefore very valuable to our
future, but the freedmen need your help, not your contempt.''

His pause suggested he took her words to heart, but
his terse words said otherwise. ''I will try and remember
that. Good evening ladies.''

He pushed his way through the crowd and was gone.

Raimond moved to his wife's side, and in response to
her welcoming smile, said, ''You have such a wide array
of admirers, *ma reine*. First Gaspar and now Brother
Julius. Where are they all coming from?''

''The Gaspars I don't mind,'' she replied, ''but
Brother Parham Julius and his ilk annoy me no end.''

Julius was not the first Northern missionary to come
South and complain about the uninhibited nature of
many of the freedmen church services. The teachers in
the freedmen schools had also come under fire. Sable
agreed that some of the teachers were unskilled, but they
were helping those who had even less learning than
themselves, and every letter learned was a step forward.
In her opinion the missionaries should be rolling up their
sleeves and jumping into the fray instead of standing on
the perimeter shaking their fingers.

Raimond asked, ''Are you ready to go home?''

She nodded. Because of all that *discussing* last night,
she hadn't gotten much sleep.

As the couples walked back to the adjoining hotel,
Raimond told Hester and Galeno about Juliana's upcoming birthday ball for Henri. Though the ball wouldn't be
held for another two weeks, Galeno consulted his wife
and they agreed to postpone their departure so they
could attend. Galeno hadn't seen Henri in many years
and wanted to stay in town so he could also raise his
glass in the birthday toasts. The couples promised to see
each other the next day, then said good-bye.

That night while Raimond slept beside her, Sable lay
awake thinking. It was now late August, and last year
at this time, she'd been a Fontaine slave struggling to

find enough to eat on a dying plantation. Mahti had been alive and Vashti living in the cabin next door. Rhine's whereabouts had been a mystery, and she had not owned one good dress to her name. Now, she had more dresses than Queen Victoria and a family and friends who cared. Rhine crossed her thoughts often. Had he found peace? If she passed him on the street, would he acknowledge her or walk past her with the nonseeing eyes of a White stranger? The sadness of not being able to answer those questions lingered in her heart.

But she had much to be thankful for. Out of the flames of Mahti's tragic death, Sable's life had been reborn like the fabled phoenix. From the camps to Boston. From a contraband queen to a wife in the celebrated house of LeVeq. Never in her wildest dreams had she imagined she would go from digging yams with her bare hands to finding a freedom that included a dessert named in her honor! Life was amazing, and she vowed to be thankful for it every day for as long as she lived. Amen.

Sable and Hester spent the next few days conducting interviews for Sable's new house staff. Although the small mansion had so many rooms that just the thought of mopping all the floors gave Sable nightmares, she'd told Raimond she didn't need help. He'd insisted. He'd cited her status as a LeVeq wife as one of the reasons she had to hire servants. Also, the freedmen needed jobs.

Sable finally settled on a housekeeper called Mrs. Bernice Vine. Sable liked her, as did Hester. Mrs. Vine was a tall, big-boned woman who'd been a house slave in Mississippi before the war. She boasted of being an excellent cook and had extensive experience running a large household.

Mrs. Vine did have one concern, however. "Will I have time off to see my daughters up in Baton Rouge?"

"Of course," Sable replied.

"I'm only asking because my last employer wouldn't allow it."

"He wouldn't allow you to see your family?" Hester asked, both outraged and surprised.

"No. He said the contract I signed didn't provide for it."

It was a common problem. Planters were taking advantage of the quasi-legal work contracts the government demanded Blacks now sign. Many former slaves were unwittingly hiring themselves out for life.

Sable asked, "How did he come to free you from the contract?"

"I freed myself. I got up one morning, packed my belongings, and headed down the road. Since my daughters were here in Louisiana, this is where I ended up."

"Rest assured, you'll have plenty of time of your own," Sable told her.

When the formalitites were completed, Sable took Mrs. Vine around to her room on the far side of the house. The new housekeeper peered around the large space. "Who will I be sharing this with?"

"No one."

Mrs. Vine's eyebrows rose in surprise. "I'll have this room to myself?"

"As long as you are with us, yes. And feel free to fix it up however you like."

Sable watched Mrs. Vine walk slowly around the room. She took a seat on the edge of the canopy bed and bounced a few times to test the mattress. She examined the newly upholstered chairs and the highly polished armoire and writing desk. "I believe I will like it here, Mrs. LeVeq."

"I believe you will too."

Sable and Hester took a walk outside later that day. Earlier in the week, they'd hired a gardener who was planting shrubs when the two women walked up.

"Afternoon, Mrs. LeVeq, Mrs. Vachon," he said, smiling.

"Good afternoon, Mr. Harper," Sable replied. "How're things with you?"

Without stopping his work he said, "No complaints, ma'am. I'm still trying to accustom myself to being called mister, though."

Sable replied, "I'm having a simillar problem, but mine is adjusting to having hired help. I'm a former slave too, you know."

"As am I," Hester admitted. "Watching someone else do the chores I'd been doing all my life took a bit of getting used to."

Harper looked them both over as if seeing them in a new light. "I didn't know that," he said.

Sable nodded. "Mr. LeVeq has been free all his life, but I have not."

Sable knew from her interview with Mr. Harper that he'd purchased some of the confiscated acres owned by the government. He had a wife, Sara, and twin little boys, Grant and Sherman. By day he worked as a gardener, then went home to them in the evenings.

Mr. Harper and Hester spent a few moments discussing landscaping plans, then the ladies settled beneath the sheltering canopy of a large tree. Hester stripped off the black crocheted gloves Sable had never seen her without and began scratching the backs of her hands, saying, "I don't think this baby likes my gloves very much. My hands itch constantly."

Sable tried not to stare at the startling sight of her friend's indigo-colored hands, but she apparently didn't hide her surprise well enough because Hester said, "When I was a child, I was a slave on an indigo plantation in the Carolinas. They'll be stained this way until I die."

"I didn't mean to stare."

"Don't apologize. I used to be very secretive about them around strangers, but Galen has helped change my attitude. I still wear my gloves more often than not when we're away from home though. Maybe the baby is trying to make me set them aside for good.''

"Maybe."

They were still seated there sometime later when they spied their husbands walking in their direction. "You know," Hester remarked, "if there were a contest to determine which one of them is the handsomest, there would have to be a tie."

"I agree. They are two handsome men, and if you don't believe it, just ask them. They'll tell you."

"They certainly will." Hester laughed.

The men had been spending their days seeing to business, meeting with ship builders, accountants, and potential customers and merchants. As they approached, the ladies stood to greet them with short kisses of welcome.

Raimond asked, "What have the two of you been doing while we were away?"

"I hired a housekeeper," Sable declared. "Her name is Mrs. Bernice Vine."

"Very good," Raimond said. "And are you going to let Mrs. Vine do her job without helping?"

"I suppose so, but it is very hard for me to have servants, Raimond. Mrs. Vine hasn't served a single meal, yet already I feel guilty making her wait on me."

"I felt the same way at first," Hester admitted as she stood in the circle of her husband's loving arms. "Maxi finally and firmly explained to me that service was her job, and that we had hired her for that purpose. For a long time she wouldn't let me even enter the kitchen, because I always wanted to help her."

"So how do you feel about servants now?" Sable asked her.

"After six years, I'm more comfortable around them, but I still jump up and help more than I probably should."

"Yes, you do," Galeno said, "but Maxi has learned to tolerate it because she loves you as much as I do."

He kissed her softly, making Sable wonder if she and Raimond would ever be so close.

The men escorted their wives back to the house. After Raimond met the new housekeeper, they all piled into Raimond's carriage to attend dinner at Juliana's.

Dinner with Juliana and Henri was a sumptous affair. Little Reba now ruled over Juliana's kitchen, and the wonderful food she prepared made Sable understand why Juliana had been so keen on hiring her.

After the dinner dishes were cleared away by one of the new kitchen maids, they sat and discussed Henri's upcoming birthday ball. Sable couldn't believe how many people Juliana had invited. "Will there truly be so many people attending?"

"There'd be even more if the house could hold more. Henri is a very well-known and popular man," her mother-in-law responded proudly. "He's been in the suffrage fight for many years and knows people of all races and from all walks of life. It will be considered an honor just to receive an invitation."

Raimond said, "Speaking of who might be attending, Mama, did you send an invitation to Jamal and his father, Yuseff?"

"I did, but considering the pace of the mail, they probably won't receive it until long after the event."

"Where do they live?" Sable asked.

"In a small principality in North Africa," Henri replied. "I've known Yuseff for many years. His eldest son Jamal attended university in Paris with Raimond and Galeno."

Galeno looked at Raimond and said, "How do you think our old friend Ezra Shoe likes Africa?"

"Probably hates it," Hester said with a giggle.

Raimond noted the confusion on Sable's face and explained, "Ezra Shoe was once a slave catcher. Back in '59 he stole Hester's free papers, kidnapped her, and tried to take her south and put her back on the block."

"But Galeno and Raimond rescued me," Hester declared triumphantly.

Galeno took up the tale. "Rather than kill Shoe for trying to abscond with my lady love—"

"Which is what I wanted to do," Raimond interrupted Galeno to point out.

Galeno grinned. "We came up with a slightly more novel punishment. We shipped him to Jamal as a present. Our old friend is always in need of someone to clean his stables."

Sable's eyes widened, "Truly?"

"Truly," Hester replied.

Juliana said, "I thought it very apropos in light of the man's nasty occupation."

"How do you know he won't try and escape?" Sable asked.

"Because death is the penalty for escaped slaves there."

"He's a slave, now?"

Raimond nodded. "If he thought the block was good enough for Hester, we thought he deserved a taste of it himself."

The next day, Raimond sat at his desk at the Freedmen's Bureau and wondered how much longer he could stomach working on its behalf. In his hand was a directive from Bureau Commissioner General O.O. Howard. It bore the name Howard Circular 15, but everyone with an ear to the wind knew the volatile decree had come directly from President Johnson's White House. The edict essentially returned all confiscated land to its original owners. As a consequence, all land deeds held by Black freedmen were no longer valid.

Raimond found the news absolutely stunning. He knew President Johnson had spent most of the summer using his power of pardon to restore lands and plantations to the men who'd been Union enemies less than four months earlier, but he'd never thought it would come to this. The Louisiana bureau alone had leased over sixty thousand acres to freedmen. Black freedmen in Tennessee were leasing sixty-five thousand acres. General Sherman's Special Field Orders No. 15, which he had issued in January 1865, had settled forty thousand contrabands on lands that stretched from the Sea Islands south to Jacksonville. Each head of household had been given a plot of land to homestead, as much as forty acres each, and a possessory title whose final disposition was to have been decided by Congress.

All total, the Freedmen's Bureau had 850,000 acres of confiscated land under its control. Now, thanks to Lincoln's successor, it did not appear the land would remain under Black stewardship for much longer.

What did the politicians expect Blacks to do? Already the military was being used in many cities, Richmond among them, to keep freedmen from entering. Hundreds of people were being rounded up by the local authorities and transported back into the countryside. In Charleston, freedmen had been ordered to leave the city and seek work opportunities in the rural areas. Never mind that those who'd attempted to find employment in the rural areas had been beaten and killed for their efforts by revenge-seeking Rebels, the city officials wanted them out of sight. Many freedmen were being told they could either sign work contracts or face jail sentences for insubordination. Contracts that offered one-tenth or one-twentieth percent profit for a full year's work of planting and harvesting were being declared valid by unscrupulous bureau agents who had only the planters' best interests in mind.

Raimond firmly believed that many Black homesteaders, especially the war veterans, would arm themselves and refuse to be run off land they'd been told was their own. Owning land was the measure of a free man, and these men would die fighting to keep what was theirs.

Chapter 13

Like everyone else, Sable was stunned by Circular 15. Obviously President Johnson had not taken the race's concerns to heart. Already in New Orleans patrols were beginning to act upon the change in policy, herding freedmen into wagons and taking them from the city. Last week, a woman who'd come to New Orleans searching for her husband, who'd never returned after the war, had finally found him just as he was being carted away along with dozens of other men. She'd run after the wagon screaming for the driver to stop, but he'd never even slowed. Her efforts to find out where her husband and the others were being shipped had been met by a wall of silence from the military and indifference from the city fathers. The Freedmen's Bureau had eventually intervened and learned he'd been sent to a plantation out past the city where he and the others would be forced to sign work contracts heavily weighted in the planter's favor.

Sable's main concern was the children living on the streets. They, along with the aged and infirm, constituted the most vulnerable members of the race. She'd intensified her efforts to gather up as many as she could before they were hunted down by the military and placed with planters who could legally hold them in thrall for the rest of their lives.

She was particularly concerned about a group of three children whose small, unconventional family was headed by a twelve-year-old manchild named Cullen, one of the most intelligent and resourceful boys Sable had ever met. Finding them on the street was difficult; they were like wraiths, sleeping in trash piles, abandoned buildings, beneath wagons. Cullen kept his sisters fed by begging coins in storefronts, stealing produce down at the market, and rifling through scraps in the alleyways behind restaurants. She'd yet to hear the story of how he and his two sisters, Hazel and Blythe, came to be in New Orleans all alone, and it was possible she never would. Unless she found them.

She spent the day scouring Freetown, the schools, the churches, and every other place where freedmen congregated, but all to no avail. As evening approached, a despondent Sable asked her driver to take her through the business district one more time in the hope Cullen was begging coins for a meal or being fed scraps by one of the restaurant cooks. She found nothing.

She was particularly worried because she hadn't seen the three children in over a week, whereas she usually came across them at least twice in the course of seven days. She always tried to convince the fiercely independent Cullen to come and live within the safe confines of the orphanage, but he would always decline, saying he could take care of himself and the girls.

He had up until now, but he was of prime age to be kidnapped and sent to work. Sable knew he was intelligent enough to be aware of that fact. So far he had avoided the nets, but the situation for young boys like himself had grown decidedly more dangerous of late, and she would feel better if she knew he were safe.

When Sable stepped out of the hack in front of Juliana's house, she froze at the sight of Cullen, Hazel, and Blythe seated on the steps. Beside them stood a worried-looking Juliana and a silent but concerned-appearing Raimond.

As she approached, Cullen stood. He was brown-skinned, tall, and painfully thin. Although he claimed to be only twelve years of age, he had the eyes of someone much older, eyes that had known ageless sorrow.

"Good evening, Cullen," she said. "Did someone tell you I'd been searching the city for you and the girls?"

"No, but Hazel's bleeding, Miss Sable, and we can't make it stop."

Sable gave Juliana and Raimond, who were listening, a quick glance before she stooped in front of Hazel. "Where are you bleeding, sweetheart?"

"Between my legs, ma'am."

Sable looked at her sturdy brown legs and saw dried blood streaking them. "How long have you been bleeding?"

"Just a day or two."

Sable knew from previous talks with these children that Hazel and Cullen were twins and that Blythe was two years younger. Hazel's age made Sable suspect the bleeding stemmed from the onset of her monthly courses but she couldn't be sure. "Have you ever bled like this before?"

She shook her head no.

"Did you fall or get hurt somehow?"

Once again, no.

Sable helped the youngster stand and turned to Cullen. "You were right to bring her here, Cullen. It's her woman's blood. The bleeding will stop in a few days. In the meantime, I'd like to get her cleaned up."

He held Sable's eyes. "I didn't trust anyone else."

"Thank you," she replied quietly. She knew from her experience with him that it had probably cost his pride dearly to admit to needing help. In the short time she'd known him he'd never come to the aid shelters for anything. He seemed bent upon relying only on himself. "Will you and the girls stay for supper?"

He looked first to Raimond and then to Juliana, as if evaluating them, then nodded.

Sable and Little Reba took the girls upstairs while Juliana went in search of something clean for them to wear. Their departure left Raimond and a silent Cullen alone in the parlor.

Raimond did not know what to make of this proud-looking manchild. He and his mother had come home to find the three seated on the porch steps. In answer to their questions, Cullen had asked first if Miss Sable would be coming there today. When Raimond replied that she would be, Cullen said they would wait. Neither he nor the girls said another word. When Juliana offered to bring them something to eat, Cullen declined. It seemed the only thing they wanted was Sable.

Now Cullen stood off to the side observing Raimond from unwavering eyes. Raimond motioned him to a seat.

The boy declined. "No. We both know I'm too dirty to sit on the furniture. I will stand."

Judging by the look and the smell of him, he hadn't had a bath in some time. "How about a bath while the girls are taking theirs?"

"No, thank you."

Raimond reiterated his offer, this time in a firmer voice. "How about a bath while the girls are taking theirs?"

Apparently Cullen had no problem interpreting Raimond's tone, though pride still shone strong in his eyes. "That would be fine, sir."

Upstairs, Juliana had no female clothing that fit the girls, but she gave them each a too-big gown and robe. The fine material flowed like a river around them when they walked, making the girls giggle, their eyes sparkling. After Sable explained to the now-clean girls all about Hazel's bleeding, Little Reba put a tired Hazel to bed. Sable and Blythe went down for supper. Awaiting them stood a freshly scrubbed and stoic Cullen wearing a shirt and trousers that had once belonged to a young Phillipe LeVeq.

Like most Black children, Cullen and Blythe were polite and respectful. Every adult at the table could see that Cullen wanted to ask for more food once he'd cleaned his plate, but pride apparently kept him from expressing the desire.

Raimond told him, "Cullen, there is plenty if you'd like another helping."

"No, sir."

"Are you certain?" Juliana asked.

"Yes, ma'am."

No one pressed him any further.

When the meal was over, Cullen said to Blythe, "Go change your clothes and get Hazel. Tell her it's time to leave."

"She's sleeping," Sable told him.

"Will you wake her, please? It's late."

"Yes, it is, so why not stay here for tonight?"

"We can't. Blythe, go fetch your sister."

Raimond stopped Blythe with a gentle hand on her shoulder. "My mother has plenty of space. You and your sisters are more than welcome to stay."

"No."

"Why not?"

"We can't."

Sable admitted, "Well, they'll have to stay because I put their clothes in the trash bin, Cullen. I can't visit the shops to replace them until they open tomorrow."

In response to his tight expression, Sable could only reply, "I'm sorry, Cullen. Their clothing was full of lice. I couldn't let them put the dresses on again, not in good conscience."

Sable saw him glance Raimond's way before returning his attention to her. "If I leave my sisters here for a while," he said, "will you see to their care?"

Sable held his dark gaze. "Explain, please."

"It is becoming more and more dangerous in the city. If I am kidnapped, my sisters will have no one. I'd prefer they live with you."

Before she could answer, Raimond drawled, "Only if you agree to stay here with them. If not, they'll have to take their chances on the streets with you."

Sable knew her eyes must be as wide as saucers. Juliana's certainly were.

The two males warily evaluated each other.

Finally, Cullen replied, "I insist upon a contract."

"I wouldn't have it any other way," Raimond answered coolly. "Shall we retire to the study?"

He gestured and Cullen followed him out.

The negotiations lasted until very late that night. Little Reba took in cognac and coffee for Raimond and lemonade for Cullen.

Sable put Blythe to bed in one of the spare bedrooms, then joined Juliana keeping vigil in the parlor. "Does Raimond know what he's doing?" she asked.

"Apparently he does. He would not make such an offer if he had no plans to honor it. Your question should really be, are you ready to be a mother to three?"

"I don't believe anyone is ever ready to take on three new children all at once, but I've already accepted them into my heart. So I believe my answer is yes."

Sable and Raimond decided to stay at Juliana's for the night and take the children to their new home in the morning. Now, seated together on the loveseat on the verandah of Raimond's old bedroom, Monsieur and Madame LeVeq watched the moon rise and talked about the three new additions to their family.

"What in the world have I done?" Raimond asked with a small chuckle.

"Opened your heart so it could encompass three orphaned souls."

He rewarded her by kissing her brow. "Cullen insisted that everything be set down on paper—everything from arrangements for the girls' schooling to when he could come work for me at the shipyard. Amazing young man. Wanted me to write down that he could begin learning to read tomorrow.''

Sable shook her head. "Did he tell you where they're originally from?"

"He didn't offer much—just that their parents are dead. Afterward, and I'm not certain when, a preacher brought them from a camp in Mississippi to New Orleans."

Sable thought back on the evening's surprising outcome. "Cullen didn't really want to stay here with us."

"I know, but I intentionally left him little choice. He'd already admitted the streets weren't safe for his sisters. They're not safe for him either, no matter how clever he thinks he is. I offered him the means to stay and to save face as well. That's very important to a twelve-year-old lad."

"Do you think his sister's bleeding played a role?"

"Maybe. At twelve, I certainly didn't have the fortitude to deal with a woman's courses. When he finished his bath, he and I talked about why his sister's body was changing, and how vulnerable to thugs she would be as she grew older. I could tell from his expression that he'd never been party to such a discussion before."

Sable snuggled against her husband's side. "He's really very intelligent, you know."

"I do. Once his schooling is finished he'll be a formidable force in whatever endeavor he chooses."

"Remember Levi Bond back in the camp?"

Raimond thought for a moment before he remembered. "Yes. There was a man who had two wives. Levi Bond married the wife the man didn't want. She had a passel of children, if my memory is correct."

"You're right, she did. Do you remember what you said about Bond at the time?"

"Nope."

"I don't recollect your exact words, but you said something like, it takes a very special man to take on a woman and her bunch of kids. Well, I think you are very special also, to take on three children and vow to raise them as your own.''

''Cullen touched my heart the moment I laid eyes on him. I've no idea how close he will let me get, but he and his sisters deserve a chance to lead full lives.'' He kissed her forehead, adding, ''We can't save all your orphans, but these three we can. In thinking back, I suppose I should have consulted you before agreeing to expand our family so dramatically, but I didn't want him going back on the streets.''

''I didn't either, and your solution is a perfect one.''

Content, Sable sat back to watch the twinkling stars.

The next morning, after Raimond and Sable shopped for clothing and beds for the children, they all traveled to the house Raimond and Sable now called home.

Mrs. Vine met them at the door. When Sable introduced the children and said they were now members of the family, the look of surprise on the housekeeper's face made Sable wonder if she would quit on the spot. Then she smiled and said, ''I always insist adults call me Mrs. Vine, but my best children friends call me Kitty. What's your favorite dessert, Miss Blythe?''

Blythe looked to Cullen for an answer and he said, ''She doesn't have one.''

Mrs. Vine's eyes met Sable's for a moment before she said, ''Well, every boy and girl should have one, so I guess I'll have to feed you nothing but sweets and treats until you decide. How about we start with the strawberry tarts I just took from the oven?''

Sable couldn't decide which child seemed most delighted.

''Strawberry tarts sound fine,'' Hazel offered.

''Then strawberry tarts it shall be.''

Mrs. Vine sailed off to the kitchen, leaving three very stunned children in her wake.

The children looked over the expansive room with its beautiful furniture and paintings, and the irrepressible

Blythe asked, "Is our new family rich or poor?"

Sable looked to Raimond in surprise.

Cullen answered, "Rich, Blythe. Richer than old Master Wheeler."

"Is Cullen telling the truth?" Hazel asked Sable.

Sable struggled a moment, trying to come up with an answer, before finally replying, "If Cullen means we are rich with love and a family who cares, then yes, we are richer than old Master Wheeler ever was."

Hazel looked skeptical but didn't say more.

Raimond herded the children upstairs to see their new rooms. Cullen would have a room of his own, but the girls wanted to share for now.

"Cullen, come help me bring in the beds," Raimond invited.

And thus began the first day in the newly expanded house of LeVeq.

In the days leading up to Henri's ball, Sable spent fewer hours doing charity work and more time with the children. There were clothes to be purchased, Brats to meet, and lessons to begin. None of the children could read, but they took to their studies like ducklings to water. Cullen seemed the most driven, and each night he fell asleep atop his books. He was no more talkative or less watchful than before, but he seemed to be settling in nicely. *Grandmere* Juliana and the new uncles did their part too: Archer took the girls shopping and then to his restaurant for lunch; Phillipe took them all down to the docks and gave them a tour of his ship. Each brother spent time helping the children adjust to their new lives, and Sable gave them all sisterly hugs in reward for their kindness.

The night of the ball finally rolled around. After a week of seemingly never-ending childrearing, all Sable really wanted to do was soak in a tub until the next day. She rallied, though, having looked forward to the grand event for weeks. Were all mothers this exhausted? She wondered.

As the bedroom door opened and Raimond walked in carrying an armful of roses and lilies, her spirits perked up. He presented the bouquet with a sweeping bow. "For you, madame, in honor of your recent motherhood."

She took the blooms with a smile and tears of gratitude. She seemed to be crying at the least little thing lately, and had no idea why.

Raimond saw her tears and gathered her into his arms. "I didn't know you were going to cry, *ma reine* . . . "

"They're happy tears, I think."

He tightened his embrace, making her feel cherished.

Looking down, he kissed her sweetly and said, "Being parents has cut deeply into our *discussion* times."

"I know. We haven't lectured each other in over a week."

He grinned. "You're keeping track?"

"Aren't you?"

In response, his hands began roaming slowly over her curves. Her dressing gown was open and he treated her bared breasts to a soft, warm palming. "Yes," he said, lowering his mouth so he could touch his lips to her half-parted mouth. "And I miss you . . . "

A sharp knock on the door made him raise his head. "What?" he yelled out.

"Raimond!" Sable chastised. "It's probably one of the children."

Sable adjusted her gown and went to the door. It was Blythe.

"What's the matter, sweetheart?"

"Hazel took my pencil and won't give it back!"

Sable chuckled and sighed all in one sound. "Tell Hazel I said to return your pencil or she won't get to watch the ball tonight."

"Yes, ma'am." Blythe stomped off.

Sable closed the door and turned back to her husband,

who stood shaking his head across the room. His eyes were filled with humor.

He said, "As soon as they can read better, I'm making a 'Do Not Disturb' sign for that door."

"I'll help," Sable vowed with a smile.

The road leading to Juliana's house was choked with all manner of vehicles, all moving at a snail's pace. It took Raimond's carriage a full thirty minutes to reach the property. The house was so filled with people one could hardly move. Sable spotted the beaming man of honor standing next to a beautifully gowned Juliana. The crush around them was so dense, it ensured she and Raimond would not get to offer their congratulations for some time, so they headed for the stairs. The children would be spending the night at their *grandmere's*. No one had any idea how long the festivities would last and Sable did not want to have to put three sleepwalking children into a carriage just before dawn. They would watch the goings-on from the top of the stairs for an hour or two, and then it would be off to bed.

After making certain the children had a good viewing spot, Sable and Raimond left the elegantly attired Cullen in charge of his fancy-gowned sisters, gave the girls kisses and last-minute instructions on minding their manners, and went down to join the ball.

Sable held Raimond's hand as he threaded his way through the crush toward his mother's side. They were stopped often by male and female acquaintances who congratulated them on their new brood. Sable saw many highly regarded members of the free elite community: merchants, bankers, business owners, doctors. She and Raimond paused to say hello to the newspapermen Louis-Charles and Jean-Baptiste Roundanez before moving on.

They finally reached Juliana's side, where they received hugs from her and an enthusiastic Henri. Sable and Raimond stayed beside them for a while, helping to receive the guests and murmuring thanks for the many well wishes. One by one the Brats made their appearances. Beau and Phillipe arrived with the young ladies they were courting. Archer and Drake arrived alone.

This event was the first Juliana had hosted since the war. According to Raimond, his mother's parties were fabled. The crowd eventually moved to the newly refurbished ballroom, where they were greeted by the melodic stains of the lively, six-piece band.

One could hardly hear the music for all the happy chatter. The buffet was well stocked with all manner of delicacies—gumbo, seafood cakes, jambalaya, and hopping john, to name a few. For dessert there were fools and cakes and the tarts Little Reba and her new staff had been preparing since dawn yesterday. Raimond filled a plate, then he and his wife slipped out onto the terrace for some fresh air.

There were quite a few people walking the grounds. Inside, the heat was stifling, but out here where a soft breeze blew Sable sighed at the cooling relief. She told her husband, "This is infinitely better than the crush in there. I seriously thought I would swoon, it was so warm."

"You should have said something. We could have escaped earlier."

"No, I'm fine now."

"Are you certain?"

She nodded.

She helped herself to some of the roasted hen on her plate. As she chewed she glanced up to find him watching her intently. Trying to talk politely around the meat in her mouth, she asked, "Is something the matter?"

"Did I tell you how beautiful you look tonight?"

"No, as a matter of fact, you did not."

"Then let me remedy that oversight. You are the loveliest woman in all of New Orleans."

She set aside her plate and closed the short distance between them, her gauzy off-the-shoulder gown rustling as she moved. "Just in New Orleans?" she asked saucily.

He chuckled. "Being humble is not your strong suit."

Her eyes sparkled with mirth. "You should talk."

He grinned and stroked her cheek. "I'm glad you're in my life, Sable LeVeq."

She placed her hand against his bearded jaw. "And I am honored to have you in mine, Raimond LeVeq."

He turned her hand over so he could place a tender kiss in the palm. "You know, I'll bet we can find a nice private spot where we might *discuss* a few topics of interest."

"Oh really? Then I propose we see the children off to bed at once and search out this *discussion* spot."

They turned to go back inside, waiting for a well-dressed woman to exit the doors before they could reenter. Both Sable and Raimond nodded politely as she passed. A quick glance at her familiar features made Sable widen her eyes in shock. "Bridget!"

The woman stopped and scanned Sable's face, then she too stared in shock. "Fontaine!" she screamed.

The two women hugged happily until Bridget noticed Raimond's cool stare.

"Major?"

Raimond inclined his head in acknowledgment, his eyes hard. "How are you, Bridget?"

"Fine. I've been fine," Bridget stammered. She stared at Sable again. "What are the two of you doing here?"

"He's my husband," Sable explained.

"Your husband?" Her voice reflected her surprise.

Bridget scanned Raimond again, almost in wonder. "We *have* been out of touch, haven't we?"

"Yes, we have," Raimond answered, "so let's find a place where we can get reacquainted."

Bridget appeared to want no such thing, but considering Raimond's mood, and the many unanswered questions left from that fateful night at the camp, she had little choice but to cooperate.

They went to Juliana's solarium. Raimond used a key on his chain to undo the lock, then ushered them both inside. He found an oil lamp and lit the fuse. The light revealed Juliana's blooming roses and lilies in all their exotic beauty.

Bridget began, "So tell me how you two came to be married."

"I've a better question," Raimond said. "Did you know Randolph Baker was a Confederate spy?"

The blunt question seemed to throw her for a moment, but she gathered herself and answered simply, "Yes."

Sable felt sick to her stomach. "You did!"

"Yes."

"Why didn't you tell me?"

"Would you have left the camp with him, had you known?"

"Of course not."

"That's why I didn't tell you. You'd've stayed there, and wound up Lord knows where, had Morse taken you back."

Sable countered, "I agree my life might have been in jeopardy, but Baker was a spy."

"Yes, he was. But he also got us to Boston safely, did he not?"

"He did, but Bridget, you should have told me."

"Why? So you could've told someone? I lived with you, Fontaine. You're too honest. I was afraid you'd give it all away."

"So my wife was not privy to Baker's plans?" Raimond asked.

"Fontaine? Of course not."

"Do you know Baker's real name?"

Bridget seemed surprised. "It isn't Baker?"

"No, he took the name and identity of a dead soldier."

"Now that's news to me. I guess I didn't know him as well as I imagined."

Sable asked, "Bridget, why would you involve yourself with a man like that?"

"Fontaine, I would have gone with old Jeff Davis himself if he could've found me a way out of that camp."

Sable understood Bridget's reasoning, she just couldn't condone it. "This whole mess has caused me quite a bit of misery. The major thought I was guilty of treason."

"Well, you weren't."

Sable looked at Raimond, whose whole demeanor conveyed his irritation.

"What are you doing here at the party?" he asked Bridget.

"My husband and I are here for the Radical Convention. He and Henri Vincent are well acquainted."

The convention would be bringing together many of the South's Black leaders and White radicals for the purpose of throwing their weight behind the Republican Party.

Bridget asked, "Are the two of you acquainted with Mr. Vincent also?"

Sable explained, "The ball is being given by Raimond's mother. This is her home."

"Isn't that something? Your family is well respected in my husband's circle."

"Glad to hear it," Raimond said.

"When did you marry?" Sable asked.

"About six weeks ago."

"To whom?"

"He's a minister named Clive Day. He has a small church outside Boston."

"A minister?" Sable asked skeptically.

"Yes, and if he finds out about my past, it will kill him. Please, don't tell him."

Sable had never seen Bridget look so serious. Her impassioned plea made Sable think Bridget might actually care for her minister husband. "Do you love him?" she asked.

"Yes. For the first time in my life, I'm in love, Fontaine, and I don't want to mess it up. Not when I'm attempting to put my past behind me. I do missionary work now, hold Bible classes for the church ladies. I'm not ashamed of my past, but if it comes to light, he'll bear the shame, and I couldn't live with that."

Sable could see that Raimond viewed Bridget with a jaundiced eye, but she asked him anyway, "Does anyone have to know? I mean, you said yourself that Baker's comrade was apprehended before he could cause any harm with Sherman's plans. Can't we just let it lie?"

Raimond knew he would never be able to deny her anything. He'd move the Sphinx into her dressing room if she asked. The fact that he had not believed Sable's claim of innocence did not sit well with him. "How do I know she's telling the truth? This minister husband may not even exist."

Sable hoped Bridget hadn't been lying because if she was, Sable planned on boxing her ears right there and then. "If we meet him, will that put your doubts to rest?" she asked. When he didn't reply, she said, "Bridget, let's go find this minister of yours and maybe afterward we can all go on with our lives."

Back inside, the heat and humidity had gotten worse, and there seemed to be even more people in the thick crowd. It took the three of them several minutes to find Reverend Day. He was much older than Sable had expected, but the warmth in his eyes as Bridget walked up spoke volumes about his feelings for her.

Bridget said to him, "Darling, I'd like you to meet some old friends of mine, Raimond and Sable LeVeq."

He shook Raimond's hand. "LeVeq, huh? Are you a member of the lovely Juliana's family?"

"Yes, sir, she's my mother."

"Ah, I am pleased to meet you."

"And I'm pleased to meet you. Bridget tells us you're a minister up in Boston?"

"Yes, and Bridget is a perfect minister's wife. What she sees in an old goat like me, I'll never know, but I'm glad she does. She's as faithful to me as my Bible."

Sable looked to Raimond as they spoke for a few more moments. Finally Raimond bowed. "It's been a pleasure to meet you, sir."

As she and Raimond waded back through the throng, Sable shouted over the din, "Well, what are you going to do?"

"You already know the answer to that. If I send Bridget to the authorities and break that old man's heart, I'll never sleep peacefully again."

His words made Sable love him even more.

While the ball continued downstairs, Sable and Raimond went upstairs to tuck the children into bed. In Phillipe's old room, they found them dressed in their night clothes, seated at the feet of Hester and Galeno Vachon, engrossed in listening to an adventure story Galeno was telling.

At their entrance, Hester looked up. The children turned too and upon seeing their parents began to clamor for attention.

Galeno said, "I was just telling them the exciting tale of the fabled Black Daniel."

"The Black Daniel was the cleverest slave stealer ever," Hazel pronounced.

"Oh really?" Raimond drawled. "The way I heard it, the Black Daniel had an even more clever best friend who had to save the Daniel time and time again, because he kept getting into scrapes he couldn't get out of."

Galeno shook his head. "Nope, I never heard that."

Chuckling, Sable headed the children to the beds Juliana's staff had moved into the room. Cullen had his own bed, but the girls were sharing.

After good-night kisses were exchanged by everyone but Cullen, who refused to accept such affection, the adults turned down the lights and left the children to their dreams.

As they walked down the hallway, Galeno said, "Hester and I wanted to say good-bye to them now because we won't have an opportunity in the morning."

At first light, they'd be heading back north to Michigan. It saddened Sable to know they were leaving. She hadn't gotten to know Hester the way she would have liked, but hoped that lack would be remedied in the future.

Hester added, "We wanted to say our good-byes to everyone else tonight as well. If I wait for morning, I know I'll cry all the way home."

Galeno eased her against his side. "She cries at the drop of a hat whenever she's carrying, so we're hoping by doing it this way, she won't upset herself so much."

Sable had gone absolutely still. Her head was buzzing with a thought so overwhelming she had to force herself to pay attention to what everyone was saying. Of late she'd been crying over the most trivial matters too. Could it be because she was carrying a child? She left the thought for now, but vowed to ask Juliana for the name of a doctor.

Raimond and Galeno embraced each other tightly. When they parted, neither seemed ashamed of the tears in their eyes.

Raimond said, "Godspeed, *mon frere*."

"*Adieu*," Galeno replied softly.

He bowed a farewell to Sable and escorted his wife away.

Sable turned to her silent husband. "The two of you care very much for one another."

"He is my brother and I am his."

"Well, we must plan to go north and visit them soon."

With lingering sadness in his eyes, Raimond said, "How about we escape this madness and I take you home?"

"If that is what you wish, Raimond, that is what we will do."

"Good. Then let's go find the buggy. We'll come back for the brood in the morning."

They'd journeyed about halfway home when Sable asked, "Are you still saddened by Galen's leaving?"

Buggy reins in hand, Raimond shrugged. "I am fine. I will miss him, is all."

And he would, greatly.

"You need cheering up."

He turned to her with the first smile she'd seen on his face since they'd left the ball. "Oh, really? You have something in mind?"

She grinned. "It's a magic trick."

"What type of magic trick?"

She slid over on the bench so they sat side by side, and replied to his question in soft, mysterious tones. "It's a mystical, magical trick that can make things grow right before your very eyes."

He chuckled at her play. "What types of things—specifically?"

"Specifically? This . . ."

She passed her hand slowly and possessively over her favorite part of his male anatomy and felt the flesh quicken to life. Holding him, she pointed out in a sultry whisper, "See . . . I told you . . ."

Raimond just about ran the horses off the road. Her warm, wandering hand made desire burst over his senses like an exploding shell. "You need a keeper . . . do you know that?"

"The queen doesn't like it when her knight is sad, so it is her desire that he be given something else to *discuss.*"

Raimond felt her seductively undoing the placket on his pants. In a voice that hovered between shock and delight, he asked, "What are you doing . . . ?"

"Freeing my knight so he can be happy again. Your

queen demands that you drive ... Pay no attention to what she is doing ... ''

Raimond tried to obey the royal directive, but as the *discussion* continued, the reins slid unnoticed from his hands and the horses came to a stop.

His head fell back against the seat as her warm mouth took him in and then slowly, slowly eased away. After a few moments of that, he growled and forced her to sit upright. ''You should be in jail!''

Sable licked her lips contentedly. ''That didn't make you happy?''

''So happy, I want to drag you over to the side of the road, Mrs. Wanton LeVeq.''

''Too many insects.''

He grinned. ''Just wait until I get you home.''

''I'll try, but it had better be quickly.''

Raimond headed the horses up the road at a full gallop. ''Is Mrs. Vine home?''

''No, I gave her the evening off. I gave *everyone* the evening off.''

''Good!''

They stumbled into the house, fondling, kissing, and ripping away their clothes. He made her ride him right there in the middle of the soft Persian rug that had been put down only that morning. Then he took her into the kitchen to introduce her to a counter they'd previously discussed. When she screamed her release, he groaned right after her, and the sounds of their love echoed throughout their home.

Chapter 14

Louisiana's long-anticipated Radical Convention convened two days later. Raimond had been chosen as a member of the state's delegation and was appointed to the committee that would draw up the convention's closing declaration. Sable and Juliana took the children to hear some of the speakers, but most days they left them in Mrs. Vine's care and joined the hundreds of other observers in the gallery. Speaker after speaker, representatives from all across the South, stepped up to the podium to demand eloquently that Blacks of all backgrounds be given the rights promised by the Constitution. The name of Lincoln was invoked many times over and the name of his successor damned.

President Andrew Johnson had not halted his pardoning of Rebel leaders and supporters. Even those who'd been termed traitors less than six months ago now had only to write to the former slave-holding president to receive absolution. Many Confederate military officers and government officials were now back in power as judges, political appointees, and local sheriffs, and they were using their positions to further accelerate the disenfranchisement of the freed slaves. Their policies and attitudes seemed to reflect the words expressed by the *Cincinnati Enquirer* at the close of the war: "Slavery is dead, the negro is not, there is the misfortune."

But most members of the race had absolutely no intention of accepting such sentiments quietly. In response to the political reversals threatening postwar progress, societies dedicated to the pursuit of civil rights were forming all over the South, bringing together freedmen, White radicals, Black soldiers, and the Black elite to ensure that the race's voice was heard.

The debates of the Radical Convention did not always go smoothly, as the delegates tried to settle on a position document. At many of the Black conventions, and this one was no exception, most of the leadership positions were held by mulatto and free elite Blacks. Some freedmen resented what they saw as an overrepresentation by the two classes and verbally aired their discontent. One delegate from Tennessee wondered publicly why the convention was even called a Black convention when there were so few true Blacks in attendance. He didn't care to have mixed-blood men—some of whom he described as "White as the editor of the *New York Herald*"—determining his political future. As he sat down there was a smattering of applause and a hail of derisive catcalls.

Sable didn't favor either side, and as the debate around the issue continued for the next four hours, she felt they were squandering time that could be better spent addressing the crisis facing the race.

Some of the delegates apparently shared her view, and chastised their colleagues for fiddling while Rome burned. They pointed out that Blacks from all walks of life were playing active parts in the quest for civil rights, not just the free, mulatto, and freedmen. In Mississippi where only a handful of free Blacks had resided before the war, the leadership was made up of Black army vets and their extended families. In Georgia and Alabama, Black ministers were more often the organizers and leaders.

Henri Vincent summed up the day's debate by sagely pointing out, "Free or freed, it hardly matters. We're all in this boat together, and we may as well accustom ourselves to rowing as one.''

He received a standing ovation.

Juliana had opened her home to the convention members, and over the course of the five days, it became Black Radical headquarters. Assisted by Sable and the wives of several other Louisiana delegates, she hosted teas, dinners, and luncheons. The delegates seemed to enjoy the opportunity to relax away from the debates, and even at midnight, the LeVeq door was open and the coffee hot.

Sable met many prominent men of all races in Juliana's parlor, one of the most memorable being the famous war veteran Robert Smalls, whose daring commandeering of a Confederate warship had to be one of the most exciting escape-from-slavery tales she'd ever heard. Smalls, now active in South Carolina politics and a delegate to the convention, told his story to Juliana and Sable one afternoon as they sat on the front porch during a convention recess.

''I'd been a slave working the Charleston waterfront for about ten years when the masters sent me to work on a steamer called the *Planter*,'' he told them. ''That was in April of '62. Before the war the *Planter* hauled cotton. She could hold up to fourteen hundred bales.''

''A large ship,'' Juliana said knowingly.

He nodded. ''A good size, yes. But after the war began, the Rebs converted it into a warship and armed it with a thirty-two pound cannon, a twenty-four howitzer, and numerous smaller armaments.''

Juliana whistled.

Smalls grinned, then continued. ''The only White men aboard were the captain and the two mates. Everybody else was Black, including the engineer, my brother John.''

Sable sat enthralled as he'd told how he'd planned his escape for a night when the three White men would be sleeping ashore. ''The opportunity came on May 12,

1862. There were sixteen of us, including my wife and three children and my brother's wife and child.''

At three in the morning they fired up the boilers and very casually set out to sea, flying the Confederate flag.

Smalls had planned his escape very carefully. He'd even acquired a large straw hat similar to the one the captain wore. His plan depended upon the Confederate forces in the harbor assuming the *Planter* had simply started the day early. They did. He passed each Confederate post by giving the proper salute with his whistle and was waved on. His ultimate destination lay with the Union fleet barricading the harbor. As the *Planter* approached the last hurdle, Fort Sumter, he donned the large straw hat and the captain's arms-crossed stance. The *Planter* gave the signal with the steam whistle, three shrill notes and a hiss, then waited. A tense moment later, they heard the last Confederate sentry sing out, "Pass the *Planter*, flagship for General Ripley." The sentry, thinking the boat was headed out to duel with the Union fleet, added as they sailed on, "Blow the damned Yankees to hell, and bring one of them in."

Once the *Planter* sailed out of the reach of the Confederate guns, Smalls and his men took down the Confederate flag and ran up a white bedsheet.

The Union fleet almost fired on them as they approached, but upon seeing the flag of truce, they held off.

"The navy officers were stunned to find only Blacks aboard, so I told them I thought the *Planter* might be of use to Uncle Abe. They made me a pilot on the spot, and later the *Planter*'s captain."

By the end of the story, a few others in the house had gathered around to listen. One of them asked, "Mr. Smalls, what would you have done had something gone awry during the running of the blockade?"

"I would have scuttled the ship," he said seriously. "And had it not sunk fast enough, we were prepared to link hands and jump to a watery grave."

*   *   *

While the convention was in session, Sable saw Raimond only late at night. She would awaken to sounds of him moving quietly around the bedroom undressing after a long day, then she would smile and sigh pleasurably as his warm body slid beside her beneath the sheets. Life had been so hectic of late, she had yet to tell him of the child that was growing in her womb. She made a mental note to let him know as soon as the convention ended and they had some time alone.

On the last morning of the convention, Hazel came into the kitchen and stood watching Sable frost a cake meant for that night's supper. Looking up, Sable asked, "Do you want something, Hazel?"

Sable continued her task while waiting for an answer, and when it did not come, she looked up again, concerned. "What's wrong?"

Across the kitchen, Mrs. Vine, working dough for the evening's bread, paused too upon seeing the serious set of the young girl's face.

Hazel said, "Cullen's gonna whip me if I tell."

"Tell what?" Sable asked.

She waited. The children hadn't been in her care for very long, but already she knew they each had distinct personalities. Cullen was moody and proud; Blythe, who appeared to be absolutely fearless, was a typical ten-year-old, with an active imagination and scores of questions. Hazel, on the other hand, seemed to be caught between wanting to appear grown-up and wise like her twin brother, and wanting to remain as silly and carefree as a child.

It was the wise, Cullen-like Hazel who was facing Sable at this moment. "Hazel, what are you trying *not* to tell me?"

"He's going to be real mad, but I'm worried about him coming to harm. He's been sneaking out at night."

"Sneaking out to where?"

Hazel shrugged. "Blythe and I don't know and he

won't tell us. He made us promise not to tell you, but . . .''

Sable placed a comforting arm around Hazel's shoulder and said softly, "It's all right, darling. You're worried about your brother, I understand. I told on my brother Rhine a few times too, and yes, he was mad. But he played with me again in a few days. So how often has Cullen been slipping out?''

"Since we came to live here. He even snuck out of Grandma Juliana's house the night of the ball.''

Sable's eye's widened. "How?''

"He lashed together all the sheets and went out the window.''

Sable stared amazed. Whatever was this manchild up to? "And you've no idea where he goes?''

"No.''

"Thank you, Hazel. Please don't say anything to Cullen for now.''

Hazel still didn't appear comfortable with her decision to reveal her brother's secret, but she nodded and departed for school.

Mrs. Vine turned to Sable. "What are you going to do?''

"What any mother would do. Find out what he's up to.''

Raimond came home late that night, dragging tired and wanting nothing more than a night of uninterrupted sleep next to Sable's warm curves. But when he entered the bedroom, and found his wife not only awake but dressed in men's clothes, he sensed sleep would not come soon that night. "And you are dressed for what occasion?'' he asked.

"Hazel says Cullen's been sneaking out at night.''

Raimond's fatigue vanished instantly. "What?''

Sable told him the story. When she finished, an astounded Raimond asked, "And she has no clue where he goes?''

"Not a one.''

Raimond found this hard to believe. "So why are you wearing those clothes?"

"Because if he leaves tonight, I plan to follow him and discover what he's doing."

Raimond shook his head firmly with denial. "No, you're not. The roads are too dangerous at night."

He knew as well as she of the reported crimes being perpetrated against people of color by roving gangs of White thugs.

"Then I suggest you come along as my protection, Sir Knight, because I'm going with or without you."

He didn't have to study her determined face for long to realize that this was not an argument he could win. "Okay. We'll both go. Just let me slap some water on my face."

They took up a vigil in the shrubbery below Cullen's window. It offered them an unimpeded view of his room and enough cover to remain hidden from sight.

Raimond knew this was supposed to be a serious endeavor, but he kept being distracted by the way Sable's trousers accentuated the sweet curve of her behind. The unconventional attire, unearthed from one of Juliana's trunks, had once belonged to Phillipe. As Sable explained to Raimond, she'd decided that dressing like a man would not only disguise her gender but also give her a freedom of movement not available to her in skirts. He believed her thinking sound, but considering the way the fabric hugged her hips, she didn't look like any man he'd ever seen.

The sound of Cullen's window being slowly opened drew his attention back to the matter at hand. While Sable and Raimond watched tensely, a long rope of lashed-together sheets was tossed out to aid Cullen's descent. It dangled against the house, eerily illuminated by the moon. Two big carpetbags were tossed out next; they hit the ground beneath the window with dull thuds. They then watched Cullen shimmy down the sheets. Once on his feet, he spent a moment glancing around the grounds, as if making sure it was safe to proceed, then picked up the heavy carpetbags.

Raimond stood up and said, "Good evening, Cullen."

The boy seemed to jump six feet in the air.

Sable stood up too.

Upon seeing them, Cullen's chin tightened.

Sable asked, "Will you explain what you're doing?"

For a moment he didn't reply. When he finally spoke it was only to say, "I must go."

He picked up the bags and took two steps but Raimond, not raising his voice, said, "Put the bags down, son."

Cullen halted in his tracks. He looked over at Raimond, then slowly eased the bags to the ground at his feet.

"Thank you. Now, Sable asked you a question, and I'd like you to answer her, please."

"I can't, because if I do you will forbid me to go."

"Well," Sable said, "it's for certain you won't be going if you don't tell me, so give us a chance, Cullen. We may surprise you."

He seemed to consider her words as he held first her eyes and then Raimond's. Finally he said, "Then come with me and I'll show you."

Cullen suggested Raimond drive the carriage because of the distance they would be traveling. So while Cullen and Raimond went around to hitch up the horses, Sable hurried upstairs to wake Mrs. Vine and inform her of the goings-on. She promised to keep an eye on the still sleeping girls, and Sable rushed back out to join the men.

Following Cullen's directions, Raimond drove them down to the New Orleans waterfront and into a run-down area of the warehouse district. Abandoned and damaged ships littered the shoreline, interspersed with the shanties and lean-tos of the homeless of all races. This was a highly dangerous area during the day, and according to newspaper reports, deadly at night. Sable found it incredible that Cullen claimed to have walked all this way each night alone. More importantly, what could be here to so powerfully attract a twelve-year-old boy?

Per Cullen's instructions, they stopped near one of the derelict ships, and Raimond set the carriage brake. It was so quiet, water could be heard lapping at the shore.

As they all got out, Raimond said, "Cullen, I hope this won't take long. An unguarded carriage will be a target for thieves."

Cullen said, "Don't worry. Pee Wee will watch the carriage."

Before either parent could ask who Pee-Wee was, Cullen placed his fingers to his lips and sent out a shrill whistle. A small, ragged child melted out of the shadows and appeared at Cullen's side. "Hello, Cullen."

"Hello, Pee Wee. This is Raimond LeVeq and his lady Sable."

Pee Wee looked to be around Blythe's age. "Pleased to meet you," he said.

"Pee Wee will watch over the carriage if you will give him a coin when we're done."

"Agreed," Raimond pledged.

They followed Cullen aboard a listing ship, then down below deck. Carrying the carpetbags, he moved confidently through the rotting vessel, while Sable and Raimond, trailing behind, stumbled and faltered over the dark, unfamiliar terrain.

Cullen pushed open a door and went inside. They followed.

A stub of a candle lit the interior of what had once been a small stateroom. It took a moment for Sable's sight to adjust to the dimness, but once it did, she found herself staring into the wary eyes of more than a dozen huddled children. There were about fifteen of them of varying ages, sizes, and shades, spread out in small groups.

Cullen said softly, "Everybody, these are my new folks."

No one replied.

Sable could now smell the foulness of the children's unwashed bodies. She had to assume they had been hiding here for some time. Just imagining their loneliness and what they were forced to do to survive from one day to the next made her want to take them all home.

Cullen bent to his carpetbags and began to withdraw food from them. There were portions of hens wrapped in linen napkins, bread, ears of corn, and three peaches— food he must have taken from the kitchen at home. He didn't have nearly enough to feed them all, but the big ones shared with the little ones, and soon each child had something to eat.

Sable knew she should be used to seeing such scenes, but knowing that children like these faced lives of hunger and hopelessness always tugged at her heart. Raimond must have sensed her mood because he came over and put an arm around her shoulders and hugged her tight.

Cullen explained, "I come each night because they have no one else."

Sable wanted to kiss him for his caring and courage but knew he wouldn't stand still for such a display.

Raimond looked down at this young boy he had claimed as son and felt his heart swell with pride. "I am very proud of you, Cullen."

Cullen's chin rose. "Thank you, sir."

Sable had no intention of leaving the children here in the dark, dank ship while she went back to her comfortable home, so she told Cullen, "They're coming home with us."

Cullen stared. "All of them?"

Raimond agreed. "All of them."

Sable took his hand and squeezed it, her eyes shining with love. He understood.

Their carriage wasn't large enough to carry all the children on the hour's drive back to the house, so Sable and Raimond piled in as many of the little ones as it would hold. The others were forced to walk, Cullen included, but he assured his parents that the older ones did not mind.

Raimond kept the pace slow to accommodate the walkers, giving Sable plenty of time to consider what she would do with the children once they were clean, fed, and rested. Her husband's family was fairly well off, but not even they could afford to clothe and feed fifteen youngsters. The established orphanages were already seriously overcrowded. She could send some of the children to orphanages elsewhere, but knew she'd spend a lot of time wondering if they were being treated fairly.

Maybe she could open her own temporary orphanage. Juliana and Henri knew lots of people. Perhaps they could direct her to families who would want to call the children their own. Hester would probably assist her in a quest for good homes in Michigan and Ontario, as would Bridget and Reverend Day up in Boston. If she could find a building to house them in while she made arrangements, and secure funds to pay for a small staff, she didn't see why she couldn't turn her idea into reality.

She looked past the small, dirty child asleep on her lap to her husband guiding the reins. He was a very special man, indeed. She knew few individuals who would open their hearts and homes this way, but he had, and she loved him more each day.

She asked him, "Were you pleased with the final day of the convention?"

"I was. We voted to affiliate with the Republicans and to ask Congress to govern Louisiana as a territory—in addition to demanding our full rights." He added, "Bridget and her minister send their best wishes. They left on the afternoon train."

"I never had an opportunity to see her after the night at Henri's ball. I wanted her address."

"She wrote it down for you. I have it in my coat back at the house."

"Raimond, I want to open an orphanage."

He chuckled at her abrupt change in subject. "Oh, really?"

"Yes. Not even the wealth of the house of LeVeq can feed and clothe all these children."

"True. So how would you begin?"

She told him her idea.

He mulled over her plans for a moment, then said, "Finding an old planter's place may be possible."

"Then you believe the idea is a sound one?"

"If I didn't, would it deter you?"

"No."

He grinned. "Then you have my full support."

Over the next few days, Sable and Raimond worked on settling the children into their home. The Brats, Juliana, Henri, and even Little Reba all helped. It took all of one day for them to be evaluated by a physician friend of Beau. The doctor declared them undernourished but otherwise in reasonably good health. Sable winced when she learned a few of the little ones bore the scars of rat bites. When bedtime rolled around, she squeezed as many as she could into the upstairs bedrooms, the parlor, and on the floor of the upstairs hallway. Juliana and the Brats contributed bedding and nightclothes.

That night, as Raimond and Sable sat out on their bedroom verandah savoring the end of yet another hectic day, Sable said, "Now we can guess why Cullen was initially so reluctant to stay with us."

"Yes, we can. There were others depending upon him as much as his sisters were."

"He's a remarkable boy, your son."

"That he is. His mother's pretty remarkable as well."

"So remarkable, she's about to add one more to the flock of children we already have."

Raimond turned to her in surprise. "You're planning on adding another orphan?"

"No, this child has parents, and will make his or her debut in a few months' time."

Raimond searched her happy green eyes, then asked excitedly, ''Our own baby?''

''Our very own. Now you and Juliana can claim the rest of the old pirate's estate.''

''To hell with the old pirate. I just want the two of you to thrive.'' He placed his hand on Sable's stomach. ''In a few months' time, you'll feel like a pumpkin.''

''And probably resemble one too.''

He kissed her softly and pledged, ''But you will still be *ma reine* . . .''

Juliana and Henri drove over the following morning. When Sable informed them of the impending arrival of yet another grandchild, the happy news reduced New Orleans's premier Black businesswoman to tears. Once the crying ceased, she imparted some good news of her own. A White radical business associate had graciously donated a house situated on fifteen acres of land for Sable's orphanage. He'd given her written permission to begin occupying the house at her convenience.

He had failed to reveal the condition of the place, however, something they learned upon their arrival at the site later that day. Although the roof was intact, the old mansion was a mess. It looked to have been occupied by either Yankees or squatters, neither of whom had bothered to clean up after themselves. The fireplace was littered with the bones of wild birds and small animals. Horses had been stabled in the kitchen, as indicated by all the fouled straw they found. The six large bedrooms upstairs bore more signs of occupation: bones in the grates and in some cases scorched spots in the floors, indicating that fires had been set there either for warmth or for cooking. Further inspection turned up a few dirty pallets, a hat bearing a Union insignia, and the broken hilt of a Confederate sword.

They were all disappointed to find the place in such disrepair, especially Juliana, who had to be held back from marching right back to the city to confront the man who'd donated the place, but Sable agreed with the ever wise Cullen, who said to his *grandmère*, "Once we clean it, it will be fine."

Soon the LeVeqs, the children, and a small crew of freedmen hired through the Freedmen's Bureau were tackling the enormous task of making the place liveable. Drake's expertise as an architect and builder proved invaluable. He instructed them on how to shore up the walls, refinish the floors, and rebuild the listing front porch.

One morning in late September, Sable and Juliana were in the kitchen shoveling out the straw and feces when Juliana announced in a wistful voice, "Henri is thinking of moving to France."

Sable paused in tossing a shovelful of straw into a wheelbarrow. "When?"

"After the new year."

Sable noticed the sadness in her mother-in-law's eyes. "I will miss him."

"As will I."

"May I ask you something?"

Juliana halted her shoveling for a moment. "Certainly."

"How long have you been in love with Henri?"

She resumed her work. "I am not in love with Henri."

"Juliana, it is unlawful to lie to the mother of your grandchildren."

Juliana grinned. "Is it?"

"Yes."

Sable waited for her to say more.

"Henri was best friend to my François."

"And?"

"And that friendship and his love for my sons are what has bound us together over the years."

"Nothing more?"

"Nothing more."

Sable didn't believe her for a moment but kept her opinion to herself.

The next day Sable parked her carriage in front of the small freedmen school her children were attending and waited for them to be dismissed. There were still a few minutes before they would come running outside into the sunshine, so to pass the time, she picked up the day's *Tribune* beside her on the seat.

The newspaper had been paying particular attention to the increasing violence spreading like brush fires across the South. Former masters and Rebels continued to exact revenge on former slaves. Henry Adams, one of the young freedmen who'd attended the convention, was quoted as saying that two thousand Blacks had been killed near Shreveport since emancipation. A freed woman named Susan Merrit from Rusk County, Texas, told of seeing Black bodies floating down the Sabine River.

Chilled by all the killing, Sable set the paper aside. The possibility that some of the violence would reach her family was a constant worry. Just the other day, Cullen and his sisters had been accosted on the way home from school by a group of mounted riders who'd declared the children had no business going to school and should be in the fields instead. Hazel and Blythe had been terrified, but Cullen had returned home furious.

The schools were becoming such targets of Rebel violence and retribution that Sable and Raimond no longer allowed the children to go back and forth to school alone. Many of the Whites who'd come South to found schools for the freedmen were pulling up stakes and heading back North—those who were still alive. It wasn't just the threat of violence that had intimidated so many into fleeing. A young White woman Sable had met a few months ago had gone to a teaching post in Lafayette Parish. According to letters she'd sent to the Freedmen's Bureau officers, she'd been shot at in both the school and the room where she boarded. Her students were also being fired upon. So far none had been killed, but one old freedman had been wounded so severely, his leg had been broken by the shells. The young woman despaired over the threats to burn her schoolhouse, especially considering that the closest military help was over two hundred miles away. Still, she refused to turn tail and run. Sable silently applauded her courage and rose to greet the children now streaming out of the schoolhouse.

Work on the orphanage house continued, and by the beginning of October, Sable and her charges were ready to take possession. She hired a small staff to do the cooking and cleaning. Drake built a small schoolhouse on the property. She did all the teaching there and opened up the classroom to other children residing nearby as well.

Sable had been so intent upon seeing to the children's care, she'd had little time to spare for her husband. Raimond suffered the neglect for more days than he cared to admit, then decided to take matters into his own hands.

His first order of business was to get rid of the children. He then arranged for a large and luxurious suite at Archer's hotel.

When Sable arrived home that afternoon, having spent the day at the orphanage, she found her husband seated in his study looking over what appeared to be a ship's manifest. He and Galeno were now back in the shipping business, and he'd resigned his post as a Freedmen's Bureau agent. He looked up at her entrance. "Good afternoon, sweet wife."

She went over and gave him a kiss on the cheek. "Hello, brave knight."

The silence of the house caught her attention instantly. "Where's Mrs. Vine?"

"I gave her the weekend off."

"Generous man. And Cullen and the girls?"

"Gone to pay a two-day visit to their lovely *grand-mére*. She promises to bring them back by Sunday. I, of course, told her she can keep them until they reach old age."

Sable grinned. "You know as well as I that neither of us could stand being without them for so long."

"Speak for yourself," Raimond drawled.

She laughed, knowing he was teasing. He had established a strong bond with all three of his adopted children and would be bereft if they were absent from his life. "So what shall we do in this blessedly quiet house for two full days?"

He waggled his eyebrows. "How about we make some noise of our own?"

Sable felt desire rise of its own accord. "What do you have in mind?"

He eased her down onto his lap and kissed her softly. "Oh, a little of this and a little of that."

"Sounds interesting . . ." she breathed, returning his sweet kiss with a sweet kiss of her own. "Where shall we begin?"

"Right here suits me just fine."

So while the children were away, the parents played.

By the time he carried her upstairs, she was already flowing with desire. Her outer clothing had been sensually discarded during the opening stanzas and she was left wearing only a paper-thin shift and her drawers as the symphony began in earnest.

He laid her tenderly atop their bed and shed his own clothing. His passion for her was displayed in all its ebony glory, and she reached out and stroked it with her hand. "Perfect time for another magic trick, I do believe . . ."

He grinned as he came closer, but as she began performing her wizardry, his eyes slid closed and all thoughts of humor fled. He had no idea where she'd learned such skills, and he somehow managed to put the question into words.

"Bridget," she replied.

"Bridget?" he echoed hoarsely while she continued to weave her spell.

"Yes," she whispered. "She said I should pay particular attention to the tip, as that will give the most pleasure . . ."

She proceeded to show him just how well she'd listened to Bridget's instructions during those nights back in the camp, and he stood there on shaking legs, reaping the benefits of his wife's sensual education.

Eventually he had to ease away, lest his pleasure culminate right then and there, and he joined her on the bed. Keeping her growing child in mind, he made love to her slowly, so slowly she was fairly begging by the time he eased himself into the warm, sweet place he favored most. They'd been away from each other for so long it didn't take long for *le petit morte* to claim them both or for their cries of pleasure to fill the silent room.

While she lay atop the bed throbbing and pulsing in the aftermath, he went down and brought up cauldrons of water he'd been simmering on the stove. He emptied them into the big bathtub. She stepped in and let the glorious warmth revive her, then stood so he could wash her clean. It took a while; his wandering hands kept dillying and dallying. When she was finally deemed clean again, she stepped out, her brain hazy with desire. He dried her leisurely, scandalously, then laid out her clothing.

She asked dreamily, "Why am I putting on clothes?"

"So we can go pick up a dress I had made for you," he told her as he washed himself in hot clean water from the last cauldron. "Of course, I'll only have to undress you later, but that's later . . ."

"And suppose I prefer not to dress or go out?" she queried brazenly, her eyes sultry.

"Then I can't give you a reward tonight for being a good girl . . ."

She smiled with the same sultriness. "Then I suppose

I will have to comply, because I am a good girl, and I do enjoy rewards."

As Sable stood in the shop wearing the dress Raimond had commissioned for her, she understood why Archer had warned her never to let Raimond choose her dresses.

"Do you like it?" he asked.

Sable looked at his expectant face and then at herself in the mirror and wondered if she should lie to the man she loved more than anyone else in the world. The dress was hideous, the cut and design as horrid as the color. "I certainly don't have anything like it in my wardrobe. Thank you, Raimond."

While he went off with a smile to pay the shop's proprietress, Sable ducked into the small dressing room to remove the gown. She'd just stepped out again with the dress over her arm when she was stopped cold by the sight of the man and woman who'd just entered the establishment. She didn't recognize the young woman, but the man was Henry Morse.

Sable immediatlely looked to Raimond, but his back was turned as he spoke to one of the clerks.

Morse's gaze brushed hers, then his eyes widened and he smiled. *He will be the jackal and you the antelope until his death.*

After excusing himself from his lady friend, Morse strolled over to Sable. "Sable, is that really you? Look at you in your fine clothes."

She didn't reply.

"What're you doing in Louisiana?"

"I was just about to ask you the same thing," Raimond said as he joined them.

"Well, if it isn't Major LeVeq. How are you, boy? Lots of folks I know are talking about you."

"I doubt it is flattering talk. I probably don't have a lot of friends in your circles."

"No, you don't."

Raimond smiled like a tiger playing with his meal.

"What brings you to New Orleans, Morse?"

"You know," he said in his thick Georgia drawl, "the hardest thing about emancipation is getting used to the lack of respect some of you show now. Before the war, you'd've addressed me as Mr. Morse or Marse Morse."

"Times are changing, aren't they?" Raimond replied. "Again, what brings you to New Orleans?"

"Damn Yankees took the Fontaine land, but I heard Louisiana has lots of land for sale, so I took the loyalty oath and bought me some. Looking to hire me some of your kind to help plant and harvest." His eyes traveled over Sable. "You always were a beautiful woman."

Ignoring the compliment, she asked, "Whatever happened to Mavis?"

"Married a Yankee soldier from Illinois. Sally Ann disowned her so fast it made my head spin, but Sally did the right thing."

"And where is Sally Ann?"

"At the house. We're married now, you know."

Sable glanced at the young quadroon who'd entered on his arm. She was looking over some expensive fabrics. Morse followed Sable's gaze. "She's just keeping me company until I get back to Sally Ann. You know I always had a weakness for golden meat."

Raimond's voice turned hard. "This reunion is over, Morse. Stay clear of my wife and you'll live a long life."

"You threatening me, boy?"

Raimond's smile did not reach his eyes. "No, Morse, that's a promise."

Morse appeared to swallow whatever invectives he was about to spill, then said unctuously, "Nice seeing you again, Sable. Maybe you can come up and visit me and Sally Ann sometime soon."

When Sable didn't reply, he nodded, smiled, and returned to his quadroon paramour.

Raimond watched him for a moment before saying, "He's going to be trouble, I can feel it."

Sable could too, but she refused to let his surprising reappearance cast a pall over what had been a wonderful afternoon with the man she loved. Putting aside all thoughts of Morse, she asked, "So, have I been good enough to earn that reward you promised?"

Her question chased away the dangerous clouds Raimond sensed building up inside himself. "Well, I don't know. Let's go over and settle into our suite at Archer's hotel and and we'll see."

Chapter 15

⁓∽∽⌒⌒

They spent the remainder of their holiday in a beautiful hotel suite making love, eating the gastronomical delights prepared by Archer's chefs, and never straying far from bed. Raimond sensed danger on the horizon and so kept Sable near, as if his arms alone would keep her safe. When the time came to return home, they were both a bit sad, but they'd had a wonderful time, and Fate willing, they would again.

They stopped at Juliana's to pick up Cullen and the girls before heading home. After parking the carriage out front, they started up the walk. Blythe came barreling out of the house like a miniature train and just about knocked Raimond down with her happy greeting. Hazel stood on the porch smiling with Drake at her side. They found Cullen inside, playing backgammon with Henri, while Juliana sat nearby offering encouragement. The rest of the Brats were also in attendance, as was the custom on Sundays after church.

After dinner, Raimond took his brothers into the study and told them about Morse and his connection with Sable.

Phillipe asked, "Do you think he means to harm her?"

"I think he means to have her, which is the same thing as far as I'm concerned. I haven't told Sable yet, but I'm going to Mobile next week for a convention. I'm counting on you Brats to keep my lady safe until my return.''

Archer drawled, ''If he knows our family at all, you'd think Morse would rather dine with the devil than accost Sable.''

''He'll be dining there permanently if he does,'' Drake promised.

Raimond inclined his head. ''I'm glad to hear we're of like minds.''

Beau asked, ''What's this Reb look like?''

Raimond began to describe Morse but paused when someone knocked on the study door. Phillipe went to answer it and found Cullen standing there.

''May I come in?''

Phillipe looked to Raimond, who said, ''Yes. I should have included you from the start. My apologies.''

Cullen entered and took a seat. Raimond told him of his concerns for Sable's safety, then once again described Morse.

Cullen said, ''Before you leave for Mobile, sir, I wish to be trained with a firearm.''

Surprise etched the faces of all but Raimond; he knew how seriously Cullen took his responsibilities, and besides, the times being so volatile, every member of the race must be able to defend hearth and home. ''We'll begin your training this evening once we reach home.''

''Thank you.''

While the brothers and Cullen continued to discuss the situation, Juliana took the girls into the solarium to repot one of her more precious plants, leaving Sable alone with Henri.

She told him, ''Juliana says you may be leaving us after the new year.''

''I am considering it. I see nothing but blood on the horizon for the race in this country. I only wish . . .''

''What?''

He shook his head. ''Nothing.''

Sable peered closely at him. "What were you going to say, Henri?"

He offered her a wistful smile. "Nothing. It is better left unsaid."

"Are you in love with Juliana?"

A furrow appeared between his brows. "How did you know?"

"I see it in your eyes whenever she enters a room. She loves you too, you know."

"I don't believe that," he said.

"Yes, I see it in her eyes when she's around you too. But Raimond and I both agree she will not act upon it because she believes it will desecrate François's memory."

Henri searched her face. "You wouldn't jest with a man my age, would you?"

"No, Henri. She truly does love you."

He passed his hands over his eyes, as if he couldn't believe what he'd heard. "Are you certain?"

"Absolutely."

He came over and kissed her on the cheek. "Sable, you have just made me the happiest man in the world. I too have been wrestling with the ghost of François LeVeq. I realized I loved her about six months after François's death, but I would have been a cad to approach her with my feelings. She was still in mourning."

"She may still mourn his memory, but we who are left behind must go on."

Her words brought to mind her own struggle to go on after Mahti's death. She'd thought the ache in her heart would never ease, but over time it had. The sorrow would walk with her always, but it no longer dogged her every thought. She gave credit for her healing to the new path opened to her by the Fates and the Old Queens, and to her love for Raimond.

Henri asked, "Do you think I should tell Ana how I feel?"

"Yes, I do. Who knows, maybe it is what she has been waiting for."

Henri seemed to consider that, then said, "You are a wise and observant woman, Sable. I hope Raimond is aware of how precious you are."

As if on cue, trailed by his brothers and Cullen, Raimond entered the room. He said, "Of course I know how precious she is, Henri."

As she smiled up at her handsome husband, Sable realized Raimond had never declared his love for her. She doubted she'd ever hear him say the three words that were the key to a woman's heart, but she knew he cared for her more deeply than she'd once thought possible, and with that she was content.

Henri looked around at Juliana's sons and announced, "Well, lads, I've decided to propose to your mother. Any objections?"

In the stunned silence that followed one could almost sense the men holding their collective breath. Finally Drake said, "Repeat that, please."

"You heard me the first time, Drake. If you have thoughts on the matter, let's hear them."

Phillipe asked, "Isn't this kind of sudden, Henri?"

Archer grinned. "Personally, I believe it's about time. Papa has been dead many years, and memories will not keep the lovely Juliana warm on a cold night."

"Show some respect, Archer," Phillipe snapped. "This is our mother you're talking about."

"Oh, for heaven's sake," Archer countered, "Mama is a living, breathing, feeling woman. She doesn't need her baby Phillipe pretending he was born by immaculate conception."

"I resent that!"

Drake laughed. "I agree with Archer. Mama has lit candles to Father's memory long enough. You have my approval, Henri."

"And mine," Beau declared.

Last, Henri turned to Raimond. "You are Ana's eldest. Do I have your blessing?"

"I would be honored to have you as *grandpére* to my children."

Henri smiled and directed his attention back to the sullen-faced Phillipe. "Well?"

Phillipe said, "You know I wish you all the happiness life can hold. Go ahead and marry her. You have my approval as well."

As Sable watched Henri embrace each of Juliana's sons, she felt tears brimming in her eyes. The ever-watchful Cullen came over to her and asked, "Are you sad?"

She dashed away the tears. "No, these are happy tears."

When Juliana and the girls returned from the solarium, Juliana said, "Hazel has a real affinity for horticulture, Raimond. She's wonderful with the plants. Blythe, on the other hand"—she gestured to her dirt-covered youngest granddaughter—"has an affinity for soil."

Blythe grinned.

Everyone laughed.

Cullen said, "*Grandmère*, Mr. Vincent wants to ask you something."

Sable countered, "Cullen, that is a private matter."

Raimond cut him a look. "Yes, it is, Cullen."

By this time Juliana appeared confused. "What private matter? Henri?"

Henri looked distinctly uncomfortable. "I had not planned on its being a public affair, but Cullen seems to have let the cat out of the bag." He too cut Cullen a pointed look.

Juliana demanded, "Well, someone tell me something!"

Henri walked over to Juliana and dropped to one knee.

Her eyes widened, and she asked in a quiet, trembling voice, "Henri, what are you doing?"

"Proposing. I wish for you to be my wife, Ana."

For a moment she searched his face. Everyone in the room could see the tears in her eyes. "Oh my," she whispered.

Juliana looked then at her sons and saw that all five were watching her with smiles on their faces. "Oh, my," she whispered again.

Henri said, "Ana, I'm an old man. My knee won't hold out forever."

"Henri, I don't know what to say."

"Say yes, Mama," Raimond coaxed. "Treat yourself to some happiness."

She brought a hand to her mouth.

"I would never seek to replace François in your life. We both loved him," Henri said genuinely, "but it is time for us now, before it is too late."

She looked at her sons again.

"Don't look to us," Drake told her. "Answer the man."

After a few more moments Juliana LeVeq finally gave the answer they'd all been waiting to hear. "Yes, Henri. I would be honored to be your wife."

Applause and cheers filled the room.

The small, quiet wedding took place the very next day, with only the family on hand to witness the happy event. All five sons gave their mother away.

Sable sat on their bed watching her husband pack his valise for the trip to Mobile. The convention would convene in a few days and he would be gone for at least a week. They'd discussed his concerns about Morse, and Sable had agreed she would be on the alert for any trouble, even though they hadn't had any contact with Morse since that day in the dress shop.

Her chief concern lay with Raimond's safety. Convention delegates were prime targets for retribution. Some of the men who'd attended Louisiana's Radical Convention last month had returned home to find their houses and businesses burned to the ground.

"You will be careful, won't you, my knight?"

"Yes, I will. I've no desire to return to you in a pine box."

"Good."

"I will also say hello to Andre Renaud for you."

Sable brightened. "My goodness, that's a name I haven't heard in a long while. How is your efficient aide doing these days?"

"He's fine, last I heard. When I came home in July he opted to stay in the Sea Islands. According to his last letter, he's now a Republican organizer, traveling all over the South."

"He'll be in Mobile too?"

"Yes. It will be good to see him again."

"Well, be sure and tell him I said hello."

"I'll do that."

Sable walked up behind him and put her arms around his waist. "I will miss you."

He brought her around and held her tight, then kissed the top of her head. "I'll miss you too, so keep yourself and our child safe."

"I promise."

She walked with him down the stairs. He said good-bye to the children, reminded Cullen to take care of the household, then went outside to where Archer and his coach were waiting to drive him to the train station.

The night after Raimond's departure someone torched the small schoolhouse Drake had built on the orphanage's property, and it burned to the ground. Combing through the rubble the next morning, Sable and the Brats found nothing salvageable. All the books, slates, desks—everything was gone. Two of the staff members quit on the spot. Sable tried hard to convince them to stay, but they refused. She couldn't really blame them; the idea of such violence coming so close to them chilled her soul. The orphans were understandably upset and many cried when she left them at the house, but she had to file a report with the local authorities. She promised the children she would return as soon as possible.

The local sheriff had once been a Confederate cavalry officer. After taking the loyalty oath he'd been pardoned and appointed sheriff by the town fathers. He'd shown little sympathy for the free or freed Black residents of the city.

He recorded Sable's report of the fire, then asked, "Did anybody see anything?"

"No."

"Then it's highly possible one of the children set the fire."

Sable struggled to hold on to her temper. "It is neither possible nor probable."

"Oh, I don't know, little lady. Some of the kids you people have in your schools would probably rather be out in the fields harvesting instead of being stuck in a schoolroom all day. I can see one of them setting that fire real easy."

Sable looked over at Drake, who'd escorted her there. He simply shook his head.

"Will you begin an investigation?" she asked the sheriff.

"I can come out to the orphanage and talk to the children, if that's what you mean."

Sable's jaw throbbed. "I doubt you will find the arsonist there."

He shrugged. "Suit yourself. If I can't conduct the investigation my way, then I suppose you'll have to wait until you catch the culprit in the act. Have a good day, folks."

Furious, Sable stormed out.

She spent the balance of the day cleaning up the debris from the fire. Under Cullen's direction, the orphans also helped. The Brats took shifts to ensure they were never alone.

Over the objections of all the Brats, Sable, Cullen and the girls insisted on sleeping at the orphanage for the

next two nights. Two brothers accompanied them to provide protection. Sable wanted the orphans to feel safe,
and her presence in the house seemed to help. Since the
arsonists did not come back for a repeat performance,
the Brats tempered their opposition and gave her their
blessing to spend the following nights there alone.

On the fifth night, Sable was awakened by screams,
gunshots, and the acrid smell of smoke. Jumping up
from her pallet on the second floor, she ran to the stairs
and descended into hell. Masked, mounted men were
riding their horses through the house, throwing flaming
torches onto drapes, furniture, and anything else that
would burn. Other horsemen were riding down on the
screaming children as if they were prey in some macabre
hunt, then snatching them up and throwing them across
their saddles like pelts. Sable ran for the tools she'd left
by the door and began swinging a shovel with a strength
fueled by her incredible rage, hitting horses, men and
anything else which threatened her charges. Through the
rising smoke, she saw one rider latch on to Blythe and
attempt to pull her up onto his saddle, but the ten-year
old fought so furiously he was forced to drop her. Cullen
was aiming a rifle, and the sounds of his firing added to
the unholy din. Then as if in a dream, she watched as
Cullen was struck in the back of the head by a rider's
club. He crumpled to the foor as if dead, her screams of
outrage shaking the heavens. She ran through the smoky
bedlam and swung the shovel as hard as she could, but
the rider saw her at the last possible moment and
blocked her blow. Laughing, he wrestled the implement
from her grasp and tried to pull her up onto his horse.
She fought fiercely amid the fire, smoke, and cries of
terror, but her effort was in vain. She felt the explosion
of a blow to her head and then everything went black.

When Sable came to, it was still dark. Her head felt
as if she'd banged it against a brick wall, and it hurt so
bad she could hardly open her eyes. She had a vague

sense of being in some type of moving vehicle, but she was too groggy to be sure of anything except pain.

Then Blythe's fearful, trembling voice calling to her made her grope her way back to consciousness. She struggled to right her thoughts through the biting agony and felt a small hand stroking her brow.

Somehow Sable found the will to speak. "Blythe?"

"Yes, Sable, it's me. Hazel's here too, and so is Cullen, but his head is bleeding and he won't wake up."

"Hazel?"

"Yes, Mama."

Sable managed a smile. Hazel was the only one who called her mama. "Are you and Blythe okay?"

A man's voice answered in Hazel's stead. "They're both fine, Sable."

Sable's pain warred with her anger. She recognized the voice, and because she did, Mahti's ominous prophesy echoed in her head: *He will be the jackal and you the antelope until his death.*

With all her soul she yearned to confront Henry Morse, but her mind slid back into darkness.

When Sable awakened again, it was full daylight. The ache in her head had subsided only minimally, but she forced her eyes open. The light hurt, but she forced herself to endure it so she could evaluate her surroundings. She was lying in the bed of a moving wagon. Beside her sat Blythe, whose dark eyes were so filled with fear and anguish, Sable vowed to send Morse to hell. Hazel flanked Sable's other side, but unlike those of her little sister, Hazel's eyes glittered with a desire for vengeance.

"How's Cullen, Hazel?" Sable forced out.

"He's still asleep."

The pounding in Sable's head increased as she attempted to turn her head, but she had to see her son. He lay at her feet. The bandage circling his head was stained with blood.

Sable crawled over to him, fighting dizziness.

Hazel said, "I bandaged his head with the end of my gown."

Sable's heart cried at seeing him lying so still. As she lowered her ear to his chest to make certain he was still breathing, she almost passed out again, but the sound of his faint heartbeat gave her hope.

"Well, Sable, good to see you up and around."

Morse.

She ignored him. Her concern for Cullen overrode all else. Softly she called to him, "Cullen?"

There was no response.

She called again, slightly louder. His body moved as if he'd recognized her voice, but he fell still again almost as quickly.

Sable turned a malevolent eye on Morse driving the wagon. "He needs a doctor."

"I'm sure you think so, but I've never known a young buck who didn't have an iron-hard head. He'll be fine in a day or two."

Sable's jaw tightened. "The lad is only twelve."

"The young heal fast."

"Where are you taking us?"

"To Paradise."

"There will be a room reserved for you in hell for this."

"Where folks like you will be my slaves."

They were still traveling in the wagon when Cullen finally awakened late that evening. His first words as he regained consciousness were a softly spoken, "I'm sorry. I promised Papa Rai I'd keep you safe."

"You did your best, Cullen. There were just too many of them."

"I'm sorry," he whispered again.

As a tear slid from his eye, her heart broke in two. "We'll get out of this, don't worry."

Morse countered pleasantly, "I wouldn't be so quick to make rash predictions if I were you, Sable, my dear.

It's my guess you'll never see that major of yours ever again.''

Bitterly Sable replied, ''Now who's making rash predictions? I will see Raimond again, even if I have to walk over your grave to do so.''

He just laughed and flicked the reins to get the horses moving faster.

As dusk approached, Morse pulled the wagon into the wild growth on the side of the road and announced they would be stopping there for the night. He'd been behind the reins since before dawn. Sable hoped to find a way to escape while he slept, but when she saw him reach beneath his seat and extract four sets of leg irons, she knew it was not to be.

Once they were shackled, he hooked them to a long length of chain whose end was attached to an iron cuff around his wrist. If they moved, the tug on the chain would alert him.

Helpless to do anything else, Sable and the children huddled together and slept.

They were already under way the next morning when Sable awakened. The sky above was a beautiful blue; it was much too fine a day to be shackled to the devil, she thought, but she thanked the Old Queens for letting her live to see it. Morse stopped the wagon and undid the shackles so they could take care of their needs, but he let them go only one at a time.

''If any of you run, I'll kill at least one of those who remain.''

Sable had no idea if he would carry through on the threat, but she had no desire to find out.

Once they were all back in the wagon, he replaced the leg irons, tossed them a few pieces of stale bread and a canteen of water for breakfast, then proceeded on down the road.

By mid-morning, the road had turned into a track, and by mid-afternoon it was nothing more than a rutted trail.

The land around them was vast and desolate. Sable didn't know this region outside New Orleans well enough to determine their exact location, but she made a point of remembering landmarks they passed—oddly shaped trees and stands of wildflowers—so she could find her way home if the opportunity arose.

It was nearly dusk when Morse finally turned off the trail. Ahead stood a ramshackle mansion. The land around it was wild and uncultivated. Knee-high weeds and thick brush covered what had probably once been cleared fields, but time and neglect had returned it to its natural state.

"Where are we?" Sable asked.

Morse answered, "I told you before, Paradise. Might not look like it now, but once it's cleared and cotton is planted, it should live up to its name."

He pulled the wagon up to the side of the house and set the brake. The side door opened and Sally Ann Fontaine stepped out. "What took you—" Her eyes met Sable's and widened. "What's she doing here?"

"She's going to be living with us, Sal. Say hello."

"You take her back to wherever you found her, and those brats as well. She's been nothing but trouble since the day she was born!"

"Can't do it, Sal. We need slaves to clear the land. These'll be the first four."

Sally Ann's face was twisted with anger. "I will not have this murderess in my home."

"You got no choice," he declared.

Hopping down from the wagon, he came around and unlatched the back of the wagon, then unlocked the irons shackling Sable and the others together and gestured for them to get out. "Let's go. Sal, I hope you got some supper on. I'm hungry enough to eat a bear."

Sally Ann's eyes continued to spit fire. "You take them back this minute, Henry Morse!"

Morse sighed and took her aside. "Sally Ann, we need help clearing this land."

"With all the slaves in this state, you can't find anyone else?"

"Sally Ann, haven't you always wanted to make her pay for Carson's death?"

"Yes."

"Well, here's your opportunity. You'll have free rein to treat her however you want. Nobody knows where she is so she'll be your slave for life."

"We're free!" Cullen declared angrily.

Morse cuffed him. "Never say that around me again, boy. God put you on this earth to be the servants of men like me, and you'd better remember it."

Sable moved quickly to Cullen's side. Seeing the blood trickling from his split lip, she snapped, "You and the rest of those masked cowards don't know the first thing about God."

Morse ignored her and turned to Hazel, who glared back at him. "How old are you, gal?" When she didn't answer he said sharply, "I asked you a question. How old are you?"

"Twelve," she told him sullenly.

"Better watch that tone, girl. Are you bleeding yet?"

Hazel didn't answer.

"Why on earth would you care about that?" Sally Ann demanded.

"I need to know if she's old enough to breed."

Before Sable could voice her outrage, Sally Ann snapped, "Henry, she's a child, for heaven's sake. If you need to rut, use that one," she said, indicating Sable.

Sable's jaw tightened.

Sally Ann's eyes narrowed as she looked at Sable more closely. "When's your baby due?"

"She's carrying?" Morse exclaimed.

"If you'd been using your eyes instead of what's between your legs, you'd've noticed."

Sable and the children were still in their nightclothes. Sable's growing stomach was easy to discern beneath the light flannel gown.

Morse stepped closer to her. "Well, well, well. Guess I'll have to wait until you whelp before I can breed you. No matter. I can wait."

He turned back to Hazel, and the smile on his face chilled Sable down to her toes. "Touch my daughter and I will send you to hell," she warned.

"He won't, or he'll answer to me," Sally Ann promised. She swept toward the door, saying over her shoulder, "I won't have them in the house, Henry. Bed them down in the quarters, then come eat."

Sable looked down the row of dilapidated cabins that had once housed slaves and was reminded of another place, another time. For the sake of the children, she did not give voice to her fear that they might, indeed, be forced to live out their lives under Morse's control. Instead, she prayed to everyone in heaven who'd ever loved her to grant her the will to survive until she could take her children home.

She settled upon the least damaged cabin. It had a partially intact roof and walls that were more or less standing upright. There was no bedding, of course, or any candles. Sighing, she turned to her son and daughters. "This will be home for a while, but only for a while. We'll get back home, I promise."

Blythe peered around the dark place. "Sable, I'm scared."

Sable pulled them all into her arms. "We're going to cry just this once, okay?"

The girls nodded, tears already streaming down their brown cheeks. Through her own tears she saw Cullen standing in a corner, his face set like stone.

"Cullen?"

He didn't answer, so Sable held the girls and prayed.

Since it was almost full dark by now, Sable tried to figure out how and where they could sleep. They'd had nothing to eat since the stale bread and water Morse had

tossed them for breakfast, and she was certain the children were starving.

Sally Ann appeared in the cabin's doorway with blankets in her arms and a pot that bore the scent of collards
in her hand. She dropped the blankets to the ground, set
the pot beside it, and left without saying a word.

The next morning at the crack of dawn she returned.
"Get up. It's time to start the day."

Sable and her children roused themselves slowly.

"Sable, I need your signature on this work contract."

"I'm not signing anything, Sally Ann."

"Either sign or I'll send these children away so fast
your head will spin off your neck. Sign."

It was yet another threat Sable didn't want to test, so
she took the pen from Sally Ann's impatient hand and
reluctantly signed her name to a contract she couldn't
even read in the dim light.

"Good. You and the children are here for life, so go
join Henry in the fields. He's waiting."

"I'm hungry, Sable," Blythe said sleepily.

Sally Ann snapped, "You work and then you eat, not
before—now get moving."

They trudged out to the field where Morse was standing. He handed them scythes and hoes. "We're going
to clear this land. Let's get started."

Six days later, when Raimond returned to New Orleans, the news that Sable and the children had been
taken by night riders almost brought him to his knees.

A stricken Archer reached out to keep him upright,
but Raimond pulled away angrily. "How could you have
let this happen?" he raged at his brothers. "There are
four of you, dammit, and between you you couldn't keep
them safe?! Damn you all!"

He wanted to turn over every piece of furniture in his
mother's house, smash every window.

The grief in his brothers' faces did not soften his rage.
"Why did you let her stay there at night? You should

have made her come home, dragged her here if necessary.''

Juliana had had enough. ''Raimond, stop this! Can't you see the pain in their faces? They've exhausted themselves searching for her and the children.''

''I don't care about their pain or their exhaustion. It's my wife who's gone, my children!''

''And how is this tirade helping to find them?'' his mother snapped. ''How many arguments have you won from Sable?''

He didn't answer.

''Not many, I'm guessing. Your wife is a very determined woman, you know that as well as I do. She was determined to spend her nights there so the orphans— her orphans, Raimond—would not be afraid. We are all worried sick, have been for six days. You love her, yes, but so do we!''

He knew his mother was right. Sable was not a woman to be deterred once she made up her mind. ''One of you should have stayed with her,'' he echoed tightly. ''She shouldn't've been alone.''

Drake admitted quietly, ''We know.''

Raimond whispered, ''I'll lose my mind if they aren't found.''

A somber silence settled over the room.

Beau told Raimond, ''We've been searching everywhere since she and the children were taken. No one knows who the men were or where they went. We found the orphans' cook and the housekeeper dead behind the house. They'd been shot.''

''How many of the orphans were taken?'' Raimond asked as his world crumbled around him.

''Six,'' Drake replied. ''Four boys, two girls.''

''They're being forced to work for some White man someplace, I'm guessing.''

''We think so too,'' Phillipe put in. ''We found homes for the other nine while you were away, but those six could be anywhere. Anywhere.''

"So could Sable," Raimond added. "And that's what most scares me—they could be anywhere by now."

"So what do we do?" asked Phillipe.

Raimond didn't know. His brothers appeared to have covered every avenue. "I know Morse has something to do with this. I feel it in my bones. Did you check the deed office?"

"In every parish within one hundred miles. There is no record of a Henry Morse owning property, or for a woman named Sally Ann Fontaine or Sally Ann Morse."

Raimond had no idea how he'd survive if Sable and the children were never found. He prayed they were still alive. There were so many things the four of them had yet to do, so many places he'd wanted them to see. The idea that he might never hold the child she was sheltering in her womb compounded his anguish. *Where were they?* He hadn't even told Sable how much he loved her or begged her forgiveness for not believing her claims of innocence regarding the Baker affair. So many things had been left undone and unsaid that he'd give up everything he owned just to hold her in his arms again. But he didn't even know where to begin looking.

Juliana's soft voice interrupted his thoughts. "Raimond, what shall we do?"

He replied in a voice as soft as her own. "I don't know, Mama. I don't know."

Raimond spent the next day retracing his brother's steps, but he turned up no new clues. He contacted friends in the Freedmen's Bureau, old army acquaintances, missionaries, and anyone else he thought could offer assistance. Archer had put up broadsides in his hotel and restaurant, and Phillipe continued combing the docks. The *Tribune* had been running a notice about Sable's disappearance, and the disappearance of the orphans, since the day after the orphanage's torching. The editors used their influence and contacted Black newspapers as far east as Richmond and as far west as Topeka, but they heard nothing in response. By the end of the second week, losing hope, Raimond felt he was going out of his mind.

Chapter 16

S able and her children had been in Paradise for over
two weeks. Morse forced them to clear land from
dawn to dusk. They'd all become slightly thinner due to
the lack of quality meals, but Sable's baby was still kicking and growing so she assumed it was fine. She guessed
that Raimond had returned from Mobile by now and was
half out of his mind with worry. She hoped he wouldn't
fault his brothers for her disappearance. She could only
blame herself for not listening when the Brats expressed
their well-founded concerns.

Sable's biggest concern at the moment had to do with
the way Morse continued to stare at Hazel. He watched
her with the same intensity he'd watched Sable when
she'd been Hazel's age. Hazel ignored him, but Sable
did not. Remembering the rumors from back home surrounding the deaths of two of his young female slaves,
she made a point of keeping her daughter in sight at all
times. Cullen seemed to be of like mind. Sable noticed
that whenever Morse approached Hazel about anything,
her brother always came to stand at her side.

Sally Ann made no attempt to veil her contempt for
Sable and avoided any contact unless it was absolutely
necessary. When Sable asked her about Mavis, Sally
Ann declared she knew no one by that name.

Clearing the fields was hard, grueling work. Morse

still had the mentality of a slave owner in the sense that he expected as much work from Blythe as he did from Cullen, and of course, the work was not going fast enough for him. On several occasions he angrily accused them of slacking and threatened to lay a whip across their backs, but as Sable so angrily pointed out to him, they were three children and a pregnant woman; they were working as fast and as hard as they could.

One day, when Sable asked if he had been among the night riders who'd terrorized the orphanage, he denied it, admitting only, "I contracted with them, told them what I wanted done, and they did it. It wasn't hard convincing them; they relish making misery for you people. Emancipation is the worst thing to ever happen to the South, and they're willing to do whatever's necessary to make sure you people don't rise above your natural place."

Sable wondered how anyone could be so consumed with hatred that they'd take it out on defenseless children, but having been a slave, she knew men like Morse and his friends were certain they were doing what was necessary to preserve their way of life. "So how did you learn about the orphanage?" she asked.

"That wasn't hard. You're fairly well known. So's your husband. After I saw you at the dressmakers, all I had to do was ask around. After my friends were done with the orphanage, they brought you and your brood to a prearranged spot outside town. I paid them and they slipped away. Now, enough questions. Get back to work."

The days began to run together. She and the children got up each morning, worked until it became too dark to see, then went back to the quarters and their beds of straw and rags. Their nightclothes had been reduced to rags after so many days of wear. Sally Ann threw Sable and the children old burlap sacks to wear over their torn and tattered nightgowns.

Because Morse was from Georgia, he wanted to plant cotton, a crop Sable knew well. Back on the Fontaine plantation, she and everyone else on the place had participated in the planting and harvesting, especially when she was young. Unlike other crops that you planted, weeded and let grow on their own, cotton had to be tended like a child. Sable remembered watching the rows being dug by the men and women, recalled walking behind the mules pulling the plows that drilled the holes for her and the other children to put the seed into. Usually seed was planted in March or April. If the cold spring rains held off, the cotton would start to come up in about a week's time and then a week later the first hoeing could begin.

Before the first hoeing, the plow went through and moved the dirt away from the plants. Grass, weeds, and the scrawniest cotton seedlings would be hoed out, leaving behind a series of dirt hills positioned about two and a half feet apart. The field workers called the process scraping cotton.

Two weeks later, there'd be a second hoeing, when the mounds of dirt were thrown toward the growing plants, leaving one hardy stalk in a two-foot hill. In another two weeks, a third hoeing would throw dirt away from the plants to kill any grass or weeds between the rows. If the weather and the insects cooperated, the cotton would be about a foot tall by the first of July when the fourth hoeing took place. This last hoeing ended with the six-foot space between the rows being plowed to the depth of a shallow creek, then filled with water. When the stalks blossomed and grew five to seven feet tall, they were ready to be picked.

Sable couldn't have been more than seven or eight when she was allowed to pick that first time, but even now she remembered how tired she'd been at the end of each day. She also remembered thinking how beautiful the cotton had looked at first, its fat white blossoms glistening in the sun, but she'd soon grown to hate it. She'd been given a bag to wear around her neck that was so long the end dragged on the ground. Many a child stumbled and tripped. Experienced workers like Vashti and Mahti could pick so fast their hands seemed to blur. Sable and the other new children in the fields, lacking the same agility, had to grab each individual blossom and pull, careful not to break the still growing parts of the stalk because broken stalks would not bloom. Bolls that were not ripe would be left until they too blossomed and were picked later.

The children also lacked the adult's experienced rhythm. Instead of going pick—drop the blossoms in the bag, pick—drop the blossoms in the bag, they had to stop, pull the bolls free and then drop the blossoms in the bag. Most times they wound up having to pick the blossoms up off the ground because they'd missed the mouth of the bag altogether.

When your bag was full you took it down to the end of the row and emptied it into baskets set at each end. One of the adults would stomp down the fluffy white blossoms, then you'd go on to another row and start the process all over again.

Sable dearly hoped to be out of Morse's foul clutches before spring. She had no desire to spend the months from April to July hoeing from dawn to dusk, or watching her children pick cotton from the end of August on, just so Morse could turn a profit none of them would share.

One morning as Sable bent over her hoe, hacking at some particularly stubborn weeds, Sally Ann came out and stood nearby. She didn't say anything, just stood. Her presence became such an irritant, Sable finally stopped, looked her way, and asked, "What is it you want?"

"Nothing really. I just enjoy seeing you laboring like a common field hand."

Tight-lipped, Sable resumed her work, intent upon ignoring her former mistress.

"The fields are where you should have been all along, not sullying my beautiful home."

"I didn't ask to be raised in the house."

"No, you didn't, that was Carson's doing. He refused to listen to me."

Sable kept up her pace, hoping Sally would take the hint and leave, but she didn't. Instead she said, "I'll never forgive him for insisting your mother be taken along on our wedding tour."

Sable didn't reply.

"I hated her, you know. That golden skin, those golden brown eyes. She had half the White men in the county sniffing around her."

Again, Sable did not reply.

"What is it about you women that our men find so fascinating? My mama used to tell me not to let it bother me when the men took slave women into their beds, but it did. Still does."

Sable finally stopped working and asked bluntly, "What do you want me to say? My mother wasn't given a choice. She was a slave, Sally Ann, remember?"

Sally Ann's chin rose. "But she refused to be bred willingly."

"What would you have done in her place? Would you have willingly given yourself to a man just because he demanded it?"

"Of course not, but you women are different, it's in your blood."

"What's in our blood, Sally Ann, is the desire for self-respect!"

Sally wouldn't meet her eyes.

"We are no different from you. We live, die, smile at our children, grieve over our dead. We are not animals, we are people."

Sally Ann turned and walked away.

A thunderstorm rolled in that night, awakening Sable and the children with lightning, wind and driving rain.

It didn't take long for the wet to penetrate their hovel. With no way to keep themselves dry, they huddled together beneath their blankets, hoping the violent weather would soon end. As Sable shivered and sheltered the children as best she could, despair rose up and gripped her hard. Would this truly be her fate? she asked as the wind shifted and rain began to pour through the broken slats of the walls. Would she and her children really have to spend the rest of their lives here? Would she give birth to Raimond's child here? She'd endured much these past two and a half weeks and she didn't know if she had the strength to take much more.

She looked up to see Morse standing in the cabin's entrance. He yelled over the storm, "Come into the house!"

She and the children ran across the muddy field to the side door.

Inside, Morse told them they could sleep on the kitchen floor.

Raimond stood before one of the windows in his shipping office looking out over the darkening river. It had rained most of the day, but now the showers seemed to be slackening. For days he'd spent every waking hour searching for Sable and the children but turning up nothing. Now he'd started coming back here. He'd thought keeping busy might help keep his mind off his missing family, but it hadn't worked. He thought about them each and every moment, no matter what he was doing or where he was. The idea that they were still nowhere to be found kept him awake nights; he hadn't had more than a few hours' sleep since their disappearance.

Where the hell were they? he asked for what seemed like the thousandth time. Not even the offer of a reward had turned up anything. He was frustrated, angry, and scared to even think about never seeing them again.

Raimond moved away from the window and went back to his desk. He looked over the manifest for a trip

Phillipe would be making in a few days to pick up a full complement of goods from an old trader friend in China. Raimond and Galeno dealt in exotic merchandise like perfumes, spices, and rugs. They catered to the rich because the rich always had money to buy.

A knock on the door caused him to look up. He was caught off guard by the sight of a White woman standing on the threshold. "Are you Raimond LeVeq?" she asked quietly as she shook the rain off her coat.

"Yes, I am. How may I help you?"

He noted that she looked as poor as some of the freedmen. Her dark dress was faded and patched, but her neatly arranged hair and freshly scrubbed pink face showed her to be a woman of some dignity.

"I came here to tell you where you can find your wife."

Raimond waited skeptically. The first day he'd posted notice of the reward in the newspapers and on broadsides tacked up around the city, many people had come to his office trying to claim the gold. Not a one had come bearing a true story. He supposed they assumed his distress over the disappearance had rendered him so mindless he would believe whatever he was told and reward them. This woman, whom he studied as he gestured her to a seat, would be the first reward seeker this week.

"Your wife and I met a few months ago," she said, looking up from her lap. Her eyes were shining with unshed tears. "She, um, fed me and my kids, over at one of the churches." She gave Raimond a watery smile. "Your wife is a grand lady, Mr. LeVeq."

"Yes, she is," Raimond replied softly. He sensed a truthfulness and a goodness in this woman he'd never experienced with any of the other reward seekers.

"I can't tell you my name, because they're kin of mine, but what they did to her—it's not right. They said they did it because they owe it to the South to make things hard for you Blacks, but Mrs. LeVeq didn't pay no mind to the color of my kids. She fed them because they were hungry.''

She wiped away her tears. ''Anyway,'' she whispered, as she extracted a folded paper from her pocket, ''here's the directions that'll lead you to where she is.''

Raimond unfolded the paper and looked at what was written on it. ''If this turns out to be true—''

''Oh, it's true. They got drunk last night and were bragging about it. Thinking of her suffering just about broke my heart. I gave them a good loud piece of my mind.'' She looked Raimond in the eye and said feelingly, ''On behalf of my kids and me, we are truly, truly sorry.''

She stood and moved to the door.

Raimond stood also. ''Do you know where the other children were taken, the six orphans who were kidnapped?''

''No, I don't. My menfolk only took your wife and children. The others could be anywhere.''

''Where do you want me to send the reward?''

''I don't want it.''

''What do you mean you don't want it?''

She shrugged. ''I don't. I'm just glad I could help her.''

She gave him a little nod of her head and left him standing there, his eyes filled with tears.

The Brats were ecstatic upon hearing the news, but a somberness soon settled over them all as they sat in Juliana's parlor to plan the rescue.

''Do you think he's harmed them?'' Juliana asked. Beside her sat Henri.

''There's no way of knowing,'' Raimond replied.

Drake looked at a map of the area where Morse had hidden himself away. ''I figure we can cover the distance in less than a day, using good strong mounts. We should probably trail a few extra horses just in case.''

Everyone agreed.

Beau asked, "Did the woman say whether Morse was alone?"

Raimond gave a negative shake of his head. "No, she didn't, so I suggest we go in masked and armed. Let's see how he likes having the tables turned."

They rode out at dawn. Raimond used the brutal pace of the ride to try and defuse his red-hot rage. He wanted to blow Morse's head off and drag the body behind his horse from New Orleans to Charleston, but he'd have to come up with another way to exact revenge. It would not do for him to kill Morse in front of his children.

Last evening when they'd all met in her parlor, his mother had expressed a similar concern. She knew that given the opportunity, Raimond would dispatch Morse to hell without batting an eye. Although she had no quarrel with that, she did not want her grandchildren to see their father kill a man unless it proved absolutely necessary. Raimond agreed.

In order not to be tempted into shooting Morse on sight he'd considered giving his weapons to Drake, but he had no intention of going in unarmed. He'd just have to keep a rein on his anger. He prayed Morse hadn't decided to pull up stakes and head elsewhere.

In many ways, this thundering ride reminded him of the time when he, Galeno and some of the Brats had ridden to rescue Hester from the slave catcher Ezra Shoe. Raimond's brother Gerrold had been with them that day. Raimond still grieved over the loss of his sibling and knew that had Gerrold not died in the war, he'd be riding at his side now too. It saddened him to know that Gerrold would never meet Sable or watch his children grow. Cullen's serious, watchful ways reminded Raimond very much of Gerrold. He believed they'd have gotten along well.

The LeVeqs arrived at Morse's plantation just past dusk. Raimond used a spyglass to scan the area. "I see a field and some ramshackle quarters but there's no sign of Sable or the children.''

"Do you see any horses or wagons that might tell us whether he's alone?" Drake asked.

"No, just one wagon. No horses that I can see. Ah, but we're in luck, gentlemen," Raimond declared triumphantly. "There's our friend Morse coming out of the house now. He's heading to"—Raimond paused a moment—"the privy. Has a newspaper in one hand and a lantern in the other."

Raimond retracted the spyglass. "Drake, how about we pay him a visit. Archer, take Phillipe and Beau and go see if there's anyone in the house. And be careful. No firing of weapons unless it's absolutely necessary."

They all dismounted and tied the horses in the tall weeds and wild vegetation before making a cautious dash across the cleared field surrounding the house. They then splt into two groups. Drake's moved quickly to the back door of the house while Raimond and Archer headed for the listing plywood privy, set off to the left.

Once Raimond saw his brothers entering the house, he and Archer quietly counted to three, then kicked over the lightweight structure.

The seated Morse didn't know whether to be angry or terrified, and settled on terrified as he met Raimond's iron stare above a drawn rifle. "Get up!" Raimond barked, his temper rising.

Visibly trembling, Morse stood with his pants still around his ankles. His legs glowed palely in the lantern light.

"Where are Sable and the children?"

"At least let me pull up my trousers."

"Answer me!" Raimond snarled through gritted teeth.

Morse jumped in response to the power in Raimond's voice and stammered, "In the quarters, in the quarters."

Just then Beau joined them. "We found a woman in the house, but no one else."

Raimond kept his eyes and weapon trained on Morse. "Tie him up, and take him into the house. I'll return shortly."

Inside the small cabin, under the sputtering light of a candle stub, Sable passed a pot of collards to Hazel. Using her hand because they had no utensils, Hazel scooped up a palmful of the greens and brought them to her mouth. Sable paused before passing the pot to Cullen. For a moment she'd thought she heard Raimond calling her name. Blaming it on her imagination, she handed the pot to Cullen.

But Sable heard it again, and this time the children did too.

"That sounds like Papa Rai calling," Blythe said excitedly.

They ran outside, and saw a man dressed in dark clothing walking toward the cabin. Sable recognized him instantly and her heart began pounding so furiously she could barely breathe. Forgetting all else, she began to run, screaming, "Raimond!"

The children began running too.

"Raimond!"

He scooped her up and held her so tight she thought her spine would break, but his presence filled her with so much happiness, she didn't mind the pain. It was over, it was over!

Raimond rocked his wife in his arms for what seemed an eternity, kissing her, holding her, whispering her name. He'd found her!

Wiping her eyes, Sable stepped aside so Raimond could have a hug- and kiss-filled reunion with his daughters. Cullen stood off to the side, silently watching and waiting, reminding Raimond of a soldier awaiting review by his commanding officer.

Raimond turned to him and held out his arms. Cullen ran to him at once. His fierce embrace put more tears in Raimond's eyes.

Cullen whispered through his own tears, "I let you down, I didn't keep Mama and the girls safe."

Raimond squeezed him tighter. "You did fine, son, and I am very proud of you. Don't ever doubt that. Ever."

Sable wiped away more tears of joy. She'd prayed every night for this moment, and her prayers had finally been answered.

Raimond turned back to her. "Did he abuse you?"

She knew what he meant and answered truthfully, "No. Cullen and I each took a knock on the head the night his friends raided the orphanage, but we're both fine."

She was so happy to see him.

He was so happy to find her alive and well.

Blythe asked, "Papa Rai, can we go home now? I'm very hungry."

Raimond smiled down at his youngest. "As soon as we finish here, sugar plum, I will take you home and Mrs. Vine will feed you whatever you like."

With all the bluntness of a child, Blythe added, "He's been real mean to us."

"Well, he won't be mean to you anymore," Raimond promised.

"You gonna whip him?"

"Yep."

"I told him my Papa Rai was gonna whip him," Blythe said proudly.

Sable had no idea when Blythe and Morse had had such a conversation, but it would be something to ask her about and laugh over later, once they were safely home.

Back at the house, the Brats had tied Morse to a chair. Sally Ann sat beside him. It was hard to determine which of the two looked more furious.

Sable shared long hugs with her brothers-in-law.

"Thank you for helping Raimond find us. I can't wait until we reach home."

"You can't take them anywhere," Sally Ann snapped. "Sable signed a contract."

Raimond looked to Sable, who said, "Raimond, meet my former mistress, Sally Ann Fontaine."

"The name's Morse now," she said.

"I'm taking my family home," Raimond assured her. "Contract or no contract."

"Sounds like something Shoe would've said," Archer pointed out.

Raimond agreed.

"Who's Shoe?" Cullen asked.

"A slave catcher your uncles and I crossed paths with a few years back," Raimond told his son.

"You know," Archer drawled, "I'll bet old Ezra Shoe would appreciate a little company. He's been there about six or seven years now, hasn't he?"

"About that," Raimond agreed.

"I'll let the children go," Morse offered, "but she stays." He nodded at Sable.

Raimond chuckled. "You'll *let* them go? You *must* know Ezra Shoe. Are you sure you haven't met him? He's a little man, about five and a half feet tall, black gums, foul odor. The two of you must be acquainted."

"So, what are we going to do with him?" Archer asked.

"Nothing," Morse answered for Raimond, snarling contemptuously. "Harm me, and every White man in the South will rise up and hunt you down."

Raimond shook his head at Morse's passionate speech. "We're not going to kill you, Morse. We're just going to send you on a long trip."

"Where?"

"North Africa maybe."

"Or," Beau said, "Considering baby brother is off to China next week, maybe our friend here would like to live there."

Raimond eyed Morse. "They do have lovely cold winters up in the mountains."

"What are you two jigs talking about?" Morse snapped.

"Sending you on that trip."

"To where?"

"Wherever we decide. Right now, I'm voting for the mountains of China. A very unpleasant warlord acquaintance of mine has a village there. No doubt the snow will make a Southern gentleman like you thoroughly miserable."

Morse began to laugh. "You can't send me any place I don't want to go."

"Sure he can," Sable countered. "My husband owns a fleet of ships that travel all over the world. He can send you to Borneo or Siberia or even Africa, if he takes a mind to."

"That's a thought too, darling," Raimond said. "Never considered the mother continent."

Morse stared. That the brothers weren't joshing seemed to have finally penetrated his thick skull. "You're serious?"

"As serious as you were when you stole my family. I'm going to give you over to someone who'll treat you the way you deserve—like a slave. Because that's what you'll be."

Morse's eyes grew like saucers.

Raimond nodded. "Ironic, isn't it? Personally, I want to shoot you where you stand, but it wouldn't do to have my children see your brains splattered all over this room, so I'm turning you into a slave instead. I've done it before. Ask Ezra Shoe."

Sable thought it a marvelous solution, one that should be standard punishment for folks like Morse.

"You can't do this!" Morse sputtered.

Archer chuckled. "People like you always underestimate people like us."

"You can't do this!" Morse yelled again.

"If you'd rather take your chances and run," Drake suggested, "I'll be a good sport and allow you a head start. I'd love to hunt you the way your friends hunted down those orphans."

Morse had the audacity to look pleadingly at Sable.

"Certainly you aren't looking to me for assistance," she told him. "If I knew how to use a weapon, you'd already be dead. Have a good life, Henry."

Morse appeared stunned as the Brats untied him from the chair and marched him outside. Sally Ann cut Sable a malevolent look but said nothing.

On the porch, Raimond spent the next few moments doing absolutely nothing but staring at his wife. Even filthy, she was the most beautiful woman he'd ever seen. He took her in his arms and held her tenderly, silently, savoring the assurance that she was safe against his heart where she belonged.

"Are you sure you're not hurt?" he asked.

"Positive. After a bath, some food, and a week or two of rest, I'll be just like new."

He grinned and stared down into her changeable green eyes. She was more precious to him than anything he could have imagined. She was priceless, irreplaceable. "After you get the bath, and the food, and the two weeks of rest, be prepared to receive a very stern lecture on being too damn determined for your own good."

She gazed up into his dark eyes; she deserved a lecture, she supposed. She stroked his bearded jaw. "Yes, Sir Knight. I'll even bring my pen and slate so that I can take notes."

Raimond draped his arm over Sable's shoulder and gave her a slight squeeze. He vowed never to let her out of his sight again.

As everyone watched, Morse was gagged and mounted atop one of the extra horses. They roped his hands to the saddle and covered him with a blanket. Drake and Phillipe would escort him back to New Orleans and prepare him for his journey east.

Raimond still wanted to kill him, but he knew that if he sent him away, Morse would never be able to threaten his loved ones again, a punishment far more fitting the crime. Some folks had to be made to walk in another's shoes before they learned life's lessons. Like Ezra Shoe, Henry Morse would be walking in new shoes for a long, long time.

Raimond decided to delay the others' return home until tomorrow so the horses could get some rest and he could spend this night holding his wife. Much to Sally Ann's anger, they all slept on her parlor's bare floor.

In the morning, as everyone went outside to prepare for the ride home, Sable stayed to speak with Sally Ann.

"We can take you back to New Orleans if you care to come along."

Sally Ann was standing before a window that looked out over the field. She slid Sable a hostile look. "No, thank you."

Sable thought back to Mavis and how she'd pledged to keep Mahti safe if anything ever happened to Sable. Sable owed it to her sister to try to look after her kin as well. "You shouldn't be out here alone."

"Just go. Haven't you done enough? I've lost *two* husbands now because of you."

Sable felt no need to apologize for the hand her former mistress had been dealt.

"He never should have brought you here," Sally Ann declared coldly. "Never! I told you you were cursed, but he wouldn't listen. Just like Carson! Now they're both gone from me."

"Maybe you should contact Mavis—"

"Don't you dare mention her name in my presence. She's dead. Dead! Married that damn Yankee. She was raised to be quality!" she declared angrily. "*I* come from quality and now my blood is mixing with some nigra-loving Yankee's, and it just makes me sick!"

She turned on Sable again. "And that's your fault too. I told Carson if he allowed the two of you to be so close something like this would happen to her. I told him!''

She fixed her gaze back on the window overlooking the fields and uttered softly, ''Now look at me. I have nothing and no one. I knew Henry Morse didn't really love me, but pretending he did, and pretending he could restore my old life, got me through my days. Now even that is gone.'' She continued to stare ahead. ''I want what I had: ease, shopping, cotillions, lawn parties.''

''Slaves,'' Sable added coolly.

Sally Ann turned her head and held her eyes. ''I'm smart enough to know my life was built on the backs of slaves, so yes—I want my slaves back too.''

''You can't have them.''

''More's the pity. I believe you people would have been served better by staying put. You're never going to be treated equal because you weren't created equal. Every race has a place and you're trying to rise above yours, but we won't let you. We're going to tell our children and they're going to tell their children and their grandchildren and we're going to follow you down through time until you accept it.''

''We'll never be slaves again, Sally Ann, not without bathing this country in blood.''

Sally Ann didn't reply.

Sable knew that her own love for Mavis was the only reason she felt obliged to ask once again. ''So, do you wish to ride back to New Orleans or not?''

Without turning around, Sally Ann stated, ''I don't need help from you, or any of your kind. You just go ahead and enjoy being equal—if you can.''

Her bitter laughter followed Sable out the door.

Sable and the children shared an emotional, heart-tugging reunion with Juliana and Henri. Little Reba was so elated to have everyone home safe, she promised the children they could come over and have their favorite desserts every day for a month. As their mother, Sable thought the offer should be amended a bit, but she didn't wish to spoil the fun by bringing that up now.

Juliana tried to convince Sable and the children to spend the night, seeing as it was already dark, but Sable felt more tired than she'd been in years, and despearately wanted to go home. Raimond had to promise his mother he would pamper and spoil the children just as if she herself were in charge before he was allowed to leave. Sable and the children kissed everyone once more, then left for the carriage and home.

As soon as they stopped in front of the house, Mrs. Vine came rushing out to meet them. The woman had tears in her eyes as she approached. "Oh, Mrs. LeVeq, it is so good to finally have you and the little ones home. The mister has been worried sick. I've tried to keep his spirits up, but it has been difficult." She shared teary-eyed hugs with the children, then said, "You know, I made some pecan tarts today, and there are far too many to fit on the plate. Would you like some after your supper?"

Blythe's eyes widened. "Real pecan tarts, like Little Reba makes?"

"I don't know Little Reba's," Mrs. Vine replied, "but I guarantee mine are better!"

"Uh oh," Sable said. "It appears as if war may break out when Reba hears this."

"Come on children," Mrs Vine said, "let's see if you can outrace an old woman to the porch!"

The children were so surprised by the challenge, Mrs. Vine got a good head start.

As they ran after her, Sable grinned. "I like her."

"I do too."

They started up the walk.

Raimond told her, "I don't want you lifting a finger now that you're home. With the baby coming, and all you've been through, I just want you to rest and get your strength back."

"Raimond, I'll be fine."

"Will you please humor me? I've missed you so much, I'll bring you the moon if you ask."

Seeing the depth of emotion in his eyes, she acquiesced softly, "All right. Your wish is my command."

He picked her up and carried her into the house.

After a long, leisurely bath and a fine, fine dinner, Sable and Raimond put their children to bed and retired to their own suite for coffee and the first chance to be alone. Sitting out on the verandah, cuddled up against her husband, Sable said, "Little Reba's going to have a fit when the children tell her how well Mrs. Vine cooks."

Raimond patted his stomach appreciatively. "My stomach is still smiling, but I am not saying a word to her."

She looked up with smiling but tired eyes. "I'm so glad to be home."

"I'm so glad to have you home."

"How'd you find me?"

He told her the story, beginning with the woman who'd come to his office. When he finished, Sable was terribly moved. "She wouldn't give her name?"

"No."

Sable had assisted in churches all over the city and sadly, hadn't a clue as to the woman's identity. She would have liked to thank her personally. "There are a lot of good people in the world, Raimond."

He drew her closer. "Yes, there are."

After a moment Sable said, "I wish I knew where Morse's friends took the other orphans."

"So do I, but I promise you, we will keep searching. Little brother has also promised to put the screws to Morse during the voyage. Maybe his conscience will get the best of him and he'll tell us where they were taken."

Sable clung to that hope. Knowing that nine of the fifteen orphans had been found good homes lightened the sorrow of losing six, but unless the others were found, she'd always feel that she'd failed them. She knew that Cullen was heartbroken over the loss too, despite his stoicism.

As they both sat enjoying the sounds of the starry night, Sable yawned and stretched. "I'm so tired, but I'm afraid if I go to sleep, I'll awaken to find you were only a dream."

He kissed her brow. "Last night, I felt much the same way."

"Make love to me?"

He raised an eyebrow. "Weren't you tired a second ago?"

She curled up and touched her mouth to his. "Is that a no?" She brushed her lips across his, teasing them slowly. His hand slid into her still damp hair and brought her closer. "Make love to me . . ." she whispered. "Show me this isn't a dream . . ."

Raimond looked down into her sultry eyes and felt his manhood throb with a familiar beat. "If you insist, *ma reine* . . ."

So Raimond gave his wife a very personal and sensual welcome home.

As fall melted into winter, Sable Fontaine LeVeq grew fat with Raimond's child; her three children thrived and Mrs. Vine turned out to be a godsend. Sable celebrated her first holiday season as a freed woman with her new relations. She and the children stared in amazement at the family's first Christmas turkey, a LeVeq tradition Raimond and the Brats had instituted after a prewar visit to Hester and Galeno in Michigan. The holidays made her wonder about her brother Rhine and where he was, but as always she had no answer.

Winter folded into spring. She and Raimond received letters from Araminta, now in the Sea Islands, and from Bridget and her reverend in Boston; Bridget was carrying her first child. They also received a hello from Andre Renaud. Most exciting of all was the poignant note from the Vachons announcing the birth of their first son, David Raimond Vachon.

Raimond felt emotion swell as he read the letter once more.

"You must be very proud," Sable murmured, kissing his temple."

"I am," he whispered softly. "I'm honored to share the name with Hester's father, David. He was a free man when he met her mother, Frances. She was a slave and he sold himself into slavery to be with her."

An amazed Sable had never heard of such a thing.

"He died soon after Hester was born. We'll have to go up to Michigan to see them after you recover from the baby."

"*If* I ever have this baby," Sable replied, trying to find a comfortable spot on the bed. "I feel like a mountain."

In early March they received a letter from Phillipe. "Morse jumped overboard and drowned," Raimond told Sable as he read on.

"What?" Sable said, looking up from the sewing resting atop her stomach.

"According to Phillipe, he let Morse up on deck as he did every morning to get some fresh air and Morse jumped overboard. I guess he found being shark bait preferable to being enslaved for the rest of his life."

He will be the jackal and you the antelope until his death. Mahti's prophecy had come true. Morse would bother her no more. "Those poor sharks are going to be sick for weeks eating all that poisoned meat," Sable replied, going back to her sewing.

Raimond chuckled. "You're probably right."

It was now April. Springtime was blossoming and so was she. "Juliana said it isn't uncommon for the first baby to be late," Sable pointed out, "but I am truly tired of waiting. I promised your mother that this baby will be here before she and Henri go off to France."

Henri and his bride were moving to Europe in three

weeks and Sable knew she would miss them dearly.

Raimond snuffed out the lamps, then came to bed and lay down beside her. Sable, who hadn't been sleeping well for the last month or so, pillowed herself against him and he pulled her close. Once she was comfortable, he kissed her brow and said, "We will just have to wait it out."

They didn't have to wait long.

Two days later, Desiré Mahti LeVeq came into the world kicking and screaming. She had a head full of hair and her father's dark eyes.

Two weeks later, Raimond entered the bedroom one evening to find Sable just putting the baby to bed.

"Is she asleep?"

Sable nodded as Raimond came over and stood beside the bassinet. He looked down at his sleeping daughter and said, "She gets more beautiful every day."

Sable agreed.

Raimond placed an arm across her shoulders and squeezed her tenderly. "You do lovely work, *ma reine*."

"I had an indulgent instructor."

He handed her a square jeweler's box. "Picked you up something."

Sable sighed. "Raimond, tell me you didn't buy more jewelry. I've got more gems than an empress now."

"I enjoy buying you presents. It's Galeno's influence. He has a habit of buying Hester little things, and I suppose it's contagious."

"Does Hester fuss also?"

"Most times, yes. You should have seen her the day he brought home an elephant for the girls to have as a pet. She threw a fit."

Sable rolled her eyes at a tale that couldn't possibly be true, then went to a chair to unwrap this latest gift.

Raimond, still gazing down at his beautiful daughter, heard the paper rattling as Sable removed it from the box, then there was only silence. He whispered to his daughter, "Your mama is speechless, *petite* Desiré. Listen, can you hear it?"

Sable was speechless, indeed, for in the velvet-lined box lay Mahti's bracelet, cleaned, polished, and gleaming. She looked into his love-filled eyes and her heart pounded. "I don't know what to say . . ."

"It was all I had of you after you left the camp. I've been meaning to return it to you, and now seemed an appropriate time. You can pass it on to your daughter."

He came over and held out his hand. "May I?"

She could feel the tears running down her face as she handed him the bracelet and let him slip it on her wrist. She then let herself be enfolded in his arms. Just as Mahti's prophecy had come true about Morse, so had Araminta's dream about the sea chest and the bracelet. In her dream the sun had come out when Raimond placed the bracelet on her wrist, and Sable did feel as if she were being bathed by its warm rays. Feeling the Old Queens smiling down, she whispered, "I love you so."

"I love you more," he said thickly. "After Morse took you, I realized I'd never told you how much I love you or how much I enjoy waking up and seeing your smile. I love you, Sable LeVeq."

He drew back and held her eyes. "I also never asked your forgiveness for not believing your story about Baker."

"You couldn't be sure, I know."

"I know this—I will love you for an eternity."

Sable basked in his strong, loving embrace and vowed, "I will love you for an eternity as well."

Author's Note

⌒〜◯◯〜⌒

The story of Sable and Raimond grew from three sources of inspiration, the first being my desire to highlight the triumphs and tragedies of the tumultuous years immediately following the Civil War. The second inspiration rose from reading a book by William D. Pierson titled, *Black Legacy: America's Hidden Heritage.* One chapter highlighted enslaved African royals. Although there were only a few snippets on queens, they were more than enough to get my imagination running. The third inspiration came from my fans. If you wrote to me and requested, or in some cases demanded, a story featuring Raymond LeVeq from *Indigo* as the hero, raise your hand. Out of the hundreds of letters I received after the publication of *Indigo,* nine out of ten wanted Raymond to have his own book. I changed the spelling of his name from the Americanized Raymond to the proper French Raimond. I hope you don't mind.

Although I featured only one verse of "The Song of the Black Republicans," the other five verses can be found in *The Black Press, 1827–1890,* edited by Martin E. Dann. According to Mr. Dann, the "song" was printed only in *The Black Republican,* another of New Orleans's Black newspapers. He could not determine how widely it was sung.

Below is a list of books I suggest you try for further reading.

Cornish, Dudley Taylor. *The Sable Arm: Negro Troops in the Union Army, 1861–1865.* W.W. Norton. New York. 1966.

Foner, Eric. *Reconstruction: America's Unfinished Revolution. 1863–1877.* Harper and Row. New York. 1988.

Gehman, Mary. *Free People of Color of New Orleans.* Margaret Media. New Orleans. 1994.

Glatthaar, Joseph T. *Forged in Battle: The Civil War Alliance of Black Soldiers and White Officers.* Free Press. New York. 1990.

Hollandsworth, James G. *The Louisiana Native Guards: The Black Military Experience During the Civil War.* Louisiana State University Press. Baton Rouge. 1995.

McPherson, James M. *Battle Cry of Freedom: The Civil War Era.* Oxford University Press. New York. 1988.

Pierson, William D. *Black Legacy: America's Hidden Heritage.* University of Massachusetts Press. Amherst. 1993.

Quarles, Benjamin. *The Negro in the Civil War.* Da Capo Press. New York. 1953.

Stampp, Kenneth. *The Era of Reconstruction, 1865–1877.* Vintage Books. New York. 1965.

Sterling, Dorothy A., ed. *The Trouble They Seen: The Story of Reconstruction in the Words of African-Americans.* Da Capo Press. New York. 1994.

Sterling, Dorothy A., ed. *We Are Your Sisters: Black Women in the Nineteenth Century.* W.W. Norton. New York. 1984.

I want to thank the following individuals for their help and support:

Cecilia Oh, my new editor—welcome aboard. Ellen E. and Nancy Y., thanks so very much. Darcy and James Barker not only took me into their home on a book-signing trip to Cleveland, but fed me and treated me like family. Bless you both for your big hearts. Special thanks to Kelly Ferjutz for her TLC; Sandra Z. Harris of Birmingham, Alabama, for the great phone calls; Ladies in Line for the fan club and their unflagging faith; Catina Colston, who reads my books at a U.S. base in Turkey; and Leontyne Thomas, my number one fan in Trinidad–Tobago.

For anyone interested in joining the *only official* fan club, please contact: Beverly Jenkins Fan Club, c/o Ladies in Line Productions, P.O. Box 252862, West Bloomfield, Michigan 48325 for more information. Everyone else may continue to write to me in care of my post office box: P.O. Box 1893, Belleville, Michigan 48112.

In closing, let me give a shout out to all of the hundreds upon hundreds of you who've taken the time to drop me a line. I do appreciate it.

Stay strong and keep reading. Until next time.

Peace,